The Promise of Deception

Isles of Illusion

Book One: The Promise of Deception

The Promise of Deception

Isles of Illusion

By

Jessica Sly

The Promise of Deception
Published by Mountain Brook Ink under the Mountain Brook Fire line
White Salmon, WA U.S.A.

The website addresses shown in this book are not intended in any way to be or imply an endorsement on the part of Mountain Brook Ink, nor do we vouch for their content.

This story is a work of fiction. All characters and events are the product of the author's imagination. Any resemblance to any person, living or dead, is coincidental.

ISBN 978-1953957-08-5
© 2021 Jessica Sly

The Team: Miralee Ferrell, Alyssa Roat, Kristen Johnson, Cindy Jackson
Cover Design: Indie Cover Design, Lynnette Bonner

Mountain Brook Fire is an inspirational publisher offering worlds you can believe in.
Printed in the United States of America

Dedication

To my Almighty Creator, for whom all my work is done. I dedicate this first step of my journey to you and offer up this book with open hands.

"Whatever you do, do it from the heart,
as something done for the Lord and not for people."
— Colossians 3:23 (CSB)

Chapter One

London, 1913

I STARED AT THE CLOSED DOUBLE doors looming through the darkness before me. Sweat gathered on my torso, worsened by the stiff corset that confined my ribs and prevented deep breathing.

A muffled din seeped through the doors and echoed through the empty hallway stretching behind me, the discussions just out of earshot. They didn't know my life was about to change, that within moments my independence would be snatched away.

Footsteps clicked before Mr. Ford emerged in my peripheral vision. I pinched my skirt to quell the rising anger within me. Then I met his gaze.

"Don't look so despondent, Adelynn." His mouth curled into a grin, crinkling the skin around eyes the cold color of lead. "This is a joyful day."

I lifted my chin. "For whom?"

"For my son, of course. But also for my wife and me, your mother, and—I should think—for your father, were he here."

I reached for the pearl necklace at my throat, but Mr. Ford wrapped his long, icy fingers around my wrist before I could touch it. I jerked, but he held fast.

"Be still." He reached into his waistcoat pocket with his free hand and drew out a ring. He splayed my fingers and slipped it into place. The rigid gold band scraped the skin at my knuckle and drew a pinprick of blood. I held my breath as I peered at the large sapphire oval encircled by a halo of diamonds. He had spared no expense.

"A shame Basil didn't have the means to supply one himself." He admired my new adornment. "But I'm confident that with this promotion, he'll be able to provide for you in your marriage without our assistance, though we've been happy to give it thus far."

"I'm sure he is grateful for your generosity," I said through clenched teeth.

"Indeed." He smirked and bent in a curt bow. "Make us proud." Then he turned and stole through one of the double doors, the cacophony of the crowd intensifying in volume before muffling once again as it swung shut.

I let out a heavy breath, fighting back tears. A pulse thumped where the ring stunted the circulation. What more could I do? Every means of escape had been exhausted.

I wrapped my arms about my middle. *Heavenly Father, deliver me from this cage.*

"Adelynn?"

I jumped.

Baze appeared at my side and caressed my elbow. "Sorry to startle you." His even tone provided a welcome calm amidst the turmoil. He searched my face with his soft caramel eyes. "You look stunning."

My cheeks warmed. I dropped my gaze and focused on the gray pattern of his brocade waistcoat peeking out beneath a black dress coat.

He touched my shoulder. "You're pale, Al. Are you well?"

His use of my childhood nickname—unconventional though it may have been—made my heart flutter. I shrugged. "A little short of breath is all. The excitement of the evening, you know."

"Well, that won't do." He shook his head, and a clump of fringe escaped his slicked brown hair and fell over his forehead. "The crowd is expecting bright eyes and beaming smiles."

"I'm not much in the mood for smiling."

He raised his eyebrows. "For me, then?" He flicked my dangling earring. "I'll get you to crack, Al. You know I can." He grinned and flicked it again.

Wrestling away the urge to smile, I tried to block him, but he caught my hand. Noticing the ring on my finger stopped him short. "Where did this come from?"

I swallowed. "Care to wager a guess?"

His shoulders stiffened. "I've almost saved enough to buy you one myself. He knew that. You must give it back. We don't need to rely on his resources any longer."

"I think he would beg to differ."

A muscle twitched in Baze's jaw. He opened his mouth, but I spoke first. "Not tonight, Baze. Please?"

He hesitated, then released my wrist. I fingered the ring's cold gems. Baze was only doing what a husband-to-be should, trying to provide for his family. But his authority didn't hold as much sway over me as his father's, not when I stood to lose all that I held dear. I didn't dare remove the ring.

Baze rubbed the slight ridge on his nose—the result of breaking it as an adolescent—and turned toward the door. We stood in silence, shoulder to shoulder. The light brush of his coat on my bare arm sent elated chills racing up my neck, but a dull ache prodded my temples.

"Baze?" I whispered.

His voice rumbled low. "Yes?"

"I . . ." Shame choked my words. I wanted to tell him everything of the conflict that churned within me, everything that had transpired to bring us to this moment. He wasn't at fault for this. He believed our engagement to be sincere, that both parties had entered the accord willingly. But telling him he believed wrong would shatter him. Could I bring myself to do that, especially after we'd spent our entire adolescence sharing memories and building trust?

Baze eased his fingertips down the inside of my forearm—electric heat flaming under my skin—until he reached my hand, entwined our fingers, and lifted them to his mouth. His firm lips warmed my knuckles where he brushed a kiss.

"You need not fear." He tucked my hand into the crook of his elbow. "We'll face this together as we always have. And we always will."

The sentiment conjured fresh tears. As I opened my mouth, the double doors swung outward. Intense light poured over us. I clutched at Baze, much tighter than I intended, but nevertheless, I said a prayer of thanks for his stability.

We stepped into the glistening room stretching nearly fifty feet across and half as wide. A bright Paganini concerto drifted from a string quartet against the far wall and lifted to the vaulted ceiling and jeweled chandelier. As we halted, the composition and the chatter quieted. Each fashionable guest turned to watch our arrival. In the new silence, every murmur resounded against the marble floor and embellished walls.

Mr. Ford took a spot beside us, his petite wife on his arm, and addressed the crowd. His booming voice carried to every corner. "It is my great pleasure to introduce my son, Basil, who, as of yesterday, was promoted to detective inspector in the Metropolitan Police Criminal Investigation Department." The crowd applauded and clinked glasses. When they fell silent, he flashed me a brief smirk.

I held my breath. Sweat trickled down the small of my back.

"It is also my delight to make the first public proclamation of my son's official engagement to the lovely Miss Adelynn Spencer. I encourage you all to wish them well before the evening expires."

More applause erupted. I tensed and tried to step backward, but Baze held me in place and whispered, "I can't believe you would try to abandon me to face these people alone."

"You're a detective inspector now," I whispered back. "You can defend yourself."

"You'll not get off that easily." He flashed a sideways grin. "A good officer always brings reinforcements." With a chuckle, he tugged my arm forward. "Come. Follow my lead."

The mingling began straightaway with a flock of the Fords' distant relatives, followed by my father's House of Lords acquaintances and a flurry of people I'd never had the pleasure of meeting. By the time

Baze's best mate and Yard companion, Bennett, and his wife, Emily, caught up to us, I was quite ready to collapse into their arms.

Bennett clapped Baze in a hearty handshake, his spectacles reflecting the chandelier light. "Good job, ol' boy. Didn't think you had it in you."

Baze laughed. "Have I ever given you reason to doubt me?"

"Don't get me started." Bennett rolled his eyes.

Emily and I exchanged amused smirks. As she glanced back at her husband, her bright smile radiated pride across her pale elfin face and into her deep blue eyes.

Bennett moved to me and grasped my shoulders. "As for you, I offer my largest congratulations—or perhaps condolences. You finally netted yourself the elusive Basil Ford." His hazel eyes twinkled. "How you ever convinced that rascal to propose, I'll never know."

The brief flutter of excitement in my chest turned to stone as I recalled the proposal. Baze had said it was his happiest moment. But it had been quite different from my perspective—his father had given me no choice but to say yes.

Bennett looped his arm around Emily's waist and tipped his head to each of us. "You've a fine wedding to look forward to. And just in time." His hand drifted across Emily's round stomach. "Our Michael shall need a close companion."

Emily lifted an eyebrow. "Oh, it's Michael now, is it?"

"Sorry." He twirled his finger into one of the rich golden curls pouring over her right shoulder. "Katherine, I meant."

"Bennett!" She swatted his chest.

"All right. Enough." Baze waved his hand as though to separate them like misbehaving school children. "There'll be no arguing here. This is a night of celebration."

Emily giggled and settled her gaze on me. She grasped my hand as she cupped her blossoming belly. Her gloved fingers, though small, felt solid and reassuring.

In the distance behind her, an approaching trio of men caught my eye. When they had closed the distance by half, I recognized Baze's three older brothers.

Baze followed my gaze and groaned. "What do *they* want?"

In moments, they were upon us, swarming Baze like a frenzy of sharks. Aubrey, the tallest yet youngest of the triad—though still a good seventeen years older than Baze—draped his arm over Baze's shoulders. "Thought you could escape us, eh?"

Bennett nudged his wife with his elbow. "Quick, Millie. While they're distracted."

Needing no further prodding, Emily hooked her arm through mine and tugged me away. I sent an apologetic look Baze's way as his brothers snuffed out the last view of him.

Leaving Bennett to rush to Baze's aid, Emily and I weaved through the crowd. We stopped near the open patio doors leading to the garden terrace shared by the Fords and my family. A light breeze shifted the drapes and carried with it mist from the steady rain outside.

When Emily squeezed my hand, her fingers came across the engagement ring. Her eyes went wide. "Good gracious, that's enormous!"

"Indeed, it is." I tried to keep hesitation from my tone.

She frowned. "What's wrong?"

"I'm merely tired is all." The ache in my temples deepened. "It's been a long evening."

"No, there's more than that." Her expression softened. "What's troubling you?"

Empathy poured from her eyes, but I shook my head and peered out at the crowd. Baze's five nieces, ranging in age from twelve to twenty, had grasped hands and now skipped around him in a humorous dance.

I let my gaze wander and singled out a lone gentleman across the room wearing a black top hat and tailcoat. He appeared to be in his early thirties, with dark raven hair and a cool demeanor. I pointed, hoping Emily would catch on. "What do you think of him?"

Though she flashed one last silent plea, Emily eventually looked to where I gestured. After a moment of sizing him up, she said, "There are definite skeletons in his cupboard."

I grinned as he sipped from a champagne glass. "Skeletons of the criminal sort?"

She wiggled her fingers. "I was thinking more of the secret espionage sort."

"Foreigner?"

"Most assuredly."

"Family at home?"

"A wife and child . . . and a mistress overseas."

I tsked. "What a scoundrel."

Emily studied the crowd before pointing. "Her."

She had selected a robust woman wearing a glittering pink gown, her brilliant white hair twisted into a magnificent design adorned with feather plumes and jewels. Her layered makeup gathered in the deep wrinkles of her face.

I tapped my chin. "Lifelong heiress, daughter of a famous millionaire."

"Married?"

"No, never. But she had a childhood sweetheart who broke off their engagement. She's spent her whole life pining for him and has since wooed many a man, leaving behind her a wake of broken hearts."

Emily pressed the back of her hand to her forehead. "A real femme fatale."

I scanned the party guests again and located an aged gentleman with a short, bent stature.

"You should be wary of storytelling. That's how rumors begin."

I stifled a squeal and jumped behind Emily. *Excellent, Adelynn. Take shelter behind the pregnant woman.*

At second glance, I recognized the newcomer as the man we had selected for our first narrative. The top hat cast shadows across his sharp cheekbones but couldn't dim his stark blue eyes.

The man smiled. "If I may ask, what type of tale did you spin for me?"

My cheeks flamed. "I apologize, sir. It's merely a little game of ours."

"I pass no judgment upon you." He held up his hands. Then he doffed his hat, bowed, and straightened in one smooth motion. "My name is Cornelius Marx." He returned the hat to his head and looked into my eyes. "You must be Adelynn Spencer, the blushing bride-to-be."

My cheeks flushed, and I resisted the urge to cover them with my hands. "Yes."

"And I'm Emily Bennett." She gave a tight-lipped smile and narrowed her eyes. "Are you a friend of the Fords?"

"New acquaintance, actually. I recently moved to the city and am looking to expand my connections." He cocked an eyebrow. "What better place to start than a party full of politicians and police personnel?"

"Well, I hope you find what you seek." I dipped in a small curtsy. "Thank you for coming, Mr. Marx."

"Before I take my leave, I would like to offer you and your fiancé a gift in honor of your new engagement." He reached inside his jacket, produced a small card, and handed it to me. It was blank, save for his name in the center, composed of a swirling script. "I am the proprietor of a new entertainment locale in town, the Empress Theatre. It will feature world-class magical spectacles, performed by one of the finest magicians I have had the pleasure of meeting. We are hosting our debut magic show next week." He nodded at the card. "Show that to my doorman, and you will be well looked after."

I tipped my chin. "That's very kind of you, Mr. Marx. Thank you."

"Cornelius, please." He bowed. "It's been a pleasure, ladies, but I'm afraid I must be off." His eyes found mine as he lifted my hand and kissed the back with warm, soft lips, raising the hairs on my arm. "Congratulations, Adelynn. I wish you every happiness from this moment forth." With a final tip of his hat, he straightened and vanished into the crowd.

Emily spun toward me. "That was awfully forward of him, addressing you by your Christian name."

"Yes, I suppose it was . . ." I massaged my forehead as the ache worsened.

"Are you all right? You've grown pale." She touched my shoulder.

Sharp pain shot through my head. I opened my mouth to cry out but made no sound. Darkness swarmed my vision.

Through the shadows, a London street materialized around me. I stood alone alongside the cobbled road. The Thames sparkled black in the distance. Behind me, the two red-bricked buildings of New Scotland Yard towered through thick fog. The glowing face of the distant Clock Tower showed nearly twelve o'clock.

Surveying the empty street, I edged a foot forward. It struck a semi-solid object. I looked down.

The body of a man lay strewn on the ground, face gray and frozen. Blood stained the pavement around him.

A laugh pierced the night. It had come from my body—but it hadn't been my laugh.

What's happening?

The scene faded. Then all fell silent.

Chapter Two

I SWALLOWED, HESITATED, THEN BLINKED OPEN my eyes.

Baze's eager expression greeted me. "You're awake."

With blurred vision, I glanced about to gather my bearings, spotting an ensemble of bookshelves near tall windows, a crackling fireplace against the wall, and a grand piano in the corner—the Fords' drawing room. I rested upon one of the lavish upholstered sofas, a quilt draped over me. Baze and his brother Frederick knelt at my side, Bennett and Emily stood at the foot of the sofa, and Mother leaned over my head.

I moved to sit up, but my dress shifted, loose. I widened my eyes and drew the quilt to my chest. "What's going on? Who unlaced my corset?"

"You lost consciousness." Creases deepened in Baze's forehead as he frowned. "Frederick said it would help you breathe."

I gulped in a breath. Lost consciousness? But how? The last memories I had of the evening were speaking with Emily, meeting Cornelius Marx, and experiencing the dream . . .

Frederick grasped the inside of my wrist with two fingers as he stroked his gray-auburn mustache. Then he turned my face toward him so that I looked into his sharp green eyes—eyes so unlike Baze's.

"Well?" Baze tapped the edge of the sofa cushion.

Ignoring his brother, Frederick lifted a finger and directed me to follow its path with my gaze. The motion sent the room spinning. He grunted.

"What?" Baze insisted.

Frederick stood, knees cracking. "Her color is returning, and her pupils are reacting to the light, but her eye movements suggest lingering dizziness. She should rest for the remainder of the evening."

"But I feel fine." How could I rest after such a vivid dream? That is, if it had only been a dream. I sat up, and the room pitched.

Baze grasped my shoulders and eased me back against the pillow. "You will do as he says."

"But—"

"You may not heed my words as an acquaintance, Adelynn," Frederick said with a sigh, "but as a physician, I must insist."

I squinted until his face stopped tilting, then struggled to sit up again. When Baze reached out, I held up a finger. "I'm by no means the first person to ever lose consciousness."

Mother leaned over the back of the sofa and stroked my cheek with gentle fingers. Light glistened off her jeweled earrings and ornate necklace. Her sapphire satin gown and styled dark hair deepened the rich color of her eyes. "You should listen to them," she whispered.

"What of the guests?" I asked. "The party?"

"You needn't worry about that, darling. Alistair is handling the situation." Mother smiled, her skin wrinkling in fine lines beside her mouth and eyes.

Bennett cleared his throat. "You'd best listen to your mother. Not doing so would almost equal an act of treason, I should think."

I rolled my eyes. "Very well. Since you all insist."

Clear relief relaxed the hard lines on Baze's face. "I'll stay with you for a while until you've settled." He glanced at the others. "May we have a moment?"

Bennett clicked his tongue. "Alone with his betrothed? And without a chaperone?"

Emily pinched her husband's arm. "Leave them be."

"Keep the door propped open if it suits you." Baze firmed his jaw. "I won't tarry long."

With Emily on his arm, Bennett knuckled Baze's shoulder and gave me a salute as he passed. Mother bent and kissed my forehead before trailing Frederick out the door.

Once they'd gone, I closed my eyes, sank back against the pillow, and massaged my temples.

Baze blew out a long exhale. "That's not quite how I pictured the evening would go."

"Sorry." I half-opened one eye and peered at him. "Are you cross?"

"I'm merely glad you're all right." He placed a hand on the armrest behind my head. "What happened?"

"Nothing happened." I twisted my hands in my lap, catching a finger on the large engagement ring. "The room was stifling. I was merely overheated and overwhelmed with emotion."

What of my dream?

What *of* the dream? It had been just that. Why draw attention to it? Still, curiosity nagged at me.

Redness crept along Baze's ears as he averted his eyes. "Overwhelmed with good emotion, I hope."

My heart warmed. "Of course. Why should you think otherwise?"

He shrugged and rubbed the back of his neck. "And how do you feel now?"

"Better, actually." I gathered up the quilt and began folding it. "In fact, I should like to go home now, if that's quite all right."

"Absolutely not." He caught my wrist and halted my actions. "Frederick said you should rest."

With a huff, I pulled free. "But it's barely a stone's throw away."

"Distance doesn't matter. I can't let you walk anywhere." He raised his eyebrows. "But if you insist upon returning home . . . I could carry you."

I lifted my chin. "Don't you dare."

"It's no trouble. Surely you're no heavier than—"

"I think it would be in your best interest not to finish that statement." I narrowed my eyes.

A mischievous grin coaxed out his single dimple. He leaned closer, holding me in a defiant stare. "And if I do?"

I pursed my lips and fought to keep a straight face, refusing to blink first, but it proved nearly impossible as his confident presence and earthy scent washed over me.

Finally, he breathed a laugh and shook his head. "Engaged. Officially." He spoke almost to himself. His gaze drifted across my features, lingering over my mouth.

"Inspector Ford!" A young man I recognized as Constable Rollie burst into the room. He jogged across the space, his bright red hair matching the flush of his face. He halted beside us, chest heaving.

Baze rocked back and stood. "What are you doing here? I thought everyone retired for the evening."

"Emergency, sir." Rollie shot me a cautious look, then rose to his tiptoes and whispered in Baze's ear.

As Rollie spoke, Baze's face whitened. He turned to me, his jaw clenching. "I need to go, Adelynn." He touched my arm. "Stay here and rest. I'll send a maid to tend to you."

My stomach knotted. "Okay."

With a nod, Baze rotated and followed Rollie out the door. It clicked shut behind them.

The mantle clock's ticking grew loud in the silence. I huffed. Yard business, no doubt. Were his new duties already demanding his every free moment? And for what? A secret police meeting? A robbery?

A murder?

The vivid image of the body on the embankment flashed before my eyes.

It was only a dream. Just a simple, terrifying dream.

But even as I repeated the words in my mind, I was already convinced—dream or no dream, I had to know for sure.

I eased to my feet and paused—no spinning, no dizziness. Satisfied that I wouldn't repeat my earlier episode, I crept to the door and peeked out. The hall outside lay empty, so I stole through the vacant corridor and filled my lungs to capacity. My loosened corset gave way only slightly until the tight design of my silk gown kept it confined.

Soon, I found the secluded door leading to the garden shared by the Ford estate and my home. When I was young, it proved to be the most successful way of sneaking in to carry out dastardly pranks on poor, unsuspecting Baze.

Outside, I lifted an arm above my head to combat the rain. Keeping close to the hedge that stretched the entire distance between estates, I trod across the familiar stone path, skirting by a pond and hulking oak tree, until I reached the safety of home.

I slipped inside and fell against the door to shut it.

Mother's passing maid released a gasp, clutching a hand to her chest. "Miss Spencer?"

"Jenny!" I stood up straight. "Would you fetch Samuel for me, please? Have him bring the car around to the front."

"Yes, ma'am." She gave a wary curtsy and complied with my order.

I hustled to my room. It sat empty but warm from the smoldering hearth opposite my bed. Thankfully, my own maid wasn't inside, though she had left the curtains closed and the comforter folded back. I tugged off my damp heels, snatched worn boots from the wardrobe, and laced them up around my ankles. Then I tightened my corset and dress, tossed on a shawl, and darted out of the room.

Most of the staff had already retired for the night, so I snuck undetected to the front door. A tingle of excitement quickened my pulse.

Our chauffeur, Samuel, huddled against the rain at his post by the car parked along the curb. "Miss Adelynn." He tipped his head as I approached. "I was surprised to receive your request. What of the party?"

"Yes, I apologize." I pulled my shawl tighter. "The party concluded early, and I have an important matter to attend to. It cannot wait."

I held my breath as Samuel's milky blue eyes studied me from under white wiry eyebrows. Was he convinced? There usually wasn't much a bat of my eyelashes couldn't accomplish, but what if he refused? Could I drive the car myself if it came to it?

"Very well." He opened the back door. "But it is late. We shall run your errand and come straight home, agreed?"

"Of course." I nodded and climbed in. While I settled in the middle of the cushioned seat, he slid behind the wheel and pulled into the street.

"Where to?"

"New Scotland Yard, please." I closed my eyes and pictured the man from my dream lying along the embankment, his face obscured in the fog of my memory. Shuddering, I opened my eyes and focused on the water droplets racing in frenzied lines across the window.

The lights of London's flats and offices had blinked out hours ago, but a faint glow still shone atop the most populated boroughs. Rain pattered on the roof of the car, and water sloshed beneath the tires. The farther we drove through Westminster, the faster my heart raced. What if a body *was* there? Was that truly something I wanted to see?

Samuel slowed the car. "It appears something's happened."

"What?" I leaned between the front seats and peered through the windshield.

Up ahead, uniformed officers crowded the embankment across the street from New Scotland Yard. A few bystanders and reporters with flashing cameras crowded around the perimeter. Baze stood in the midst of his fellow policemen, one hand on his hip, the other rubbing his forehead.

Perfect . . .

I swallowed. "Pull over here."

"This looks like a crime scene," Samuel said as he eased up to the pavement. "Perhaps we should return to the estate."

"It's all right." I opened the door and slid out. "I'll only be a moment."

"Miss Spencer, you shouldn't—"

I shut the door. Cool rain moistened my shawl and sent a shiver through me. Gathering my skirts, I marched straight for Baze.

No sooner had I stepped onto the pavement than an officer blocked my advance. He puffed out his chest. "Pardon, miss, but this is a restricted area. I'll need you to clear out."

I tried to see around him, but what his height lacked, his width made up tenfold. I gave up and looked him in the face. "Listen, Constable—"

"Sergeant."

"Excuse me, *Sergeant*." I cleared my throat. "But my fiancé is over there. Detective Inspector Basil Ford. He's expecting me." I pointed over the sergeant's shoulder. When he turned to look, I dashed around him and scurried to the unit where Baze stood. My gaze trailed to the crouching men. Bennett knelt among them, scribbling on a notepad.

A man lay prostrate at their feet.

It can't be.

My knees locked, halting my steps. It was him . . . the man from my dream. And now, his face free from the haze of my memory, I recognized him. Jonathan Mallory—an instructor from childhood. Raindrops clung to his ashen skin. Red blotches marred his stark white waistcoat and circled the hilt of a knife plunged deep into his chest.

In the distance, someone called my name. But I couldn't move. I swallowed bile and blinked rain from my eyelashes. When I shut my eyes, the image remained, exactly as I had seen it. I teetered but managed to stay on my feet.

A hand latched onto my arm. I gasped and would have tripped backward had Baze not held me upright.

Rain sprayed from his lips as he spoke. "What are you doing here?"

"I . . . I needed to see . . ."

His fingers tightened on my arm. "Adelynn, get back in the car."

I tried to respond, to move—anything—but my muscles stiffened. Everything was exactly the same—the man, the embankment, the Clock Tower. How could I explain this? Dreams didn't show visions of the future, did they?

Lord, why? Why would you send me this horrible dream? What am I meant to do?

"I'm serious, Al." Baze huffed, bent his knees, and scooped me up into his arms.

I snapped out of the daze and pumped my legs. "What are you doing? Put me down. Put me down right now!" But as Baze stomped toward the car, I had no choice but to hang on.

Samuel waited until we reached the car, then opened the back door. "Evening, Mr. Ford."

Baze deposited me in the seat, none too gently, and slammed the door.

"Wait!" I pounded on the window as Baze returned to the crime scene. "You can't just walk away from me, Basil Ford!"

Samuel opened the door and settled into the driver's seat. "Better leave him be, Miss Adelynn. Your stubbornness is no match for his resolve."

I crossed my arms and sank into the seat, my face flushed and pulse pounding. Samuel was right, much to my chagrin. He had witnessed enough of our adolescence to know firsthand Baze's instincts toward me—scrambling up a trellis to sweet-talk me down, tending to me while I recovered from a broken arm, drying my tears after a group of boys had poked fun at my freckles. His resolve was strong, yes, but his nerve was appalling, picking me up like that in front of the other Yard men.

I watched the scene drift past the window, catching a glimpse of Jonathan Mallory's limp foot through the sea of officers.

He was dead. And I had seen it before it ever occurred.

Chapter Three

BAZE GLARED AFTER THE CAR AS it retreated toward home. As if he hadn't enough to worry about, now Adelynn was following him to crime scenes. What in blue blazes had she been doing here? Not only was their engagement now public knowledge, but this was his first crime as a proper detective inspector. She knew how long he'd anticipated this promotion. If they expected their marriage to work, she needed to rein herself in.

One of the sergeants snickered. "Caught yourself a feisty one, eh, Ford?"

Baze flashed a scowl, quieting the officer, and set back to work recording his own notes. No witnesses. Belongings still on his person. A single injury, albeit fatal.

Despite the mounting evidence, the pieces refused to connect in his distracted mind. It didn't help that instead of seeing the dead man's rigid face—despite it being a face he recognized—Baze's thoughts flooded with images of Adelynn at the party in her formfitting gown. Her powder-blue eyes had sought his for reassurance as the world finally learned of their engagement. Jeweled strands woven through her auburn hair and secured at the back of her head left her smooth, slender throat exposed and radiant. And as he had carried her to the car, her soft body had pressed against his chest, enough to steal his patience for the upcoming wedding.

Bennett tucked away his pad, rose, and joined Baze. "Surely that wasn't Adelynn I saw you dragging away a moment ago."

Baze sighed. "Unfortunately, it was."

"She likely won't take too kindly to your handling her that way."

Bennett waggled his eyebrows and elbowed Baze's side. "You'll cause a scandal, touching her in that way before you've said your vows."

Heat expanded in Baze's stomach and rose to his ears. "It's too dangerous for her to be out here, not to mention improper. She wasn't listening to me, so what else was I to do?"

"Oh, you don't have to defend yourself to me." Bennett grasped Baze's shoulder. "But don't be too hard on her. Engagements, and marriage itself, are a massive adjustment. You'll need to learn how to work as partners. It takes time. Trust me."

"That doesn't mean she should have come here."

"Well, no, but that's Adelynn." Bennett winked. "Would you love her the same if she were any different?"

Fire built under Baze's collar. He coughed and fumbled to form words.

"Don't overexert yourself, mate." Bennett knuckled Baze's shoulder and pointed to the body. "Back to business?"

Baze exhaled, thankful for the change of subject. "What did you find?"

"Doesn't appear to be foul play."

"No?"

"No. Look at the way the knife is angled." Bennett imitated the position and made the motion of stabbing himself in the chest. "It's congruent with the way one might hold it in order to stick himself, but Dr. Hamilton should be able to confirm when he arrives." He whisked off his spectacles, rubbed them free of water with a sleeve, and replaced them. "Not a very clean way to go."

Baze grimaced. "*Is* there any good way to go?"

"No, I suppose not." Bennett scratched his head. "The chap looks familiar."

"Jonathan Mallory. He was Adelynn's maths tutor, but he provided lessons to me when my father determined I needed extra instruction." Baze stretched his neck side to side, but his muscles only seized in response, made worse by the burden of his rain-laden coat. His first incident as detective inspector and the deceased was someone he knew. What he wouldn't give for a hot bath and a cup of tea and milk.

"Ah, yes, so you knew the victim. I suppose I should interview you, then." Bennett unsheathed his tablet and pencil. "When was the last time you saw the man?"

"Not since I joined the force seven years ago." Baze rubbed the bridge of his nose with a finger, lingering on the slight ridge in the bone. "He was a proper gentleman. A widower. No children. But loved life."

Bennett chewed the end of the pencil, brow furrowing. "Something doesn't seem right."

Baze shrugged. "People change."

"Perhaps they do." Bennett quieted, but the crease in his brow indicated he still brooded on the thought.

"I know that look." Baze jutted his chin at his partner. "What's on your mind?"

Rolling the pencil between his fingers, Bennett sighed. "I can't explain it. But this feels wrong, like there's more to it. It appears a suicide, but . . . what if we have a perpetrator on the loose?"

Chills marched up Baze's spine. He cleared his throat. "Let's not speculate on something that doesn't seem likely. We should wait until Hamilton arrives."

"I suppose." Stashing his writing implements in a pocket, Bennett knelt next to Mallory's body. He placed a hand on the tutor's torso, beneath the knife, and bowed his head. Quiet words drifted from his mouth. "Almighty God, commit his spirit into your hands. Bring agents of evil to justice and heal the pain of this dark world."

Baze clenched his jaw and looked away from the scene. Prayer—as if prayer worked. Bennett believed it did, but Baze couldn't accept that a God possessing such sovereignty would heed the words of mere mortals. Baze already had a father who imbibed himself on power, and the man only used that power for his own gain. Why should a heavenly father be any different?

When Bennett finished, he stood and turned toward Baze.

Baze tried to sweep the judgment from his features before Bennett noticed—but to no avail.

Bennett cocked an eyebrow. "What's wrong?"

"Nothing."

"Liar."

Baze narrowed his eyes. "I don't understand why you feel the need to utter such words. You know it's in vain. The man's already dead."

"Oh, it's done a heap of good. You should try it sometime." Bennett rapped a knuckle against Baze's skull. "It might get through to that stubborn head of yours."

Baze leaned away. "'Twould do me no good. The Almighty doesn't respond to unbelievers. And it's just as well."

Before Bennett could respond, a squat man in an oversized coat swept them apart, wild white hair lifting from his scalp as if to defy the precipitation. "What have you found, my boys, what have you found? Ah, yes. I see. I see." He crouched beside the body and waved his hands at the two sergeants still recording evidence. "Shoo. Off with you. Off!" He dug through his leather handbag, produced a magnifying glass, and set to work.

Bennett folded his arms. "It's too wet to procure his fingerprints, Dr. Hamilton. You'll have to do the job after he's been transported to the mortuary."

Incoherent mumbling rushed from Hamilton's mouth as he pored over the body.

Baze shook his head. Department Christmas parties never elicited so much as a flinch from Hamilton, much less a smile, but give the man a body and he was giddier than a child with a bag of sweets.

A sharp whistle drew every officer's attention to where Superintendent Richard Whelan's large form loomed at the side of the road. Fists planted on his hips, he singled out each man with a fiery look. "Finish your work here, then report inside. That's not a request."

Baze grimaced. What now? The man rarely misplaced his anger, but what he was cross about this time was anyone's guess.

"Come on." Bennett clapped Baze on the back and started toward New Scotland Yard.

Once the body had been carted off to the mortuary and every man assembled in the claustrophobic room at the Yard, Whelan took his place at the front and squared his broad shoulders. The officers quieted as he folded his hands behind his back. "Take a look out the window, gents." His voice rasped, likely the result of a lifetime of smoking. "Tell me what you see."

Everyone looked. Seconds passed before Rollie said, "The Victoria Embankment, sir."

"And can anyone tell me the distance between the embankment and New Scotland Yard?"

"About one hundred feet perhaps," Rollie said.

"Right you are." Whelan's eyes flashed, and his mutton chops quivered as his face flushed red. "So can anyone tell me how in the blazes none of you witnessed a fellow offing himself in plain sight?"

Rollie's mouth opened, but Baze rammed an elbow into the junior officer's ribs.

Whelan caught the movement and narrowed his eyes. "Negligence. Laziness. Stupidity. Take your pick, but I won't be having any of 'em in my precinct, understand? If the press come sniffing about, leave 'em to me lest one of you twits blows our credibility."

With a grunt, he stomped out the door. The tension eased as the men released a collective sigh.

Baze groaned and massaged his neck. "Well, I suppose that could have been worse."

Whelan poked his head back into the room. Officers stumbled and jumped to attention. "Ford!"

The crowd spilled away like a waning tide and left Baze standing alone.

Whelan narrowed one eye and grunted. "Congrats on the promotion."

Wind from across the Thames blew cool air and rain against my neck. In the distance, the Clock Tower emitted a single lonely chime. Smothered in darkness, just beyond the reach of the dim electric streetlamp's condemning aura, I pulled up my collar and drew my hat low over my brow. I tucked my hands into my overcoat's deep pockets as I watched the officers work. My knuckles brushed the cold metal of a knife.

Even from my position behind the horde of onlookers, I could make out the details of the dead man. I stared at the hilt sticking out of his ribcage. He had died so easily. A single pop with the knife brought him to the ground, gasping, twitching, then lying quiet.

I eyed his body, starting at the polished shoes and traveling up to his mud-plastered trousers, bulging waistline, bow tie and—

Don't look at his face.

I stopped my gaze from drifting farther.

Salvage your humanity.

I grimaced. What humanity could possibly remain in my shriveled soul?

You must find a way to go back home.

Memories snatched me away from this dismal scene and dropped me atop an emerald hillside of soft grass above a frothy bay by the sea. Gulls called. Waves crashed. Wind whistled.

A shout from an officer pulled me back to the scene at hand. The superintendent barked a reprimand at his men. Their first test and already they drew admonishment? Perhaps we overestimated them.

I turned, but before stepping off the pavement onto the cobbled street, I allowed myself one glance back at the man's face—a mistake. Remorse stabbed my chest exactly as the dagger had done to his. But why did such a storm rage within me? English noblemen like him were all the same. They cared nothing for the trials of common folk or foreigners, my kin. The English had seemed so concerned for our well-being when they commandeered my country's parliament, so where were they when nearly a million of us died from starvation and disease during the potato famine? Where were they as we tried to escape by boarding cramped, unsanitary ships to a better land with food?

And now, mere months ago, the House of Lords had blocked our most recent attempt at independence and to establish home rule in Ireland. It was hardly a surprise. They only cared about power.

I strolled along the empty street and gazed at the churning, cloudy skies. A longing twisted in my breast, a longing for green knolls, for hedged pastures—for home. I had been promised a better life if I did this. My people were promised a better life. No matter the turbulence in my gut.

No matter the trail of death that followed.

Chapter Four

THE CURVED PICCADILLY CIRCUS SHOPPING PARADES teemed with eager crowds. Fast-moving carriages, motorcars, and petrol- and horse-driven omnibuses added to the commotion. The unusually brilliant spring sun warmed my shoulders as Emily and I weaved through the other pedestrians.

Emily gripped bolts of unadorned linen to her chest. "This child had best stop growing." She projected her voice over the bustle. "I don't think there will be enough fabric in all of London to accommodate my size."

I glanced at her belly, no larger than a child's football, and chuckled. "Oh, come now. You're sure you are eight months? I should think five at most."

She smiled. "Very well. Perhaps I'm exaggerating." Her expression fell a tick. "I assume Baze told you about last night's ruckus in front of New Scotland Yard. Bennett couldn't disclose all of the details, of course, but they found a deceased man along the embankment, right in front of police headquarters."

As a child darted through a puddle of water lingering from the previous night's rainfall, splattering dark, muddy droplets across the pavement, I pictured the gruesome scene I had encountered. Bile burned in my throat. "How awful."

"Indeed. And Superintendent Whelan had a row with the squad after the fact. Bennett said the man was quite ready to overturn a desk in frustration."

"I suppose a crime outside of police headquarters doesn't reflect well."

We strolled onto Regent Street in the direction of St. James Park, and the crowds thinned. Emily slowed and tilted her head. "Do you hear that?"

I matched her pace and listened, picking up a faint, high-pitched chant growing louder by the second. Up ahead, a large stream of women dressed in their Sunday best came around the corner and marched toward us. Some held signs, but they all exhibited sashes slung across their bosoms that read "Let Women Vote."

Emily and I walked single file to let the troupe pass. They shot us a variety of looks—scrutiny, curiosity, sympathy. As soon as the chanters disappeared from sight, I shook my head. "Their campaigns are everywhere."

"Yes, there's certainly no shortage of people who have a cause for which to fight these days."

My stomach twisted as I remembered how fervently my father had defended each man's right to independence with his work in the Irish courts of law. He had fought to put an end to the prejudice experienced by the Irish, something for which the average Englishman hadn't a care—even as riots broke out in Ireland and the occasional rebel took to London streets. I had watched Father's work from afar, afraid to involve myself in the affairs of others, especially when the power lay so far atop the hierarchy of government and society. What could I possibly do?

"Well, regardless of whether this new case is a murder or not, Baze's promotion will leave him short on time and attention to give you." Emily adjusted the fabric bolts against her stomach. "You must try to be patient with him."

I leaned over and took the fabric from Emily's hands. She gave a relieved smile as I propped the bolts against my hip. "We're not married yet. He isn't obligated to be at my side at all times."

"Yes, but you will be married soon enough. 'Twould be good for you to grow accustomed to how his life works now rather than after you've said your vows." Emily rolled in her bottom lip and passed a gentle hand over her stomach. "There will be many late nights. There will be nights where he doesn't even come home until the dreary hours of dawn. You'll eventually learn to sleep those nights, but the worry will always remain, hiding at the edge of your dreams."

I waited for her to continue, to elaborate, but she didn't. Instead, she swallowed and massaged her right side above her stomach. She winced.

"Are you all right? Is it the baby?"

She breathed a laugh. "He has his rather large foot wedged in my ribs at the moment."

I grimaced. "That sounds . . . unpleasant."

"This dress makes it so terribly difficult for him to move, but he does his very best, I assure you." She pushed the palm of her hand into her belly and huffed. "I pray he'll settle soon."

"He?" I smirked. "You think it's a boy."

Emily's cheeks pinked. "Bennett hopes for a boy." She looked ahead. Her eyes widened. "Adelynn, look out!"

I faced forward but not in time. I collided with a man walking in my path. My heel twisted sideways, the bolts of fabric dropped from my hands, and I stumbled backward. As he clutched my arm to prevent my fall, I gasped and looked up into his glacial eyes.

"Well, if it isn't the future Mrs. Detective Inspector."

A chill gripped me. "Mr. Marx!"

"Cornelius, please," he said and released me, then bent and retrieved the fabric. After handing it to me, he smoothed his crimson waistcoat. Loose waves of his coal black hair fell from beneath his top hat and molded around his neck. "Quite a lovely day for a stroll, is it not?" He gave a lingering, sideways glance at Emily's stomach. "Though, a woman in your condition should take care not to overexert herself. What would Mr. Bennett think?"

Her cheeks flushed pink as her jaw clenched. "I don't think that is any of your business, Mr. Marx."

"Quite right. I was merely looking out for your well-being." He raised his eyebrows and lifted his hands. "May I?" Without waiting for her answer, he placed his hands on her stomach, the large span nearly covering the entire surface.

"Mr. Marx," she snapped and grasped his wrists, "that is wildly inappro—"

"You're a great testament to the strength and wonderment of the female kind, Emily Bennett." His voice lowered. "Such a miraculous event, the creation of another human being. We men must do our part to protect you."

Rage faded from Emily's eyes. Her grip on his wrists loosened.

Sensing an awkward shift in the atmosphere, I cut in. "What brings you here, Mr. Marx?"

With a grimace, he removed his hands from Emily's belly and stepped back. "No more of this Mr. Marx nonsense. I never cared for the decorum that society forces upon us. Cornelius. I insist."

"Very well." I tipped my chin. "I shall try."

"Good, good. To answer your inquiry, I was on my way to the Empress to watch the rehearsal for our debut magic show next week." He brightened. "Would you ladies care to join me? I could give you a special preview."

I shook my head. "Actually, I think we'd better—"

"It's not far. You'll be in and out in a snap."

We couldn't very well go with him. After all, he was a stranger—and a stranger with clearly no respect for societal boundaries. Who was to say what we would find at this so-called theater? Could we trust this man? Though his suave demeanor enticed me to lower my defenses, how much did we really know about him? Perhaps we should have Bennett or Baze inspect the place first to confirm its authenticity.

I held up a hand. "We thank you, Cornelius, but we really—"

"A small peek couldn't hurt," Emily blurted.

"Excellent." Cornelius clapped his hands.

Before I could protest, he squeezed between us and offered his arms. "Allow me."

I narrowed my eyes in Emily's direction. She shrugged and gave a sheepish smile. What was she doing? She was usually more cautious than I. What had come over her?

"We mustn't tarry," Cornelius said.

"Our driver is expecting us at our rendezvous at two o'clock," I said. "He shall notice if we don't arrive."

"I'll have you back in plenty of time to meet your appointment."

"Very well." As I tucked the fabric under my arm and inched my other hand through his proffered elbow, gooseflesh swept across my arms under the pink sleeves of my light silk walking suit, and I shivered.

He led us forward, through another shopping district, and onto a side street. We emerged on Haymarket, parallel to Regent Street.

For some odd reason, Emily looked everywhere except at our guide, despite the fact that she'd been the one who accepted this precarious invitation. So, I assigned myself the task of interpreting this mysterious stranger. I cleared my throat. "What's your story, Cornelius?"

"My story?" He kept his gaze forward.

"Yes. Your story. Emily and I took the liberty of kindly crafting one for you last night. Perhaps you could set us straight?"

"Not much to tell, I'm afraid." His arm muscle tightened, squeezing my hand deeper into the crook of his elbow. "I'm sure your tale is far more engaging."

"Try me."

He cracked a small smile. "I was raised in a wealthy family. I grew up never wanting for anything. Then I moved here, purchased a theater, and am now escorting two lovely women to see the fruits of my labors."

"Surely there must be more to it than that."

"Afraid not."

I narrowed my eyes. "What secrets are you keeping?"

He gave me a sidelong look. "We hardly know each other, Adelynn."

"And yet you're escorting us to your private rehearsal, Cornelius."

His smile widened. "Touché."

We walked beneath an awning and briefly pressed closer together to let others pass. My pulse quickened. To distract my mind from our nearness, I continued my line of questioning. "Siblings?"

He cocked an eyebrow but obliged. "Only child."

"Schooling?"

"Educated."

"Wife?"

"No, and no mistress overseas either, as you and Mrs. Bennett speculated last night." He chuckled as my cheeks warmed.

I cast another glance at Emily, but she walked with her gaze to the ground, so I continued. "What about—"

"As engrossing as this conversation is, Adelynn," he cut in, "I must stop you here."

I bristled. "I'm not finished."

"No, but we are." He slowed us to a stop and gestured upward with his chin. "Welcome to the Empress Theatre."

A four-pillared marble portico towered nearly two stories over us, bearing gold lettering on the front of the roof that read "Empress Theatre." Steps of the same rich cream-colored material led up to twin red oak doors. Glittering light flashed through the door windows and gave us a taste of the brilliance inside.

The longer I stared at the columns, the more they seemed to lean over me, tantalizing, threatening, as though wanting to topple and crush me. Unease dried my mouth and prickled my skin. I looked down and away, but the feeling remained.

What had prompted such a reaction? First suspicion, now fear. Was I the one out of balance? Or was there something through those doors of which we should be wary?

Lord, enter this place with us.

"Let's not dawdle." Cornelius urged us forward.

As we ascended the steps, he slipped his arms from our grasp and swung the doors wide for us. Inside, a vaulted ceiling stretched high above, stealing my gaze away from the wide, magnificent staircase in the center of the room.

Cornelius led us past the staircase to a propped door, our heel-clicks on the marble floor echoing in the vast, empty space.

Two men dressed in crisp black suits squeezed through the door and headed in our direction. I looked once, then looked again. Their faces were identical, with the same sleepy brown eyes, flat mouth, and etched brow lines. However, one sported a mole above his lip.

"Ladies, these are Killian"—he pointed to the one with the mole—"and Niall. Two of my ushers. Gentlemen, I'm giving these two lovely ladies a tour of our theater."

Killian jabbed a thumb over his shoulder. "Kelly's about finished."

I slowed. An Irishman?

Cornelius shot us a look. "Come. Quickly now."

On the other side of the doorway, the enormity of the theater struck me with such force that my steps faltered, my jaw slack. The ceiling must have been at least four stories up, with vibrant frescoes spreading across the massive surface. Sculpted molding spiraled to a dome where a giant crystal chandelier cast spectacular particles of light. Boxes lining the walls rested upon golden statues of angels wrapped in folded linen and feathers. Velvet maroon curtains cascaded above the boxes. Rows upon rows of seats filled the auditorium.

And then the stage caught my eye. In classic proscenium style, an arch capped the deep space, and a shadowed gap in the front opened into an orchestra pit. Brass footlights in the shape of elegant shells lined the platform edge and housed dormant candles. The imposing crimson curtains hung open, and two men stood facing each other about ten paces apart, one with a gun pointed at the other.

I halted. What were they doing? Was this part of an act?

"I'm ready." The unarmed man's quiet voice carried easily through the space.

Before I could even form the word *no*, the other man fired. The weapon popped. Emily and I jumped.

The unarmed man's hand flew up in front of his chest. Smoke rose from the end of the gun, signaling its discharge, but the man stood unharmed. He couldn't have caught the bullet. Such a feat wasn't possible by human hands, not without severe injury.

As though hearing my thoughts, Cornelius turned back to me and smiled. "Not everything in stage magic is as it appears." Gesturing his hand for us to follow, he started down the slanted aisle to the stage.

Emily and I shared looks of awe and trailed behind him.

As Cornelius neared the stage, he clapped slowly. "Excellent work. Excellent. Let's have a gander."

A few paces from the stage, their faces came into view. With smooth skin, round eyes, and soft features, the man with the gun wasn't a man at all—but a woman dressed in a man's loose trousers and baggy shirt. Her short hair added to the illusion, but her feminine physique gave her away.

The other man—this one truly a man—nodded toward his female assistant. "Excellent work, Siobhan. That was even better than last time." A thick Irish accent poured through his lips.

Siobhan tipped her head at him, but when she noticed us, she scrunched her nose. With a sniff, she stomped across the stage and through the curtains.

The magician shrugged and leaped down in front of us in one deft move and smoothed his navy-blue waistcoat. "Don't mind Shiv. She doesn't take to strangers too well."

Cornelius held up an open palm, and the man dropped a small object into it. Turning to us, Cornelius produced a gleaming bullet between two fingers.

I shook my head at the magician. "How did you achieve such a feat?"

Finn wagged a finger. "That would be tellin'."

The corners of the magician's mouth deepened into a grin, but his cloudy gray eyes conveyed a solemnness that contrasted his amused expression. Dark hair curled over his forehead, and that, coupled with a shadow of scruff on his jaw, gave him an air of mystery—definitely the sort who'd be caught up in the world of magic and illusion.

He rubbed his chin as though self-conscious and then extended his hand. "Me name's Finn Kelly."

I turned and placed the fabric bolts across several seats, then accepted his greeting. "Adelynn Spencer." His firm handshake pained my fingers. I winced and folded my arms to nurse my hand.

Finn turned to Emily. But as his gaze lingered on her face, then darted to her belly, he hesitated, hand held suspended between them. He cleared his throat, moved his hand to his pocket, and tipped his head. "Charmed to meet you, Mrs. . . . ?"

"Bennett. Emily Bennett." She returned the nod. "Thank you for having us."

He aimed a thumb over his shoulder toward the stage. "You liked my trick?"

Emily sized him up with a glance. "You certainly go for shock value, Mr. Kelly."

"That indeed, Mrs. Bennett." He bowed.

Cornelius looped an arm around Finn's neck. "Why don't you show these fine ladies a special trick, something simple perhaps. After all, they've come all this way to see a performance."

"Of course, Cornelius." Finn ducked out of Cornelius's hold and tipped his head toward Emily and me. "If you'll excuse me a moment." He vaulted onto the stage and rushed through the curtains.

Cornelius faced us, expression keen. "Finn is a master of his craft, to be sure. You're gettin' a premier look at what is to come."

I replayed his words in my head, recognizing a cadence similar to what had passed through Finn's lips. "It seems you've adopted a bit of the Irish accent."

Cornelius stiffened. "I apologize. I only employ good folk from those green shores, so I suppose it influences my own accent when I'm in their midst." He placed his hand over his heart and wrinkled his brow. "I don't mean to be distracting."

I frowned. "On the contrary, I think it's lovely. You needn't be ashamed."

Cornelius tilted his head, something akin to surprise—perhaps admiration—alight in his eyes. "You're probably one of the only English souls I've heard describe it as such. The Irish aren't particularly welcome here."

I fiddled with the pearls around my neck. "Yes, I am certainly aware."

It was an accent—and a plight—with which I was well acquainted. Father used to break into the Irish inflection to entertain me, mimicking the common tongue he had heard so often while working abroad. He'd been ridiculed for it by his peers, for fighting alongside the Irish to reach an accord in their clamor for independence. Yet, it had been more than mere jeers and gossips. He'd lost his life for it.

The curtains parted, and Finn jogged through. "I do be apologizin' for the wait." He dropped onto the floor in front of us, a bouquet of red roses in his grasp. Ruffling his dark curls with his free hand, he extended the flowers toward Emily. "For you, madam."

Emily accepted the roses with care. "That's very kind, Mr. Kelly."

"Give them a smell. They're real, sure?"

She buried her nose in the flowers and breathed deep, closing her eyes for a moment. "Mmm, they're real."

Finn extracted a deck of cards and shuffled them with dizzying speed. "Now, there is a legend of fairies in me homeland. We call them the *aos sí*. They dwell all across Ireland, in burial mounds, in ringforts, in lochs." His fingers splayed the cards and held them out to me. "Choose one, if you will."

I snatched a card from the pile and allowed myself a brief look at what I'd drawn—jack of hearts—before locking my gaze on Finn. That was the secret, wasn't it? The magician distracted the audience with a grand display while he pulled off the trick in secret. I was determined to spot the method.

"As a boy, I encountered one of those fairies, and I do be believin' that they've influenced me magic ever since." Finn collapsed the deck and stashed it within his coat, then stretched his open hand toward me. "Give us the card, now."

Narrowing my eyes, I handed it over.

He gave it a glance and spun it in his fingers. "Sometimes those fairies, they're on their best behavior." The card twirled faster. "But sometimes, they do be playin' pranks." He swept his hands together, then whisked them apart and held up empty palms—the card nowhere to be found.

Emily and I gasped.

Cornelius smiled and leaned an elbow against the stage edge.

Finn tsked. "As expected." The corner of his mouth curled upward as he approached Emily. "They've a fondness for flowers." He wiggled his fingers around the bouquet she held upright. "Do you suppose . . ."

As he circled his hands above the roses, a white object began rising among the crimson petals. Ever so slowly, a card emerged.

I stood paralyzed, mouth agape, breath trapped in my lungs.

When the card had risen halfway, Finn seized it from the bouquet and flicked it upright between two fingers. The jack of hearts.

I clapped loudly, grinning ear to ear. Emily shifted the bouquet and joined my applause.

"That was incredible, Mr. Kelly," I said.

With a grin, Finn bowed. "You have me fairy friends to thank."

Emily extended the bouquet to him, but he shook his head. "Keep it. Call it a partin' gift."

"Is there anything more you could show us?" I clasped my hands together. "Some tricks from your act, perhaps?"

Finn opened his mouth, but Cornelius cut in. "I'm afraid we cannot reveal anything further." He stepped in front of Finn, leaned close, and lowered his voice as though bestowing a secret. "But if you come back for our debut performance, we shall give you a demonstration you won't soon forget."

Chapter Five

BAZE ADJUSTED HIS COLLAR, SMOOTHED HIS hair, and straightened his stance before entering his father's study. Alistair reclined behind his desk with steepled fingers, a newspaper in front of him. He looked up without comment as Baze closed the door and approached.

Baze tried not to shrink back during what felt like an incredibly long trek across the room, but his father's accusing glare held him locked like prey in a hunter's scope. What more could the man possibly demand from him? And at what point would Baze eventually snap?

Stopping in front of the desk, Baze held eye contact. "You sent for me?"

One eyebrow twitched. Alistair slid the newspaper forward, his eyes never leaving Baze. "Can you tell me what this is?"

Baze swallowed and lifted the paper. Right above the fold, he spotted a photo—Jonathan Mallory's crime scene and Baze hefting Adelynn in his arms in the foreground—with the headline, "New detective inspector has hands full with death and dames." Embarrassment and anger flamed his cheeks. He tightened his hands until the paper crinkled.

"Speak!"

Baze flinched. "She wasn't supposed to be there. I don't know how—"

"Your engagement's only just been made public, and already it looks like you can't control your own fiancée." Alistair pressed his fingertips to the desktop and rose slowly. "Do you realize how this affects your reputation? How this affects *my* reputation?"

Old fears clawed their way back to the forefront of Baze's mind.

Memories of this same condescending look fired up every instinct to retreat. He resisted the urge to feel the bridge of his nose and the jagged bone that reminded him daily of his failure—and how close he had been to abandonment.

"I'm sorry, Father," Baze said with as level a voice as he could muster.

"Sorry? No, you are not sorry until you see to it that this never happens again."

"Adelynn is headstrong. She is not likely to—"

"She is a woman." Alistair's nostrils flared. "Her only role is to acquiesce to your demands and produce sons to carry on your name. It is your job to ensure she knows this, by any means necessary."

Unease and inadequacy clutched at Baze's throat. Could he bring himself to tell Al such a thing?

Could he live with the consequences if he didn't?

Baze dropped the newspaper to the desk. "I shall speak to her. It will not happen again. You have my word."

Alistair's eyes lost their sharp edge. "I worked hard to build the reputation of the Ford name from nothing. You and your brothers will never have to experience the trials I did. Your brothers have capitalized on the privileges I afforded them. They're wealthy and successful. I expect you to achieve the same."

"Of course, Father." Baze tipped his head. "If that will be all . . ."

Alistair narrowed his eyes but waved a hand. An invisible vice squeezed all the air from Baze's lungs as he spun on a heel and hastened to the door.

"I have provided everything for you," Alistair called after him.

Baze halted, strangling the doorknob.

"I can take it all away just as easily." Alistair paused, prompting Baze to look back. The revulsion flaring in his father's eyes ensnared him. "Do not give me a reason to do so."

◆

"Have you heard about that new Irish magician?"

I opened my eyes and looked at Margaret's reflection standing behind my own, both of us framed in the mirror of my mahogany vanity. She reached for a pin amidst an unorganized pile, then twisted a section of my hair up and secured it in place.

I turned my head, but she touched my cheek and guided my face forward. I made eye contact through the mirror's reflection. "I have, in fact. How did *you* hear of him?"

"Oh, the city's chittering on about it. He sounds like a rather mysterious character." She slid a flower-shaped mother-of-pearl comb into the auburn curls layered at the back of my head. "Apparently, tonight is his first performance. I do wonder how many will attend."

I watched her finish the hairstyle and tried not to compare my freckled nose, small mouth, and sky-blue eyes to Margaret's pure milky skin, deep green eyes, and full features. Despite my seniority of a few years, she had the appearance of a mature woman.

"It looks lovely." I moved my head to admire the ornate design. "Thank you."

"We're not quite finished yet." She gestured to my cotton and lace combinations—a mixture of a chemise and drawers.

I drew in a deep breath as if to combat what was to come and stood.

With practiced hands, Margaret fastened the corset around my midsection in one smooth motion. As it stretched from mid-thigh to bosom, it flattened my stomach while accentuating my hips and bust. I grasped the varnished bed post and braced my legs as she tightened the laces.

"What do you think?" she asked.

"Of what?"

"Of what." She giggled. "Of the Irishman. I heard his kind are a rather ragged bunch. Should be quite the sight to see him on stage."

I tapped my thumb against the post. Finn had been anything but ragged. Poised, charismatic, genuine—that better described him. But my opinion of the Irish hadn't differed all that much from Margaret's before last week when I met Finn. Father had labored to help smooth relations between our two lands in the midst of their struggle for independence, but I'd never truly seen deep into his world with the Irish—never cared to. What did I really know of them?

"I think he appears to be a gentleman," I said and left it at that.

I was already fifteen minutes late by the time Margaret helped me into my evening dress—a coral-colored patterned silk with beaded tulle overlays and a black velvet belt that draped down the back of the gown. After she took her leave, I paced a few laps around my room and said a prayer before gathering the courage to venture out.

Though I took brisk, controlled steps, my heart pounded as though I'd sprinted the full length of the city. The Fords had joined us for dinner on many previous occasions. But now that my engagement—and Mr. Ford's influence over me—was public, the stakes had changed.

My stomach felt heavy as I rounded the corner and entered the dining room. The Fords and my mother paused mid-conversation and watched my approach. Judging from their empty bowls and the delectable smell, they were well into the second course of oxtail consommé and cream of barley soup.

One of the footmen nodded and pulled out my chair. I took my place next to Mother and noted Baze's empty seat. So I wasn't the only one with better things to do.

The staff entered the room in a flurry with the next course. My stomach growled as they removed my uneaten soup and replaced it with a fresh plate of poached salmon, mousseline sauce, and cucumbers, then filled my glass with chilled sherry.

As I removed my gloves, placed them in my lap, and covered them with a cloth serviette, Mr. Ford flashed a tight-lipped smile. "So nice of you to finally join us, Adelynn. I do hope we aren't keeping you from anything important."

"Of course not, Mr. Ford." I smiled back, reached for my cutlery, and aimed my fork at Baze's vacant seat. "But I do wonder what your son could be up to at this hour."

Mr. Ford's eyes gleamed as he severed his flaky salmon with his fork. "Finishing details with the case, I'm sure. He'll come along shortly."

I'm sure he will. I stabbed a cucumber slice, stuffed it in my mouth, and batted my eyelashes.

Mother cleared her throat. "Adelynn, the Fords were just telling me of the plans they have for you and Basil after the wedding."

I'm sure they were. I sliced off a piece of fish and gnashed it between my teeth. "And what plans might those be?"

Mr. Ford reddened as I continued chewing. Mother pinched my thigh beneath the table. What had come over me this evening? Though, if throwing my manners to the wind made Mr. Ford squirm, then what was I waiting for? Toss out the utensils and loosen the corsets.

I swallowed. No. I couldn't risk it. Mr. Ford had made that clear.

Mrs. Ford smoothed the black curls framing her petite face, leaned forward, and looked into my eyes. "I had hoped to wait until both of you were present, but, well, Basil's occupation is unpredictable." She glanced at her husband, then back at me. "We purchased a small residence in Kensington for you to use after the wedding. At least until Basil can invest enough for a larger home."

Mr. Ford cocked his head. "Or perhaps you could dip into that grand fortune your father was so kind to leave to you."

I nearly inhaled my next bite, but Mrs. Ford didn't give me a chance to comment. "You should be quite happy there. There's plenty of room to raise a family. And, of course, we don't expect repayment for the property."

Yet another part of our lives over which they would hold leverage. "Thank you. I'm sure it is a lovely home." My insides screamed otherwise.

A door clicked in the distant foyer. The butler spoke, and then a man answered. Though the words were indistinguishable, the familiar timbre of Baze's voice carried through.

The four of us chewed in silence and waited a few heartbeats before Baze stepped through the dining room doorway, his chest heaving.

Mr. Ford's stare locked on him.

Baze's face flushed, and he averted his eyes. "I apologize for my tardiness. Sincerely. I was delayed at New Scotland Yard by important matters that couldn't wait. I need to return posthaste, but I wanted to deliver my apology in person." His gaze drifted to his father. A faint wince crossed Baze's face. "I apologize once again. Please excuse me." He bowed, then spun and hurried from the room.

"Disgraceful." Mr. Ford sniffed and flung his fork on his plate with a sharp clang, causing the rest of us to flinch. "He'll find any excuse to wriggle out of his commitments."

I took a slow bite of fish. No. I doubted Baze was avoiding his duty on purpose, especially when he risked incurring Mr. Ford's wrath. Judging by Baze's slightly disheveled appearance and shortness of breath, something upsetting had likely occurred. Perhaps he would eventually return to the precinct as he said, but if he were truly as troubled as he appeared, he would retreat to Father's private study. Over the years, the study had become a refuge for Baze as he sought my father's soothing words to heal him every time he'd been stung by his own father's sharp tongue. Even now, though my father's presence no longer filled the study, Baze continued to return.

After waiting a moment to allow Baze time to reach his destination, I dabbed my mouth with the serviette and skidded my chair back along the wood floor. "Please excuse me for a moment."

Not waiting for their permission, I hurried out of the dining room and took an immediate left to escape from view.

I checked over my shoulder before continuing through the short hallway until I came to the door of my father's study. I touched the pearl necklace at my throat as I grasped the brass knob, a rustic complement to the dark cherry grain of the door. I'd only visited the study once since his death. Everything had been left exactly as it was before. Even the maids took care to return each item to its place after dusting.

I pushed the door open on smooth, silent hinges to reveal a single walkway between three rows of full bookshelves on each side, with a glimpse of Father's desk at the end and the constant yet comforting scent of pipe tobacco. I let the door swing shut behind me and walked reverently through the aisle, my footsteps muffled by the long Persian rug. Memories flooded my mind—sitting on my father's lap as he worked fervently on paperwork, stealing books from the shelves to read late into the night, and playing competitive games of sardines with Bennett and Baze, the study a perfect hiding place.

For a moment, I imagined Father sitting here, filling out forms, signing papers, reading the latest newspaper. He would puff on his pipe, which lit his eyes briefly with every fiery simmer. Then he would pause and look up to where I hid behind a bookshelf. He'd laugh and call me over and hoist me up onto his lap.

Loneliness tightened my insides.

As I rounded the last shelf, Baze came into view, slouched in one of two red velvet armchairs aimed toward a cold fireplace. A glass of whisky rested on a brown paper-wrapped parcel on the side table between the chairs. If he knew I was there, he didn't acknowledge my presence, only stared forward with a glazed expression.

I crept behind him and leaned around the back until he edged into view. "Found you."

Baze jumped and clutched the armrests. Upon seeing me, he sighed and groaned. "That was cruel, Al."

Hiding a smirk, I eased into the empty chair. "What was so important that you would miss the chance to indulge in *riveting* conversation with our parents?"

"Did you only come here to patronize me?"

"Did you only come here to sulk?"

He shot me a stern look, downed his whisky, and grimaced.

"Fine, don't tell me." I folded my hands in my lap and waited, playing with my engagement ring and shifting it off a bit to release the pressure over the deep indent in my skin. I stared at Baze as he stared at the empty fireplace. The coffee color of his slightly frizzed hair matched the hue of the day-old shadow across his jaw. As he lifted a thumb to chew the nail, I became mesmerized by the smooth strength of his mouth. Images of him, a younger him, sitting close to me filled my head, then a quick touch of the lips—

My stomach seized. I swallowed hard and looked down at my hands. *Now's not the time for such thoughts.* I picked at the sapphire gem of my engagement ring. Dredging up old memories would only complicate things even more . . . because they reminded me why I loved him. But my feelings were irrelevant. They had to be if I had any hope of dealing with Mr. Ford.

Baze sighed and dropped his whisky-wielding hand to the armrest. "I can't get something Bennett said at the crime scene out of my head. We haven't found any evidence to suggest it was anything other than a suicide. I've spent all evening sifting through the details." He leaned forward, resting his elbows on his knees. "Yet, Bennett thinks something more lies beneath the surface."

The hair rose on the back of my neck as images of Jonathan Mallory's body flashed in my head, images of me standing over the body as though looking through another's eyes. "Why does he think that?"

"A gut feeling, he said." Baze ran a hand through his hair. "But I can't go on intuition. This isn't some serial mystery in *The Strand.* A real man died by his own decision. We should let him rest in peace and not look for a twist that isn't there."

"But are you sure it's not—"

"Which brings me to my next point." He aimed a finger at me. "What were you doing out there?"

The conversation had shifted so fast, it took me a few seconds to adjust. I widened my eyes. Was now the right time to tell Baze about the dream? If it all sounded utterly daft to me, wouldn't it appear even more so to Baze?

"Answer me," he said, his voice soft but stern.

I managed to force words out. "You won't like my answer."

"I mean it, Adelynn."

"Very well." I stared hard at my ring. "That night, at the party, when I swooned . . ."

"Keep going."

"I had a dream." *No turning back now.* "I saw Jonathan Mallory lying there by Scotland Yard and witnessed it as though from another's perspective."

Baze tensed, looking at me with inquisitive eyes under a furrowed brow. "You dreamed this?"

"Yes . . . or something like a dream. I wanted to be sure it was only that. That's why I went there that night."

He studied me for a long moment and then said, "You realize how insane that sounds."

Nausea soured my stomach. "I don't care if you believe me."

"Then why did you tell me?"

"I don't know."

In truth, I ached for him to believe me, to affirm my sanity and offer to join this quest to learn the truth of the dream and how it related to the dead man. Wishful thinking.

Baze cleared his throat, set the whisky glass on the side table, and picked up the wrapped parcel. He handed it to me. "This is for you. Call it part of your wedding present."

I tried not to let disappointment filter across my face. Perhaps it was for the best that he'd steered the conversation in a different direction. A detective inspector couldn't have a fiancée believed to be insane.

I loosened the twine and stripped the paper away to reveal a hardcover novel. White lettering against a cobalt background spelled out "The Lost World by A. Conan Doyle."

"It's Sir Doyle's newest series. You're always reading those Sherlock Holmes stories, so I thought you would fancy something different."

"Thank you." I lifted the book to my nose and breathed in the aroma of freshly printed paper. Perhaps absorbing a new story would distract my thoughts from the dilemma at hand. When I looked up, I caught Baze watching me with a half-cocked smile.

"There's one more gift."

"Really?" Heat radiated through my chest. "And what might that be?"

He raised his eyebrows. "You'll have to follow me outside."

"Curious." I allowed a little grin. "Lead the way."

Baze stood and helped me to my feet, but rather than offer me an elbow, he grasped my hand and entwined his fingers with mine.

The warmth and natural feel of his hand in mine shot currents of heat through my back to the nape of my neck. Every instinct urged me to pull away, but my delight in our touch ran deeper, stronger. So I stayed.

Baze led me out the front door. A shining two-seater car sat parked in the circular drive. Its ivory sides and rims shone in the streetlights, a stark contrast to the chocolate interior and the tar-black wheels. The rounded gold radiator gleamed and reflected our images and the mansion behind us.

Baze squeezed my hand. "What do you think? It's brand new this year. The manufacturer cut me a deal."

"It's beautiful." I flashed a sideways glance. "Are we merely going to admire it, or will you grace me with a demonstration?"

He rubbed the back of his neck. "Our parents will wonder where you are. It would be impolite to leave without informing them."

"Oh, *now* you're concerned about our parents." I rolled my eyes. "They'll be fine." I tugged on the gold chain hanging from Baze's waistcoat pocket to pull out his stopwatch and glanced at the time. Half past eight. I replaced the watch. "You know, if we hurry, we could make it just in time."

He smoothed his pocket and frowned. "Just in time for what?"

"For the premiere magic performance at the Empress Theatre. It's a new venue in town. I met the owner at our engagement gala. He offered us free seats."

"That was a generous gesture." Baze narrowed his eyes. "Why don't I remember meeting this chap?"

"Because you likely didn't. You were quite distracted with your nieces' dance, and rightfully so." I fought off a giggle at the memory of Baze standing helplessly trapped within their twirling circle, going ever round and round. "So what say you?"

"It's tempting." He put a hand on his hip and scratched the back of his head. "They already think I've gone, but I don't feel comfortable pulling you away from an engagement to which you've already committed, not when my father is probably already seething by my absence."

"Very well then." I sighed. "I'll scurry back inside like the faithful offspring that I am, and you'll go off and hide, abandoning me to endure monotonous conversations about all the plans they have for our wedding. Or"—I raised my eyebrows—"we could get in that car, attend the performance, and revel in the excitement of the unknown. Where's your sense of adventure? Or has your new title replaced exhilarating fun with dreary decorum?"

Baze exhaled through his nose and stared at me so hard I wondered if he might bore a hole through my head. As I gazed back into his brown eyes—smooth as French silk in the streetlight—they softened. Without a word, he stepped next to the car and opened the passenger-side door. He shot me a challenging look, but the slight dimple in his cheek betrayed his amusement.

Swelling with triumph, I climbed in the car and settled in the firm but comfortable seat.

Baze shut the door. "Stay here. I need to inform the butler that you're leaving so he can relay the information to our parents."

"What are you going to tell him?"

He raised an eyebrow. "I'll think of something."

I waved a hand. "Could you also have Margaret fetch my reticule?"

As he sauntered away, the anticipation of what we were about to do—sneaking out into the night like we did when we were children—sent my heart racing. But circumstances weren't as they used to be. Would I ever be able to separate my feelings of the past with the reality of the present? Events like this couldn't keep happening. After tonight, I needed to refrain from such spontaneity.

When Baze returned, he slid into the driver's seat and placed the reticule on my lap. The engine roared to life, then relaxed into a whirring purr. He grasped the steering wheel and shifted the car into gear, then shot me a skeptical glance. "This show had better be worth it."

I crumpled the purse in my hands. "I've been assured it's one we'll not soon forget."

Chapter Six

A SUITED VALET MET US AT the door as polished gentlemen and ladies in sparkling gowns streamed into the theater. Baze eyed the young man. "Your name?"

The valet blinked up at Baze. With childlike blue eyes and a round face without a hint of whiskers, the boy couldn't have been more than sixteen. "Collin Donoghue, sir." His thick Irish accent nearly masked his words.

"Mr. Donoghue, can you assure the safe return of this automobile?" Baze asked.

"Yes, sir. I promise."

Baze seemed to ponder before handing Collin the key.

"Thank you, sir." Collin ducked his head and hopped into the car.

I bristled at the stern tone Baze had taken with the boy, but before I could scold him, he grasped my hand and directed it to his arm.

As we approached the entrance, I gazed up at the marquee. The brilliant electric sign seemed to beckon me inside. Posters covering the windows on either side of the open doors displayed a fantastical illustration of Finn Kelly in a swirl of cards, colored smoke, and feathers. A dove flew beside him, wings flared. In large, stylized letters, "The Dubliner" stretched along the bottom of the posters.

One of the twin ushers, the one without the mole—Niall, was it?—greeted us inside. Dressed in a black suit with a bow tie, his hair slicked back, he smiled, and wrinkles webbed from the corners of his eyes. "Good evening, miss. How may I direct you?"

"I was told to give you this." I reached into my reticule and produced the card Cornelius had gifted to me at the Fords' gala.

Niall's eyebrows rose, then he placed a gloved fist over his middle and bowed. "Right this way."

He led us into the main hall, lit dimly with golden lights that created a tranquil, comforting ambience. More men dressed like Niall lined the outside walls, each waiting to assist guests. He led us up the staircase.

I lifted my skirts and watched my step as I ascended, thankful for Baze's arm. Though my heeled shoes didn't have substantial height, I'd always been uncomfortable in them. Give me slippers—or better yet, bare feet—any day.

We followed Niall to the right and stepped lightly along the thin red carpet leading the way down the middle of the hall. We passed multiple openings on our left, accented with draping curtains to allow privacy for the guests inside. When we reached the end of the hall, Niall directed us to the last opening.

"Please, make yourselves comfortable. I will be close at hand should you need anything." His mouth twitched. "Enjoy the show."

Inside, we found ourselves in the box closest to the stage, positioned high, overlooking the rest of the crowd. Several rows of seats filled the box, clearly meant for more than two guests. I released Baze's arm, walked to the front row, and settled into one of the lush velvet cushions.

"Best seat in the house, I'd wager." Baze sank into the seat beside mine and looked at me askance. "You certainly made an impression on your theater friend."

I ignored him and leaned forward to watch the audience gather. Sweeping music provided a calming undertone to the crowd's conversation. In the middle section of seats, a large man sat wedged in a chair near the end of the row. The chandelier lights danced across his bald head before he placed a top hat upon it. His wife sat beside him, dressed in a sequined gown, her hair twisted in an array of beads.

"Mr. Clifton is here." I pointed.

Baze followed my gesture. "Your father's mate from the House of Lords? Strange seeing him here. I thought he abhorred the Irish."

"He does. Curious that he'd attend a show that's blatantly so."

"Perhaps it was a special invitation like yours." Baze gave me another condescending look.

I huffed and tried to take a deep breath. Unfortunately, my inhale cut short as my ribs hit the confines of my corset. It was about this time in the evening when Margaret would help me undress—or I would tug at the laces myself. I took another breath in through my nose, but the strain made my torso and neck ache.

Baze gave me a sideways glance. "Are you well?"

"Yes," I said, perhaps a bit too quickly.

"You've been acting strange since the engagement party." He paused, then whispered, "Is that what's bothering you?"

"I'm not acting strange. It isn't bothering me."

"But you seem—"

"'Twas a lovely evening." I forced a smile. "I have nothing about which to complain."

"Al—"

"Your parents' hospitality and generosity know no bounds—"

Baze pressed a hand over my mouth. I targeted him with a glare but didn't struggle.

"You don't have to do this," he said. "If you don't want to talk about it, then you simply have to say so."

When he freed my mouth, I lifted my chin. "Very well. I don't want to talk about it."

He grinned. "Now, was that so difficult?"

I rolled my eyes and drew in a breath. As the ache in my neck deepened, I winced.

He held out an upturned palm. "Give me your hand."

I faced forward. "No."

"Adelynn."

"I'm fine."

He snatched my hand from my lap, grasped it firmly in his own, and began massaging the inner muscle of my thumb. His warm strength swirled up my arm and wrapped my core in delight. Gradually, the tightness in my neck lessened. I'd forgotten the little medical tricks his brother Frederick had taught him.

I closed my eyes and breathed low and deep—already finding it easier—and tried to coax my thoughts away from Baze, of his tight hold and how my hand pressed against his thigh.

Shadows and lights danced across the back of my eyelids. The din of the theater hushed and became a humming backdrop to the ringing in my ears. Light grew brighter, casting out the shadows, erasing the black, until it became blinding. Then it flickered to utter darkness.

I blinked my eyes open. I now stood outside, and my vision hazed. I was in an alley of some kind, the night sky void of stars. Directly in front of me, not five feet away, Mr. Clifton stood with his knees knocking. Sweat poured from his pink forehead, his eyes wide and wild.

"Please," he managed, his voice quaking. He waved his hands in front of him as if to ward off an attacker. He held a knife in his left hand. "Please let me be. I'll give you anything. I have money. Lots of money!"

"Oh, I think we're past that point, laddie," I said, my voice hollow, distorted, and thickly Irish. "I'm afraid you cannot continue."

"No! I beg you."

"You have no other choice." I grinned.

"No, wait!"

Mr. Clifton grasped the dagger with both hands and plunged it into his own chest.

Black tendrils fingered their way across my sight until everything went dark again. I couldn't feel, couldn't hear, couldn't smell.

Wait—fingers massaged my hand, spreading warmth through my body.

I jolted, opened my eyes, and whipped my hand away from Baze. He jumped. "Sorry. Did I hurt you?"

I inhaled sharply and searched for Mr. Clifton in the crowd. He still sat there, his head bent toward his wife in conversation. He waved his hands in a cryptic manner, no dagger in sight. Everything appeared normal. So what had I just seen? A premonition? A vision of the future? Is that what I had seen at the engagement party? And did it mean Mr. Clifton was destined for the same fate?

I sat quietly on a chair against the far backstage wall, head bowed over my folded, gloved hands, knees supporting my elbows. I listened. People pooled into the auditorium like a pestilent wave. They'd be watching intently, eager to be fooled by magic. I had only to sit back and make sure they witnessed a good show.

I pressed my thumbs into the corners of my eyes. Those rich fools, wasting money on fleeting pleasures while an entire population couldn't afford to buy bread. But why should they be concerned? They were the cause.

Laughter swept through the crowd. The hair on my neck stood on end. I rose slowly, ventured through the sea of props and stagehands, and peeked out from behind the dense curtains. The auditorium swelled nearly to capacity, dotted with men in black suits, accompanied by women with their chins lifted. Dust tickled my nose, and I fought against the urge to sneeze.

My gaze rested on a middle-aged gentleman sitting near the center of the crowd. He rested a hand on his round stomach and jiggled as he laughed at something the woman next to him said—the epitome of rich, entitled, and moronic.

The first victim had been an unfortunate but necessary test. To garner the attention of the police . . . and Adelynn. Tonight, the curtain would be rising on the real show, to really test the mettle of the players. I turned away from the curtain and rubbed a finger under my nose to suppress the itch. A rush of nausea gave me pause.

Every respectable magic show needed a compliant volunteer— chosen by the magician, of course. It was my job to see to it that this audience had an outstanding show. Our volunteer didn't know it yet, but he had been specially chosen for the grand finale.

Chapter Seven

"AL, WHAT'S WRONG?" BAZE ASKED AGAIN. "You're ghastly pale."

Licking my lips, I tried to collect myself. "I saw—"

The chandelier dimmed. Music swelled. Audience members quieted. The crimson curtains reflected the glow from the footlights out onto the audience. My heart beat against my chest like the thundering hooves of a racehorse. I needed to inform Baze about what had happened. The last time I had seen a body in a dream, it turned up in real life. Show or no show, Mr. Clifton was in danger.

I leaned toward Baze and whispered, "I need to speak with you."

He gestured to the stage. "The show is about to start."

"Never mind that. This is important."

The vibrato of a solo violin drew my attention to the stage. As the orchestra's full sound joined and enriched the melody, the curtains parted just enough to allow Cornelius through and then swished shut.

Smiling, Cornelius waltzed to the edge of the stage until the lights cast long shadows over his suit, elongating his already tall frame. Covered with a top hat, his dark hair hung straight to the tops of his shoulders. He lifted his chin to peer at the audience in the second-floor boxes. His shaped eyebrows rose above his eyes, deep pools of molten silver in the low light.

"Good evening, my friends." Cornelius's clear voice projected through the large space. "It is my pleasure to welcome you to the Empress Theatre and thank you for coming. We have been working tirelessly to make sure this is a show you won't soon forget. Our resident magician, The Dubliner, despite his name, comes to you from Liscannor, County Clare, Ireland."

A few murmurs trickled through the crowd. In the corner of my vision, Baze shifted.

Cornelius clapped his hands together and backed up a few steps. "Now, let's get on with the show, shall we? You'll be dazzled. You'll be deceived. And you'll witness things you can't even begin to comprehend. That, I can promise you."

He squeezed through the curtains. Then, before I even had a chance to breathe, they yanked apart and sped across the stage, revealing its entirety. Cornelius was gone. A man-sized blue box sat vertical and isolated in the center of the stage. Nearby stood a rectangular table covered in a black cloth.

That's it.

As much as I longed to know what kind of trick involved the box on the stage, I had to tell Baze what I had seen. If I remained silent and misfortune befell Mr. Clifton, I was not certain I could forgive myself.

I stood, grasped Baze's hand, and leaned backward to heave him out of his seat.

"What are you doing?" he whispered through his teeth, but I tugged him up the wide stairs and out the door past Niall.

"We'll just be a moment," I whispered to the doorman as we passed. Out in the hallway, I looked both ways and led Baze to the left. When the hall came to an end and we could go no farther, blocked by a wall decorated with what looked like half of a stone fountain, I twirled to face Baze.

"I don't understand you," he said before I could speak, hands on his hips. "You were so excited to come tonight, and now you're perfectly okay with missing the opening act."

"I had another vision," I said.

He let out an aggravated sigh, voice stern. "Adelynn."

"Listen to me. Clifton died. I saw him."

"No, Al. Clifton is sitting in that auditorium next to his wife, watching the show."

"Then I've seen a vision of what is to come." I stared hard into his eyes, daring him to contradict me. "My first premonition turned out to be more than simply a dream. Why should this be any different?"

He groaned and scrubbed a hand down his face. "Because people don't see visions of the future."

"Why not?" Uncertainty hitched my voice as applause filtered in from the auditorium. "What if God sent me these visions? What if I'm seeing them so I can warn you?"

"It doesn't work like that."

"How can you be sure?"

Baze gritted his teeth. "God doesn't meddle in our affairs like that. He can't be bothered."

"You're just bitter." I jabbed a finger into his chest. "But it doesn't matter what you think. I saw what I saw. Mr. Clifton is going to go into an alleyway, and he's going to stab himself. Just like Mr. Mallory."

"I've had enough of this." Baze moved to step around me.

I snatched his arm. "At least talk to him after the show."

Baze glowered but didn't pull away. I could almost see his thoughts whirring and meshing like the gears of a clock. He exhaled through his nose. "Very well. But once we see that he is hale and hearty, I don't want to hear another word about this."

"Thank you."

He shook his head, then took my hand. As he led me back to our seats, I glimpsed the stage. The box still sat in the center, but now, long, sharp swords pierced its sides. Clothed in an elegant black suit and top hat, Finn Kelly circled the box and slid another sword into the side.

I swallowed. Was someone inside?

When he finished, Finn posed beside the box and gestured toward it, prompting nervous applause from the audience. Then he stabbed another sword through the box, this time eliciting a feminine grunt from within.

I halted, my eyes fixed on the box. I'd heard of tricks like this, but I'd never seen them performed. How was it possible to remain unharmed? I held my breath as Finn grasped the sides of the box and spun it around until it circled a full rotation, giving everyone a look at the hilts and sword tips sticking from its sides.

Finn lifted his arms and bowed—no applause this time. He extracted the swords with spine-tingling scrapes of the blades against wood. When he had removed them all and rested them in a heap on the table, he gave the audience a one-sided smile and unlatched the door. It swung open to reveal a woman crammed inside—the same woman I had mistaken for a man earlier.

Finn extended his hand and helped her climb out. Her dark green and black leotard hugged her deep curves, while her heels lengthened her already long, bare legs. When she smiled at the audience, her bright red lips made her white teeth shine.

After escorting her to the edge of the stage, Finn clapped his feet together and lifted his free hand. "Let's give me lovely assistant, Siobhan, some appreciation." He and Siobhan bowed together. The pink feathers in her hair swayed with every move of her head.

The audience erupted in applause. I let out a long sigh as Baze and I took our seats.

"Thank you, Shiv." Finn released her, and she backed away a few paces, then stood with a bent knee and hand planted on her hip.

Finn gave a sharp whistle and held out his index finger. A rustle of activity erupted behind the left-side curtain before a dove glided through the air and perched on his outstretched finger.

Finn smiled and stroked the bird. "Lads and lasses, may I introduce the love of my life, Maeve. She's been with me since my very first show, and she's goin' to help me with somethin' extra special tonight." He wiggled his fingers, and Maeve hopped between each one, her wings a white blur.

I sat mesmerized, both by the beauty of the dove and the timbre of his accent. I watched the dove's wings flutter as I noted the way Finn elongated his o's and combined some of his th's into t's.

"You see, Maeve has been with me through many hardships." The bird flapped about his head and settled on his shoulder. "She was with me on my crossin' to England when I was a young man and later when I watched the Irish lose their chance at freedom in the House of Lords, once again." Maeve flitted her tail and sprang down to his forearm. "She was with me when I made my first English acquaintance, the first without prejudice." With a smirk, he held up a flat palm, coaxed the dove into the center, and covered her with his other hand. "Of course, real prejudice never truly leaves. 'Twould be a miracle if such a strong force could simply disappear."

Finn crumpled his fists, then flashed his fingers toward the audience. A burst of white paper confetti burst from his hands, the dove nowhere to be seen.

My jaw grew slack. As if on cue, the orchestra quieted, and the chandelier lights brightened.

Siobhan headed down the stairs on the far side of the stage and made her way up one of the aisles. Her costume sparkled in the dazzling light as she stopped beside Mr. Clifton. With a wide smile, she posed and waved a hand toward him.

"Ahhh." Finn walked to the very edge of the stage. "Mr. Henry Clifton of the House of Lords. How appropriate. Sir, if you would, might I borrow your hat?"

I latched onto Baze's arm.

Mr. Clifton grunted and made no move except to cross his hands over his lap. But when he looked about and found all eyes in the audience on him, he grimaced, snatched the hat from his head, and dropped it into Siobhan's hands.

As Siobhan made her way back to the stage, Finn tucked one arm under the other and twirled a finger of his free hand. "Are you enjoyin' the show tonight, laddie?"

I stiffened, the distorted voice of the man in my vision ringing in my ears. *"Oh, I think we're past that point, laddie."* Could he be the one whose eyes I saw through? I didn't want to think of Finn as a suspect. But luckily, both he and Mr. Clifton were here in the theater, and as of yet, there was no proof that anything would happen.

Mr. Clifton's ears burned red. "You've yet to show me something that has dazzled, Mr. Kelly." His voice churned, gritty as gravel, no doubt a side effect from years of smoking and alcohol.

"Perhaps you simply haven't opened your mind to the possibilities." Finn's eyes lit with delight as Siobhan handed him the hat. He twirled it several times and aimed the empty center toward the audience. "A fine piece, Mr. Clifton. Let's see what we can find, now."

Firming his lips and wrinkling his brow, Finn held the hat upside down and swirled a hand over the opening. In a flash, his hand dropped in and returned holding a small gray ball between two fingers. He raised his eyebrows and shook his hand. When he stopped, he now held two balls. Another flourish revealed a *third*.

"Not quite what I had in mind." Finn rolled the balls between his fingers, making the movement continually faster until they merged into one single ball. After stashing it his suit, Finn switched the hat to his other hand and repeated his previous motion.

He reached into the hat, then yanked his hand out. It emerged amid a flurry of Maeve's white wings. She darted through the air before roosting on Finn's shoulder.

Mr. Clifton's face paled as the audience clapped and sent awed looks his way.

"I appreciate your takin' such good care of me girl." Finn tossed the hat to Siobhan, then grew a mischievous smile. "If only you took such care with your votin' record."

Through rousing applause and laughter, Siobhan strutted through the aisle and handed the hat to Mr. Clifton. He balked, but the lights dimmed, and the orchestra crescendoed, indicating Finn had already moved on to the next trick.

I ran my tongue over my teeth to cure my dry mouth as I watched Mr. Clifton smash the hat back on his head. The lord half-sprinted, half-tripped up the aisle, toward the back exit of the auditorium.

I jumped to the edge of my seat and smacked Baze's arm. "He's leaving. Go after him!"

"Al, calm down."

"Fine, I'll go after him." I lurched to my feet, but Baze caught my elbow and pulled me right back down.

"I'm going." He rose and sent me a stern look. In the darkness of the theater, his brown eyes softened into the shadows of his face. He jabbed a finger at my seat. "Even if I don't come back until the end of the show, do not move from this spot."

I frowned. "What do you think might happen?"

"Nothing. I just know you."

"Well, if nothing will happen, why should I stay put?"

Clenching his jaw, he bent in front of me, placed both hands on my armrests, and stared me straight in the eyes. "Promise me, Al—or I'm staying here."

"Very well." I tucked my legs like a lady should and crossed my hands over my knees. "I will not move from this spot unless you say so. Now hurry up before you lose him!"

Baze straightened and shook his head. Without another word, he hurried from the box.

I allowed myself a deep breath. Was Mr. Clifton really a target? But then why had he stabbed himself? Could the man I had impersonated in the vision have forced him into it? And what if I had just sent Baze into the mouth of danger?

No, Baze was a detective inspector with the Met. If anyone could prevent a crime—prevent murder—he could. Still, part of my conscience prodded at me, insisting danger lurked nearby.

I watched the show for a time and marveled at the tricks. Finn's stage presence, humor, and delightful accent enticed my mind away from the current predicament.

As Finn finished another trick, the audience clapped. Siobhan grabbed Finn's cane and tablecloth and hurried offstage. Finn held his arms in her direction. "Let's hear it one more time for me beautiful assistant." More applause sounded.

The stage lights dimmed a bit as he walked his familiar path to the front of the stage, brushing his palms together. "This next act is not for the faint of heart. If you have a squeamish stomach or are disturbed by peril, I suggest you be seein' yourself out."

Long seconds passed. No one moved. Silence carried through the wide, shadowed space, broken only by the occasional creak of a seat or amplified whisper. As his eyes darted from person to person, the corner of Finn's mouth twitched. Walking backward into the depths of the stage, he said quietly, "You are all committed now. Don't look away. Don't blink. Dark happenin's are at work tonight. And if you look hard enough"—he pulled a long satin sheet from his sleeve, shook it out, and looked directly up at my box—"you might discover the secret." With a flick of his wrists, the sheet billowed around him, blocking him from view, and then fell empty to the floor, Finn nowhere to be seen.

I caught my breath along with the audience. Pain shot through my palms—I had dug my fingernails into my skin. It was one thing to make a dove or a rubber ball disappear, but a full-grown man?

My throat constricted, and I reached for Baze, but his seat was empty. I froze. I'd become so caught up in the performance, I had forgotten he left to check on Mr. Clifton. What could be keeping him? Baze could only do so much out there . . . unless something had happened to him. As much as I wanted to see the end of Finn's trick, I couldn't stand the unknown. Was Baze all right, or did he lie bloody and dead in an alley?

Fear squeezed my chest tighter than the corset ever could. Promise or no promise, I needed to find him.

Gathering my skirts, I rose and sprinted to the entrance of the box. Niall wasn't standing by the door as I exited. I blinked to let my eyes adjust from the dark theater to the warmly illuminated foyer and hurried down the grand staircase. "Baze!" I whisper-shouted, my voice echoing. "Basil Ford, where are you?"

Niall's twin, Killian, still manned the front door, and the young valet, Collin, lay stretched on a divan between two pillars. He glanced my way and jolted to a stand.

I opened my mouth to ask him if he had seen Baze, but the moment I stepped off the stairs, Baze entered through the front door. Water droplets freckled his suit and teased his hair from its previously kempt appearance.

As soon as he saw me, he hesitated. Annoyance flared in his eyes as he reached me. "Do you listen to anything I say?"

"On occasion." I planted a hand on my hip. "How long does it take to see to someone's well-being? I worried that Mr. Clifton's killer had gotten you too."

Baze grasped my arm and pulled us away from the staff. His voice lowered. "There's no killer. Mr. Clifton is alive and well, I assure you."

I stepped back. "Then what, pray tell, have you been on about all this time?"

"We got strung up in conversation about politics." He grimaced. "God forbid he talk about anything besides politics."

"Where is he?" I glanced over Baze's shoulder at the front door and at the darkness outside the window.

"He said he would have a smoke and then return."

"You left him alone?"

"Al, he's a grown man. He's perfectly capable of seeing himself in. Now if you don't mind, I'd like to return to the show."

Nausea roiled my stomach. The mystery and adventure of the evening had vanished. "Actually, I'd rather return home."

We stared into each other's eyes for a long moment before Baze shrugged and massaged the bridge of his nose. "If that's what you want."

I eyed his weary expression, his submissive stance. Since when did Baze give up without a fight? Had all the talk of killers and my visions put him on edge? Or maybe he and Mr. Clifton had talked about more than Baze let on.

"Mr. Donoghue." Baze wagged two fingers at the valet and extended the parking ticket. "Would you please retrieve my car?"

"Yes, sir." The boy took the ticket and rushed out the door.

Standing straighter, Baze offered me an elbow—which I gladly accepted—and led me into the front foyer. The doors sealed behind us, giving us privacy from the doorman. Gooseflesh rose on my arms, the temperature in this alcove colder than in the main foyer.

After a sideways glance, Baze removed my hand from his arm, shed his coat, and draped it over my shoulders. The captured heat of his body and the mild scent of cedarwood and citrus enveloped me, sending an elated shiver up my spine.

Quiet rumbles from outside drew both of our gazes up to the low, gray clouds.

Baze lowered his head and shifted, his arm brushing mine. "Thank you for inviting me to come tonight."

"You're welcome." I smiled and pulled his coat tighter around me, imagining it was his embrace instead. "You're the only one whom I would have invited."

"Really?" He caught my gaze and held it for a long, agonizing moment. Then he searched my face and lowered his voice. "When are you going to tell me what's bothering you? I know you didn't want to talk about it, but you haven't been the same since the gala."

This time, I forced my smile. "Not tonight. Perhaps one day, but you aren't yet ready to hear it."

His eyebrows drew together. "What do you mean I'm not ready to hear it?"

"Exactly that."

"Adelynn, if you're not happy with our engagement, or if you're cross with me—"

"Baze, stop. It has nothing to do with you."

A half-truth. Tears threatened to form. He truly had no idea. We'd talked about marriage before, long ago, as we'd dreamed about the future. But it had all changed when his father swooped in and took me captive, stripping away my freedom and threatening to take much more unless I complied with every order and did exactly as he commanded. It was imperative that Baze continue to believe this whole affair a mutual agreement . . . for I couldn't bear the hurt he would endure were he to learn otherwise.

Headlights flashed across the window glass as Collin pulled our car next to the pavement. I shrugged out of Baze's coat and passed it back to him before pushing through the door ahead of him. Cool raindrops dotted my face. Collin dipped his head as he passed and ducked inside.

Usually, I would have stopped by the passenger-side door—the gentleman in Baze wouldn't allow a lady to open her own door—but this time, I unlatched it myself. Baze hesitated behind me, apparently unclear about whether to help me in or not. He opted for the latter.

As I set a foot on the car-step, a scream pierced the air. My foot slipped. I toppled forward into the seat, then recovered. "What in heaven's name was that?"

Before I could gather my bearings, Baze had a pistol in his hand.

"Adelynn," he barked. "Stay here." Then he slunk along the building to a side street and disappeared around the corner.

A mental image of Baze encountering someone with intent to injure him—or worse—propelled my feet forward.

When I rounded the corner, I slammed straight into Baze. He stood stock still, staring at the ground, his pistol-bearing hand hanging limp at his side. I lifted to my tiptoes and peeked over his shoulder.

Mr. Clifton lay sprawled on the ground in a pool of blood, a knife protruding from the middle of his chest, one loose fist curled around the hilt.

My breath rushed from my lungs. The knife, the alley, Mr. Clifton—I experienced it all again like a déjà vu display of horror. A sick, twisted nightmare. I'd witnessed two visions now that had each come to pass. How many more were to come?

Chapter Eight

BAZE WATCHED HIS TEAM OF CONSTABLES and inspectors document the scene and interview theatergoers and passersby. No matter how deeply he breathed, he couldn't rid himself of the regret that burrowed deep in his chest. He'd stood with Clifton not half an hour ago, and now the man lay dead.

Despite the absurdity of the situation, Adelynn had known—somehow. But entertaining the idea that she was having visions, whether from God or not, would border on the insane. A detective acted on the evidence before him and didn't chase after silly notions of seeing the future.

Out of the corner of his eye, Baze studied Adelynn as she lingered by the wall at the entrance to the alley. The flash of a journalist's camera briefly lit her inquisitive features, and Baze's earlier conversation with his father about keeping her in line shouldered its way to the front of his mind. His palms grew clammy.

This needed to stop. Coming here to the theater had been a mistake. He couldn't allow her to coerce him into participating in her schemes. They needed to learn to abide by the set standards, both now and as eventual spouses.

When Adelynn noticed Baze watching her, she threw her gaze to the sky as though feigning disinterest. She tried to smooth the curled hair that had escaped the fastener holding the rest at the back of her head, but her tending only served to make it messier.

In spite of his annoyance, he fought the urge to smile. Even now, as a grown woman, she retained the adventurous qualities of the little girl who used to pilfer his trousers and yank her hair out of its styled updo. Could he really bring himself to dampen that spirit, even if it meant enduring social scrutiny and gossip if he didn't?

Shaking his head, he turned away from her and faced Clifton's body. Bennett squatted next to it, murmuring his prayer. "Almighty God, commit his spirit into your hands. Bring agents of evil to justice and heal the pain of this dark world."

Baze waited until Bennett had finished before approaching and kneeling. Clifton's face had been frozen in time at the moment of death, his eyebrows plastered high. His body, now gray and pallid, had stiffened since discovery. Pale light from a nearby streetlamp gleamed across his wide, hazy eyes. A trickle of spittle trailed from his open mouth.

Despite the grisly details of the scene, Baze managed to maintain detached emotions, for this could never compare to the murder he'd been assigned barely a year ago. The scenes burst through Baze's mind unbidden—growing numb at hearing the victim's name spoken, stumbling through the dusky morning fog on leaden limbs, and rounding a corner to find the prone and bloodied figure of Thomas Spencer, the man who had been more of a father to him than his own. Thomas had been on his way home—to his wife, to Adelynn—when his life had been snatched from him. Images of Thomas lying motionless in his own blood had solidified in Baze's mind, as had the feeling of helplessness, knowing there was nothing he could do to bring him back.

"Based on a first glance, it certainly looks like this poor fellow offed himself." Bennett's steady voice cut through the memory.

Throat tightening, Baze willed the rest of his feelings away. He followed Bennett's gesture to Clifton's hand still curled around the dagger. Baze nodded. "Indeed it does."

"However," Bennett said, giving Baze pause, "considering the dead fellow from last week, we may need to consider other options."

Baze's stomach tingled. Adelynn's insistence on the validity of her visions—and her belief that they may be God-given—wrestled to the forefront of his mind. He struggled to force it back down. Could he admit the existence of a heavenly father? Of course. But could he speculate that the same heavenly father could willingly, selflessly, invoke visions of the future? For that, he reserved skepticism.

Baze tugged at his bow tie. "You can't draw conclusions from two unrelated incidents."

"Unrelated, so you say." Bennett pushed his spectacles higher on his nose. "Two suicides in one week? And committed in the same manner, no less."

Resisting the urge to groan, Baze merely sighed, miffed that Bennett insisted on bringing up his earlier speculation. "It's too early to link these events."

"Perhaps." Bennett shook his head. "You said you talked to him for a good long while. Did he seem of the mindset to do something like this?"

Recollecting their conversation, Baze tried to pinpoint an off spot. Clifton had exhibited agitation, most likely from being made a fool in front of hundreds of people—and by an Irishman. But that was the topic of the hour. Clifton hated the Irish. That much wasn't a secret to anyone. In a changing society and a world becoming more diverse, it wasn't so unbelievable that it could have driven him to this end.

"The motive was there," Baze said.

"Well, this knife holds the key." Bennett clapped Baze on the shoulder. "We'll need to ask the missus about it."

"Yes . . ." Baze stole a look at Adelynn. She'd inched closer, watching with wide, curious eyes. Baze pinched his brow. "I'll be just a moment," he muttered and stood.

With precise steps, he approached Adelynn and blocked her view. She frowned, but he spoke first. "What do you think you're doing?"

She brushed a hand over her cheek where tear trails had dried. "Clifton was a friend."

"Then you should remember him as he was. Alive." Baze dug in his pocket and extracted the car keys. "Come. I'll take you home."

She sniffed and shook her head. "You're needed here."

Baze sighed. "It's more important that you're out of harm's—"

"Perhaps I could be of assistance." The new voice made them both jump.

The man who had introduced the show approached. Light rain glistened in his slick black hair. For the moment, he only had eyes for Adelynn—which kindled Baze's irritation—and as the man examined her, his icy eyes seemed to emanate a faint glow, as though lit from within. The corner of his lip curled up in a smirk, revealing pearl white teeth and a sharp incisor.

"I would be honored to offer my chauffeur to take Miss Spencer home," he said, placing a hand over his chest. "I shudder to think what such a grisly scene would do to the mentality of a highborn lady."

Baze shook his head. Mentality? Indeed, it affected her mentality. It fed her lust for adventure. Baze flashed his car keys. "Thank you, sir, but I am driving her home."

"I insist." The man waved a hand. "Your duty is here, as is mine."

"I'm sorry, but who are you?"

"Forgive me." Stealing a look at Adelynn, the man bowed from the waist. "Cornelius Marx, the proprietor of the Empress. And you are Detective Inspector Basil Ford. It's a pleasure to finally make your acquaintance."

"Yes . . . Adelynn mentioned meeting you at our engagement party." Baze stiffened as he shook Marx's hand. "How did new blood on the London scene procure such an invitation?"

Marx's eyebrow lifted. "Your father and I have become fast friends, Baze. You don't mind if I call you Baze?"

"It's Inspector Ford," Baze said, bristling. "It's been a pleasure, but we must depart." He nudged Adelynn's arm and nodded at Marx.

Marx stepped in Baze's path. "As I already said, I am more than happy to offer my chauffeur. You have a job to do here. 'Twould be a shame to take you away from your responsibilities."

The way Marx looked at Adelynn—intent, confident—made

Baze's skin crawl. If Marx thought Baze would entrust her into a stranger's supervision, he was sorely mistaken.

As Baze made ready to push past the man, one of the sergeants approached. "Sorry for eavesdroppin', Inspector," the sergeant said, "but I am available to take Miss Spencer home so that you may stay here."

Marx's smile faltered, which nearly led Baze to embrace the sergeant. "Thank you. Your initiative is much appreciated." Baze handed him the keys before turning to Adelynn. "Go straight home."

She heaved a stilted sigh. "Where else would I go?"

"I mean it. It's nearly midnight. This isn't the time for gallivanting through the city."

"Not to worry. I'm far too weary for adventures such as that." She patted her thin torso. "Besides, I'm aching to change into something more breathable."

Baze's eyes followed her hand and lingered where it rested beneath her bosom. His face grew hot. He inhaled and lifted his gaze to her face, and it snagged on another of her features, this time her tender pink lips. He licked his own, suddenly dry. Were her lips still as soft as the first time he'd kissed her so many years ago?

"I pray that you will uncover evidence that leads you to the cause of Mr. Clifton's death," Adelynn said, snapping him away from his thoughts. She shot Marx a look and then leaned closer to Baze. Fire burned under his collar, but he held his ground. "And please, at least consider the possibility that I'm right."

Baze grimaced. She meant the possibility that her visions were true, that she'd witnessed it all before it occurred. No, that he could not do. Not yet.

The sergeant offered Adelynn his arm. She glanced at the officer, to Baze, then rested her hand on the sergeant's sleeve. As they made their way toward the street, she cast a longing gaze back at Baze before they disappeared around the corner.

Baze turned to Marx. "Has anyone taken your statement?"

Marx swiveled, hard soles scraping the cement. "They have not, Baze, but I'd wager you're about to ask for it."

It took everything in him not to reprimand the man. Something about Marx bred mistrust, but it was difficult to pinpoint.

Baze fished a pen and pad from his inner coat pocket. "Where were you at a quarter after ten?"

"Backstage with my crew, ensuring the success of the final act. Ask any of the them and they will verify it."

Baze maintained eye contact as he scratched some notes. "Is that where you were throughout the whole performance?"

"It is. I run a smooth operation and see to it firsthand."

"And who selects audience participants during the acts? Do you watch from backstage and instruct Mr. Kelly whom to choose?"

"I do not. I rarely watch the audience. 'Twould shatter the illusion if audience members glimpsed faces peering through the curtains."

"I suppose it would." Baze finished scrawling a note. "Were you acquainted with Mr. Clifton before tonight?"

"I hadn't had the pleasure." Marx's lip twitched. "Tonight is the first time I have laid eyes on the man."

"You never saw him enter the theater or take his seat?"

"As I said, I was backstage." Marx smoothed an eyebrow. "I'm afraid you've nothing more to glean from me, Baze. Would you mind if I got back to tending to my stage crew? They're in a rather frightful state, knowing a man died on the night of our first performance."

Baze pressed the pen tip firmly against the paper. "Actually, Mr. Marx, I've still some questions if you don't mind." They locked eyes, and the iciness of Marx's gaze wrapped Baze's spine in a shiver. "What is your relationship with the Irish?"

Marx hesitated, fire igniting in his eyes. "Pardon me, but I fail to see what that question has to do with this case. If this was a suicide—"

"Lord Clifton had quite a few enemies among the Irish, especially in the Irish Republican Brotherhood, due to his opposition of the Home Bill. From what I've observed, you employ several Irishmen here."

"You observed correctly. In fact, all of my employees are Irish."

"Then you understand my suspicion. It wouldn't be much of a coincidence that Clifton is dead outside of an Irish safe house. So if you would answer the—"

"Inspector Ford!"

Baze flinched and turned toward the shout.

Young Constable Rollie hurried to Baze's side and fumbled a salute. "Mr. Clifton's widow is crying something fierce, and she refuses to come back to Scotland Yard for comment. What should I do?"

Baze closed his eyes and stole a short but deep breath, then faked a smile at Marx. "We shall have to continue our interview at a later date. Please expect my call."

"Indeed. I look forward to it." The smirk returned to Marx's face as he bowed his head, tipped his hat, and headed to the theater doors.

Baze rotated toward Rollie. "Where is Lady Clifton?"

"Around the corner." Rollie picked at one of the polished gold buttons of his uniform. "Never dealt with a dead person before, Inspector. Lady's awfully upset. I don't quite know what to do."

"Yes, I imagine she is." Baze placed a hand on Rollie's thin shoulder. "I will talk to Lady Clifton for you, but you will accompany me and watch. And so we're clear, we haven't yet determined the cause of death."

Baze faced the alley and squared his shoulders. He willed himself forward, but his legs grew heavy. This made his fifth case involving a death that he'd had to personally attend to since starting with the Met. Each time he had talked to family members of the deceased, they had cried, hugged, and grasped at him for support. Generally, skills improved with practice, but this was a skill he wasn't sure he'd ever master—or ever wanted to, for that matter.

With soft footfalls, Baze turned out of the alley to see Lady Clifton leaning against the building, her hands covering her face as her shoulders shook. Baze halted a few feet from her and felt Rollie stop close behind him. Baze spoke low. "Lady Clifton, I offer my deepest condolences."

A hiccup and a sniffle interrupted her cries.

"I know this is painful," Baze continued, "but I'm afraid I need to ask you some questions about your husband."

After wiping her eyes with the back of her wrist, smearing her makeup in large black smudges across her cheeks, she looked at him. "As you wish, Inspector."

Baze nodded. "What had Lord Clifton's demeanor been like as of late? Were there any recent changes in his mood?"

She furrowed her brow. "No. Same as always. He did the same activities as always. Everything was normal."

"And what was the status of your marriage? Did you notice anything that might have indicated that he was unhappy?"

She curled her lip, exposing her teeth. "You think this was a suicide."

Baze stumbled at her hardened stare. "This investigation has only begun, Lady Clifton. We aren't certain how your husband perished, but early examination seems to indicate such." He cleared his throat as Rollie fidgeted. "So, please, if you would answer the question. Anything you can tell us may help us determine what happened."

Lady Clifton jabbed a crooked finger in Baze's face. "My husband did *not* kill himself, young man. He was perfectly happy with his life. In fact, he feared death."

Baze resisted the urge to retreat from the nicotine fog of her heated breath.

"Continue your investigation, Inspector, but do not enter my presence again until you have determined an indisputable cause of death." She whirled on her heels and scurried to a vehicle parked on the side of the street, collapsed inside, and sped away.

"Hag," Rollie muttered.

Baze threw the constable a glare. "She's just lost a husband."

"But think how much money she's come into." Rollie slid his fingers up the back of his red hair. "If it were me, I wouldn't miss him."

Baze shook his head. Did the lad have any sense of propriety? He made his way back to Clifton. Rollie followed, and as the body came into view, Rollie shuddered. Baze approached Bennett, who stood going over a list of notes.

"Find anything new?" Baze asked.

"Afraid not." Bennett shook his head. "The vicinity is free of clues, and the body itself doesn't show anything out of the ordinary, aside from the dagger sticking out of his chest."

"And the verdict?"

"Clifton is left-handed. He was found with his left hand clutching the dagger and a blood spatter on his forefinger and thumb. No one reported any suspicious individuals leaving the scene." Bennett exhaled heavily. "Everything is leading to suicide—but my gut tells me otherwise."

Baze bit back his urge to squash Bennett's instincts. "If the evidence points to it, then why question it?"

"I'd like to see what Hamilton has to say after a full autopsy." Ben looked him in the eyes, light from the nearby streetlamp glinting off his spectacles. "Something about this that doesn't feel quite . . . normal." He lowered his voice. "I can't explain it, but it's as though there's another kind of power at work here."

Baze gave a nervous laugh and peered at Rollie, whose eyes widened. Surely Bennett couldn't be in his right mind. This case was cut and dried, exactly as the Victoria Embankment case had been. Nothing out of the norm, no witnesses, no suspects, no indication of foul play.

"I had a vision of the man who died." Adelynn's urgent words broke into his thoughts.

He stiffened. Now that she'd planted the idea, he couldn't escape it. But she couldn't possibly have seen what she claimed. Things like that simply didn't happen.

Chapter Nine

PARKED WITHIN VIEW OF THE EMPRESS, I chewed a nail and stared down every passerby as though they were to blame for my spying. The theater remained deserted. Not a light shone from behind the glass windows. For being a mere two days after Mr. Clifton's demise, the area was far more deserted than I'd expected.

Go have a look.

I steeled myself against my own suggestion. What if someone were inside? How could I explain my presence? I couldn't very well tell them the truth, that I was investigating an alleged murder because of something I'd seen in a vision. Even the thought sounded daft. And what then? Would they show me the door or involve the police?

Samuel cleared his throat. "Miss Adelynn, as pleasant as this street is, I assume we came here for more than sightseeing?"

"Yes, you're right. I'll only be a moment." I opened the car door and stepped onto the pavement. Resting my hands on my hips, I sent Samuel a look indicating he should stay put. He held up his hands, shook his head, and looked the other way.

I faced the theater, my confidence boosted by my authoritative cream-colored walking suit. The ensemble featured black trim, from the base of the ankle-length skirt to the tunic-style jacket sleeves to the silk cord buttons. I'd requested fancier ornaments from Margaret and had been rewarded with sparkling emerald earrings and a large black hat embellished with a huge white feather. If I were to walk into a battlefield, I might as well be dressed the part.

I straightened my spine and marched to the Empress front doors before I could talk myself out of it. Heart racing, I yanked on the handle.

The door refused to budge.

My adrenaline dulled. Pressing my face against the glass, I squinted into a void of shadows and knocked. The tinny glass sound ended with no echo. Groaning, I rolled my eyes at the sky. There had to be another way in.

Moseying my way to the entrance of the alley where Mr. Clifton's body had been discovered, I kept an eye on people roaming the pavement. An old man lumbered along with a corgi trotting out ahead. Three suffragettes, with sashes blazing, congregated at the street corner. A gentleman and his lady approached arm in arm, gazing only at each other.

When they passed out of sight, I darted into the alleyway. I strode beside the wall, careful to avoid the dark stain on the cobbled ground. As I moved deeper into the alley, the shadows cast by the overarching buildings grew darker. I shivered. Despite offering protection from the wind, the alley didn't provide an ounce of sunlight to compensate.

Finally, I spied a door handle protruding from an inset in the wall ten paces away. A glance back confirmed my privacy before I hurried to the door and tried the handle. No success.

I peered up at the hazy semicircle window in the door. Even with the height of my modest heels, I couldn't quite see inside, so I lifted to my tiptoes and peered in, tugging at the dusty sill with my gloved fingers. The grime caked to the glass made it impossible to see within. I wrinkled my nose. Couldn't a ritzy establishment such as this afford someone to clean this simple door?

"What are you doing?"

I yelped and stumbled backward into a man's arms—Bennett.

He helped me regain my balance and adjusted his crooked spectacles. "The building is noticeably vacant. Surely you're not trespassing."

"Surely . . ." I cleared my throat. What would I tell him? *How* could I tell him? Truth be told, I was spying on those in the theater. Two deaths had occurred, the second connected to this theater somehow, and my visions indicated more to the story than met the eye. Baze wouldn't see that. Would Bennett?

"Al, are you all right?"

I blinked out of my daze and secured his gaze with my own. "I have something to tell you."

Strolling along the gravel paths of St. James Park lined with gnarled cypress trees and fragrant cherry blossoms, I gripped Bennett's arm. "Please listen closely with no interjections. I must explain it in full before you offer your opinion. It will sound absurd, but you must keep your mind open. I beg you."

He raised his eyebrows and smiled. "I'm listening."

The path steered us around the lake, and I explained everything, starting with the vision I had at the gala and finding the same scene later that night. I told him of Mr. Clifton, of what I had seen beforehand, and of the uneasy feelings I experienced whenever in close proximity to the theater. As the words flowed from my lips, hearing them said aloud, I doubted them. I sounded like a madwoman.

By the time I finished my tale, we found ourselves standing in the center of Blue Bridge, looking east. The foliage of the nearby island provided a lush foreground to the Horse Guards and government offices beyond. Bennett simply stared at the swans paddling across the glassy lake surface. I bit my lip, certain he was contemplating whether to turn me over to an asylum or warn Baze about the deranged woman he was about to marry.

Bennett folded his fingers and leaned his forearms against the railing. "And what does Baze think about all of this?"

Knowing New Scotland Yard lay just beyond the government offices, I crossed to the opposite side of the bridge, preferring the grand view of Buckingham Palace to the guilt of what I withheld from Baze. I gripped the railing as Bennett joined me. "I'm not sure he believes me. He thinks it all my imagination."

"And what do you think?"

"I think it's real . . . somehow. Maybe by divine intervention. But that's why I'm here. To find answers."

Bennett crossed his arms and leaned backward against the railing. "Indeed, God gave foresight to those He deemed worthy in biblical times, so it's not outrageous to think it happens even today."

Had I heard him correctly? I fiddled with the pearls at my throat and waited for him to continue.

He brushed his chin with a thumb. "God only knows why you see these heinous acts before they occur. If these keep happening, we must know why. Right now, as far as I can tell, you're the only one who might have an inkling of the truth."

I fought back a wide smile. *He believes me!*

Gripping the railing, I calmed my quivering voice. "I wish to befriend those at the theater and gain their trust. They must be connected. And if I can find that connection, perhaps I can put a stop to future deaths." I picked at a fleck of chipped paint. "With these visions, I feel responsible."

Bennett narrowed his eyes and watched a well-dressed couple pass by us. Then he nodded. "Clearly, I'm not going to stop you from investigating this on your own, so I want you to report to me." He wagged a finger and looked me right in the eyes. "But I forbid you to visit the theater—or any other location you deem significant—unless you are accompanied by an officer. I'll assign one to your safekeeping. This could be dangerous, and I don't want you going anywhere alone." He adjusted his spectacles. "And if you have another vision, tell me immediately. Perhaps we can act before it comes to pass."

"Thank you, Bennett." I nodded and swallowed. "And . . . please don't tell Baze about all of this, about what we plan to do."

"I shall keep it between you and me. I promise." He placed a fist over his heart, then touched my shoulder. "Though, I don't think you should fear Baze's retribution should you share it with him. He could never dismiss you."

"I'm not so sure." I shrugged. Baze was already put off by my claims. If he knew Bennett and I were joining forces, it would send him over the edge.

Bennett pursed his lips and looked skyward. Fragments of blue peeked through the gray clouds. "Did he ever tell you the reason he chose to refer to you as Al when we were children?"

I turned toward him. "It's a play name we used as kids to make believe."

"That's half true." He smirked. "Somewhere along the way of our blossoming trio, he became drawn to you, and being the young boy he was, it embarrassed him. After all, girls were far too prim for an adventurous lad like himself. Baze fashioned the nickname so that he could see you merely as one of the boys."

Warmth spread through my body. "But you both still use the nickname today."

"Yes, but he no longer sees you as one of the boys."

My heart pounded in my chest. "I should hope not."

"You know what I mean."

I studied my groomed fingernails. I did know, but it would be easier if Baze still viewed me as "one of the boys."

I cleared my throat. "How does Emily fare?"

Bennett's eyes lit with delight. "She is well. Growing larger every day."

I swatted his shoulder. "You had better not tell her that."

"'Twas only an observation." He tweaked my nose with a knuckle. "Just as this line of questioning is your tactic to change the subject."

Forcing a laugh, I pushed back the longing squeezing my chest. "Perceptive as always, Inspector."

I followed them to St. James' Park—Adelynn and the inspector. They engaged in small talk, based on what I could hear from twenty paces back. The busy afternoon concealed my presence well enough. Tipping my hat to a passing couple, I watched Adelynn and the inspector cross to the center of the bridge and pause.

Leave her be.

The quiet voice deep within my conscience buzzed in my head. No matter how strong the dark desires were growing in me, it somehow found a way to surface.

Give up this quest. More people will die—innocent people.

I perched on a nearby bench and occupied myself tossing breadcrumbs to the ducks. Give up? That was something I could not do. Not when they'd taken so much. Innocent, they were not.

I closed my eyes and thought of my home in the country with the rolling hills, the harbor, and the sheep. It'd been more than a decade since I'd set foot on the green land, but I could still smell the fresh air, tinged with salt from the sea.

A caress of wind brought me back in time, back to the Cliffs of Moher where it all began.

Puffins squawked and dove in and out of the cliff walls. White sea spray crashed against jutting rocks at the base hundreds of fathoms below. The walls curved in and out in exaggerated waves, each surface wrought with multicolored lines and marred by burrows and weather scars. A stone tower stood guard in the distance. Wind rushed by and stole my breath as I watched the scene unfold before me.

Ciaran and I stood alone, both of us who'd barely seen ten summers. Ciaran teetered in the gales, standing mere inches from the cliff's edge with dried tear stains on his cheeks. I watched from where I stood inside the flagstones extending both directions over the hilly clifftop.

"Are you going to jump?" I asked.

Ciaran shut his eyes. "Me family's all gone. I don't want to be alone."

"You're not alone. I'm here."

Ciaran stared long and hard at the waves dying on the shore below. But then, little by little, he swiveled until his back faced the ocean. Wind tugged at him as though begging him to change his mind. I smiled and reached out. Ciaran lifted a trembling hand.

A gust spilled around us. Ciaran swayed and stepped backward. His heel caught empty air.

My stomach lurched. I gasped and opened my eyes, which returned me to the overcast afternoon park. Phantom pain ignited in my shoulder, where bone had popped and ligament had torn. At least I'd managed to drag Ciaran back over the edge to safety.

I looked to the bridge but found that Adelynn and the inspector had disappeared. This was no time to be distracted by daydreaming, no matter how critical a part the memories played in my production. We'd almost died that day.

Who was to say I would make it out of this current predicament alive? By the dark and ruling powers that be, this could very well go south, especially if Adelynn involved the Metropolitan Police or Criminal Investigative Department. But she should be careful of what she desired. If she wanted to involve the police, by all means, we could certainly oblige.

Chapter Ten

WE MET DOWN THE STREET FROM the theater so we wouldn't rouse suspicion. Samuel dropped me off at the corner where Bennett and another young man waited. I pulled my shawl tight against the nip in the air.

"Adelynn, good of you to come." Bennett gestured to the other officer. "I'd like you to meet Sergeant Peter Moseley."

The young man took my hand in a firm shake and gave a slight bow. "Charmed, miss." He straightened and placed a hand on the baton hanging at his hip.

Though he might not have been much older than me, he sported a dark goatee, a touch of recession in his hairline, and intelligent eyes that belied his age. He wore the typical navy high-necked tunic and trousers of a Met officer but lacked a helmet. A delicate hummingbird brooch gleamed on his left breast pocket.

"The pleasure is mine." I curtsied. "I understand you're to be my bodyguard."

"Where you lead, I shall follow, miss."

"Come now, Sergeant, loosen up." Bennett smacked Moseley on the shoulder.

Moseley blinked, face stoic. "'Tis a fool's errand, this quest. Police work ought to be left to the police."

"Ehm, right." Bennett sighed as I pressed my fingers to my lips and concealed a laugh. "Too loose, mate."

"I'll do as you command, Inspector."

Bennett shook his head but cracked a small smile. "A stickler, this one, but he's one of the best. Sure you still want to do this?"

"Positive," I said.

"Best be off then. I'll be round if anything should arise. Don't hesitate to send for me."

"I won't." We exchanged knowing looks before he strolled off and left me with the sergeant. I took a breath and put on a smile. "Shall we?"

"Lead on."

I bit my lip to avoid reacting to his terse answer and marched toward the theater. With each step, a growing chill took hold in my core. Why did I feel so uneasy?

Probably because you could be walking straight into danger, Adelynn.

But there was something more. I couldn't explain the feeling, but it seemed as though a heavy presence had settled in the vicinity. What kind of presence, however, I couldn't guess. I clutched my string of pearls. *Dear Lord, go with me into this place.*

I squared my shoulders and angled toward the sergeant. "What do you prefer to be called? Sergeant Moseley? Sergeant? Peter?"

He walked with a straight spine and hands clasped at the small of his back. "You can call me whatever you like, miss. I've no preference."

A disdain for decorum directed my first instincts toward his given name, but in this case, perhaps formality was best. "Why did you decide to become a policeman, Sergeant Moseley?"

"I wish to help people," he said immediately as though he had expected the question. "More than that, I wish to keep them safe from injustice."

"It sounds like there's a story there."

He sighed. "I long for justice in London, and I would like to help enforce that justice. But the inspector insisted I'm better suited here."

I tried to suppress a wince. "I'm sorry you're stuck with me."

Something flashed in his eyes. His cheeks reddened. "You needn't fear for your safety, miss. Though my heart yearns for the field, I commit myself fully to my duties. I will protect you wholeheartedly should you be threatened."

"Oh, I don't doubt that." I stopped under the shadow of the Empress portico and shivered. "However, you may be closer to the field than you think." Taking an invigorating breath, I strode to the doors and breezed inside.

Finn's voice echoed through the empty foyer from within the auditorium. With Sergeant Moseley close on my heels, I followed the conversation past the center staircase and through one of the two sets of double doors into the auditorium. Finn stood in the middle of the stage with a large box on wheels behind him. Siobhan posed next to it, dressed in ragged trousers and a baggy shirt, a far cry from the risqué ensemble she had worn in the real show. It took but a glance at her milky white skin, angled jaw, and thick lashes to see that she was beautiful. Why did she feel the need to cover it up?

I located Cornelius seated in the front row and headed down the aisle toward him. Though I trod quietly, Finn caught sight of me. Cornelius must have noticed his glance and looked back over his shoulder. Within a few moments, he stood at my side. "Adelynn, this is quite a surprise," he whispered.

"Yes, forgive me. I should have sent word."

"No need. It's always a pleasure." He nodded in Sergeant Moseley's direction. "And who is your companion?"

"Sergeant Peter Moseley with the Met. He's assigned to my safekeeping. After those two recent deaths, one can never be too careful."

"A wise decision. Welcome, Sergeant." Cornelius offered his hand, but Sergeant Moseley merely nodded. Cornelius slowly withdrew his gesture and raised an eyebrow. "A tad skeptical, eh, Sergeant?"

"It is my job to be skeptical," Sergeant Moseley replied.

"Right so, you policemen are always internalizing intel. What can you tell about me?" Cornelius took a step back and opened his arms wide.

Sergeant Moseley shifted and furrowed his brow.

"Tell you what. Let's play a wee game." Cornelius grinned and ushered us away from the stage. "Reading people happens to be my specialty, as it is your specialty as a sergeant in the Met, I imagine. Let's have a go at each other." He shot me a quick wink. "Adelynn can be the judge."

Sergeant Moseley cleared his throat. "If you don't mind, Mr. Marx, I prefer to keep my observations to myself. For policing reasons, you understand."

"Oh, where's the sport in that? Play the game. There's no harm in it."

Sergeant Moseley's demeanor shifted to a more relaxed posture, and his eyes grew hazy. "Very well," he said, prompting a quick but nevertheless satisfied smile from Cornelius. "By the manner in which you speak, you're educated but not from London originally, perhaps not even from England. Wales, I'd wager, by the irregular cadence of your accent. You're not a physical man but rather rely on your wits and intelligence to succeed." He stole a look at Finn and Siobhan before focusing back on Cornelius. "And despite the unrest with the Irish, you seem quite at ease here among them, indicating a long, intimate history between yourself and their kind."

"Very close," Cornelius said, his lips tipping into a smile. "My turn." He narrowed his eyes and tilted his head left, then right. "You're young, sharp, and cordial. Based on your rank and age, you were well involved in the force at the time of the gunfight on Sidney Street several years ago, which caused much of the force to arm themselves. Though, unlike many of your comrades, you have opted to carry a baton instead of a gun. So, one must ask oneself, why would any officer forgo a gun in times such as these?"

As Cornelius took a step forward, Sergeant Moseley retreated one pace, his ears burning scarlet. "There are many possible answers to this, the most likely scenarios being that you still believe in an unarmed force and keeping up confidence in the common folk—or you fear the potential destruction caused by guns. While I don't doubt your high moral character, the latter is more likely, measuring from your expression. But it goes one step further. You don't merely fear the potential of guns. You saw their power once before, demonstrated on someone for whom you cared deeply." Excitement deepened in Cornelius's eyes. "Tell me, Sergeant. That hummingbird brooch you wear clipped to your pocket doesn't have anything to do with it, does it?"

Nostrils flaring, Sergeant Moseley's eyes glossed. He blinked and stuttered but didn't form a coherent sentence.

I couldn't bear to let the moment continue. "You both did a fine job." I stepped between them and faced Cornelius. "But I would like to speak with you about the reason for my visit."

Cornelius held Sergeant Moseley in his gaze for a moment longer and then smiled at me. "If you would follow me, I know the perfect location for our tête-à-tête." He led us down the aisle and to the staircase on the left.

Siobhan postured herself at the top with folded arms and a grimace, halting us halfway. "What's she doin' here?"

"Shiv!" Finn called from his position at center stage.

Cornelius, however, didn't bat an eye. "She is our guest, Siobhan, and you will treat her as such."

"Disturbin' the peace, no doubt." Siobhan's eyes hardened as she took in the sight of me. "Meddlin' where she don't belong." She radiated so much hostility that her jaw quivered.

I stared right back, hopefully channeling just as much fervor. What was her vendetta? We'd only met once before. How could I possibly have done anything to put her off? Well, if she wanted to start a row, I could certainly oblige.

Cornelius touched my shoulder—a gentle, warm touch that calmed my inner fire—then climbed the stairs to Siobhan's level. He gestured for me to follow. As I passed by, Siobhan wrinkled her nose, so I did what came naturally and wrinkled my nose back at her.

"Now, ladies, there's no need to be uncivil." Cornelius shook his head.

"No uncivility, I assure you," I said. "At least from me."

Siobhan clenched her teeth and made a move toward me, but Sergeant Moseley stepped between us. "Please step back, miss." He glared down at the small Irishwoman.

"I like the way you think, Sergeant." Cornelius took my hand, placed it in his elbow, and led me the rest of the way up the stairs. "If you wouldn't mind entertaining one another for a short while, I've something to show our guest."

Sergeant Moseley made to argue, but before he could, Cornelius whisked me through the curtains to backstage. Dust stung my eyes and pricked my nose. Humid, stale air enveloped me like a shroud. A cool trickle danced across my skin and stood my hair on end.

Cornelius pointed upward. "How would you like to see the stage from above?"

"I've seen it. I was seated in one of the boxes for your first performance. It presented a magnificent view."

"That's not quite what I meant." He smiled. Though I stood close to him, I could barely make out his face in the dim light. Yet, as he glanced my way, the striking blue of his eyes flashed. "There's a ladder here." He took my wrist and coaxed my hand forward until it touched a wooden rung.

"Where does it lead?" I whispered.

"There's one way to find out."

Sergeant Moseley burst through the curtains. I backed away from the ladder, but Cornelius held out a hand toward the sergeant. "No need to fear, my good man. I simply want to show her the catwalk. It will be plenty visible from the stage."

Sergeant Moseley huffed. "I answer to Miss Spencer, Mr. Marx."

I touched the sergeant's arm. "It's all right. Once we ascend, you can go back to the stage and watch us."

Narrowing his eyes, Sergeant Moseley crossed his arms.

Cornelius didn't seem put off by the sergeant's intense stare. He chuckled. "I shall go first and meet you at the top, Adelynn."

I breathed a sigh and smiled at Sergeant Moseley. As I waited while Cornelius climbed, I reminded myself why I'd come—to gain their trust and find new opportunities to explore the establishment more. Perhaps this small diversion would help me achieve my objective.

"All right, Adelynn," Cornelius called from above. "I'm ready for you."

With a nod toward Sergeant Moseley, I scaled the ladder with ease. Despite my skirt and heels, the rungs proved mere child's play after a full adolescence of traipsing about in large trees with sparse branches. I'd never known when one might break, and with a race on the line and Baze to beat, I'd become adept at finding solid footholds.

At the top, Cornelius took my hand and helped me to my feet. We stood atop a walkway no wider than a single person, which forced us to stand close. I took a deep breath and caught myself relishing his comforting scent of verbena and sandalwood.

Light shone from below. Heavy sacks and ropes tied to posts lined the entire railing. Holding both of my hands, Cornelius stepped back on his heels to guide me forward. Once we progressed to the center of the walkway, he turned me away from him. The entire auditorium expanded before me in full red and gold glory. Below, the stage sprawled like a continent upon the ocean. *Is this what God sees as He watches over us from heaven?*

"Extraordinary, isn't it?" Cornelius cast his gaze about the auditorium.

"Indeed." I spotted Sergeant Moseley now entangled in a rousing discussion—or argument—with Finn and Siobhan. He glanced up, so I waved. "What do you use the catwalk for?"

"We typically don't employ it in a show. Back when the theater hosted dramatic productions, it was used for backdrops and props. But it's certainly a splendid place to come and reflect."

Or a place where I could easily get murdered.

I tried to ignore my inner musings, but the seed of doubt sprouted. The Lord would have to work extra hard to keep my mind at ease.

Clenching my trembling fingers, I leaned away from Cornelius, hoping it would appear as a simple shifting of weight.

He gave me a sideways glance. "You are frightened."

Don't betray your emotions.

I tucked a stray strand of hair behind my ear. "Not at all."

"It wasn't a question." He rested an elbow upon the railing. "I can read people, Adelynn. Fright isn't hard to deduce."

My curiosity piqued at the thought of someone being able to see through my façade. "And what else can you tell about me?"

"I know that you are unhappy as an engaged woman."

The blunt statement caught me off guard. "B-Baze is a good match."

"Oh, a good match indeed. And your childhood sweetheart, I'm told. So why the hesitation?"

I stiffened. How much could he possibly know, and where did he get his information? He couldn't read all of that in one look.

I swept fringe away from my forehead, eyes averted. "Every woman is hesitant before her wedding, I imagine."

Cornelius's voice grew low and controlled. "Tell me, has your fiancé discovered the reasons behind those two unfortunate deaths?"

Another subject change, another spike of emotions. "No, they suspect suicide, but they're not ruling out the possibility of foul play." My throat tightened. *Snitch!* Why had I said that?

"I thought as much." He pushed off the railing and stood straight and still. The light from below reflected in his eyes. "Why are you here, Adelynn?"

"Well, I . . ."

Moment of truth. I knew what I wanted to do. Now I had to sell it.

I put on a sheepish smile. "'Tis only my curiosity, of course, but I would like to learn about the inner workings of your theater. The show utterly captivated me, so I want to know what goes on behind the stage, to meet those you employ. A few introductions wouldn't require much of you, I promise."

He tilted his head, the corner of his mouth twitching. He took a few steps until his body heat warmed me. "Why are you *really* here?"

I looked deep into his eyes and found myself paralyzed. His emotions were impossible to decipher. Jest? Suspicion? Either way, he somehow saw through my ruse.

"I am here because I care about the people of this city," I said quietly. "If there is a killer on the loose as the police suspect, I will do what I can to help bring the fiend to justice. The last death occurred right outside these walls. This was the logical place to start."

He exhaled through his nose. "I admire your wish to help the police seek justice for those lives lost, and I vow that I will do all I can for you, even if that includes allowing you to roam our halls and become further acquainted with my staff. But you must take care to think hard on the matters in which you meddle." Concern seeped from his voice. "There are malevolent forces at work in this world, Adelynn, and sometimes, when the lights go out and the people file through the doors into the night, those forces continue on behind these curtains. I would hate to see your pure conscience sullied."

Soft shadows danced in his wintry blue eyes. I swallowed a lump, feeling every part of its agonizing crawl down my throat. I knew God's protection covered me, but that didn't mean the darkness didn't unsettle me.

The sudden desire to draw close to Cornelius, to soak up his calm strength and reassurance, enveloped me. I stiffened and—reluctantly—willed it away.

"I would like to return to the stage."

He looked to the ladder and back at me, then advanced. With each of his forward steps, I backtracked until we stood less than a foot from the edge. "After you," he whispered.

Somehow, with weakened knees and numb fingers, I managed to descend and find stable ground. Back on the stage, Finn and Siobhan had gone, but my stalwart bodyguard remained. I felt Cornelius's presence behind me and whirled. "Thank you for your time." I tried not to sound too shaken. "My driver is coming soon, so I must take my leave."

"I understand." He gave a slight bow. "'Twas a pleasure, and I hope to see you again very soon." Just as he had done at the engagement gala, he took my hand and pressed a gentle kiss to the back. But this time, his lips lingered. I stiffened until he straightened and released me. "You must forgive me for not escorting you to the door. I am overdue for a previous engagement." His mouth tipped, eyebrow cocked, before he retreated backstage again.

I shuddered. I couldn't explain the dense aura that had settled over the theater after Cornelius's last words on the walkway, and I wasn't keen on remaining to investigate the sensation. Not now. Not before I'd had a chance to reflect and pray.

I lifted my eyebrows at Sergeant Moseley and gestured to the stairs. "Shall we?"

He followed me off the stage and up the long sloping aisle. Just as we reached the door, Siobhan stepped through and brought me to a halt.

"Yes, please, be on your way, Miss Priss."

I glared, my hands curling into fists. "Cornelius approves of my visit. I have every right to be here."

She stared for a few seconds, then stepped closer. "You'd best watch your back. We're a family here. We're a brotherhood. And we don't take kindly to those who disturb the peace." Something soft—pleading even—glinted in her eyes, gone so fast, I wondered if I'd imagined it. "Go back to the comfort and safety of your mansion."

Brotherhood? She couldn't mean . . . the Irish Republican Brotherhood? My limbs went numb. Quick, sharp memories raced through my mind—a soft knock, a distant wail, a gruesome photograph, and a funeral come too soon. I swallowed a swirl of nausea.

Sergeant Moseley stepped in. "That is quite enough." His tone challenged her to defy him. "We'll be on our way."

With a gentle but firm hand on my elbow, he escorted me through the foyer and out into the crisp air.

I exhaled and looked to Moseley. "Thank you."

He nodded. "Are you all right?"

"Yes, I will be."

The buried memories of the IRB's wrongdoings against my family continued clawing at the locked door of my mind, seeking release. I forced them away and thought back to Siobhan's words, to that last look she'd given me. Siobhan's declaration hadn't been a threat so much as a warning. She knew something. Could she know who the killer was? Or was the killer Siobhan herself?

What kinds of dark deeds were happening in this place?

Chapter Eleven

HOLDING MY BREATH, I ENGAGED THE knocker of the Ford residence and stepped back. I twisted my fingers against my stomach, catching them on my insufferable engagement ring. A slight chill tinged the eventide air, and the weakening sun cast pale rays over the mansion. Gooseflesh dotted my arms beneath the sleeves of my maroon velvet gown.

After several minutes, the door swung open, but rather than the butler, Baze greeted me. He gave a delighted smile and escorted me inside. "You're early."

As I crossed the threshold and noticed the butler standing farther down the hall, I raised an eyebrow at Baze. "Don't you have work enough without taking the butler's duties?"

"Can't a man answer his own door from time to time?" He cracked a boyish smile, then winked at the butler. "You don't mind, do you?"

The thin man shook his head, amusement painting his features. "Anything you say, Mr. Ford."

"Excellent."

What had come over Baze? I had been trying to absorb the events of the previous day at the theater when I received his invitation for dinner. And now he insisted upon serving me for the evening? To that, I had no witty quip.

"Dinner isn't quite ready." He swept his arm toward the hall stretching behind him. "May I show you to the drawing room?"

I fought back a smile and narrowed my eyes. "Lead the way."

As he guided me into the sitting area, the familiar décor coaxed out a childhood memory of when Baze, Bennett, and I had been engrossed in a competitive game of blind man's buff. We had blindfolded Bennett and spun him mercilessly in the middle of the luxurious rug before darting behind the Jacobean sofas and chairs to escape him. He stumbled after us, arms outstretched—and ran straight into one of the mahogany side tables. It toppled and shattered a lamp into thousands of glass shards. The Fords had long since replaced the lamp and its matching partner, but all else remained the same.

I snorted softly, grinned, and shook my head.

Baze raised an eyebrow. "What's so amusing?"

"Nothing." I waved a hand. "I'm simply remembering."

His gaze drifted across the space, and his features relaxed into a contented smile. "We created a lot of memories in this place, that's for sure." When his eyes fixed on one spot, his expression grew serious, reflective.

Following his stare to the French doors leading outside, I glimpsed the vibrant groomed hedge that stretched between our homes, visible through the full-length windows. My mouth went dry, and my skin warmed. The hedge—where we'd shared our first kiss . . .

I cleared my throat and turned away. "You never mentioned why you invited me here tonight. I'm positively brimming with curiosity."

It took a moment for him to tear his gaze away from the hedge and focus on me. "I haven't seen you since the night of Clifton's death. I wanted to ensure you were all right." He reached a hand toward me, then retracted it and dropped it into a pocket. "Are you? All right, I mean?"

"I've experienced death before, Baze." Bitterness twisted in my chest. "This hardly compares."

He winced and looked down at the floor. I followed suit, wishing I hadn't spoken so bluntly. He'd been the first one to arrive on the scene of Father's attack that night, an event likely seared into his memory. Knowing now what a murdered man looked like, it wasn't hard to imagine what he'd found, especially given the brutal way in which Father had been killed.

The gleaming ebony of the Bechstein grand piano near the edge of the room caught my attention. I grasped Baze's arm and tugged him toward the instrument. "Play me something."

He resisted. "You've heard me play."

I increased my pull. "Not for a long time. Please?"

A mischievous twinkle flashed in his eyes. "Why don't you play something?"

"I don't know anything."

"Yes, you do. I taught you." He slipped out of my grasp and pressed a hand between my shoulder blades.

Digging in my heels, I pushed against him. "That was years ago."

"Muscle memory is stronger than you think. Give it a go." He leaned around me and raised his eyebrows. "For me?"

Those eyes . . . oh, how quickly they disarmed my every argument. I sighed and settled on the bench, opened the cover, and poised my hands over the keys. He would pay for this later.

The first notes were easy enough to remember, and to my delight, the rest flowed as naturally as taking a breath. Light, jovial phrasing sprung from the instrument—a simple piece, yes, but the first and only one I'd ever learned. Baze's careful perusal of my performance tightened my muscles and strained my playing. As I neared the last measure, panic set in. *What's the final chord?*

I halted, fingers hovering above the keys, the sustain pedal allowing the notes to linger, mix, and fade. Disappointment shallowed my breath.

Baze's warm presence enveloped me from behind, his chest brushing my back. He slid gentle hands down my forearms and aligned his fingers with mine. He leaned over my shoulder and whispered into my ear, his breath tickling my neck and igniting my senses. "G Major." His fingers pressed mine onto the proper keys. A rich, concluding chord wrapped me in delight.

"Beautiful." He swiveled and sat beside me, his back to the piano. He lifted a hand and turned my face toward him. His eyes traced my features until they settled on my mouth.

I held my breath and stiffened. Not now. We couldn't do this now.

But I want to.

Yes, I did, and that's what frightened me. If I opened up to him now, I wouldn't be able to preserve any strength when it came to his father. Mr. Ford would claim victory.

I turned my face forward. "Why am I here, Baze?" I gave him a sideways glance. "And don't say it was merely to invite me to dinner. There's something you're not telling me."

Baze contemplated a moment, jaw muscles flexing, and then nodded. "Al, I don't quite know how to say this"—he took a quick breath—"but I need you to rein yourself in, for both of our sakes and for the sake of our impending marriage."

Alarmed, I searched his face. Did he know? Had Bennett told him of my plan? "I'm not sure what you mean."

"The night of Jonathan Mallory's death, you infiltrated a police crime scene and made a fool of the both of us. Then with Clifton, you couldn't leave well enough alone."

So he didn't know.

"I didn't seek out Mr. Clifton. That was a coincidence."

He sighed. "What I'm trying to say is, I'm a detective inspector with the Met, and you're to be my wife. Not only that but our families are well known and influential throughout the city. The press have already started to report your interference, and if it continues, London gossip could take it to the extreme." He adjusted his bow tie. "I've a reputation to uphold, and I can't expect to continue climbing the ranks if this continues."

I swept an invisible dust mite from the piano keys. He was right, of course. That's what society wanted and demanded. But this wasn't what I anticipated hearing from *Baze*, not the Baze who'd once encouraged my wildest fancies when we were teenagers, who'd laughed along with me as I jested about the staunch rule-followers.

"I can't believe I'm hearing this," I whispered.

"You should learn to become accustomed to it. It's what society requires."

I wrung my hands in my lap. "So you expect me to hide away for the rest of my life? To remain silent and only come out when you need to show me off to further your *reputation*?"

His skin paled. "You know that's not what I meant."

"Do I?"

He made a face. "We can't pretend anymore. We're not children. Once we're married, we have to assume our roles. Society has standards, and we have to abide by them to succeed in this world."

This wasn't Baze. Not so long ago, he'd called us partners. His father's influence was growing stronger than I ever anticipated. But why should I have assumed any different?

"Al, say something." His strict tone had lost its edge.

I shot a scowl his way. "I thought you wanted me to assume my role. Submissive, silent wife."

"Adelynn—"

I slammed the keyboard cover shut, stood, and marched toward the first door I laid eyes on. To my chagrin, I found myself in Mr. Ford's study, dark and suffocating. Out of spite, I yanked a book off the shelf and rifled through its starchy pages with shaking hands. That lasted but a moment until Baze entered after me.

"Al, don't be like this. I don't see what's so wrong."

"No?" I raised my eyebrows. "You didn't see what was so wrong when I tried to warn you about Mr. Clifton's demise either."

Baze slashed his hand through the air. "That has nothing to do with this. Those visions, or whatever you call them, are purely a fantasy."

"Tell that to Clifton's widow."

"They're not real, Al. It's all your imagination. You sound like a madwoman."

"How dare you!"

Before I realized it, the book left my hand and hurtled toward his head. He batted it out of the air and gaped. I felt just as surprised as he looked, but it was too late now.

Besides, he deserved it.

His face flushed. "What's *wrong* with you?"

"What's wrong with *me*? You're the one who's calling me crazy and telling me to rein myself in." I snatched another book off the shelf and lobbed it at him.

He ducked out of the way and glared. "You're clearly not listening."

"I'm trying to help. Can't you see that? Why would I make any of this up?"

"I don't need you telling me how to do my job." His voice rose.

"If you would do your job, I wouldn't have to."

I reached for another book, but it wasn't until it left my hand that I realized it was much heavier than it should have been. A brass bookend sailed through the air and found purchase on Baze's forehead. He grunted and dropped to one knee, holding his head with an astonished expression.

Anger drained as I watched a trickle of blood seep from a cut above his eyebrow. I rushed across the room and fell to my knees beside him. "I'm so sorry." I yanked the handkerchief out of his pocket and dabbed the wound. "I didn't mean to. I simply got wrapped up in the moment."

"Always violence with you." A slight grin tugged the corners of his mouth. He tapped a light scar on his cheekbone near his ear. "I remember this same temper causing me quite some agony during an innocent game of conkers."

"You're hardly innocent yourself." I brandished my palm, where a scar jutted down between two fingers, dealt when he'd pushed me to the ground while racing between our homes. "Did your mother never teach you to treat a lady with respect?"

"Don't play the lady charade." He raised one eyebrow. "You deserved it."

"And I dished it back." I stared in defiance, suppressing a smile.

As I started to withdraw my hand, he caught hold and pulled it back toward him. He traced my scar with a thumb. Then he covered it with a light kiss. "I'm sorry if I came across as demeaning."

My palm tingled where his warm lips had met my skin. Gooseflesh raced up my arm, and longing formed a tight ball in my stomach. "And arrogant. Not to mention patronizing."

"All of those, yes, but please let me explain myself." He lowered his voice and squeezed my hand in both of his. "I'm afraid I did a frightful job conveying my meaning a moment ago."

"A terrible job, really." I rolled my eyes. "Go on then."

"I want . . . No. I *need* you to take a step back. I don't want you drawing unwanted attention. It's important to me that you settle into your role, now and after we're married." His tone jumped in pitch and became rushed. "Not only for my reputation but to keep you safe. My job is dangerous, Al. I have enemies, and I'm bound to make more. Once you're my wife . . ." His jaw tensed. "I could never bear it if something happened to you."

The words settled in my heart like a balm. This was the Baze I remembered, free from his father's grip, if only for a moment.

Baze leaned toward me and searched my eyes. "Can you promise you'll do this for me?"

But what of Bennett, Sergeant Moseley, and the relationships I was forming at the theater? I couldn't give that up now, but I couldn't let Baze know about them either.

I nodded. "I will try."

"That's all I ask."

To hide any betraying expressions, I collected the two books I'd thrown, silently bemoaning the fact I had treated them with such callousness.

As I lifted one of the volumes, a small scrap of paper slipped from between the pages and onto my lap. It unfurled to reveal neat handwriting and . . . *my name?*

I cast a look at Baze, but he was focused on picking up the bookend. I snatched up the paper and opened one of the books, pretending to skim the words while using it to block the view of sliding the paper down the front of my bodice.

Baze tapped his wound and examined his finger. "You know, this can only mean one thing."

"And what's that?"

"Retribution."

"Oh, I should like to see you try."

"I accept your challenge." He laughed and helped me to my feet. But rather than let me go, he slid a gentle hand around my waist and pulled me against him. Staring deeply into my eyes, he caressed my cheek with his other hand. His gaze drifted to my mouth. Surely, he could feel my heart thrumming against his chest.

I held my breath as he tilted his head and bent toward me. Should I allow him this moment? Or should I—

Pain struck my forehead, and my knees buckled. Darkness enveloped me.

Just when I thought I'd lost consciousness, my eyes blinked open. The Empress Theatre towered over me, and Sergeant Moseley stood ten paces away. I chuckled as he eyed me warily.

No, Lord, not another vision.

"Are you lost, Sergeant?" I asked in a mocking Irish lilt with a voice that wasn't my own.

"No, sir. Just finishing my rounds and then I'll be off." His eyes shifted.

"And what exactly be you lookin' for?"

"I'm afraid I can't discuss an open case." Sergeant Moseley's hand hovered over his baton.

I grinned. "What if I told you that you were lookin' in the right spot, Sergeant?"

The color drained from Sergeant Moseley's face. "It was you."

"Very perceptive."

He stood still for a moment as though debating what to do, sizing up the threat of his adversary. He inched a hand toward his cuffs. "I'm placing you under arrest for the murder—"

"Oh, please. We both know you're not capable of a feat such as this." I rolled my eyes and produced a pistol with a gloved hand. Sergeant Moseley froze. I placed it on the ground and kicked it toward him. It skidded across the cobblestones and bumped his toes. "Pick it up. You know what to do with it."

I expected Sergeant Moseley to ignore my command, but to my horror and confusion, he bent and retrieved the weapon with a shaky hand.

"How long has it been since you handled such a weapon?" I tilted my head. "Since you accidentally discharged your own and left your fiancée paralyzed, perhaps? Such an unfortunate incident, so it was. Ah, well, such be the way of the world."

Sergeant Moseley gripped the gun with both hands as the barrel crept upward and pressed against the vulnerable flesh under his chin. He trembled, and tears gathered in his wide eyes. Sweat dripped down his temples.

"You've failed your assignment from Inspector Bennett, I'm afraid. No need to draw this out any longer. They'll be better off."

Sergeant Moseley pulled the trigger.

Chapter Twelve

BAZE STARED AT THE CORPSE AND patch of blood oozing onto the pavement. Other officers worked in silence around him. His gaze became fixed on the delicate hummingbird brooch pinned to the body's left breast pocket, its emerald hue marred by red.

Peter Moseley. Too young. One of the Met's best, so eager to don the uniform, patrol the streets, and provide justice to the city.

But the gun, the wound, the arc of blood—Moseley shot himself. There was no doubt.

Baze's throat constricted. He clenched his teeth until his molars ached. Maybe if he had rushed to the scene immediately after Adelynn had come to, after she'd frantically explained the horror of what she'd seen, he could have prevented this. But he had doubted her and thus had first gone to headquarters to find Bennett.

What am I thinking?

An acidic ball of remorse burned deep in his belly. Despite how it happened or how he came to learn of it, this man's blood was on his hands. The duty to protect his squad fell on Baze's shoulders, and he had failed in that.

Rubbing the crooked bridge of his nose, he glanced up at the Empress Theatre portico looming in the dim light of dusk. Two men had died in its vicinity—but were they connected?

Bennett's soft prayer drifted to Baze's ears from where he knelt beside Moseley. "Almighty God, commit his spirit into your hands. Bring agents of evil to justice and heal the pain of this dark world."

Frustration brewed as Baze listened to his partner's righteous plea. The world remained dark. The perpetrator remained at large. Clearly,

Bennett's appeal fell on deaf ears, holy as they may be. Why did Bennett continue in vain? How could his faith endure so fervently when Baze's own had shattered like fragile glass years ago? *What am I not seeing?*

"Baze." Bennett's clear voice broke through his reverie.

Unable to find the strength to respond, Baze could only gesture for him to continue.

Bennett's tone grew low. "There's something in Moseley's mouth."

The blood drained from Baze's face. "What?"

Bennett gently worked Moseley's jaw, unhinged and hanging loose, and extracted a crumpled piece of paper. Seconds dragged by as he smoothed out the note and read it to himself, expression impassive. Then he swallowed and offered it to Baze.

Cold saliva coated Baze's fingers as he took it. Feathery, flowing handwriting marked the paper: *You'll need a good Eye to spot the next clue, Inspector Ford.*

Hot anger surged to the tips of his fingers, followed by suffocating fear.

If Moseley shot himself, where had the note come from? And there couldn't be clues unless . . . unless there truly was a murderer behind this. But the evidence indicated Moseley had dealt his own death as had the others. Could someone be coercing them into taking their own lives? Farfetched, but perhaps not as impossible as Baze had first thought.

Bennett straightened and nodded toward the note. "What do you make of it?"

Baze tried to still his shaking hands. "I don't know."

Stroking his chin, Bennett tipped his head from side to side. "You know, I've mentioned how I think there's more to these deaths than we think, and this note only strengthens my conviction." He gave Baze a wary look. "And I spoke to Adelynn about her visions."

"What?" Baze's mouth fell agape. "She told you?"

"Well, you certainly weren't doing anything with the information."

"Because it's complete balderdash."

"And that's precisely why she chose to tell me. You brushed her aside. You wouldn't acknowledge her." Bennett placed a heavy hand on Baze's shoulder. "She's only trying to help. And given the circumstances, she's offering us a plausible explanation."

Baze lowered his gaze, mouth dry. Had it really come to this? Had he pushed her away to the point that she sought others for validation? She'd once been able to come to him with anything, and he'd accepted and supported her with no questions asked.

But the war raging within him interfered with their relationship. He was trapped in a standstill battle between wanting to succeed in being the proper Ford his father had groomed him to be and being the compassionate man Adelynn needed.

Baze drew in a deep breath and met Bennett's gaze. "Do you believe her?"

"Maybe I do." Bennett cast a sad glance at Moseley. "But if that note proves anything, it's that we've got a madman on the loose."

Baze watched Hamilton examine Moseley's naked body that lay flat on a table, a sheet draped over the sergeant's lower half. Bennett pored over a report from the Fingerprint Bureau. The chill of the mortuary burrowed into Baze's bones. Fatigue weighed his shoulders and feet. Beyond the single murky window, the fading stars and vivid cobalt sky signaled early morning, mere hours before the break of dawn.

Bennett shook his head and threw down the paper. "They're all Moseley's prints. No one else touched the gun."

"So it's confirmed then." Baze rubbed the back of his neck. "He killed himself."

Hamilton waved a hand. "Yes, yes, I could have told you that, my boy. Look at the way the entry wound follows through to the top of his head." He spoke in quick, excited tones and made the motion of holding a gun in his hands. "It indicates he held the firearm like so when he pulled the trigger."

"We understand." Baze growled. "But the note specified a clue."

"This takes time, young man." Hamilton looked down his long nose at Baze. "I've only just begun."

Bennett joined them at the table, staring calmly with a finger over his lips. Light from the low-burning lamp flashed across his spectacles and deepened the ridges in his brow. While Hamilton held a magnifying glass to a blood spatter on Moseley's ribs, Bennett circled around to Moseley's head. "What did the note say again?"

Remembering the cursed phrase turned Baze's stomach, but he choked out his answer anyway. "You'll need a good eye to spot the next clue, Inspector Ford."

"Eye . . ." Bennett rubbed his chin. "The word was capitalized, was it not?"

Baze followed his studious gaze to Moseley's face—more specifically, to his eyes. Though they were shut, something seemed off. The left one protruded slightly, the skin purpling around it. Bennett touched a finger to the eyelid and slid it open. Where Moseley's eye should have been, a wooden sphere bulged in the socket.

"Hamilton," Bennett whispered. "Pass me the forceps."

With the instrument in hand, Bennett carefully extracted the sphere and held it up to the light. A small hinge and slight break in the surface indicated a container of sorts. "I think we've found your clue."

Bile rose in Baze's throat. He gestured to the sphere. "What's inside?"

He and Hamilton drew close, hovering over Bennett's shoulder as he used a second instrument to pry open the delicate lid. A crumpled flower with five cobalt blue petals unfurled.

For a moment, no one said anything. A flower. That was it—the clue indicated in the note? Was this some sort of sick joke?

No, a foolish question. Any individual who could do anything like this was sick beyond repair.

"I shall take that, my boy, thank you." Hamilton snatched the sphere from Bennett. "I'll analyze the flora and wood type. That should give us some more insight, eh? Why don't you lads return home and get some rest? You'll need your strength to rein in this madman."

Chapter Thirteen

PULLING MY SHAWL TIGHTER, I CLUTCHED the paper that bore the address and stared up at the looming tenement. Its tired, crumbling bricks and broken, dusty windows suggested abandonment. The surrounding buildings clustered around one another, blocking the sky and turning the street into a claustrophobic cage for the beggars and harlots. The sour stench—likely originating from rivers of waste in the gutters and lack of bodily hygiene—turned my stomach.

The letter I'd found in Mr. Ford's study had shaken me to my core. It held cruel evidence that his deception and manipulation ran deeper than I ever imagined—that he wasn't acting alone in his extortion. I scanned the letter for the hundredth time.

Dear Alistair,

You will not regret choosing Adelynn Spencer as your son's betrothed. Her family's wealth and influence in this city will increase yours tenfold and give immeasurable power to your name. But first, you must gain her compliance. For that, I have the answers. Her submission is all but assured. Meet me at the below address at half past three this Saturday.

All the best.

And of course, no signature.

Two scrappy children using twigs to draw on the pavement attracted my attention. Their gaunt, pale faces expressed indifference. For a moment, my own plight seemed trivial in comparison. Yet, here I held evidence that I was a mere puppet in a grand scheme—powerless.

But that was why I had come—to steal back some of that power.

Samuel stepped into my line of sight. His wrinkles deepened in the dim light and smog. "Are you sure you want to do this, Miss Adelynn?"

"I must, Samuel." I crinkled the paper in my hand to remind myself of the objective, then turned back toward the tenement. "Thank you for accompanying me." Proper etiquette dictated I should have also brought a chaperone, but not knowing what I might encounter, I couldn't subject Emily to this investigation.

As I stepped forward, Samuel cleared his throat. "May I say a brief prayer?"

I smiled. "Absolutely."

He bowed his head, and I did the same. "Dearest Almighty Father." His voice rumbled with warmth. "Go with us into this place. Protect our hearts and our minds, and keep our bodies from harm. Amen."

"Amen."

We shared a reassuring look before facing the tenement. I pushed inside, and a stale, foul smell enveloped me. Doors and hallways emerged from the darkness. Rat nests and dirt littered the floor. Outside noise grew muffled while the sound of wheezing and racking coughs heightened.

You should have brought Bennett.

Quiet.

You're going to get murdered.

Poppycock.

To distract my mind from conflicting thoughts and fear, I silently said a prayer for those who dwelled here. Who could possibly live in such conditions?

"To be sure, it is a humbling experience to see those who were not born into privilege and wealth," Samuel murmured.

I nodded and checked the address. Number 301. Third floor?

As we ascended the rickety stairwell, I tried not to picture what would greet me at the end of this journey. Someone had urged Mr. Ford to choose me for his plot, and they had known exactly how to coax me to comply. The person must be known to me. There could be no other explanation. But who of my acquaintances would have the gall or motive to do this, all while living in a rundown hovel?

And what would I do if I located said acquaintance? Reprimand him or her? Would it suddenly give me the courage to march up to Mr. Ford and put a stop to this madness? The fact remained that he knew my heart's desires, and he was exploiting them.

We reached the third floor before I had time to speculate further. It didn't take long to find the door. One of the brass numbers hung crooked on its screw. I poised my knuckle and knocked.

Silence followed. Perhaps no one lived here anymore . . . or ever had. What then? I hadn't thought that far ahead. I supposed we would retreat home, my thirst for answers unquenched.

Footsteps from inside alerted my senses. The rusty knob grated and turned, then the door swung back on squeaky hinges.

Cornelius stood in the doorway. An ensemble of tattered trousers, a tweed jacket, and mussed hair produced an image of a common worker, not a ritzy magician. His eyes lit with excitement, soon followed by confusion. "Adelynn, to what do I owe the pleasure of your company?"

"C-Cornelius." His enticing voice rang in my ears. "What are you doing here?"

"I live here."

Heat crept into my cheeks. I'd expected to see someone I knew, but I wasn't prepared to see *him*. For a moment, I was at a loss for words and only managed to fill the void by making brief introductions between Samuel and Cornelius.

"Well, come in, then." Cornelius stood back with an eager smile and held the door wide. "I've many questions."

"As do I," I said under my breath.

The interior of the small, two-room flat was in better shape than the corridors—but only just. The living space held a crackling hearth, wooden rocking chair, plush armchair, and two beds pushed against the opposite wall. In the corner, a gramophone balanced on an end table too small for its base. Most else lay bare, albeit tidy and smelling significantly better than the rest of the building.

"What can I do for you?" Cornelius faced me with a quizzical expression.

No sense delaying the inevitable. I looked at Samuel. "I hate to ask this, but would you mind terribly—"

He held up a hand. "I understand, Miss Adelynn. I shall leave you with some privacy."

"Nonsense," Cornelius cut in. "You're a guest now, and my guests aren't made to stand in the hall. I've just wet the tea, and there's a lovely lounge chair in the second room. I'll put on some music. It should be privacy enough. Besides"—he winked at me and gave a respectful nod to Samuel—"a young woman of class should never be alone with a gentleman she hardly knows."

"Cheers to that." Samuel returned the nod. "Thank you, sir."

Cornelius waited until Samuel had disappeared into the second room before crossing to the gramophone and winding the machine. Within moments, a lively ragtime piano tune emitted from the brass horn.

I couldn't help but grin. "You fancy Irving Berlin?"

"I do indeed. His music always brightens the room." He gestured to the armchair. "That's not the most comfortable seat, I'm afraid, but you are welcome to it."

As I accepted the offer and sank onto the faded cushion, he pulled the rocking chair close and sat—our knees but a few inches apart.

"Now, tell me what this is all about." His brows sank low, darkening his eyes. "How did you get here, and why? This corner of the city is no place for a lady. At the very least, you should have brought police protection and a chaperone, not a mere chauffeur."

I twisted my fingers, ashamed of how the question drudged up recent emotions of Sergeant Moseley's death. "It was all I had." My voice cracked.

"I am sorry for your loss." Cornelius met my eyes, his own softening. "What is so important that you would risk your safety?"

I tried to answer, but my voice hitched. Biting my bottom lip, I crumpled the note in my lap.

Cornelius eased a warm hand over mine and coaxed the paper from me. He read it silently and frowned. "I don't understand."

Come clean now, I supposed. What more did I have to lose?

"My engagement was arranged by Alistair Ford, which may not sound out of the ordinary on its surface. It's not uncommon in wealthy families." I cleared my throat and rolled my shoulders back. "But he's threatening my family and me to keep me compliant. He's controlling every action I take. He claims to have information that would soil my father's name and tear my family apart by scandal. I don't know why. Status. Power."

My voice caught. "I found that note tucked inside one of the books in his study. I thought . . . I thought maybe if I could find the person who wrote it, I could fix this."

It took everything to keep the tears from falling. I was so close—sitting in the room of the person who may have sent this letter. If I could confront him, look him in the eyes . . .

Cornelius folded the note and handed it back to me. "I'm afraid I recently moved to this establishment. It had been vacant for quite some time. There's really no way to track down the one who lived here before." He fiddled with a gold band on his middle finger. "I'm sorry."

That was it then. I didn't know what I'd expected. Someone had fed information about me to Mr. Ford, and now I would never know who that person was. I crinkled the paper with my fist.

"You love the inspector, do you not?"

The question was so abrupt, bold even, that I couldn't quite form an answer and merely gaped.

Cornelius slid his fingers into my palms and squeezed, staring into my eyes. Despite the warmth radiating from his hands, a chill began at the base of my neck and wrapped around my scalp.

"I've devoted my life to the art of reading others," he said. "What I see in you now is love, I presume, for the dashing Baze Ford."

I resisted the urge to pull away as my heart beat faster and I became aware of his closeness.

"If you truly feel this way, then why should an arranged marriage to him cause you distress?"

Why, indeed. It was a question I asked myself every day. And every day, I never came to a certain conclusion. "Perhaps it's the fact that no matter where we go, even after the wedding, after we have children, Mr. Ford will always be there pulling the strings. I don't know if I can live like that."

"Have you not alerted your fiancé to the predicament?"

"I might try, but Mr. Ford's influence goes too deep. To break Baze's perception of his father would be to break their entire relationship. And then I would lose him . . . lose Baze."

Cornelius nodded, then tightened his grip on my hands and looked to the side. "I was betrothed once, an arranged marriage like yours. It wasn't a result of blackmail, of course, but the expectation was still there. It was a perfect match by all accounts. She was beautiful and wealthy, but I soon realized that I wouldn't tolerate anyone's dictation of my life but my own. So I fled. I never looked back. I found something new." He shrugged and met my gaze. "Perhaps you could too."

In his eyes, I found certainty and fervor. As though beckoned, I leaned toward him until our faces were inches apart. The sweet scent of sandalwood and verbena ignited my senses and made my palms perspire. A slow smile spread across his lips, attracting my gaze.

Adelynn Spencer, you're engaged!

I yanked my hands out of his and looked away, all too aware that he still stared at me.

The front door groaned and popped open. Finn entered in a flurry, curls wild and windblown. "You won't believe what—" He stopped the moment he saw me, and his gaze flicked to Cornelius, who pressed a slow finger to his lips. Finn looked back to me with wide eyes. "Adelynn. What a surprise."

"You live here?" I glanced at the extra bed.

"We've been flatmates ever since I found him poor and destitute in Dublin." Cornelius leaned back and slapped his hands against his thighs.

A tiny chill spiraled around my spine. Generally, my first instinct was to ask for more details, but a wariness steeled my tongue. What was this sudden unease?

No, it wasn't sudden. It had been present for the duration of this visit, but now that Finn had appeared, it laced my limbs with insistence. Perhaps it was a warning. But a warning of what?

I rose, careful not to touch Cornelius in the process. "I have overstayed my welcome." I looked at Finn. "I'll let you get settled."

"You are always welcome, Adelynn." He said it with such earnest that I almost believed him, but sincerity struggled to shine through his cloudy eyes.

"Thank you." I backed toward the door and called, "Samuel, I'm ready to depart."

Chapter Fourteen

WHEEZY COUGHS SHOCKED BAZE FROM HIS slumber. He shot straight up in the chair. Files catapulted from his chest and floated haphazardly to the floor. The sharp ache in his neck and twinge in his lower back jogged his memory. He'd fallen asleep in this chair, here at his desk. But how long ago? He glanced bleary-eyed at his pocket watch. Nearly two hours wasted.

It was almost impossible for him to turn his neck to the right, so he bent it side to side in an effort to loosen the clenched muscle. It released a few pops.

"Perhaps you should head home, Ford," came a deep, husky voice, followed by another bout of coughs.

Baze scanned the rows of thick, empty desks before he set eyes on Superintendent Whelan. The senior officer adjusted the coat draped over his elbow and gestured with his hat at Baze. "You've been staring at those files for days now. Best give it a rest and try to get some other work done, or at the very least head home for some shut-eye."

Trying to rub awareness back into his face with his hands, Baze scooted closer to his desk where more piles of papers slumped in chaos. "There'll be time for sleeping later. This case is more important."

"I think the last two hours prove you wrong." Securing his coat around his paunch, Whelan knit his brow. "You're no use to us if your body's shutting down on you. We need you sharp, Ford."

With a sigh of defeat, Baze nodded. "Yes, sir. I'll wrap it up soon."

"See that you do. Don't make us regret rushing into your promotion." With a tip of his hat, Whelan stomped out of the precinct. The slamming door behind him made Baze flinch.

They wouldn't regret putting him here. Because he wouldn't fail. Not now, not when the case had completely blown open. The murderer was starting to get a big head, starting to boast about his conquests. If he wanted to play a game, very well. Baze would play along, especially if it meant bringing this madman down and avenging the three souls who had perished at his hands.

A chill from the empty room, echoing with pings of rain on the window glass, worked its way to his core. Desks cast uneasy shadows across the walls. He fought against shivers.

But what if he did fail? What if this monster escaped justice like the Ripper had done thirty years ago? Criminals had outsmarted the Met before. And it was clear they weren't dealing with someone in his right mind. Anyone who could do this to another human being was psychotic.

Baze couldn't afford to fail, not with everything at stake. Livelihood, safety, his squad—Adelynn.

I need help. God, I need help. Would you . . .

No. He refused to let his mind go there. He refused to surrender to another father who would use him, who would control him.

Releasing an aggravated sigh, he pushed back from the desk and picked up the spilled papers. Searing anger injected warmth back into his body. He dumped the pages on his desk, snatched his coat from the back of the chair, and marched to the door.

As he swung around the corner, Hamilton materialized from the darkness. Baze yanked back. A small cry escaped his lips. "Hamilton, you cad." He tried to hide his alarm. "Give a chap some warning."

"Apologies, my boy." Hamilton waved a hand as though it were no bother. His thinning white hair drifted across his scalp, raindrops clinging to the strands. "However, this couldn't wait. Time is of the essence, you know."

"Yes." Baze straightened his waistcoat. "What is it?"

With a proud smile, Hamilton produced a torn page from a journal depicting a deep blue flower—the same flower they had taken from Moseley's eye. Baze swallowed back nausea.

"*Gentiana verna* of the family Gentianaceae," Hamilton said. "Or in Irish, *Ceadharlach Bealtaine.*"

"And in English?"

"Spring gentian." He tapped the photo. "It's quite rare here in northern Europe. Most notably, it's found in Ireland in the counties Galway and Clare and dispersed through the Burren, that deliciously mysterious stretch of rocky ground in the Irish countryside."

"So we're looking for an Irishman."

"It would seem so."

"County Clare, you said?"

"Yes, my boy."

That magician—Finn Kelly. Hadn't he been introduced as hailing from somewhere in County Clare? Excitement sent Baze's heart racing. This was the most direct connection so far. "Thank you, Hamilton. This indeed helped."

"As I knew it would."

"Keep your eyes sharp from here on." Baze traced his gaze over the smooth outline of the flower petals. "This man is growing bolder."

Hamilton clucked his tongue. "Or woman."

"You think it's a woman?"

"The handwriting on the note was poised and delicate, more likely to belong to a woman, though I suppose it could belong to a few men. But if that were true, it would have to come from a very learned man, one well versed in literature and writing."

Thoughts swirled in Baze's head, making it nearly impossible to focus. A woman? Or a man with a high level of education. There was a woman at the theater. And was Kelly educated enough to warrant such a signature?

"There's one more thing that may interest you." Hamilton folded the page and tucked it into Baze's jacket pocket. "This little flower is the subject of old folklore. The tales say that if the flower is ever picked, death will soon follow." He raised his eyebrows. "Whether you believe in coincidence, superstition, or divine providence, my boy, we can be sure of one thing. We have the flower, and death has most certainly shown its face. The only question that remains is, will it strike again?"

"Thank you, Samuel." As I slid across the seat and stepped onto the pavement, the nearby streetlamp cast a dim halo over me. "I should only be a moment."

"I am in no rush, Miss Adelynn." Samuel smiled as he shut the car door and crossed to the driver's side. "Take all the time you need."

I smiled back and headed toward Bennett and Emily's red-bricked townhouse, which stood squeezed in a row of several others. A single light glowed in the window. Good. They hadn't yet retired for the evening.

After the visit to the tenement—and with the events of Moseley's death—I needed a solid friend to confide in. Bennett and Emily were certainly that. Besides, I needed more advice on how to proceed. This investigation was far from over, but the stakes were rising.

I stopped at the evergreen door and slammed the knocker. After a moment, Bennett answered the door. Light poured out around him and pierced the darkness. I smiled as I stepped across the threshold and took in the scent of warm tea and fresh-baked scones. "I'm terribly sorry to call at this hour, but I—"

"Adelynn?"

Baze's voice. I looked about and found him almost immediately, sitting cross-legged in front of the sofa with Emily pacing behind it.

I widened my eyes. "What are you doing here?"

He looked equally as incredulous as I felt. "What are *you* doing here?"

I stomped toward him, but when I noticed files lying open on the floor in front of him—filled with gruesome photographs of Sergeant Moseley and reports with the word *homicide* featured prominently—I drew to a halt. "What is that?"

Bennett shut the door and skirted around me. "Now, let's remain calm. Perhaps we should all sit down and talk things through before overreacting."

"Do you think Sergeant Moseley was . . . murdered?" I nearly choked on the word, flashes from his death replaying in my mind. All along, I'd been pleading with Baze to believe me, believe that the cause of these horrible deaths was more sinister than he'd concluded. Every time he rejected me, my heart grew heavier, my resolve stronger. But now, had he accepted my claims? "Baze? What does this mean?"

Emily shuffled to her husband's side. "Love, why don't you join me in the back room. I've got a bit of washing to finish up."

He raised an eyebrow. "Millie, I hardly think this is the time—"

"Now, dear." She squeezed his arm and nodded at me before dragging him out of sight.

Once I heard the door close, I knelt on the floor in front of Baze and examined each photograph and written report. Sergeant Moseley had certainly shot himself—but there had also been a note left on his body.

I swallowed and stared into Baze's bloodshot eyes. When was the last time he slept? I firmed my voice. "What does all of this mean?"

The ticking of a distant clock filled the silence as he gazed back at me. Muscles tensed in his jaw, then relaxed. Finally, he whispered, "You were right. There's a killer out there."

Panic ripped through me. Now that he had said it aloud, despite his confirming my suspicions, I wanted him to take it back. A killer—there was a killer walking freely among the public.

I flipped the nearest photograph of Sergeant Moseley face down, trying to banish the image from my mind. "S-so, what of my visions?"

"I'm considering the possibility"—he sighed—"they may be real."

Emotion clogged my throat. My hands trembled. Terror gripped my body and paralyzed each muscle. *Lord, I didn't want this to be true. Why are You letting this happen? Stop this madness!*

"What are you doing out at this hour?" Baze's low, calm voice took the edge off my fear.

Somehow, I managed to work my tongue. "I needed to speak to a friend. I have much on my mind."

When his hand eased around mine, I started. He drew it to his lips and kissed my fingers, leaving a warm mark that cooled in the air. Then he cradled my cheek, his fingers reaching behind my neck, into my hair. The heat of his palm raised gooseflesh on my skin.

A small touch of color bled back into his face as he studied me. "Adelynn, I used to be the one you sought in the past." His callused thumb stroked my cheekbone. "I know emotions have escalated these past couple of weeks, but I hope I can still be the one you come to. I *want* to be the one you come to."

"Baze—"

"Let me finish." He pressed his thumb over my mouth. "It's driving me mad to see you so distant, and I don't understand what I've done to make you despise me."

I focused on his unbuttoned waistcoat. "I don't despise you."

"Then tell me what I am to do. You're clearly unhappy. Tell me how to rectify it. Is it something I've done? Have you changed your mind? Do you want out of the engagement?"

"That's not an option," I said before I could stop myself.

He winced. "I'm not forcing you into this."

"I'm sorry." The words came out breathy and weak. "I wasn't implying . . . I mean that to say . . ."

He took his hand away to brush aside the hair dangling over my forehead and trace the outline of my ear, then returned it to my cheek. "I know where I stand, Adelynn. I've loved you since that first moment we shared in the hedge, and I've only fallen deeper in love since. There was a time . . ." His voice hitched. "There was a time when you said you loved me too. If you've changed your mind, if your feelings have changed—truly changed—I need to know it now." His eyes searched mine.

I dropped my gaze. He'd see the truth in it if I didn't. My feelings hadn't changed, and that's what made this so much harder.

His hand applied slight pressure on my neck, pulling me forward. I looked up in time to see him lean into me. His lips pressed to mine—gentle, soft, steady.

My emotional barrier slammed shut. I turned my face away. His phantom touch tingled on my lips. His hand shook, loosened, and fell away. My neck grew cold. The realization of what I'd just done to him made me ill. "I'm sorry . . ."

The door in the back of the house creaked, followed by Bennett's excited voice. "What about Stella? Or Evelyn? I'm quite partial to Evelyn."

"Bennett, I told you not to go out there yet," Emily hissed.

"How much time do they need? I, for one, would like to get some sleep." He appeared around the corner. "Pardon. I hope I'm not interrupting."

"No, we were done." Baze got up, leaving me alone on the floor. "I'm going back to headquarters."

"That's not such a good idea." Bennett followed him to the door. "You haven't slept for almost twenty-four hours."

"There's no time. I have work to do."

The door slammed, shaking the walls of the home.

My floodgates opened. Tears poured forth. Emily sank onto the couch behind me and stroked my hair as I cried. Bennett rushed out the door after Baze.

Chapter Fifteen

"ANYTHING ELSE I SHOULD KNOW?" BAZE straightened his collar and leveled a stern look at Rollie as they loitered outside the interrogation room.

Fatigue dried his eyes and weighed down his limbs, but he had to stay sharp. He and Bennett had managed to snag Finn Kelly and Cornelius Marx for an interrogation. He couldn't afford to squander their opportunity to acquire answers.

"No, sir." Rollie handed him a manila folder with a list of the information he had just divulged about their suspects. "That was all I've found out so far."

"Good work." Baze paged through the papers. "That will be all."

"Very good, Inspector."

As Rollie made his retreat, Bennett moved forward and slapped Baze's shoulder. What was he so chipper about?

"Are you ready for this?" Bennett curled his hand around the other and cracked his knuckles. "Two in one."

Baze tried to draw up the scenario of interviewing two suspects at the same time. He'd prefer a solo interrogation, but Marx had a stronger pull than Baze had realized and convinced Superintendent Whelan to allow it.

Baze sighed. "As long as we convict one in the end, it makes no difference to me."

"We'll flush him out." Bennett sobered. "No one kills one of ours and gets away with it." He faced the door, then turned back to Baze. "Have you spoken to Adelynn yet?"

Baze stiffened, reliving the tense moment when Adelynn had

rejected his advance mere days ago. After he bolted, Bennett had run after him, but Baze had managed to evade the confrontation and isolate himself at New Scotland Yard. Spoken to Adelynn? No. Why should he even attempt reconciliation when she'd made it clear she didn't want him around?

Baze shrugged. "Haven't had the time."

"Pardon me if I sound overbearing, but that's the only way you'll work this out."

"She doesn't seem too keen on working this out." He curled a hand into a fist, bending the folder in his fingers. "She refuses to tell me what's wrong."

"Give her some time. Millie and I have learned that sometimes stepping away from an argument and coming back clearheaded is the best way to mend a disagreement."

"I doubt time will mend this rift."

Bennett rolled his eyes. "At the risk of sounding melodramatic, I believe you'll get through this. You merely need to put in the effort." He knuckled Baze's shoulder. "Where's the hopeless romantic I used to tease relentlessly? He would never leave a lady in distress, especially his one true love."

Baze clenched his jaw, resisting Bennett's attempts to appeal to his optimistic, stargazing younger self. That persona had all but been extracted from him. "I'd like to crack on with this interrogation if you don't mind."

Bennett stared a moment before letting out a frustrated sigh. "As you wish."

They entered the room. Kelly sat at a single table in the middle of the windowless space, rapping his fingers on the surface, while Marx stood leaning against the back wall, arms folded. A dim light directly above cast shadows across their faces.

Marx nodded in their direction. "Gentlemen."

Baze bit back the urge to raise his voice. "Have a seat." He and Bennett settled in their own chairs and waited.

Marx never wavered as he sat, a solid display of calm and confidence on his face. On the other hand, Kelly rested his forearms on the table and picked at his thumbnail. Sweat collected on his brow.

Just as Baze slapped the folder on the table, Marx started in. "I was under the impression these fatalities were the result of self-harm."

"A note and bodily mutilation disproved that theory." Bennett produced two pens and a sheet of paper with a single sentence written on it. "I need you gentlemen to reproduce this line, please."

As Kelly set to work, Marx tilted his head. "Trying to match the handwriting, I assume?"

"Perceptive." Baze noted both men's use of their right hands, then collected the finished sentences. A quick glance told him neither was a match, but closer inspection later could reveal condemning patterns.

Kelly cleared his throat. "I've been goin' home early every night this week. I was nowhere near the theater when this man was—"

"I'm not interested in knowing where you were." Baze flicked open the folder and slid a photograph of the blue flower in front of Kelly. "Do you recognize this?"

As Kelly studied the image, his features softened. Out of the corner of his eye, Baze noticed Marx's expression grow distant and contemplative. Kelly sniffed. "It's a flower from Ireland."

Baze nodded. "County Clare, to be exact. You hail from that region, do you not?"

"I do, but I'm not seein' the connection to your investigation."

Bennett spoke up. "Peter Moseley's eye was gouged out, and one of these flowers was left in its place."

"This is your evidence thus far?" Marx snorted. "Finn hasn't been back to his homeland in more than a decade. How do you propose he came by one of these flowers?"

"That's what I intend to find out from him." Baze leveled a stare at Kelly, who had returned to studying the flower.

Kelly met Baze's gaze. "As Cornelius explained, I have not been home in many years."

"Then perhaps one of your brotherhood assisted with the deed."

"I'm afraid I don't—"

"You're not an easy man to investigate, Mr. Kelly, but my men visited your Irish hovel and caught a glimpse of this." Baze fished out a second photograph, this one depicting a green flag with half of a golden starburst hanging on the side of a tenement. Kelly inhaled and held a breath while exchanging glances with Marx.

Baze stifled a grin. He was backing them into a corner. If he and Bennett could keep up the assault and play the right cards, they could end this.

Marx cleared his throat and fiddled with the gold ring on his finger. "Inspector, if you're suggesting that my organization is affiliated with the Irish Republican Brotherhood, then you are sorely mistaken."

"We weren't suggesting your organization is linked to the IRB." Bennett leaned back, folded his arms, and looked directly at Kelly. "Just one man."

Kelly shook his head. "Even if I was a member, I couldn't divulge that information."

"Would you really let an oath to a secret nationalist society jeopardize your freedom? This is murder. If you're found guilty, you will hang."

Marx drummed his fingernails on the table. "You're assuming he's guilty of a crime you've barely begun to understand. To be found guilty, one must have evidence brought against him proving the accusation, of which you have none. Only conjecture."

"Our finest men are investigating this case." Bennett lifted his chin. "If there's something to be found, we'll find it."

"You're assuming there is something to be found."

"Everyone has secrets."

Marx's eyes flashed. "I assume you speak for yourself as well, Inspector Solomon?"

It took a moment for Baze to process the name. He hadn't heard it for many years. In fact, he'd only heard it uttered a few times before the owner of it had put an end to its use. He risked a glance at Bennett and found him rigid and pale.

"I'm terribly sorry, Inspector." Marx pressed his fingertips together. "But it is your name, it is not?"

Bennett took a long breath. "It is."

"Named after your father, I imagine?"

"You can imagine."

Marx tilted his head. "I wonder, what would make a man loathe his father to the point of abandoning his name?"

Bennett curled one hand into a fist. "I am not the object of interrogation today, Mr. Marx. I would like to proceed."

Baze would have ended the conversation that very moment were it not for the growing hostility emanating from Bennett—face flushed and nostrils flaring. Perhaps if riled enough, he could squeeze more information out of these magicians.

"You heard the man, Finn." Marx rested an elbow on Kelly's shoulder. "Do you have anything to add to their interrogation?"

Kelly stared at the table. "I don't."

"There you have it. We've made our peace." He leaned forward, leveling an unflinching stare at Bennett. "Now if you'd be so kind, Solomon—you don't mind if I call you Solomon, do you?"

"Call me what you wish." Bennett shrugged. "My identity isn't determined by a name."

"And yet you feel the need to pester everyone with the oh-so-very-important selection of your unborn child's name." A muscle in Bennett's jaw tensed as Marx raised an eyebrow. "Why not take the traditional route? Surely Solomon Bennett Senior would be proud to have a grandchild carry his namesake."

Now the magician was baiting him. Somehow, he'd learned the buried details of Bennett's upbringing. The only question was, would Bennett give in to the man's provocation? He rarely discussed his past, even with those closest to him.

Baze scrutinized the magician—who displayed an eager, haughty expression—before casting a quick glance at his partner.

Bennett tapped a finger on the table and held Marx in a blank stare.

Finally, he cracked a small smile. "Bennett was my mother's maiden name, Mr. Marx, a fact of which you are most certainly aware."

Marx responded with his own smile. "How curious for a woman not to take her husband's name. Of course, there are only two likely scenarios to answer that question—that you were either the product of promiscuity . . . or prostitution."

Baze vaulted to his feet, preparing to throttle the magician for such a barbed statement, true as the former might have been. But Bennett stilled him with an outstretched hand. "Mr. Marx, do you have anything to add to your statement concerning the murder of Peter Moseley?"

Marx held Bennett's gaze, unblinking. "Not at this moment, Inspector."

"Very well. You are free to go." Bennett pushed back the chair, the legs screeching across the hardwood floor, and stood. "Don't leave the city. You are still very much a part of this investigation, and we may call on you in the future."

"As you wish, Solomon."

The name elicited a barely noticeable wince before Bennett breezed out of the room, leaving Baze under the scrutiny of the two magicians. Avoiding eye contact, Baze followed suit and headed to the door.

He'd barely made it two steps before Marx said, "Give Adelynn my best."

It was everything Baze could do to keep from turning around and diving across the table to silence the man. Today wasn't the day for such things. If they were guilty in any way, their punishment would come.

Outside the room, Baze found Bennett leaning against the wall, staring at the ground, arms crossed. Baze stopped in front of him. "What are you thinking?"

Bennett chewed his bottom lip and furrowed his brow. "They're smart."

"Do you think one of them is guilty?"

"I don't know." Bennett pushed off the wall and brushed past Baze. "But we're going to find out."

Chapter Sixteen

A BURST OF WIND WHIPPED THROUGH my skirt as I stepped under the shadow of the Empress Theatre's portico. The gusts roared in my ears. I gripped my hat against my head and stepped toward the door.

"Did you really think I'd let you come here by yourself?"

I let out a yelp and whirled.

Bennett approached with crossed arms. Misting rain clung to his wool coat and fogged his spectacles.

I clutched my pearl necklace and swallowed. "How did you know I would be here?"

"Because I know you." He removed his spectacles to wipe away the condensation, then returned them and directed a frown at me. "You shouldn't be here. Not after what happened with Moseley."

The mention of the sergeant stung. A passing car blared its horn. I jumped and wrapped my arms around myself. "I knew the risks when I accepted this task. You were tolerant of this plan then."

"That was before the man assigned to your protection was murdered." He closed the gap between us by a few paces. "My men and I can handle it from here."

"But you can't get as close to them as I can." My voice broke. "And I'm responsible for Sergeant Moseley's death."

His eyes softened. "Adelynn, you know that's not true."

"But if I hadn't insisted on doing this, if my visions had come sooner—those useless visions—then he wouldn't be dead." My nose tingled as hot tears formed. "I have to see this through."

"The danger is real, Al. You may not survive this ordeal if you continue."

"Three men are dead, Bennett. Not only that, but I saw them all happen." My body trembled. "I know exactly the risk I'm taking."

He maintained his stern expression. "Then let me help you."

I stiffened. What if Bennett was also wounded—or worse—while serving as my guardian? It was one thing to put myself in danger, but as had already been demonstrated, people around me weren't safe. I couldn't let him do that.

As if guessing my objection, Bennett grasped my shoulders and squeezed. "I put my life on the line every day I walk out the door. It's the risk I accepted when I chose to do this job. I'm honored to do it. And I would be honored to serve and protect you—especially if it means we flush out a criminal and bring him to justice."

Gratitude warmed my chest. "Thank you, Bennett."

He smiled and used a knuckle to whisk away my tears. "Now let's go get our man."

We shared unspoken acknowledgement and passed through the theater doors. Finn greeted us inside the grand foyer, wringing his hands and squaring his shoulders. I pushed all fear out of my mind, smiled, and gestured to Bennett. "Finn, this is—"

"We've met." Finn nodded in Bennett's direction, his mouth a straight line. "Inspector."

Bennett returned the gesture. "Mr. Kelly."

"I was hopin' you'd return." Finn turned to me and signaled for us to follow. "I've somethin' to show you."

My curiosity piqued. "What is it?"

"A wee secret from our show."

I took quick steps to keep up with Finn's long strides, and Bennett trailed behind us. We entered the auditorium, marched down the aisle, and went up to the stage.

Finn spun and walked backward. After a few paces, he stopped and gestured to a spot in front of him. "Step here."

I lined my toes up with his, but he grasped my shoulders and yanked me closer, so close that I could see fibers in his suit and smell the earthy, salty scent. "Sorry," he mumbled. "This door was only made for one. We must stand close to fit."

Door?

"Hold tight now." A rapid tap of his heel vibrated the floor. For a moment, nothing happened. Then the floor descended beneath our feet. My insides rushed up toward my throat. I squeezed Finn's elbows. Wooden beams and dust whooshed around my head. Light gave way to dark. When the floor beneath us creaked to an abrupt stop, I stumbled back a step, but Finn caught my arms to steady me. The rush quickened my heartbeat. A wide smile stretched across my face.

He raised his eyebrows. "How did you like it?"

"Exhilarating." Two gulps of air steadied my breathing. I looked up through the hole in the ceiling and locked eyes with Bennett, who peered down with concern. In one swift movement, he crouched and swung over the edge, hanging on with his fingertips. Then he dropped beside us and smoothed his coat.

Finn threw an arm out as though to shield me from Bennett—a ridiculous notion. "You were not included in this invitation, Inspector."

Bennett straightened, stood toe-to-toe with Finn, and puffed out his chest. "Either I accompany you or she doesn't."

Finn held his gaze for an extended moment—then faltered. He took a step back and inclined his head. "Very well."

Bennett helped me off of the platform onto the floor as Finn lit a dim oil lamp and held it aloft. It illuminated more of the space, revealing a rectangular room lined in thick wooden columns. Several tables littered with an array of props sat near the trap door. A dark doorway gaped at the end of the chamber.

I pointed. "Where does that lead?"

"Tunnels run beneath this place." Finn swung the lantern my way. "Some lead outside. Some lead to nothin'. Others will bring us back to the main floor. And there are others, still, that may be leadin' to undiscovered secrets." He winked. "Would you like to see?"

Curiosity shouldered its way past my unease. "Absolutely."

As we turned to go, I caught a glimpse of Siobhan's shadowed form on the other side of the trap door contraptions, her hand wrapped around a lever that appeared to control the pulley system. Yet, her eyes were completely on me, glowing dim in the light from above. I squared my jaw. Heaven forbid I show that woman any weakness. If she and I had a quarrel, she need only confront me, not skulk in the shadows seething with contempt.

Finn tapped his foot. "That will be all, Shiv. Thank you."

"'Twas me pleasure." She hopped up on the trap door, leaned over to whack the lever, and pulled inside as the floor lifted and thrust her back on stage. We plunged into darkness, shattered only by Finn's flickering lantern.

He chuckled. "You need not fear her so. She has a tough outer shell, but dig deep enough and you'll find a kind heart and fierce loyalty."

I studied his hardened jaw and firm brow. This was such a different side of him—calm, calculated, and somber. A far cry from the jovial, alight personality he channeled on stage. Which persona was the real one?

He swept his arm toward the door. "Now, if you'll follow me, m'lady."

I hesitated and glanced at Bennett. He returned my look with narrowed eyes. It wasn't lost on me that we had been so adeptly trapped below stage with no exit. Anything could happen in those tunnels. But Bennett was here. He could protect me if danger should present itself . . . unless it ensnared us both.

Don't think on such things. Clear your mind and pray.

Finn started through the tunnel. I walked by his side, and Bennett trailed a few steps behind.

A silver chain around Finn's neck glinted in the firelight. His collar had always been crisp and straight, so I'd never noticed it before, but now with a casual waistcoat and jacket, the chain slipped into view. I reached for it. He noticed my motion and halted, but I stopped as well and managed to snag the chain and pull a pendant out from inside his shirt. Nicks and scratches marred the knotted cross forged from tarnished silver.

Finn tugged it from my hands and dropped it back down the front of his shirt. A humorous twinkle appeared in his eyes. "You're not one to follow proper etiquette, I see."

Bennett coughed behind me—stifling a laugh, no doubt.

I rolled my eyes and gestured to the chain. "You're religious, then?"

"I'm not." He started walking again, footsteps loud in the silence of the tunnel. "It was me mother's. A sentimental trinket. Nothing more."

"You don't share her faith?"

"Faith is a myth." He snorted and ruffled his raven curls with his fingers. "Faith promises redemption only for those who have enough. And why should we pretend when we know there be some who can never even be redeemed?"

"That's not how it works." I frowned. "There's hope for everyone. It doesn't matter what you've done."

"If you knew what some were capable of, you wouldn't say that."

A mix of grief and rage constricted my stomach as I pictured the injustice that had been done to my family, how it had stolen my father from me.

I snatched Finn's arm and yanked him to a halt. "My father was murdered by individuals who were capable of unthinkable cruelty." I jabbed a finger at his chest. "And now I'm made to watch as more men are killed. Don't tell me I don't know the horrors of which people are capable. I know too well."

Finn wrinkled his brow. "What happened to your father?"

Old wounds and memories opened, impressing further pain upon my heart. I raised my fingers to stroke the pearls around my neck.

Bennett's hand warmed my back between my shoulder blades, and his gentle voice filled the darkness. "You needn't answer, Adelynn."

I shook my head and breathed in to calm my voice. "He was killed by a gang of Irish nationalists. Radical members of the IRB." I grasped the pearls tighter. "But if any of those men turned from his ways, he could be redeemed. No matter the black mark, it can be wiped away."

"Now you're bein' naïve." Finn took a step backward. "Each of those men deserves the gallows. Nothing more."

"In this world perhaps," I said softly. "But in the eternity beyond, mercy is available for everyone—he need only accept it."

"So you're tellin' me if those men were standin' here before you, were lookin' you right in the eyes, you'd absolve them of all guilt?" Anger burned in his murky eyes. "Do you sincerely believe that? Or are you just spoutin' spiritual rhetoric that's been pounded into you?"

I opened my mouth but quickly shut it as I pictured facing the men guilty of stealing my father from me. I'd imagined it many times, what I would do if the moment ever came to pass, but now faced with the choice, did I truly believe it—that everyone deserved forgiveness? Objectively, I knew the correct answer, but translating that into action proved harder than I'd anticipated. Conflicting choices warred within me. *Lord God, soften my heart.*

"See?" Finn snorted and curled his lip. "There's a clear boundary between redeemable and completely condemned. Those men are unforgivable. My soul be no different."

Pity joined my jumbled mess of emotions. What could he possibly have done to resign himself to this fate? My blood turned to ice. There was the obvious offense, the mystery we'd been trying to solve all along—but I wasn't ready to label him as the guilty party.

I shook my head slowly. "Your mother clearly taught you about her beliefs. What made you stray so far away?"

The light seemed to go out of his eyes even as he raised the lantern. "A story for another time."

He pressed on through the tunnel. I formed a protest but decided it best to let it go—for now. Bennett and I traded glances before following. If Finn was involved with the murders in some way, he could be dangerous, and angering him would only add to the danger.

We passed multiple splits in the way forward, and I marveled at how such an expansive maze could exist beneath the London streets. The ceiling seemed to grow lower, the walls closer, as we continued. Musty smells tinged the air and labored our breathing. Soon, we came to a steep spiral staircase and climbed. The blackened wooden steps creaked and whined under our weight.

At the top, Finn opened a wooden hatch before climbing the rest of the way and assisting me out. Clear air filled my lungs as we emerged into a tight hallway with dim lamps, dusty red carpet, and faded wallpaper. Several doors lined the hall. Floating dust particles tickled my nose. On one side, the hallway led to a door left slightly ajar.

"This takes us back to the foyer." Finn waved a hand and made straight for the end of the hallway.

I examined each door as we passed. "What's in the rooms?"

"One is Cornelius's study. The others are nothing of consequence."

As I passed the open door, I took a quick peek inside and glimpsed a flash of green. Nausea gripped me. I turned from Finn's lead and surged into the room.

On the opposite wall, centered in the small room, a deep emerald flag hung above a blackened fireplace, emblazoned in the center with half of a golden sunburst. The IRB's emblem. I gasped and stood paralyzed. Cold sweat gathered on my brow as memories of my father's funeral flashed in my mind.

Bennett appeared at my side, eyes wide. "No affiliation with the IRB, you said?"

Finn ignored him and held up his hands. "Adelynn, let me explain."

"If you'll be explaining anything to anyone, it's to me." Bennett took a step toward Finn, but I grabbed his arm and held him in place.

Tears streaked down my cheeks. "Take me home, Bennett," I whispered. "Please, I want to go home."

Bennett held Finn in a glare for a moment before looking down at me. His expression softened. "Of course, Adelynn." He pulled out of my grasp and placed his strong arm around my shoulders. Then his tone grew stern as he fixed his gaze back on Finn. "You'd do well to prepare a statement, Mr. Kelly. I'll be back to follow up."

It was as I had suspected. Adelynn couldn't help but snoop around for evidence. I stared at my bedroom ceiling. Each muscle and joint in my body stretched, relaxed, and loosened as I lay prostrate on my bed. Even the knobbed wool blanket beneath me seemed to be a cloud from heaven. Sleep pulled at my senses and dragged down my eyelids, but my mind still whirled with the possibilities.

What if she discovered the truth to which we were leading her before all the pieces were set? That's where we were ultimately pushing her, but she was proving more resourceful than we anticipated. Though, the notes to Inspector Ford should keep the police busy at least.

A moth danced around my single lit candle, scattering shadows across the ceiling. The flame burned low on its tilted wax base, swaying slightly. A small trail of smoke trickled upward.

Would it be enough once we secured a small fraction of justice for our fallen brothers and sisters? What would we do once it was all over? Move on to the next target? Adelynn wasn't the only individual in England to blame, but her bloodline had started us all on this path.

The longer I inhaled the smoky scent from the candle, the more my head cleared. Thoughts slowed. Heat radiated through me, slickening my skin with sweat. Was it all worth it in the end? The manipulation? The murder? Weren't we just as cold-hearted as the English?

We weren't. This was different.

But then again—it wasn't.

I closed my eyes and concentrated on taking deep breaths. What should I do? What was right? This uncertainty was a frequent visitor as of late. It would wake me in the middle of the night, body in a cold sweat, weeping over the shed blood.

And now I faced one of those moments of turmoil, of indecision. So many unanswered questions. And yet, I knew one thing.

Adelynn couldn't find out any more. She had to be sidetracked— or incapacitated.

My breath came slow, and I put myself back in Ireland, no longer green but gray and dismal. Lichen-encrusted crosses jutted through the mist. Ciaran and I stood beside two oblong mounds of fresh soil on the hillside. Stone markers bore crude etched names above a shaky "Mama" and "Papa."

I knelt in the damp grass and gingerly placed a flower on each mound. Blue petals sang in delicate contrast to the black dirt's gaping maw, a distorted aroma of sweet flora and bitter earth. Fog rolled in as a faint humming trickled over the knoll and sent me off to sleep.

Chapter Seventeen

EMILY AND I STROLLED THROUGH THE grassy paths at Hyde Park. Nannies in white frocks pushed bulky prams with skipping children in tow. Two suffragettes planted themselves near the fountain and waved large signs with block letters. I squinted against the sun, thankful for pockets of shade beneath the trees.

Despite her condition, Emily's pace far surpassed my own. "You're moving rather quickly," I said in jest. "Surely, the doctor would insist that you rest."

"Actually, I was reading a delightful new pamphlet on motherhood, *Prenatal Care* by Mrs. Max West." Her breath came in short bursts, but her voice bounced with a jovial tone. "It recommends that light exercise is good for the mother and the baby."

I huffed. "At least slow down. You sound fatigued."

"The baby's simply left little room for my lungs." She pressed the side of her bump beneath her ribs. "I am fine. I assure you."

We passed an elegant swan, her long neck extending past the height of my waist. She kept watch along the banks of the Serpentine while her fuzzy gray cygnets grazed around her.

"Not long now." I grinned and nudged Emily's side. "How eager you must feel in anticipation of this little one's arrival."

"Yes . . ." She slowed, her arms tenderly encircling her round midsection, until she came to a complete stop, head bowed, bottom lip quivering. "If I can carry this one through to the end."

As I remembered the events of the past, stinging regret brought me to a halt beside her. She'd been through this before. Twice. Both lost before she'd made it midway through the pregnancies. I should have chosen my words more carefully, been more empathetic. This was a time of celebration but also one of trepidation. Even if the baby came to full term, the mother remained at great risk. Death was not uncommon for mother or child—or both. What could one say to a mother in that situation? Was there even a right answer?

"Emily, I apologize. I should have—"

"It's quite all right." She waved a hand before placing it back on her stomach. "You were only asking what one normally asks." Children near the prams giggled and chased one another. Emily's gaze grew distant. "I can't put Bennett through that again."

"'Twasn't your fault."

I uttered the instinctual phrase in earnest hope to deflect some of her blame, but every explanation I crafted to follow died at the tip of my tongue. It was nothing she hadn't heard a million times before.

"Was it not?" she murmured as though to herself. "Bennett was there for the second one, you know. Pain woke me shortly after midnight, and he helped me through the difficult delivery. When our daughter arrived, she was no bigger than Bennett's palm." She breathed in and then released a tense sigh. "Even before our engagement, I started praying for a healthy child when the time for children came. Bennett remains fervent in his confidence, but mine has begun to wane."

I grasped her hands. "You mustn't think like that. Sometimes, the evil of this world strikes us down and takes away things most precious to us." A knot formed at the bottom of my throat as I pictured my father and the last time I'd seen his face—loving blue eyes, deep laugh lines, and showstopping smile. "Lean on your husband. Lean on his faith. No matter the outcome, God will see you through it."

Emily watched the wandering cygnets and their diligent mother for a time before looking back to me and squeezing my hands. "Thank you, my friend."

The hair on my neck stood on end. Alarmed, I scanned the park, noting where those nannies had stopped for a rest, where the elderly couple fed pigeons on a bench, and where Samuel had parked so he could keep watch. But this feeling—I couldn't quite place it.

"Adelynn, are you all right?" Emily touched my shoulder. "You've gone quite pale."

"Yes, it's nothing." I urged a smile to spread my lips. "Come. We should get you home." Linking arms, we turned around—

And ran straight into Finn.

Emily and I drew back. I clutched her arm. All the feelings from the other day rushed back, of spending intimate time with him, discovering his secrets.

Finn's eyes widened. As he looked from me to Emily, redness crept into his cheeks. Focusing again on me, the initial shock dwindled from his features. "Cornelius and I were returnin' from a business meeting. I'm glad to have found you here. The other day—"

"We're leaving." I snatched Emily's hand and dragged her in the other direction.

"No, wait!" Finn darted around us and planted himself in our way, a look of pleading in his hazy gray eyes. "Please. Hear what I have to say."

"Do you know what those men did to my father? Men from the Brotherhood, your kin, as I recently discovered." I raised my voice. Finn's wince spurred me on. "He was on his way home after months abroad in Ireland. He was coming home to *me*." Large tears distorted my vision. "They followed him from port and dragged him into an alley. They beat him. And then they stabbed him." I gripped the pearls at my throat and heaved until I could catch my breath. "Nothing was stolen. Nothing held for ransom. It was a deed of the most heinous brutality, born simply of spite and revenge."

"I'm sorry," he said, his voice but a wisp on the wind.

I gnashed my teeth and swiped at the tears scorching my cheeks. I should send for Baze or Bennett, compel them to haul him to Scotland Yard to pry any guilt from the depths of his soul, which he insisted was condemned. Perhaps it was after all.

"Adelynn, you must believe me when I say—"

"I don't care to hear anything you have to say."

A figure materialized beside us as though from thin air. Cornelius's hand clamped down on Finn's shoulder. "If you don't mind, ladies, I'd like to speak on Finn's behalf." He gave Finn a gentle shove and flashed a grave look.

Without any semblance of a protest, Finn sent me a parting glance—eyes shrouded in fog and uncertainty—before withdrawing.

Cornelius offered a half-hearted smile and gestured to a nearby bench. "Please."

Emily placed a gentle hand on my shoulder as we sat, her delicate brows wrinkled in a frown. Cornelius dropped before us on one knee, resting his arms on his propped leg. "I know of your discovery, Adelynn, and I apologize. Had I known such a symbol had been erected in my establishment, I would never have allowed it. I've since removed it from the premises. I understand the distress it caused you."

Distress barely began to cover it. But I nodded for him to continue.

"Finn's father was a member of the IRB," Cornelius said. "You've heard of the Phoenix Park killings?"

Emily stiffened beside me. I grasped her hand and held it in my lap. "Yes," I said.

"His father was one of the perpetrators." Cornelius watched me, but I managed to keep a straight face, even while my insides soured. "He escaped justice and moved to a rural village. Finn was born soon after, but then it seems justice had a strange sense of humor. The man lost his wife in childbirth and, later, his twin girls to tuberculosis. His past caught up with him when Finn was ten. He was hanged." Cornelius twisted the gold band on his finger. "You have to understand that in those times, for an orphan, Finn didn't have a lot of options. He fell in with other members of the IRB, who accepted and cared for him. But that's never what was in his heart. It was all a method of survival."

As he leaned toward us, the sun glinted off his pale eyes, brightening them so that the irises almost seemed white. "Finn's been my flatmate, my employee, and my friend for the better part of a decade. He's not the ruthless IRB spy you think him to be."

Wasn't he? How could I be sure anymore? Who could I trust in all this? Even Baze, whom I'd confided in, wouldn't heed my words. And now Cornelius dangled these statements in front of me, hoping I would accept them as truth.

Emily rubbed my arm, waking me from my musings.

I sent a brief smile in her direction, but when I looked at Cornelius, a heavy emotional weight dragged my mouth into a frown. "I wish I could take you at your word, Mr. Marx." I squeezed Emily's hand as though to draw confidence from her. "But as with Finn, I've only known you for a few weeks."

"I understand." Cornelius flashed a fleeting smile. "I will not fault you for your mistrust. I would harbor the same hesitation." He stood, and the sun cast his tall shadow between Emily and me. "But if you truly wish to see the truth of Finn Kelly for yourself, then come out to the Molly Malone the night after next."

I rose, tugging Emily with me. "The Molly Malone?"

"An Irish pub in Whitechapel. There's to be a *céilí*, a lively gathering of dance and music, and Finn will be lending his musical talents to the event." Cornelius mimed the fingering of a vertical instrument, then touched his chest with one hand. "When they play, musicians bear their hearts for all to see."

Despite my mistrust, I knew the statement to be true. I pictured Baze bent over the piano, sweat trickling down his brow, fingers dancing across the keys, and emotion as clear as crystal radiating on his face.

Cornelius's voice brought me back. "If you truly think Finn a threat, come witness it for yourself. But that's up to you." He took a step back and bent in a stiff bow. "Ladies. Until then."

Chapter Eighteen

TICK-TOCK. TICK-TOCK. MR. FORD'S grandfather clock interrupted what would have been welcome silence as I waited, seated in front of his desk in the dark study. It wasn't like my father's—a warm, book-filled place of comfort and reprieve. Instead, Mr. Ford's crimson walls held guns and pelts from game he'd killed on exotic hunts.

Only a moment, he'd said. *Typical.*

I breathed methodically to calm my stomach. The longer I waited, the more I worried about the circumstances surrounding this call. I hadn't done anything to deny his wishes, so I couldn't imagine what this would be about. Unless . . . had he heard about the moment Baze and I had shared the other night, when I had rejected his advances?

The door opened, and Mr. Ford breezed into the room, followed by Baze. As though a king settling into his throne, Mr. Ford lifted his chin and sat rigidly in the leather chair behind his desk.

"What's this about, Father?" Baze took a seat in the chair beside mine. "You know we're in the middle of an investigation. I haven't got much time."

"That's precisely what I would like to talk about. In the wake of these horrific past weeks, your mother and I have grown concerned for your safety." Mr. Ford steepled his fingers. "Which is why I have decided to move your wedding date to two weeks hence."

I gulped in a breath. Move the wedding date? How could they think to propose such a thing, especially in the midst of all this madness?

Baze glanced my way and then back at his father. "Forgive my insubordination, but I don't believe now is the time for that decision. There is a killer on the loose."

Mr. Ford's jaw muscle twitched. "I must insist."

"And I must decline again." Baze leaned forward. "I just lost one of my men, and the culprit is still at large. My wedding is not one of my priorities."

"But that is precisely why I expect you to comply." He watched Baze down the length of his nose, narrowing his eyes. "You've failed to catch the killer thus far. Who's to say you'll ever catch him? If your past performance is any indication, you've a better chance of joining a debutante ball than succeeding in this mission with which you've been tasked."

I expected Baze to jump in once more with a rebuttal to the absurd statement, but he remained silent and still, expression morphing into that of a reprimanded schoolboy. He stared, caught in his father's dominant snare.

"Your last chance at redemption is to wed Miss Spencer and produce an heir." Mr. Ford sniffed. "Or perhaps you will fail at that too."

A primal instinct awakened in me, the overwhelming urge to charge the desk and scratch at Mr. Ford's smug face. Somehow, I bottled the desire and settled for stringing together defiant insults in my subconscious.

Baze took a slow breath. "Set the date and send out the invitations. We shall wed in a fortnight."

I whirled toward him. "Baze!"

"Good boy." Mr. Ford grinned.

I bolted out of my chair. "I'll have no part in this."

Baze thrust his finger toward my seat. "Sit down, Adelynn."

"No. Why are you acting this way? You said yourself, this isn't the time—"

Baze surged to his feet and seized my wrist. A cry escaped my lips. His tone grew low. "You'll do as I say." Unfamiliar coldness shifted behind his eyes.

Mr. Ford watched our exchange intently, expectantly.

What had come over Baze? His father's taunting had triggered something in him. I wasn't about to break through that with any measure of persuasion, not with his father's presence still suffocating the room.

"Do what you will, then." I yanked from Baze's hold and turned on my heels. "I'll see myself out."

Once free of the room, I blew out a heavy breath. Tears nearly spilled out with it. What I had just witnessed, the breadth and destruction of Mr. Ford's influence, struck fear in me. Baze had fallen completely under his control and, by that, had subjected me as well. Was there no way out? No way to pull Baze back from the brink?

I only made it to the parlor before Baze's large hand slipped around my wrist—this time gently—and pulled me to face him.

"Al, please don't go." His chestnut eyes pleaded, regaining some of their familiar character and losing the callousness from a moment ago.

For an instant, he had me cornered, using the same methods he always had when we were children—with those expectant, forlorn eyes peering at me from under dark knitted eyebrows, as though the world would come to a halt if I didn't comply with his every request.

But I couldn't make a stand right now. There was history between father and son that I couldn't understand, not without help. I needed to know more. His brothers—one of his brothers would know.

"Al." His voice hitched while his hand squeezed my wrist. "Please."

A little piece of me curled in anguish as I forced myself to look away. "I'm sorry, Baze. I have to go."

"No—"

I pulled from his touch and didn't look back.

Chapter Nineteen

"NIGHT, FORD." THE LAST SERGEANT TO check in at headquarters, Andrews, gave Baze a formal nod and vacated the building. It was about time Baze headed home as well, not that he needed to conclude any work. This had all been for show—sitting here, rifling through papers, going through the motions.

Lingering smoke from Andrews's cigarette pricked Baze's nose. The sunset burned through the window in dusty orange beams. It warmed his shoulders but couldn't reach the ice in his bones. That look his father had given him transported him back to his teenage years, back to that wretched alley. The pain from his bloodied body had paled in comparison to the anguish caused by the revulsion in his father's eyes. Had his brothers not intervened, Father would surely have stripped him of his title, status, and family right then and there.

Baze had sworn he would never do anything after that to give his father reason to cast him out, but—as always—he failed. Why should he expect anything else at this point? Despite everything he did, everything he tried to do, nothing was enough. Perhaps he truly wasn't worthy of the Ford name.

He crumpled a page in his fist to keep himself from ripping the lot to pieces and overturning the desk for good measure. He rubbed his eyes and leaned back, balancing on the rear legs of the chair.

A fist slammed down on his desk. Baze yelled as he lost his balance and toppled backward.

"I've told you not to tempt fate like that." Bennett chuckled as he leaned over Baze, sunset glaring off his spectacles. "'Twas only a matter of time before I caught you off guard."

Groaning, Baze sat up and righted the chair. "Shouldn't you be at home?"

"I was on my way." He jabbed a thumb over his shoulder, humor still dancing in his eyes. "Had to check in with the boss. I've been called to do some impromptu investigating tonight."

Baze eyed him. "Why so late? Are you on a new case?"

"It's a secret assignment." Bennett helped Baze to his feet. "I ran into Hamilton on the way in, and he asked me to fetch you. Said he made a startling discovery. Sounded urgent."

Sore muscles protested as Baze stretched. "Care to join me?"

Bennett grinned. "Wouldn't miss it."

Down at the mortuary, they walked through the chilled room of tables—some for instruments, some for corpses. Bennett leaned in closer. "What do you think of Sophia? Or perhaps George for a boy?"

Baze elbowed him away. "You're thinking about that now?"

"One must be prepared." Bennett tapped his temple. "Nature could take over any day now."

"We have other things to focus on right now."

"So that's a no, then?"

"Nutter."

Hamilton paced beside a prepared table with a covered body. Sweat beads lined each wrinkle in his brow and glistened under his wispy white hair. When he saw the two approach, he gestured enthusiastically for them to come closer. "Good, good. I was afraid Bennett had lost his way. Come quickly, my boys, come."

Hamilton threw back the sheet. It revealed Moseley's mangled face, conjuring sharp images of blood on the pavement and the wailing heap of his mother when Baze informed her of her son's death.

Lightheadedness returned as Hamilton prodded open the remaining piece of Moseley's jaw with a set of silver tongs. Even Bennett went a bit white.

"Come close. Come close." Hamilton wagged a finger at Moseley. "Look. There."

As they leaned in, Baze tried to breathe through his mouth to dull the smell of rot, but it consumed his senses.

Inside Moseley's mouth, the bullet had done its job. Twisted flesh and bone curved inward toward his skull in a gaping hole. Red light streamed in from the missing portions of his face.

"What are we meant to see?" Baze asked, the contents of his stomach swirling and rising.

"There." Hamilton pointed. "The right side of the palate. In the tissue."

It all looked pink, torn, and blistered, but as Baze peered closer, he recognized a swollen shape etched in the tissue. The numeral 3.

Baze and Bennett retreated at the same time and gave each other puzzled looks. "So what does it mean?" Bennett asked.

Hamilton touched his fingertips together and turned to his workbench. His silence chilled the room even further. Without a word, he handed Baze a developed photograph of Clifton's naked body from the waist up, clearly depicting his gruesome stab wound. "What do you see?"

This time, it only took Baze a short moment to find a small, almost indistinguishable mark carved among the curled white hair between Clifton's clavicles—the numeral 4.

Hamilton tapped his fingers together again. "And Jonathan Mallory, the first victim, had a five etched into his thumbnail."

Sweat dampened Baze's shirt as he added the numbers in his head. "It's a countdown."

"It would appear so."

"That blasted madman is numbering his victims." Pain shot through his knuckles before he even realized he had struck the table's surface.

Bennett stroked his chin. "But if it's a countdown, then he still has two victims left, assuming zero doesn't count."

Suddenly, Baze could think only of Adelynn and ensuring her safety. God only knew who this killer would target next. "We have to catch this man," Baze murmured. "I should take a squad down to that wretched theater and arrest them all."

"You know we can't hold them without evidence." Bennett grimaced.

"Then what are we to do?" With a growl, Baze raked a hand through is hair. "I've studied the photos, the testimonies, the notes a thousand times. This man might as well be a phantom."

"Pull yourself together, Ford." Hamilton snatched up a ruler from the table and smacked Baze across the side of his head. Baze grabbed at his stinging ear and gaped at the doctor. "This is clearly a living and breathing being with a malformed soul. Don't let his madness pollute your instincts and your character." Hamilton poked Baze's chest with a finger. "God gave you the gift of discernment, my boy. Use it. The answer is out there, but your eyes have been clouded and can't see it."

Baze hung his shoulders. "Then how do I uncloud them?"

"You simply need a little inspiration and God's divine touch. And I think I might have some for you—the former anyway." Hamilton's milky eyes twinkled. "I received a tip this morning that there is to be a large convergence of the Irish people at one of the pubs in Whitechapel. What's it called? The Molly Malone, I believe."

Bennett blanched. "The Molly Malone?"

"Indeed. Might be a good continuation of your investigation. Perhaps there will be a bloke willing to talk. And the theater employees may even be in attendance."

"I'll actually be passing through that area tonight." Bennett cleared his throat. "I'd be more than happy to investigate. You've been stretched quite thin, Baze. You should stay—"

"No, I'm going with you." Baze stood straighter, resolve solidifying within him. "I want to be there in person to look those Irishmen in the eyes as they answer my questions."

Bennett shook his head. "Tonight's not a good night—"

"My mind's made up." Baze clapped his partner on the chest. "I'm going."

Chapter Twenty

SCATTERED LIGHT AND FAINT MUSIC SEEPED from the small pub. Its shutters hung askew over cracked windows while the shingles on its low roof stuck up every which way. Painted in faded gold letters against a green background, the words "Molly Malone" decorated a crooked signpost above the door.

As I stood on the pavement facing the pub, I blew into my hands and rubbed them together. Bennett should be along any moment, but how much longer could I linger? I bounced on my toes and ruffled the scratchy skirt of the simple dress I'd borrowed from Margaret so that I might blend in with the lower class. I could sit in the car with Samuel until Bennett arrived, but the evening slipped away with each passing moment. This wasn't a time for waiting.

I stepped forward. When I pushed through the heavy wooden door, a gust of soft air warmed my cheeks and encircled me like a coverlet. I shivered and breathed in the delectable smells of seasoned roast and hearth fire. Men and women, some barely of age and others decades past, filled the seats around scattered square tables and lined the wall-length bar. A group of musicians clustered in the corner played a light-hearted jig. One wielded a penny whistle. Another held a flat drum vertically on his thigh and struck it with a cylindrical wooden beater. Father had once brought one of those drums home with him after a particularly long trip to Ireland—a bodhrán, if I remembered correctly. The whistle piped above the hearty din and laughter of the bunch. Soon, a fiddler joined in with a singsong melody and double-stops.

That's when I noticed Finn sitting in the middle of the quartet. He played some sort of bagpipe instrument. Rather than use a mouthpiece,

Finn brought the instrument to life by pumping air through bellows with his elbow and fingering quickly on an upright chanter pressed to his thigh. The sound resembled the cadence of a bagpipe but was more lyrical in tone.

Finn laughed and bobbed his free leg in time as they upped the tempo. I'd seen his stage smile, even caught a brief glimpse of a real smile away from the public persona, but it paled in comparison to this one. It consumed every feature with overflowing emotion, etched deep in his cheeks, wrinkling the skin around his eyes, and revealing light dimples I had never noticed before. No baggage, no guilt—simply joy.

My heart softened. Cornelius had wanted me to see this side of Finn, and now I believed it. How could someone with this much happiness create so much heartache? I refused to believe it was possible. *Lord, let it be so. Let his heart be innocent.*

The sound of my name filtered through the music. Cornelius waved from a table near the bar. I picked my way through the crowd—receiving a few whistles from drunk patrons—and joined him at the table with Collin and Siobhan.

As soon as she saw me, Siobhan curled up her nose and stood. "I'm going for a smoke." She brushed past, bumping my shoulder. I sucked in a tight breath and bit my lip but chose to let it alone.

Cornelius waved a hand as I took a seat. "Don't pay Shiv any mind. She doesn't care for anyone really. I'm her employer and she can barely tolerate me." He raised his eyebrows. "'Twas good of you to join us."

"It was an invitation to which I couldn't say no." I put on a half-smile. "You presented it so convincingly."

Hoots and hollers drew my attention back to the musicians—to Finn. When I caught his eye, he brightened and winked, then shouted, "Let's go, me lads," as the musicians transitioned to a new jig. I sat mesmerized by the fluttering style of his fingers on the chanter.

I pointed. "What is that?"

Cornelius leaned forward and raised his voice over the music. "It's an uilleann pipe."

I caught my breath. "It's beautiful."

"Aye. There's nothin' quite like it."

I studied Cornelius's face, his contented look and relaxed expression, as though this atmosphere allowed him to drop his guard. His speech sounded different here among these people. The Irish inflection he borrowed was more detectable—the way he kept the earthy vowels and tight consonants near the front of his mouth.

I grinned. "Dare I say it, but the Irish brogue sounds downright natural coming from you."

He raised an eyebrow, and a smooth smile stretched across his mouth. "I hardly do it justice, but I have lived among their kind for many years, so I have developed an affinity to their cadence in my own speech. I'll be takin' that as a compliment."

"As you should. It suits you."

He tilted his head. His eyes grazed across my face, easing across my lips and up again to hold my gaze securely in his. For a moment, I found myself stuck in those deep icy pools. They held curiosity, admiration—and desire.

I snapped my gaze away, cheeks flaming, but my stomach growled and provided a welcome distraction. I swallowed as I watched others gulp down drinks and laugh over full plates of food.

"Good heavens, how rude of me." Cornelius put his fingers to his lips and whistled at the bartender. "Bring some mutton stew for the lady and a round of beers for the lot."

Out of the corner of my eye, I caught Collin studying me, but when I gave him my attention, he dropped his gaze. With youthful round features and innocent green eyes, Collin should have been in school, not working in a theater and spending his evenings in a pub.

I put an elbow on the table and propped up my chin with my palm. "So, tell me your story, Collin. What brought you here?"

Redness blossoming on his cheeks, he looked to Cornelius.

I smiled. "If you're put off by how my fiancé treated you at the show, I apologize."

"No, I'm afraid that's not quite the problem." Cornelius glanced at Collin, who gave a nod, then continued. "Though much of Ireland now speaks the king's English, there are small colonies scattered throughout the countryside that still teach Irish as the primary language. Collin is from one of those colonies."

I blinked. "Then how did he end up here?"

"His parents died several years ago. With no other living relatives, he made his way to Dublin and found a ship heading to England. I found him stowed away aboard a ship docked in Liverpool while I was tourin' the country. Was all skin and bones. So I took him in. Gave him food and lodging in exchange for his work."

"He be teachin' me English." Collin's speech, though hesitant and buried by his accent, came out smooth.

I crossed my arms on the table. "My father used to teach me basic Irish words and phrases, but I'm ashamed to say I never caught on."

Collin's eyes lit up. "He knows Irish?"

I bit my lip, tears welling as eagerness radiated from Collin. "He spent his life advocating for the Irish cause. He passed away last year." My voice hitched. "Would you mind teaching me some?"

For a moment, Collin stared blankly until Cornelius whispered a phrase in a language heavy with consonants.

Collin broke out in a toothy smile. "*Dia dhuit.*"

I nodded and frowned in concentration as I attempted to pronounce it. "Gee-uh gwitch?"

"Close. *Dia dhuit.*"

"What does that mean?"

"God be with you." He tipped his head. "And hello."

"I'll have to remember that one."

Collin edged closer, eyes large and expectant. "*Go raibh maith agat.*"

I clumsily repeated—or tried to repeat—the words. "What did I say?"

He beamed. "You said, 'Thank you.'"

I stated the phrase again, stumbling as Collin tried to help me. The bartender's shadow covered me as he placed a steaming bowl of thick stew and a crust of bread in front of me, then delivered us each a pint of dark beer.

Before he could leave, I tripped through the phrase Collin had just taught me. The bartender eyed me for a moment down his bulbous nose and then let out a hoarse, bellowing guffaw.

I frowned and looked to the men.

As Collin snickered, Cornelius tipped a hand from side to side. "Your pronunciation could use a wee bit of work."

The stew tasted salty and meaty, warming my throat and stomach. As I ate, Cornelius told tales of the short time he'd spent in Ireland, stopping every so often to clarify in Irish for Collin. He explained how he first met Finn at a riot in Dublin, after the second failure of the Home Bill's passing. It was a peaceful demonstration until an anonymous instigator injured one of the policemen. Violence erupted, and Finn was caught in the middle of it. Had Cornelius not shown up, Finn would have gone to prison, probably for life.

I stole a look at Finn. He played with his eyes closed as he kept in time with the latest melancholy reel, this time in a minor key. He didn't seem the type to resort to violence, nor even the type to attend a protest in the first place. But I supposed hardship could make a person do terrible things.

Cornelius eyed my empty bowl, then my full glass of beer. "You haven't touched your Guinness."

"Oh, I'm not really partial to alcohol." I slid it away.

Cornelius pushed it back toward me. "It's on the house, Adelynn. 'Twould be rude to refuse."

I lifted my chin and straightened my shoulders. "'Tisn't ladylike."

He smirked. "That hasn't stopped you before."

The challenge in his voice pricked my pride. I narrowed my eyes. "Perhaps a few sips."

The black beer flowed smoothly down my throat and spread

warmth and calm through my core and out to my limbs. Its creamy texture left a bitter finish in my mouth, but the flavor—a hint of coffee and chocolate—was surprisingly enjoyable. Foam stuck to my top lip.

Cornelius handed me a serviette and raised his eyebrows. I wiped my mouth with as much dignity as I could, then pursed my lips and shrugged. "Well, it's not the worst thing I've tasted."

His eyes twinkled as he laughed. He and Collin lifted their glasses for a toast with mine. "*Sláinte!*" they shouted and drank.

A sharp whistle pierced the air. The mood shifted. Energy buzzed. Music transitioned to a timed, lively jig. Finn tossed his head back and laughed. As if rehearsed, people shoved aside tables to make a large space in the middle of the floor. Cornelius and Collin stood and pushed our table away, leaving me sitting out in the open.

Cornelius offered me a hand.

I examined the bustling scene. "What's going on?"

He snatched my hand and pulled me to my feet. The momentum toppled me forward against him. He chuckled. "It's time to dance!"

I pushed off of him, stomach tight. "I don't know how to dance—not this kind, anyway."

The music crescendoed. Through a dazzling smile, he said, "Just follow my lead."

Time was lost as we twirled and spun, grasping hands, forming lines, stomping in one-two-one steps as we shifted and traded partners. My feet and face ached—my feet from learning the new steps, my face from smiling so wide. Cornelius stuck by my side and kept hold of me with trained hands and a firm stance. After only a few songs, I had the steps memorized.

Finally, as my dry throat burned, my legs shook in exhaustion, and my lungs seemed ready to burst right through my corset, I stepped out of the group. Cornelius followed close behind. I couldn't stop laughing as we rested by the bar.

"That was amazing," I shouted, barely able to hold myself up. Weakness shook my legs and sweat stuck the light cotton dress to my skin. Hair fell about my face, loose from its comb. I tried to collect and pin it back, but I could hardly keep my arms aloft.

"Allow me." Cornelius took the pins from my hands and turned me to face away from him. After a few tugs and shiver-inducing comb-throughs with his fingers, he said, "How's that?"

I tested his handiwork as I swiveled back around and found a tight updo. I raised an eyebrow. "Such an odd hidden talent."

He shrugged. "I had two younger sisters while growing up and no mother. Someone had to learn how."

Skin on the back of my neck prickled. As I remembered a past conversation, faint alarm snuffed out my delight. "I thought you were an only child."

The grave countenance that came over him stirred even more alarm in me. Whether he displayed regret or defensiveness—or both—I couldn't decide. My stomach constricting, I glanced toward the door. *Bennett, where are you?*

Clearing his throat, Cornelius shrugged again, and his features softened into a more agreeable expression. "I don't like to speak of them. Tragic childhood and all that." Before I could inquire further, he rapped on the bar with his knuckles and shouted at the barkeep. "Riordan, one for me and a special one for the lady, please."

Two glass mugs—one frothing with beer, the other a clear liquid—slid into his hands. He offered the clear one to me. "It will help your breathing and soothe your muscles."

Gratefully, I accepted and downed the drink. I'd expected water, but this scalded my throat. I coughed but reveled in the burn. Relaxation passed through my body, and the need for quick breaths passed. Even my thoughts slowed. My senses blurred, and the world became distant, hazy.

Cornelius tilted up my chin with a knuckle. "How do you feel?"

Imbalance buzzed through my head. I tried to answer but found my tongue thick and useless.

He surrounded me with a supportive arm. "It will pass. Come. I requested a ballad. I'll teach you the steps."

But the feeling did not pass.

Chapter Twenty-One

FINALLY, AFTER HUSHING BENNETT MULTIPLE TIMES, Baze's drive grew quiet. Bennett had insisted that Baze rest and let him handle this alone. But Bennett rarely denied help, a believer in always bringing someone to watch his back. Was Baze's exhaustion really so evident that Bennett would sacrifice his own safety?

Bennett propped an arm on the car door and tapped his foot. "Are you sure you know where you're going?"

Baze rolled his eyes. So much for a quiet evening. "I memorized the route."

Indeed, as they rounded a curve onto a smaller street, the map materialized in his head. One more turn and they would arrive.

"Last chance to go home." Bennett's spectacles shifted on his perspiring nose.

"Lay off it."

"Very well, but at least answer me this. Do you prefer Andrew or Elias?"

Baze took the next turn sharply, throwing Bennett against the door. He fought off a satisfied grin as Bennett scowled.

A warm glow from the pub up ahead illuminated a huddle of men stumbling about near the street corner. When Baze pulled up to the opposite curb, he killed the engine and opened the door. A chilled breeze and lively music greeted him. With a shiver, he stepped onto the pavement and surveyed the area. A familiar car parked a few spaces ahead held the silhouette of an unmistakable chauffeur.

Baze halted. Cold tendrils of fear blossomed within him. "What is Samuel doing here?"

"Samuel?" Bennett came around to Baze's side of the car, mopping his brow with the back of his wrist. "Where?"

Samuel's presence was enough to rouse suspicion, but Bennett's strange behavior and deflective attitude confirmed Baze's fears. He seized Bennett's jacket collar and jostled him. "You cad!"

Bennett wrinkled his nose. "Easy, Baze."

"Al's in there, isn't she?" Baze shoved him but kept hold of his jacket. "And you knew about this. This was your 'secret assignment.'"

Bennett swallowed and shifted his jaw before nodding.

Baze paused to let the information sink in. "What in God's name is she doing here?"

"She asked me not to divulge that information." Bennett tried to pry Baze's hands away. "Let go."

Anger swelled. Baze clutched tighter and hefted Bennett to the balls of his feet. "What do you mean? What is she . . ." He gritted his teeth. "No, never mind. We'll speak about this later. I need to get Al out of there." He dropped Bennett and jabbed his chest. "If anything happens to her, it's on your head."

Bennett batted Baze's hand away. "If you hadn't insisted upon accompanying me, I could have arrived sooner and ensured her safety."

Baze clenched his hands into fists and faced the pub, fury tightening to resolve. This woman would be the death of his sanity.

The room radiated heat and sweat collected in my pores. My heart palpitated as Cornelius and I moved to the flowing ballad, but a sense of calm relaxed my muscles. It felt safe in this moment, my hand in his, his palm on my lower back.

As my thoughts whirled and my vision hazed, my tongue loosed. "Who is it?"

Cornelius raised an eyebrow. "Pardon?"

"Who's the murderer? The police think it's someone in the theater. Is it Siobhan? Is it *you*?"

Expression unreadable, his bright, icy eyes cut through my haze.

His lips stretched to a gentle smile. "Perhaps it is time you retired home to bed. Your exhaustion has clouded your judgment."

"No, I want to stay." I squeezed his hand and slid my other from his shoulder to the back of his neck. My mouth tingled and grew dry. "Don't make me go."

His fingers prodded the small of my back, pulling me close until no space remained between us. Hard heartbeats tapped my chest—his heartbeats.

"You're a fascinating woman, Adelynn." His hot breath warmed my cheeks. "So, it puzzles me. Why do you remain with the inspector? You're unhappy, that much is clear. And it's plain to see that he takes you for granted."

"No, he doesn't." My speech slurred, and no matter how hard I tried to enunciate, it still came out lopsided. *What is wrong with me?* "He's a good match. My mother has said so. His parents have said so."

"What do you say?" He caressed my back with his thumb, sending electricity through my hips. "Don't be afraid to take what your heart wants, Adelynn, even if your head is telling you not to."

Excitement and eagerness filled my bones. All images of Baze faded away, replaced with Cornelius's smile—here, now. I released his hand and gripped his face with both of mine, his smooth jaw free of stubble. We stopped dancing.

Somewhere, deep in the pit of my stomach, my gut screamed, "No!" But both my head and my heart urged me on—as though an outside force moved my limbs and whispered thoughts to me.

As I focused on his lips and rose to my tiptoes, the song changed. The new melody quickened in pace but calmed my mind. All previous thoughts cleared, allowing me a small reprieve and a chance to regain some control. Gingerly, I dropped my hands to his shoulders and whispered, "I know this song."

"'Tis a farewell song of Ireland." His quiet tone matched mine.

"What's it called?"

"Parting Glass."

Somehow, this song had drawn me out of my dazed state. My head still pounded, and an ache took hold in my stomach, but I could think clearly. I'd let my guard down, had almost been drawn in. What could I have been capable of?

Lord, protect my heart and my mind. Keep outside influences at bay.

Like the dousing of a candle, all tempting thoughts fled and left me clear-minded—and in the arms of a man who wasn't my fiancé.

The stomach pain deepened, growing sharp. My vision swirled. I clutched at my abdomen and bent forward.

"Steady now." Cornelius held me upright against his chest. "I think your time here is done for tonight. Let me escort you to your car."

A hand dropped down on Cornelius's shoulder. "Release her, Marx." Control leveled the familiar voice, but the ire lacing it sent a shiver up my spine.

"Baze?" I squinted at him, holding my middle with both arms. "What are you doing here?"

With fury etched on his face, Baze gripped my upper arm. "You've no right to ask me that, Adelynn." He yanked me from Cornelius's hold. Had it not been for Baze's numbing grasp, I would have collapsed. "I've just learned you've been sneaking behind my back and putting your life in danger. And now I've come all this way to find you with another man. Have you no dignity?"

I whimpered as pain twisted up into my chest. "Baze, please. Let's talk about this later."

Cornelius took a step toward us. "Can't you see she is unwell?"

Baze aimed a scathing look at him. "This does not concern you."

"Please, Baze. I must go home." I clung to his arm now, if only to keep myself from toppling over.

By now, several men had drawn closer to us, staring at Baze with hungry eyes. Somehow, Finn managed to keep the musicians engaged and playing as though to distract from our squall.

"I suggest you let Adelynn go." Cornelius's expression turned to stone, eyes cold and unblinking.

"I'll thank you not to tell me how to handle my fiancée."

One of the Irishmen approached and put a hand on Baze's shoulder, but he stepped out of it, whirled us around, and flashed his badge. "Police. If you touch me, I will arrest you for assaulting an officer." His hold tightened, and I moaned. As though realizing the pain he caused me, his eyes softened, and he let go.

I seized the opportunity to stumble to the entrance, hunched over as the stomach pain sharpened. The room pitched side to side. Up ahead, I spotted Bennett near the door. Approaching, I could only manage, "How could you?"

Regret crossed his features. "I tried to stop him."

"It doesn't matter," I said, almost to myself. "I need to get home."

Outside, cool night air revived my lungs and seemed to lift a bit of the pain. When the door swung shut, the music fell to a tolerable hum. I took a deep breath and released a cleansing sigh.

How could such a grand night have taken such a dark turn? It had begun with that drink. What toxic substance had been added to it? And then Baze . . . he always appeared and spoiled all the good I tried to accomplish. He was already in charge of my life by default. Couldn't he leave me to my own pursuits at the very least?

The music jumped in volume. Baze snapped, "No, Bennett, stay here." Then the music softened again. I tensed as Baze turned me toward him. "We're not finished, Al."

I glared up at him, leaning into his hold more than I wanted. It took all of my strength not to double over. "I need to go home."

"How long have you been sneaking around behind my back?" He let out a growl. "What have you been doing?"

As much as I didn't want to continue this conversation, Baze knew now, and unless I set him straight, he would fill in the remaining details with his own conclusions.

"I've been trying to find answers. You refused to listen to me when I told you about my visions." I took another deep breath. "I was open and honest with you right from the start, but you turned me away."

"So lying to me and waltzing headlong into the lair of a could-be killer was your answer?" He spat the words.

"It was more than what you were doing."

The statement came out harsher than I'd intended, but another wave of pain and dizziness struck me before I could backtrack.

Baze grasped my arms to prevented me from pitching to the side. "I'll take you home." His tone calmed but retained its bitterness. "Now."

I pushed against his chest. "No, Samuel will—"

"I'm not asking for your permission." He held fast. "This is an order."

My voice quivered as I spoke low. "Just as you ordered me to marry you in a fortnight?"

A muscle jumped in his jaw. "I tried to discuss it with you, but you insisted on walking out."

"So I'm in the wrong because I walked out, despite your doing nothing to defend yourself—defend me—against your father?"

"Enough." He jostled me, sending my head spinning. "You don't know the whole story."

"Then tell me." I managed to yank away. "Tell me what your father did to secure such a strong hold on you. Then maybe I'll understand. I *want* to understand."

"You need only understand this." He jabbed a finger at his chest. "My thoughts and actions are my own. He holds no influence over me."

I gave a terse laugh. "Your father has his teeth sunk deep into your life. But I can't tell if you simply refuse to see it or if you truly are so naïve."

"I said that's enough."

"I'm not finished yet." I raised my voice and tried to straighten, but the pain and dizziness kept me bent over. "I've held back this long for the sake of your heart, but now I see it can't be avoided. Right from the start of our engagement, perhaps even before, your father has been pulling the strings to control us."

"No." He scoffed. "It was my decision to ask you to marry me. You said yes to me, not him."

"I said yes because of him, and you only asked because of him." I waited for a rebuttal, but he clamped his mouth shut. A sob brewed in my chest. "Your father is influencing everything we do. Why can't you see that?"

"I don't know what you're talking about."

I fought back tears and searched for another way to make him understand. Then, before I could stop myself, I said, "Your father threatened me, Baze." Heat rose to my cheeks. "He threatened to remove me from my mother and strip my family's—and my father's—reputation away to leave us with nothing." Baze's complexion paled as he went rigid. Was there a chance I could break through this fear that gripped him so tightly? "I don't have the authority to stand up to him, but you do. You have to put an end to this."

"I . . . I can't." He curled his hands into fists. His eyes glistened. "We have to do as he says. We'll be together. Why does it matter how? You love me, don't you?"

Hopelessness spread like an infection within me. I swallowed away a sob and peered through tears at the face of the man I had cherished since childhood. "I love you with all of my heart, Basil Ford, and that's what makes this so difficult."

He winced and stepped toward me. "Adelynn—"

"No." I drew back. "I'm done reasoning with you. I need to go home. Don't follow me, Baze."

I stumbled across the street, cries filling my chest. I nearly fell over but managed to make it to the car in time to catch myself. All I wanted to do was collapse in the seat and pretend the outside world didn't exist. Maybe that would make all this pain melt away.

Before I could open the door, I glimpsed the empty driver's seat. I blinked. Perhaps my vision was tricking me.

"Samuel?" I asked, then called out louder. Using the car as support, I crossed to the driver's side. The door hung ajar. A black splattered trail twisted along the pavement and disappeared to a side street. My lungs and throat clenched. I swayed on my feet.

With every ounce of my remaining strength, I followed the liquid stain. Around the corner, I scanned the scene through bleary eyes. Samuel lay crumpled in a heap twenty paces away.

I fell by his side and lifted his head. Dried blood matted his snow-white hair. Was he breathing? I couldn't tell. "Samuel." I shook his limp arm. "Samuel, please!"

Cold fingers clamped over my mouth. A scream stuck in my throat. An arm curled about my torso and lifted. Street and sky spun. Arms and legs flailed. I broke free, stood on my own two feet. Something yanked around my neck, choking, biting. *Pop.* White beads rained down.

My necklace!

"Back away from her or I'll shoot!" Baze's faint voice sounded muffled, as though underwater.

I jolted forward to my knees. Footsteps sprinted away.

"Go after him, Bennett!"

Warm, gentle arms smelling of cedarwood surrounded me.

"He's gone." Bennett's voice echoed in the distance.

"Blast."

I floated up in Baze's arms. His face tilted in my vision. Their voices started cutting out.

"It appears . . . she's . . . drugged."

"Get Samuel . . . doctor. I'll take her home."

Baze's concerned eyes flashed in my blackening vision. "You'll be all right. I'll keep you safe."

Chapter Twenty-Two

I STOOD AT THE EDGE OF the stage, hands in my pockets, feeling nothing but cool air despite the lit stage lights directly at my feet. In a way, I preferred the emptiness now to the energy and exuberance of an audience. So much unknown. So much peace.

Usually, as I reflected in the desolation, I'd feel turmoil, a sick feeling in my gut—but tonight, I felt nothing. Was it finally happening? Was I losing my heart—my mind? Had my will finally been beaten, eradicated?

Hollow footsteps preceded Siobhan's tight, clipped words. "She almost died."

I looked at my shoes—scuffed leather and frayed laces. "Are you disappointed or relieved?"

"You almost killed her." Her tight words punctuated the darkness.

"I wasn't the one who attacked her."

"But you didn't stop it from happenin'."

I breathed a terse laugh. "And you think I have that kind of power?"

"We both know the answer to that."

A dull ache throbbed behind my eyes. Resolve faltered, but I managed to keep my composure.

There it was. The conflict. So my spirit had a bit of fight left in it after all.

I smiled. "I thought you didn't like the little heiress."

She huffed. "I don't. But I know what's right and what's not. This is wrong. Evil even. And you're too far brainwashed to see it."

I half turned and cast a look her way. She held her shoulders back and chin squared. The seams of her shirt hung off her shoulders while the rest of it poured over her hips like a dress, drowning her small frame. Her cropped hair stuck out around her ears.

"So what are you goin' to do?" I tilted my head.

She scowled. "I can't really do much without endin' up dead myself, can I?"

"True."

"But you can do more." She extended a hand as though to offer peace. "You can put an end to this."

"I'm afraid I can't."

"Why?"

Pain struck my head, a ripping of two consciences, both crying out for control. As I arched forward, sweat coated my skin and plastered my shirt to my back.

Siobhan dropped in front of me and grasped my arms. "Do you even remember who you are, who you were before he got a hold of your mind?"

I looked up. The blue-green flecks in her eyes transported me back to the emerald countryside of home, lying nestled in the soft grass within a stony fence, watching the airy clouds skim across a blue blanket of sky. Sheep bleated and roamed, teeth crunching as they grazed and shook out their woolly coats. I could see it all Rolling ocean foam. Sheer cliffs. Green country.

But where was I? Who was I?

The scene faded to dark. Inky clouds blotted out the stars in the black, moonless sky. Waves clawed at the feet of the cliffs. I climbed the soggy wooden stairs with soft footfalls to where Ciaran stood at the top of the tower facing the sea, his arms propped on the stone wall. He picked at his bitten fingernails. A thick dark substance clung to the ridges of his hands.

"You'll be hanged for this," I shouted above the roaring wind.

Ciaran looked at me out of the corner of his eye. "Then come to England with me. We'll hide among them, strike them from the inside."

"Are you mad?"

"Possibly."

"But Maeve—"

"Forget Maeve!" Ciaran grabbed my arm and wrenched, twisting me down onto my knees. "Maeve is gone. You'll never see her again. I made sure of it . . . for your own good." Ciaran let go, but I stayed on my knees, bulging tears spilling down my face as I pictured my fiancée's beautiful features. A grin twitched on Ciaran's lips as he cupped my chin and forced me to look up into his eyes. "Accept this callin'. Fight for your people. Follow me."

Something inside me sputtered and went out. The powerful gale stole my breath and dried my tears into salty trails. "I will follow you."

Another shot of pain brought me back to the present. The black night evaporated into the dusky curtains and flickering shadows of candlelight across the stage. Siobhan supported my arms and stared into my eyes.

I shook my head and stepped away from her. "The man I used to be is gone."

"I don't believe that." Siobhan's voice shook. "He's merely lost."

I replied in a whisper, "Then how do I find him?"

"You stop all this madness." She gestured to the belly of the theater from where thousands of eyes always watched and judged. "You listen to what your own *heart is tellin' you. You must stop this before someone you love gets hurt."*

I exhaled a laugh. "I love no one."

Siobhan shifted her jaw, her fingers flexing. "I can't keep up this charade forever. The police will come, and the game will end eventually. You will be caught."

"We shall see."

Chapter Twenty-Three

I WOKE TO THAT SONG FROM the pub resounding in my head. "The Parting Glass." The melody my father used to sing to me each time he left home for the distant, green shores of Ireland. I grasped at the bed covers as I recounted the lyrics and tried to recall his clear, tenor voice.

So fill to me the parting glass, and drink a health whate'er befall,
And gently rise and softly call, good night and joy be with you all.

Each breath siphoned painfully through my throat, a reminder that the assailant had tried to strangle me with my necklace. Then he'd snapped it. The pearls were lost, gone forever—and with them, my father's memory slipped further away.

I blinked my eyes open and stared at the ceiling. Tears streaked down my face and into my ears. My head pounded like the frenzied beat of the bodhrán. The pain constricting my heart grew tighter.

"Papa, don't go." My hoarse voice cracked and barely lifted above a whisper. I prayed with all my heart that he would come home, trying desperately to keep the image of his smiling face in my mind's eye—his soft blue irises, salt-and-pepper hair, and strong, clean-shaven jaw.

I closed my eyes and imagined him surrounding me with his sturdy embrace as he sang me off to sleep and murmured into my hair, "Good night, Addie."

Lips trembling, I mouthed, "Good night, Papa."

A gentle knock vibrated the door next to my bed. I started and sucked in a breath.

"Darling, it's me."

"Yes, come in." I swiped at my eyes with the bed sheet and attempted to sit up, but my lingering headache anchored me to the mattress.

Mother entered, followed by a maid carrying a tray of tea and biscuits. After the maid placed the tray on my nightstand, Mother dismissed her and faced me. She stood erect and distinguished, not a hair out of place nor a wrinkle in her sapphire satin dress. Then she bent and brushed aside the fringe from my forehead. Her deep green eyes searched mine. "How are you feeling?"

I bit my lip as I endured her gentle scrutiny, then finally swallowed and spoke. "Humiliated." I blinked against new tears. "I'd love nothing more than to stay in bed for the rest of my days."

"*Tsk.* What a waste that would be." With deft hands, she propped my pillow and helped me sip from the cup. Warm steam opened my sinuses as the herbal nuttiness and dash of honey fended off my aches.

For a moment, she paused as though unsure how to proceed. Indeed, I wasn't quite sure myself. I'd been charmed, embarrassed, drugged, and nearly strangled. The evening had spiraled into chaos after that drink. Had Cornelius requested the drug, or had it been the barkeep's doing—or Siobhan's? She'd disappeared when I arrived and never returned . . .

"I spoke with the doctor." Mother offered a biscuit—freshly baked based on the warm aroma. "Samuel should make a full recovery. The attacker hadn't struck to kill."

"Thank God." I sighed and turned down the food. "What of the attacker?"

The shake of her head confirmed he had escaped. Her hand curled around mine. "Actually, I was coming to see if you were well enough for company."

My stomach tied in knots. What if it was Baze? Was I ready to see him so soon after our argument? From what I could remember, he had carried me away from the attacker, but that didn't mean he wasn't still cross.

Mother smiled sadly as though understanding. "Basil stayed long enough to ensure you were sleeping soundly before taking his leave."

As expected, I supposed.

"Then who is here for company?"

"Do you not remember, love?" She caressed my forearm. "You

awoke not long after midnight absolutely beside yourself. I'm not sure if it was triggered by a dream, but you were adamant that we send for Percy Ford first thing in the morning."

"Percy?" Memories of my row with Baze trickled back, of confronting him about his father. It hadn't been a dream that prompted my request, but Mother needn't know that. "Send him in."

"You're sure?"

"Yes. The fog of yesterday has cleared." I paused. "Would you help me into a dressing gown?"

Once I was halfway decent and tucked back into bed where Mother insisted I remain, she left to retrieve Percy. Silence overtook me. I touched the raw, aching skin at my throat. The necklace should have been the least of my worries. I'd almost been kidnapped—or killed. But that necklace had held a piece of my identity. The perpetrator had tried to take my body, but he stole so much more.

Percy knocked and then entered. Though of a stocky build, with a large mustache that wrapped around his jawline, he was the brother who most resembled Baze. Both took after their father. Percy's brown eyes stood out starkly against his graying hair. Would Baze's do the same when his hair eventually whitened?

"I am sorry to hear of your assault, Adelynn." Percy removed his hat and gave a slight bow. "But I'm pleased to see you came through the ordeal relatively unscathed."

Twisting my hands in my lap, I flared my nostrils. "It will take more than that for them to break me."

"I would expect nothing less from you." He rocked forward on his toes. "What can I do for you? The messenger didn't give details."

"I want to know why Baze is so enslaved to your father."

It took a moment for comprehension to register on Percy's face. He furrowed his brow. "To what are you referring?"

"You know more than you're letting on, Percy." I leveled an intense stare at him. "He bends to your father's every whim, and if he tries to resist, all it takes is one rebuke from Mr. Ford to force compliance."

"Ah, well." Percy rocked forward again, then back. "You may not like it, Adelynn, but that's how it is. He's simply doing what's expected—"

"Stop playing coy!" I smashed a fist into the mattress. "Your father mentioned an incident in an alleyway during our last encounter. Please, Percy. If I am to attempt to steal my life back from your father, then I need to know what I will encounter. Baze may be in the dark, but you've witnessed everything that's happened to my family and me. You know what we're being forced to do. But without comprehending what kind of hold Mr. Ford has over Baze, I can't even begin to try to break it."

Percy studied me, drumming his fingers on the rim of his hat. Would he oblige? No, that couldn't be a question. I needed him to.

With an exhale through his nose, Percy dropped his shoulders and nodded. "Very well, but it's not a story that I like to tell."

"Thank you." But even as I reveled in the small victory, I braced myself for the agony that Percy's words might bring.

"You have to understand that in the eyes of my father, Baze was lacking from the start." Percy fiddled with the brim of his hat. "My wife and I had recently returned from our honeymoon when we found out Mother was with child. Father already had three successful sons, so Baze was tossed by the wayside, left to the governesses and maids. But it was later in life when Father's expectations turned from the three of us to Baze." Percy shifted his weight from side to side. "After my daughter was born, my wife and I were unable to have more children due to delivery complications. Then Aubrey and Frederick both had two daughters. Do you see where I'm headed with this?"

"No sons." The pieces linked in my mind. Suddenly, all of the conversations, all of Mr. Ford's talk of children—his insistence that Baze and I marry soon to produce an heir—made sense. Combine that with his oozing narcissism and it all came together. A numbing wave washed over my body. "Baze is his last hope for carrying on his name."

"Precisely."

"But . . . that doesn't explain why Baze so readily complies with his demands."

Percy pulled out the chair of my vanity and sat facing me, arms on his knees. "Adelynn, what do you remember about the time Baze broke his nose?"

I frowned, picturing the slight tweak in the bridge of Baze's nose—which he often stroked with a finger when anxious or deep in thought. But how was that relevant to the current conversation?

Then, as I imagined Mr. Ford's conniving smile, my stomach soured. Beat his own son? As malicious as Mr. Ford acted, could he really go that far?

My headache throbbed and sweat gathered on my brow. "He fell from a tree. I think he broke a few ribs and blackened his eye as well."

"You are correct, but his injuries weren't from a tree. That was a clever ruse to hide the truth."

My skin prickled as I realized my fears were about to come to fruition. How could Mr. Ford do such a horrible thing?

"And it wasn't Father either. Though, it may as well have been."

I gulped in a breath and squeezed the comforter in my fist.

"When Baze was sixteen, he had high aspirations to pursue architecture. He was always sketching buildings and designing blueprints. One of his favorites was the bank at which I worked." A small smile stretched Percy's lips. "He came to visit me after school. It began like it usually did. He sketched. We chatted about his classes." The smile disappeared. "But this particular day, I had a hefty withdrawal to deliver to Father. I was about to send it with a courier, but Baze insisted he deliver it. He wanted to please Father."

Percy took a long, shaky breath. "Baze was followed and assaulted by two thugs. They thrust him into an alleyway, beat him unconscious, and took the money. God only knows the extent of what he endured." Percy pressed a finger to his lips and shut his eyes. "The damage done to his body rendered him bedridden, and Frederick attempted to reset his nose—but you know as I do that it never quite properly healed."

I tried to speak, but a lump had formed and stuck in my throat, bile rising beneath it. Assaulted. Beaten. Why had Baze never spoken about this before now?

"Father blamed Baze for the entire incident and told him so. He resolved that Baze would join the police force to learn how to defend himself." Percy grunted. "The police don't accept teenagers, of course, but Father eventually managed to coerce—or bribe, rather—the commissioner into accepting him when he turned eighteen. He shipped Baze away the first moment he could."

I remembered the day all too well. Baze had barely looked at me as I cried, clinging to him, begging him not to go—not when we had so recently acknowledged our affection for one another. Now, my heart broke for him. He'd been cast out, sent off to be groomed to his father's liking, no more than a stallion crammed into a pen, awaiting auction.

So then why me? Why not choose any proper lady for a wife? If an heir was all he needed, I wasn't the only option, not by a long shot—as much as it pained me to imagine Baze wooing another woman. The letter I'd found had cited my family's wealth and influence. Was that all there was to it? Was Mr. Ford's narcissism so strong that the prospect of securing me erased all other notions?

Percy's voice sliced through my musings. "I'm sorry that you had to learn of it this way, Adelynn. Baze refused to talk about it after that day, and to be honest, it's not a memory that the rest of us like to relive."

I relaxed my fist and wiped my sweaty palm on the sheet. "What do I do? How do I rescue Baze from this?"

Percy rolled in his bottom lip. "I think you need to take it straight to my father."

"Confront him?" My stomach knotted at the thought of facing Mr. Ford straight on.

"I've known you for a long time, Adelynn. You have spirit. If anyone could strike a blow to his pride, it's you. Aubrey, Frederick, and I have tried to talk sense into him. And Baze certainly isn't going to do it. Father's influence is too tightly wound."

I took a shuddering breath and winced as my neck twinged. "Thank you, Percy."

Situating the hat back on his head, he stood and headed for the door. When next to me, he paused and lay a heavy but reassuring hand on my shoulder. "God be with you."

God be with me indeed.

Chapter Twenty-Four

LOW, MINOR NOTES OOZED FROM THE open piano, its copper strings vibrating with each thump from the felted hammers. Aches stiffened Baze's fingers, but he continued to pound on the cold ivory keys. The music poured forth as an extension of the conflict in his soul.

He loved Adelynn, that much was clear. But this engagement, this theatrical production, was all a farce. And his father served as the director, according to her.

Baze had done it all wrong from the start. He should have told her he loved her from the moment he realized he did. Mental images danced before his eyes—there, inside the hedge between their homes. Thirteen-year-old Baze perched on his hands and knees, crowing in young Adelynn's face that he'd found her and it was her turn to seek.

The music shifted, grew melancholy, as she hugged her knees to her chest and stared at the ground. "I don't feel like playing anymore."

He crinkled his nose. "You're no fun."

"Father sailed away today." She sniffled. "I won't see him for three months."

He'd felt foolish. She was hurting, and he had to make it better somehow.

So he kissed her mouth. It was a quick kiss—wet, foreign, and warm. Her lips may have been made out of velvet. He sat back and gulped, ears aflame. She gaped, wide-eyed, cheeks scarlet.

Transitioning into the next somber song, Baze licked his cracked lips. He reached for the glass atop the piano—continuing the melody with his right hand—and took a burning swig of the whisky. From that moment on, Adelynn had been a permanent resident in his heart and mind. Through his assault. Through academy training. The years apart solidified his desire and need for her to be in his life.

And when he returned home, fresh out of training and a rookie constable with the Met, she was the first one he'd sought—but Father had found him first.

"Now that you're a proper officer, you need a wife if you want to earn respect in this world." Alistair had placed a firm hand on Baze's shoulder, squeezing slightly. "I've just spoken with Miss Adelynn Spencer. You were sweet on her, if I'm not mistaken. Fortunately, she has wealth and influence. You should ask for her hand posthaste."

Engaging the soft pedal and relaxing his pressure on the keys, Baze put himself back in that moment when he'd found her—in typical Adelynn fashion—hiding out in the hedge. He never knew whether she had been trying to avoid him or if something else had upset her—he'd never asked.

She had swiped at her cheeks and sucked in a breath as he ducked into the hedge. He couldn't stop the smile from stretching across his face as he settled in front of her. "It's really good to see you."

She bit her lip and twisted her hands in her lap, avoiding his gaze. "And you as well."

Excitement had swelled within him, so strong that he couldn't contain it and ended up blurting, "Marry me, Al." She widened her pretty powder-blue eyes and stiffened. He grasped her hand. "You're all I could think about when I was in training, and I want you to—"

"Yes," she whispered.

He paused. "Yes?"

She offered a small smile. "Yes."

Pride and triumph swelled in him. He leaned toward her, but as he bent for a kiss, she lifted her face. Their noses collided. Embarrassment bubbled up in his chest and rose to the top of his head. He sat paralyzed.

But Adelynn had laughed—a loud, robust laugh that chased away any semblance of distress from her features.

When she quieted, he cleared his throat, cheeks blazing. "I'd like to . . . try again, if I may."

She giggled. "Don't miss this time."

Oh, he hadn't intended to. He cupped her jaw in his hands and tilted her face opposite his. And then he kissed her, lightly at first, then deeper as she responded in kind.

He'd felt such happiness at the prospect of their future together. All for naught now. He was such a fool.

China clinked behind him. His fingers tripped on the keys and caused a muddled blast of dissonance. Wrapping a hand around his pistol, he swiveled and scanned the room.

Sipping from her best teacup, his mother lounged on the couch. "Don't stop, darling. That was lovely."

Sighing, he released his weapon and slammed the keyboard cover shut. "You startled me."

She shrugged. "Sorry, dear."

"How long have you been listening?"

"Quite some time."

With a glare at the mantel clock, he sighed. He'd been playing for more than an hour. Now that he'd stopped, the throbbing in his fingers and forearms reflected the long performance. Had he known she was watching, he wouldn't have played so freely, so emotionally.

"It's been months since I last heard you play." Mother's wrinkles deepened as she smiled. "It was nice."

He grunted. "I'm glad you enjoyed it."

She set her teacup on the side table and patted the cushion beside her. He hesitated but eventually joined her. "What's troubling you, my son?" She chuckled. "Or are you going to tell me all that was purely for entertainment?"

Why did Mother have to be so perceptive? His throat tightened. "I lost her."

"Lost who?"

"Adelynn." He took a deep breath and looked her in the eyes. "Mother, what has Father done?"

A knowing smile—sad, intelligent—crossed her face. "It doesn't matter what your father has done or not. Your actions are up to you. If you've lost her, go find her."

"But it's not that—"

She pressed her fingers to his lips, then brushed the hair from his forehead. His skin tingled under her touch, reminding him of the rare moments of his boyhood when she, not the governess, would tuck him into bed and caress his face—his eyebrows, his nose, his chin—to send him off to sleep.

"You love that girl, Basil." Her petite palm cradled his cheek. "Anyone can see that. Forget what has happened, abandon your fear of what *could* happen, and fight for her."

It made sense. He loved her, so why shouldn't he go after her? Adelynn had to know that there was no one else in the world he loved more, and he would do anything to protect her, even if it meant confronting his own father for the truth.

"Your father threatened me."

Adelynn's words reverberated in his mind. The thought of anyone harming her sent his adrenaline racing. He didn't want to believe his father was capable of such a thing, but as he thought back over the pain and damage of his teenage years, it started to become clear.

He caught Mother's hand in his and kissed the back, her thin skin soft and cool under his lips. "Thank you, Mother."

She laughed softly. "Don't overthink. Just do." She kissed his forehead, stood, and breezed out of the room.

His gaze drifted across the space to where the door to his father's study hung slightly ajar between two floor-to-ceiling bookcases. The man probably brooded within.

Baze could never fully pursue Adelynn until he understood his father's role in all this. For so long, his emotions had lain dormant, pent up from the moment his father sold him to the academy to be conditioned as a proper Ford. And if that man had indeed threatened her, Baze wasn't sure he'd be able to control his urge to protect her with his life—even if that meant stepping out against his own father.

With confident steps, Baze crossed to the door and grasped the handle with a crushing fist. As he made to open it, a woman's taut voice came from within.

"This engagement has drained whatever independence I used to possess. It's stealing away my very life. I can't tolerate it any longer."

Baze froze. *Adelynn?*

Chapter Twenty-Five

BAZE WAS PLAYING THE PIANO—A slow, melancholy song—when the butler escorted me into Mr. Ford's study. I plopped down in the chair behind his desk. Its lush leathery cushions reflected the rich façade he always tried to keep up.

Briefly, I closed my eyes and inhaled deeply. *Lord, give me strength. Whatever happens, give me strength.*

Sitting in Mr. Ford's chair, behind his desk, in his study, I held all control this time. I would make sure of it. This would be my conversation, my conquest.

I'd chosen to wear a long-sleeved maroon gown, velvet, strung with lace around my neck and a silver sash at my waist. Solemn. Dramatic. A gown made for battle.

The gold handle twisted, the door opened, and Mr. Ford stepped in, looking fresh and energetic in his neatly pressed suit. He stopped in the middle of the room and cocked a groomed eyebrow. "My, don't you look diplomatic."

I squared my jaw. "Thank you for seeing me, Mr. Ford."

"'Tis always a pleasure, Adelynn."

I gestured to the seat opposite me, but he held up a hand. "No, I am much more comfortable standing, thank you."

"Very well." I pressed my fingertips to the desk and stood. I refused to let him look down on me while we spoke. "The engagement between myself and your son is hereby terminated."

He studied me, his lips parting into a white smile. "I'm afraid you're not in a position to make demands."

"I'm not asking for your permission."

"You would trample Basil's heart so callously?" He narrowed his eyes in mock concern. "Such a little viper you are."

"It's because of my love for Baze that I must do this."

"Touching."

"This engagement has drained whatever independence I used to possess." I pressed a fist against the desk. "It's stealing away my very life. I can't tolerate it any longer."

"Stop being dramatic." He chuckled. "If anything, it's made you a better woman. Much more compliant."

"You know as well as I the folly in that statement." I flared my nostrils. "And Baze . . . I know everything. You took advantage of him in his most vulnerable moment. You poisoned his mind with lies to mold him into your own personal puppet. After today, after I tell Baze everything, you won't have any more power over us."

A laugh burst from his lips. "You don't have the courage to tell him the truth."

I raised my eyebrows. "Don't I?"

He folded his arms. "The reality is, Adelynn, everything I've done has been for my son's benefit."

"Your benefit, you mean."

"My reputation remains intact, yes. Had I let him wallow after his assault, he'd have become a disgrace to my name. That wouldn't do." His eyes darkened. "I had no choice but to step in. I gave him wealth, status, and you. That it meant manipulating him or using *creative* persuasion to keep you in check makes no difference to me."

Nausea struck me. "That sort of talk could get you arrested."

"I wouldn't worry about that." The smile crept back onto his face. "Not when my son holds influence with the police. It's like you said. Basil is my own personal puppet."

Disgust clamped my throat shut. If Baze could hear this, he'd be devastated. I couldn't let this continue. I needed to protect him.

I stared straight into Mr. Ford's eyes. "I came here out of courtesy, but again, I'm not asking for your permission."

Mr. Ford spoke in a low, leaching tone. "If you go through with this, you'll lose everything. Your reputation. Your family. You know as well as I your father's death pushed you to the brink. One more nudge and you'll topple over the edge. All that awaits you there is loneliness and despair. You wouldn't want that, now would you?"

I struggled to keep my face from showing pain. "My fears are irrelevant. Severing your influence is all that matters." I pulled out the letter—the one with instructions on how to force my compliance, written by an unknown conspirator—and held it up for him to see. "Your contact is wrong. My marriage to your son will not bring you greater standing in the world, not when you've already sunk so low. This individual gave you false information. It may have worked for a time, but I will not be swayed by this coercion any longer."

Mr. Ford sobered and advanced a step. "That's enough now, Adelynn. You're no longer amusing."

"If you think I will continue to endure your abuse on account of my fears, you're sorely mistaken." I moved around the desk to confront him without a barrier. "You have been made a fool, Mr. Ford. I will not marry your son. You will stop harassing my family. And you had better pray to the Almighty that I never inform the police of the extent of your extortion and deceit."

Mr. Ford lunged forward, seized my arm, and snatched the letter out of my hand. His vise grip sent a numbing shock spiraling to the tips of my fingers. "Listen to me and listen well, Adelynn." Spit sprayed through his teeth onto my face. "I started from nothing. I have worked too hard, sacrificed too much, for my legacy to die now. So you're going to be an obedient little girl and marry my son, give him an heir, and keep your mouth shut."

"Let go." I yanked against his grasp, but he held fast.

"I'm not afraid to beat you into submission, if that's what it takes." His grip tightened.

The side door creaked open in my peripheral vision. I whirled toward the intruder with a sharp gasp.

Baze stood in the entryway, his face expressionless, unreadable.

No! We were supposed to have been alone. When had the music stopped? *Lord, please say that he heard nothing.* But judging from his rigid stance, he had heard more than enough.

"How long have you been standing there?" Mr. Ford shoved me aside. "Get out. This doesn't concern you."

Baze held his father in a chilled stare as he eased toward us, each careful click of his soles on the hardwood floor driving an emotional stake deeper and deeper into my heart.

"If you've nothing to say, then get out." Mr. Ford jeered. "You're the same as the day we found you beaten in that alley. You were a coward then, and you're a coward n—"

Baze threw his fist into Mr. Ford's face with a fleshy snap. The older man cried out, tripped backward, and clapped a hand over his nose. Blood trickled between his fingers.

Baze seized his father's arm, twisted it behind his back, and kicked out the back of his legs, which brought him to his knees. Mr. Ford moaned. Baze drew his pistol and aimed it at his father's head.

"Baze, no!" Images of the gun firing and Mr. Ford slumping to the floor ran through my mind.

Releasing Mr. Ford's arm, Baze kept the weapon pointed at the man's head and snatched up the letter. He glanced at the words, but then looked again—as though realizing he'd missed something—and read them in a rush. Panic pulsed in his eyes, but he blinked it away and stashed the letter in his coat pocket.

I stepped toward him, knees weak. "Baze, please say something."

Baze crossed the distance between us in two strides and grabbed my left wrist. He tucked his pistol under his arm and wrenched off my sapphire engagement ring in one deft swipe. Flesh tore from my knuckle. Blood seeped. I yelped and curled it up to my stomach.

Baze lobbed the ring into the waste bin where it ricocheted like a gunshot. He brushed past me and murmured, "Go home, Miss Spencer."

Chapter Twenty-Six

BAZE GNASHED HIS TEETH AS HE shoved his father through the precinct doors. The men behind their desks looked up from their work to watch his staggered procession. Even Superintendent Whelan peeked out from his office to investigate the commotion. Baze kept a firm grip on his father's collar and pressed on.

Bennett jogged forward from the back of the room, eyes questioning. "What's the meaning of this?"

Baze ignored him and headed to one of the interrogation rooms. He wrenched the door open and threw his father inside.

Alistair stumbled but recovered quickly. He examined his surroundings with flared nostrils, dried blood staining his curled lip. "You really think you can hold me here, boy? I have influence in this city." He tightened his tie. "You have no proof of anything."

Baze ignored the man and made to leave, but Alistair drew close, enough so that Baze could smell his stale breath. "Adelynn could have been yours, along with the wealth and influence that came with her compliance. But you couldn't keep her under control. And because of your failure, she'll soon be on her way into another man's arms." Alistair turned up his nose. "You're a disgrace to my name."

Baze rotated toward his father, their faces mere inches from one another. Yet, somehow, Baze managed to remain rooted to the spot and stand straighter. At such close proximity, the details of Alistair's face and his resemblance to Baze were unmistakable.

A sticky lump caused Baze's words to stutter out in a whisper. "Why have you done this? Why have you gone to such sinister lengths to ensure your lineage carries into the next generation?" He gripped a fistful of his father's shirt. "You threatened Adelynn. You've been manipulating me. What could possibly be so important about a single name that you would destroy lives like this?"

"Our name means everything." Alistair grasped Baze's wrist with cold fingers. "I can't expect you to understand."

"Humor me." Baze released Alistair's shirt and wrenched out of his hold. "You're in my custody. You've nothing more to lose."

Alistair folded his arms. His low, wiry brows shadowed his eyes. "I came from nothing. You can't even begin to imagine the hardships I endured to reach the status we hold now. If you only knew what I had to sacrifice, you wouldn't judge so harshly. You would heap gratitude upon me for the steps I took to correct your teenage disobedience and groom you into the man you are today."

Baze fell back a step, incredulity slackening his jaw. "Disobedience . . . *disobedience?* I was only trying to please you. And then I was attacked. Nothing I could have done would have prevented it from happening."

"You made a foolish decision. You were reckless."

His voice cracked. "I was a *boy.*"

"Boy or not, had I not intervened, you may very well have toppled everything I spent decades trying to achieve."

The lump returned as Baze's eyes filled. "Did Percy, Frederick, and Aubrey have to endure such an iron fist from you? Or was your ire reserved for me simply because my conception was accidental?"

Alistair looked at the floor, his jaw shifting. "You might not believe me, but the circumstances surrounding your birth held no sway upon the way I treated you."

"You're right." Baze exhaled a bitter laugh. "I don't believe you."

His father lifted his head and locked their gazes. The steel gray of his eyes dimmed slightly into a softer shade closer to Baze's. "Each of your brothers received equal treatment. I may have been harsher on you, but that's because I saw your potential. I saw how you could benefit our family and catapult us into even greater success."

Baze pressed his lips together as he fought for control of his voice. Finally, as his vision blurred, he managed, "Do you see me as anything more than merely a means to an end?"

Alistair's posture relaxed as he dropped a heavy hand onto Baze's shoulder. "Stop holding onto the hope that I'll utter a confession of unconditional love that will revive our bond as father and son. It is not who I am. And I can't change that."

"Can't . . . or won't?" Baze looked deep into his father's eyes, yearning for a glimpse of regret—but he found nothing. His stomach plummeted. "I have nothing more to say to you."

Alistair's fingers tightened on Baze's shoulder. He opened his mouth, but Baze shrugged away from him.

Chest knotted, Baze burst from the room and slammed the door behind him. He veered across the hall into the adjacent room and shut himself within. Emotion built as he gripped his head and paced. The confession uttered from his father's own lips took hold in every corner of his mind. He halted, looked to the ceiling, and shouted, "Is that how you see me too? As a stupid lackey to control for your own amusement?"

"Baze?" A knock sounded on the door before Bennett entered. "What's going on? What's happened?"

"I'm just a pawn to him." Baze paced again. His words came swift and slurred. "He's a conniving snake who would use me for his own advancement. He's been manipulating me my whole life. And Adelynn—he threatened Adelynn."

"I can't quite understand you." Bennett held out his hands. "Try to calm down."

"This whole engagement with Al was a ploy to force us to give him an heir to carry on his blasted name." Baze wavered on his feet, breaths coming hot and heavy.

Bennett gestured to a chair and touched his shoulder. "Baze, sit down."

"Heard his confession with my own ears." He brushed aside

Bennett's hand and waved an index finger around as though to accuse someone, anyone. A drunken numbness buzzed in his brain. "Then I arrested him and told Al off in one fell swoop."

The realization of the truth settled like a dumbbell on his chest. All of it came rushing out in air and tears. He tripped backward into the chair, elbows on weak knees, wet face in trembling hands.

It was all over. Whatever hope he had of marrying Adelynn and salvaging a relationship with his father—gone. There was no getting it back this time.

"We will find a way to remedy this," Bennett said softly, lowering himself into the chair opposite Baze. "But you need to clear your head first."

Baze looked up. "Oh, but it's much worse." He produced the letter from his coat pocket—the one Adelynn had kept hidden from him— and smacked it on the table.

As Bennett stole a look, the color drained from his face. "What is this?"

"It was written to my father. This individual claimed to know exactly how to manipulate Al. And my father succeeded." Baze settled back in the chair and scrubbed his face with a palm.

Bennett stared wide-eyed. "But . . ."

"I know."

"The handwriting is identical to the killer's."

Chapter Twenty-Seven

I HADN'T INTENDED TO TRAVEL TO the theater after leaving the Fords' home. I'd merely begun wandering and found myself on the premises. The swollen cut on my ring finger throbbed. My mind spun with outrage and grief. With a killer on the streets, it certainly wasn't the smartest of my endeavors, but I couldn't stay home. It reminded me too much of why my heart wept

So I hailed a cab—and ended up at the Empress. The magical spectacle would be a welcome distraction.

But inside the main hall, my footsteps echoed within empty walls. With no one around, why had the door been unlocked? My heart skipped a beat. Perhaps this was my chance to find some long sought-after evidence. If this indeed was the killer's domain, then there had to be a sign of him somewhere.

Inside the auditorium, blinking candles cast long shadows across the wide stage, the only source of light in the embracing blackness. I picked my way carefully down the sloping aisle, touching each passing chair for balance. The darkness tricked my mind into thinking I saw shapes moving in the shadows. *Lord, protect me from this darkness.*

"What are you doin' here?"

A yelp burst from my lips and echoed up to the high ceiling. I spun.

Siobhan stood farther up the aisle with her hands on her slender hips, eyes blazing.

I exhaled and slumped onto an armrest. "You frightened me."

"Good." She approached and leaned over me, sharp blue eyes reflecting the agitated candlelight. "Now what are you doin' here? You're not welcome."

"I was looking for Finn." It seemed a plausible story.

"Have you learned nothin'?" Siobhan drew back with a grimace. "I warned you it was dangerous to come here."

"Oh, was that a warning?" Heat rose to my cheeks. "It sounded more like a threat to me."

"You flatter yourself." Siobhan pressed the back of her hand to her forehead in a mock swoon. "You're simply an ignorant heiress meddlin' where she doesn't belong."

I scowled and shot to my feet. If this woman wanted to start a quarrel, very well. I would let her have her quarrel. It was about time I got the opportunity to speak my mind.

"What have I done to turn you so against me?" I planted both fists on my hips. "Since the day I met you, you have been hostile and cold."

Siobhan stood taller. "Because you do not belong here."

"I shall go where I very well please. Who are you to tell me where I belong?"

"Ooh, the heiress has bite." She smirked.

"Yes, this heiress has bite, and she is fed up. You've no right to bark orders and toss around threats. You don't know me, but you've already made assumptions about my life and cast judgment. Do you have any sense of decency?"

Siobhan bit her lip, eyes dark. She continued with a low voice. "You are right. I have no decency. I have no morals. You've no idea what I've had to do to survive in this life." She looked into my eyes, and looking back into hers, I read shame and regret. "As a child, I worked mending garments in a factory, under contract and trapped. Then I sold my soul and company on street corners." A muscle tensed in her neck. Her eyes glistened. "And now I am here, bound between magic and murder, still trapped in servitude. I've seen things you can't imagine, Miss Priss. You, with your life of luxury and wealth."

I swallowed, overcome by welling sorrow. Such a horrible life. I couldn't imagine.

"I'm sorry." I wrung my hands. "But my life is not as cozy as you like to believe. Money is no comfort when your family is being stripped away bit by bit." Hesitant curiosity sparked in Siobhan's eyes, so I forged ahead. "My father was murdered a year ago by the very people he had worked his whole life to protect. Before that, I was forced into an engagement for the sole purpose of producing an heir. Had I refused, I'd have been outcast and raked through the coals of society. The only thing I can possibly do now is to find the one responsible for these recent murders to salvage any sense of normalcy I can."

Siobhan chewed her lip, and after an extended moment, she nodded.

Was this respect? Acceptance? This woman had such a rough exterior, could I really have cracked the shell?

"It would be in your best interest, Miss Spencer, to leave." She frowned at the carpet. "Things are at work here. Things you can't understand. As long as you stay here, you are in danger."

My stomach flipped. "You know something."

"Please leave."

"Siobhan, you must tell me." I scooped up her hands in mine. "You could save innocent lives. Tell me what you know."

She turned her face away. "I cannot."

"If it's a matter of safety, I can acquire protection for you through the police. Please, I'm begging you."

She lifted her eyes, muscles stiff. She rolled in her bottom lip.

Finn's voice shattered the suspended silence.

"What are you ladies on about? Your squabblin' could wake the dead." He jumped down from the stage and approached.

Siobhan pulled away from me, her features hardening.

Finn's hand curled over my shoulder—heavy and reassuring. "Siobhan, you aren't harassin' our guest, are you?"

"Of course not." Her eyes flicked to me, then quickly back to him as she walked backward. "If you'll excuse me."

I tried to follow, but Finn held me back and shook his head. "I should ask what you're doin' here at this hour, but I'm not surprised to see you." He gently grasped my wrist and tugged me toward the stage. "Come."

Baze paced in front of the photography board. Multiple images of each victim littered the surface, with notes and observations pinned around them. His feet ached, but he refused to stop. The constant motion kept his sorrow from pooling and festering inside. He'd been forbidden to enter the room while his father was being interrogated about what he knew of the mysterious contact. So what else could he do, if not try to connect the victims to one another?

"You sure you want to do this now?" Bennett mumbled from where he leaned against a nearby desk.

"Quiet." Baze's voice cracked. He massaged his temple.

"You're going to wear a path in the floor."

"It's just as well." Baze stopped to face the board. He traced invisible lines between each victim with his gaze. Jonathan Mallory. Henry Clifton. Peter Moseley. And now, the letter written to his father added a new layer of complication to the web. What was the connection?

Bennett sighed and crossed his arms. "What reason would the killer have to write that letter and blackmail Adelynn?"

Baze unfolded the letter and examined it. Whoever penned it must have studied Adelynn . . . or knew her personally. How else could he have known exactly how to gain her compliance with outrageous demands—as though marrying Baze were so outrageous. Was this letter's revelation the sole reason for her acceptance? She claimed to love him, but how could he believe that now?

He crumpled the letter in his fist.

Bennett leapt to his feet. "Oi, that's our best lead."

Baze looked at the image of Jonathan Mallory, Adelynn's maths tutor. A seemingly random victim, yet the first of the countdown. Next came Henry Clifton. Even though the lord fought against everything Thomas Spencer stood for—he outright opposed the Home Bill and insisted the Irish didn't need independence—they were close outside of politics. So close, in fact, that he'd been a constant in Adelynn's life.

And Moseley . . . Baze's throat constricted as he looked at the formal photograph of his dead comrade. Bennett had ordered him to protect Adelynn on her mad escapades—as Baze had so crudely discovered. But the point remained. Moseley had been close to her. He'd been her defender. And he'd died as a result.

Breath rushed from Baze's lungs. "Adelynn!"

"Come to your senses, have you?"

"No, no. She's the connection." Baze held his breath as he drank in the photographs. He saw it now. It laughed in his face, as plain as a sailing vessel on the Thames. Adelynn was the link.

Bennett joined Baze in front of the board. As he studied the photographs, realization dawned on his face. "You might be right."

"There's also the matter of her visions." Baze massaged the back of his neck. "The details she describes are too intricate to be coincidence."

Bennett removed his spectacles and rubbed his eyes. "Then that begs the question, why make her a target? What enemies could she possibly have?"

"I don't know." Baze searched the photos as though they would outright confess. "But this killer's on a countdown and only has two victims left. Maybe he's already killed again. But Al is the final target. I'm sure of it. These connections, this letter, are meant to throw her life into chaos, and those visions . . . those blasted visions."

Acceptance allowed him to see clearly. Adelynn had been telling the truth all along. Somehow, she was connected—more so than he realized—and it started with those visions.

Baze turned toward Bennett. "Will you see to it that a constable is placed at Al's house? Place another at your home. Anyone close to her is a target."

"Of course." Bennett picked at his thumbnail as he looked at the board. His gaze grew distant. Was he was thinking about Emily, so close to giving birth and all on her own while he worked?

As Bennett rotated to leave, Baze caught hold of his sleeve and pulled him back. "Bennett, don't go anywhere without backup." They locked eyes. "He's targeting people close to her."

A crease formed in Bennett's brow. "The same goes for you."

Baze cleared his throat. "And I need another favor."

"Anything."

"Will you . . . talk to Al? I need to find out what she knows."

Bennett narrowed his eyes. "You are perfectly capable of holding a conversation."

"You know why I can't."

"No, I don't." Bennett knuckled Baze's shoulder. "Which brings me to the point of your being utterly daft."

Baze glared. "I beg your par—"

"None of this is her fault. You read the letter. You were there when she confronted your father. He had her backed into a corner."

Baze spread his arms, incredulous. "She should have told me."

"She tried. Did you believe her?"

"She never came outright and said it." Baze growled. "Why wasn't she clear?"

"What choice did she have?" Bennett aimed a finger at Baze's chest. "You may not want advice, but here it is. Forget what your father did. Forget what she did. Take that blasted ring you had made and ask her for her hand, sincerely this time. That's the only way your torment will end." Bennett collected his coat from the chair and stormed out.

Baze kicked the edge of the desk. It set his toes on fire, and burning tears jumped to his eyes. He bit his lip to will them away. How could Bennett think all this could be so easy to forget? He hadn't been the one to lose his father and fiancée all in one breath. Baze couldn't forgive her that easily. She could have told him the truth at any moment in their relationship, but she chose to let him believe their affections were mutual. He was not the one in the wrong.

"Richter," he called to the other detective inspector sitting with his feet propped on a desk. "Would you mind accompanying me to the Empress Theatre?"

The sergeant dropped his feet to the ground and smoothed out his graying mutton chops. "What are you up to, Ford?"

"We're going to question the employees." Baze snatched up his coat. "I want to put an end to this."

Chapter Twenty-Eight

As I followed Finn up the stairs and across the stage, bathed in the warm glow of the footlights, a tangle of regret wound in my chest. The last words I'd spoken to him had been out of utter rage—and misdirected rage at that. I'd lost my father, yes, but Finn had lost everything. I could only imagine how the weight of his affiliation and status stalked him wherever he went.

"I'm sorry," I said.

Finn stopped and turned back with a frown. "What do you have to apologize for?"

"I judged you immediately after I saw the IRB flag. But Cornelius told me your story . . . and then I saw you at the pub." I wrung my hands. "I was wrong to accuse you so hastily."

A look of confusion—or maybe disappointment—crossed his face briefly before he put on a small smile. "You've nothin' to be sorry for. You had every right to lash out. But I appreciate your acknowledgment nonetheless." He grasped my hands and pulled me a few more steps toward center stage. "Wait here."

He disappeared backstage and returned moments later, holding a rope about a foot long. Small beads of perspiration dotted his upper lip. His hair was unkempt and unevenly curly, but his eyes held excitement.

"Hold out your hands," he said.

"Why?"

"Humor me."

I could already tell where this was going, but I obliged. I held my breath as he wound the rope around my wrists and laced it tight until my fingers tingled. He grinned. "Can you escape?"

Twisting my hands, I yanked, but the bonds held fast. "No."

"Good." The grin still plastered to his face, he started untying the knots.

Was that it? But nothing had happened. With my hands free, I massaged my wrists. "What kind of trick was that?"

He offered me the rope and placed his wrists together. "Your turn. And don't be afraid to pull it impossibly tight."

I narrowed my eyes and set to work binding him. Sharp, scratchy fibers chafed my palms, but I tugged with as much strength as I could muster. Once finished, I crossed my arms and raised my eyebrows. It was impossible. He couldn't conceivably escape from that.

Finn rotated his wrists and spread his arms apart. Though his hands turned red and swelled a bit, he managed to slip one through—free. My jaw dropped as he dangled the rope from his unbound hand.

"It's a classic trick we use to escape our bonds on stage. It doesn't matter how tight you are tied. You can always escape."

I thrust my arms forward. "Show me."

He laughed. "The trick begins before I even start binding you. Place the underside of your wrists together." He poised the rope as I did so. "Now as I begin to tie, squeeze your fists and push out against the ropes."

As he bound my wrists again, I concentrated on doing as he instructed, but as tight as the ropes were, it was hard to strain against them. When he knotted the last bit, he sat back. "Can you escape?"

Again, I twisted and yanked, and this time, the rope gave slightly. Biting my lip, I pulled one hand with as much force as I could, despite the stinging on my skin. My hand popped free. I let out a triumphant laugh. "That's incredible!"

"No tellin'." He tapped a finger to his lips. "A magician's secrets are all he has."

"Everyone should know that trick." I slid the rope off and handed it to him. "It could be the difference between life and death."

Any semblance of happiness melted from his features, leaving him dark and unreadable. A stab of fear squeezed my muscles. He clenched the rope with tight fists, uncertainty raging war behind his eyes, before he tossed the rope aside and offered a hand. "I will escort you home."

I tried to process the sudden jump in attitude. What had I said? Or rather, what thoughts had entered his mind?

I shook my head. "I'm not ready to return home,"

"That doesn't matter. You must go." He avoided eye contact and pushed past me toward the stage edge, then jumped to the floor below.

I peered at him, his body blending with the shadows. They darkened his once bright eyes and stole away any remaining pleasantry.

"Have I stated something that upset you?"

"You haven't." He reached up. "I'll help you down."

But I didn't move. I might as well come out with it. It was why I had come here. If he turned out to be dangerous, so be it.

Baze's condescending and foreboding words played in my head, but I willed them away. Not this time.

"You're hiding something."

"Am I?" Finn's eyebrows lifted as he lowered his arms. "What brought you to that conclusion?"

"I can feel it."

He paused as though thinking, then heaved himself back onto the stage and towered over me. Without my height advantage, I wanted to back away, but I managed to stay solid and remain in his shadow.

"It seems you've been feelin' quite a lot around here," he said with a low tone. "Somehow, you're resistant to any darkness that slithers your way. Despite the terrible evil displayed in these recent acts of violence, despite the suspicion surroundin' this place, you keep comin' back." He grimaced. "You're either one of the bravest women I know . . . or one of the stupidest."

Indignation stirred within me. "I keep coming back because I want justice, and my instincts keep leading me here, perhaps rightly so. Because as you said, this place is absolutely rife with suspicion." I poked his chest, and my finger struck the solid cross pendant hidden beneath his shirt. "You're keeping secrets, and if you continue to withhold information, guilt will ravage your conscience until you're absolutely consumed by it."

"That's assumin' I'm not consumed already." He swatted my hand away. "Sometimes, things simply *are*. They can't be changed. So it doesn't matter what I say."

I gestured to the chain hanging about his neck. "I'm sure your mother taught you about forgiveness, that if you confess, you can have peace. You can have *life*. Why else would you keep wearing that cross, if not because a part of you believes what it represents?"

"I already told you, it be just a trinket. Nothin' more."

"Then put it to the test." I moved closer, raising my chin. "Tell me what you know, and then pray for deliverance. See if that doesn't remove this burden you're carrying. See if He doesn't grant you mercy."

Finn seemed to ponder, chewing his bottom lip. Then he met my gaze. With a gleam of despair in his eyes, he shook his head slowly. "A magician never reveals his secrets."

The reality of the situation dawned, unveiling a truth I'd been searching for but yet had prayed wouldn't prove real. He was involved. How or in what capacity, I didn't know, but he was involved with the murders.

But what of the Finn I'd seen at the pub? That joyous man with a lighthearted smile and deep, full laugh. Could that person really be capable of such evil? And if so, what could have pushed him to that point?

I scrambled for words. "I-I have to go."

"Let me see you out."

"No!" I said a little too quickly. "No, that isn't necessary. I came alone, so I can find my own way back."

Doors slammed in the foyer. Footsteps and voices echoed. "Spread out. Find Cornelius Marx. Let's round them up."

I nearly cried out when I heard that voice. "Baze."

Finn grimaced. "What's he doin' here?"

Did I say that out loud? No matter. I had to leave immediately. Baze was already furious. God only knew how upset he'd be if he discovered me here.

I dropped to my haunches as gracefully as I could and slid off the stage. Voices echoed from the right-hand doors, so I went to the left. Just as Baze's men entered, I snuck out the opposite entrance and bolted for the door.

But when I reached the outer exit, I stopped. Now might be my chance. Baze had come for all of them, and he would make sure they were all where he could see them, which would leave their personal quarters empty. If I could find any evidence linking them to the crimes, this would all be over. No more fear. No more death.

I turned back.

Chapter Twenty-Nine

As Baze stomped down the auditorium aisle, Finn Kelly approached with folded arms. "We're closed, Inspector Ford." Kelly blocked Baze's advance. "Can I see you out?"

"I'm here on police business." Baze squared his stance. "Please gather your staff."

Kelly scowled, but as he opened his mouth, Marx appeared, pushed between them, and stood chest to chest with Baze. "You have no business here, Inspector."

Baze stepped away from the man. "I have orders to bring your staff in for questioning."

"You won't find anything." Marx's tone held an edge that matched the frown on his face. His disheveled appearance suggested he'd been caught off guard.

"I shall be the judge of that." Baze checked to make sure Richter and his other men stood in position by the door. Aside from shuffling sounds made by the men, the auditorium sat in eerie silence.

"You have already questioned us." Marx spoke through tight lips. "What more could you glean?"

"As I said, I shall determine what is relevant." Baze cast a stern glance between the magicians. "Now, if you would be so kind, please gather your staff. All of them."

"They don't all reside here. It will take some time." Marx glared.

Baze met the man's gaze and crossed his arms. "I have all the time in the world."

Tense, silent seconds passed. Baze's heart pounded.

Redness crept into Marx's cheeks. The magician blinked, breaking their stare, and motioned toward Kelly. "Do as the inspector ordered."

When the theater staff had gathered and sat in the front row—bleary-eyed and grumbling—Baze and Richter faced the group. Marx paced nearby, running fingers through his unkempt hair, but his gaze stayed fixed on Baze.

"I'll take you one at a time." Richter wagged an index finger at Collin. "We'll start with you, son. Come with us."

Fear sparked in the youth's round eyes, but he stood and trailed Richter without a word.

Marx turned to follow, but Baze extended a halting hand. "One at a time, please."

With a sigh, Marx narrowed his eyes. "Collin speaks only rudimentary English. If you wish to extract more than merely a yes or no, you'd do well to let me join you."

Every ounce of Baze wanted to tell him off, but the man had a point. They wouldn't get much information from a confused adolescent. He jerked his head to allow Marx to accompany them.

As they entered the foyer, Baze observed Collin. The boy walked with hunched shoulders and head hung, eyes fixed on the floor. Baze doubted this boy could be the killer. He was too reluctant. Too oblivious. Then again, it could all be a ruse. Marx claimed the boy didn't speak English, but one could easily feign innocence.

Richter dragged a chair over, screeching across the marble floor, and planted Collin into it. Then he produced a pad of paper and scrawled a lengthy sentence. "Copy this." He pushed the items into Collin's hands. The boy stared, face scrunched in confusion.

Marx scoffed. "This is a waste of time. Collin was never taught how to read or write."

Baze caught his breath. What kind of life had this boy seen?

"He doesn't need to know all that." Richter snapped his fingers in the boy's face and pointed at the paper. "He only needs to copy it."

Biting his lip, Collin set to work mimicking the writing. Ink wobbled in the wake of his unsteady pen nib, but he managed to complete the task after several uncomfortable minutes. When he handed back the pad, he sat rigid and doe eyed. Something stirred in Baze's emotions, whether compassion or pity, he didn't know, but despite the circumstances, he wanted to let the boy go.

Too late. Richter towered over Collin and started in on him. "Where were you on the night of the opening show? And no tricks, boy. I'll have your tongue if you lie to me."

From the lack of change in Collin's face, he didn't understand the threat. Only after Richter grunted at Marx did he translate the words into Irish.

Collin pointed at the ground. "Here."

"And what were you doing here?"

"Asleep."

Richter rolled his eyes. "Can anyone corroborate that?"

They waited for Marx to translate. "The others," Collin said.

"As in your theater mob?" Richter chuckled. "Anyone outside of your little gang that can verify that?"

Collin looked to Marx, who shook his head. The magician's eyes grew increasingly bloodshot, and he tapped his fingers on his folded arms. Baze couldn't quite get a read. Normally, he could determine emotions, but this man . . . he was a blank slate.

"All right, kid, I'm only going to ask you this once." Richter bent over, put his palms on his knees, and leaned in until his pointed nose nearly touched Collin's cheek. "Who. Is. The killer?"

Marx didn't translate, and Collin didn't move. Richter waited for a moment, then spoke in a guttural growl. "I know you understood that, you little bogtrotter. Answer me before I arrest you on the spot."

Collin tensed until his teeth chattered. He managed to keep a stoic face, but tears welled in his eyes.

Baze's stomach turned. "That's enough."

Richter waved a hand. "Don't interrupt, Ford."

Baze grabbed Richter's shoulder and forced him to straighten. "Your tactics aren't effective." He glanced at Marx. "Let me have a moment alone with the boy."

Marx shook his head. "I can't leave him alone with you. He's a child."

"Yet, if he's found guilty, he'll be tried as an adult and hanged. Let me have a moment alone, and maybe I can prevent that."

Marx opened his mouth but abruptly swung his head to look at something in the distance, his eyes icy and severe, body paralyzed. Then, as if coming out of a trance, Marx blinked and exhaled. "Very well, Baze, you may have your moment." Marx stole into the adjacent hallway.

Shaking off the odd behavior, Baze raised his eyebrows at Richter. "Trust me."

Richter scowled but nodded. "I s'pose I'll interview another one, then, shall I?"

"Good man."

Once Richter had gone, Baze raked his fingers though his hair and glanced at Collin, unsure of what to say. Collin wrung his hands, eyes downcast.

Clearing his throat, Baze retrieved another chair, placed it opposite the boy, and sat with folded hands, elbows on his knees. He used a gentle tone. "Where are your parents, Collin?"

Collin avoided eye contact. "Dead."

Baze suppressed a wince. "How?"

"Illness." The boy swiped at his cheek.

"And what about siblings? Brothers? Sisters?"

"Brother."

"How old?"

Collin gestured to Baze. "Your age."

"And where is he? Why are you not with him if he's capable of caring for you?"

Collin shrugged. Baze held back a groan. This boy didn't belong here, especially if he had family out there.

Collin huffed and looked up. "Can I go?"

Baze tapped his thumbs together and held the boy's gaze. "Listen, son, if you know anything at all about the killings, I implore you to tell me. More people will die if we don't catch this monster."

Collin flattened his lips and stared, eyebrows drawn and dark. So intimidation wouldn't work—unless the boy truly didn't understand, but something told Baze he knew more than he let on. Then how could he coax a confession?

"If you're in trouble," Baze started, not quite sure where his words would lead, "we can protect you." Something perked in Collin's eyes. Baze was on the right track. "Perhaps you think this killer may come after you if you talk, but if you help me, I can keep you safe. I'll track down your brother and get you back to Ireland unharmed."

Collin's eyes grew large. "Back to Ireland?"

Baze smiled. "Yes, I give you my word."

Hope flashed on Collin's face for a fleeting moment before he regressed into uncertainty. He dropped his gaze back to the floor.

"Collin, you could end all of this." Baze placed a gentle hand on Collin's wrist. "Tell me who it is. Do that, and I promise I will get you home."

For a moment, Collin relaxed as though submitting. But then he scowled, shot to his feet, and shoved Baze back in his chair. "Get out!" He bolted for the auditorium door.

Chapter Thirty

FLOORBOARDS CREAKED AS I CREPT THROUGH the darkened offices. Aside from a few candles shimmering from some of the rooms, all was dark. I left behind my most recent search and ventured back into the hallway. So far, I'd come up empty.

Maybe this was all in vain. Maybe I searched for something that didn't exist in the first place. My stomach coiled. No, it was here, whatever it was. I could feel it, deep, burning.

The next room chilled me. Unlike the others, with trunks flung open and desks overflowing, this one held a tidy setup of a wardrobe, roll-top desk, and bed against the far wall as though the occupant often stayed here. There wasn't a wrinkle on the handmade quilt over the bed, not a piece of clothing out of place. A swaying flame illuminated an oil lamp on the desk.

I knelt and rifled through the trunk, careful not to leave anything out of place. It contained a few books, two porcelain figures, and a tin whistle. Could this be Finn's room?

While I paged through one of the books, *Sleight of Hand* by Edwin Sachs, I came to a small blue flower pressed between the weathered pages, its five vivid petals splayed to showcase each one. A token of love? Family, perhaps? I hadn't the time to speculate further.

I replaced the book, closed the trunk, and faced the desk. As I drew closer, I spotted a sealed envelope addressed to a Shay O'Sullivan sitting atop a stack of stationery—and recognized the handwriting. It matched the note written to Mr. Ford.

Shock and excitement paralyzed me. If authentic, this correspondence could put an end to it all. I reached for the envelope.

A man cleared his throat in the hallway. Light footsteps approached the room. My breath raced straight out of my lungs. I stumbled back.

But the envelope! No time. *Hide.*

I leaped to the wardrobe and shut myself inside. A row of crisp shirts and the stifling scent of mothballs swallowed me. Breathing low, I counted each painful second as footsteps entered the room. Numbness encircled my leg, but I dared not shift for fear of making a sound.

For once, why couldn't I have been a proper lady and gone home? Instead, I was trapped inside a killer's lair, about to be discovered and viciously murdered. Would Baze avenge my death? Perhaps he no longer cared.

Papers shuffled. The floorboards groaned. A chair's legs scraped against wood, but I couldn't tell if he sat. Was he turning in for the night? They were all supposed to be with the police—unless they had finished already.

He coughed directly on the other side of the wardrobe door. I squeezed my eyes shut. The thick air made me lightheaded. I would topple at any moment if I couldn't adjust my position.

But then the footsteps clipped away, fading, lessening, until everything fell quiet once again. Seconds, then minutes passed before I allowed myself to peek out the door. Empty.

Urgency propelled my legs forward to the desk. The envelope was gone. *No!* But I couldn't dwell. No time. Whoever had come might return. I raced to the exit—

And ran straight into Cornelius.

He loomed in the darkened doorway, expressionless. He stepped forward. At the same time, an invisible force pressed me backward until we stood in the middle of the room. The candlelight ignited his eyes. I tried to breathe, speak—anything—but I was frozen in every sense.

Cornelius's arms hung at his sides, barely touching the hem of his untucked shirt. Without a jacket or waistcoat, his hair falling in crude waves, he looked a far cry from his usually pristine appearance.

"How can I help you, Adelynn?" His voice oozed around my senses and suffocated my clear thoughts.

"Cornelius," I stuttered. "I was . . . I mean, when the police—"

"Don't explain yourself." He took another step, which pushed me back against the desk. When he smiled, the light gleamed off his uncommonly white teeth. "I know why you're here." With movements as sweet and restrained as molasses, he traced his fingers down my left arm. My skin tingled. His thumb caressed the scabbed knuckle of my ring finger. "Your heart's been broken, and you're seeking solace."

"No, I . . ." My head pounded. Thoughts jumbled. "How do you know?"

"London may be a large city, but news still travels fast on the tongues of gossips." He tilted his head. "The inspector so carefully controlled your life. But you're free of him now." His voice dropped to a whisper. "You can do as you please."

Warmth encircled the chill around my spine. *I can do as I please.* But what did that mean? What did I truly want?

Desire swelled in me—the desire to finally make my own choices and the desire to have someone love me deeply for who I was. And, in this moment, the desire to have that love demonstrated.

I traced his angled features with my gaze, eventually focusing on his mouth.

"Don't let fear control you any longer, Adelynn." Cornelius's voice was merely a breath now. "You control your own actions. Take what you want."

Darkness swarmed my mind as desire swallowed me whole.

I grasped fistfuls of his shirt and kissed him. My force knocked him back a step, but he recovered and responded with calculated movements. Fiery tremors laced my limbs. His rough, cracked lips rasped against mine, tingling with peppermint. I tangled my fingers into his soft hair and explored deeper, tasting him, savoring him. I'd been wanting for so long. I could no longer have Baze, but Cornelius could give me everything I yearned for.

His lips hardened into a smile against mine.

Stop!

I shoved him back. We panted, chests heaving. Clear thoughts rushed back, bringing with them images and feelings of what I had just done. Poisoned emotions roiled in my stomach.

His cheeks flush, Cornelius examined my face and brushed his thumb over my bottom lip. He grinned and whispered, "Good girl."

Smacking a hand over my mouth, I lurched past him—eyes clouding, heart tearing—and fled.

The interrogation had been a complete waste of time—for the authorities, anyway. We told them nothing in terms of what they needed to know. But they told us everything.

I tugged the mechanism that closed the trap door to prep for our final show.

The police showed us their hand. They still didn't know who committed the crimes, but they knew we were involved. Exactly like we wanted.

And Adelynn, sweet Adelynn, she was coming close to cracking open this mystery. Oh, so close. But she left empty-handed, her heart molested. She wouldn't return here again, but in her stead, she would likely send someone else—and we would be ready.

As I moved the loose ropes into place, setting them where they could be accessed easily, I paused and squeezed my eyes shut. A headache pulsed behind my sockets. Thick air closed in around me. I pinched the corners of my eyes to stop the beginnings of tears. My conscience gave a defiant push, tried to emerge from the depths, but the darkness had a stronger hold and yanked it back down—smothering it, snuffing it out.

This was it. I stood on the edge, one step away from the end of all this.

There is yet redemption for you.

I winced as light squeezed into my mind, offering a small reprieve from the suffocating darkness. My homeland came into view—lush, green, alive. Suddenly, all I wanted to do was abandon this mad quest and return there. Perhaps I could even find happiness.

You can.

I opened my eyes and looked at the chain. The images faded. I couldn't leave—not yet.

The final act was about to begin.

Chapter Thirty-One

CORNELIUS WOULDN'T LEAVE MY MIND—THE heat of him, the dominance in his touch. Had I not snapped out of my trance, I would have given myself over to him completely.

A cough jolted me out of my thoughts. I closed the book in my lap and caught a glimpse of the sergeant standing outside the door of Father's study. For a moment, his cropped brown hair and distinct profile reminded me of Sergeant Moseley, and the memory sowed further anguish within me.

Hugging the book to my chest, I slumped low in the armchair and stared into the gentle fire. Guilt soured my insides. What kind of woman was I? I'd succumbed to my worldly desires, turning a blind eye to pure thoughts. *Lord, how could you ever forgive me for this?*

The door creaked, and soft footfalls crossed the room. Mother's mellow voice edged into my reveries. "Tired of Sherlock Holmes so soon?" As she stepped toward the opposite chair, she squeezed my knee and then sat.

I traced a fingernail along the book's spine. "I can't seem to comprehend his mysteries today."

"Mmm. Life's mysteries are complex enough on their own."

If only she knew.

Mother tilted her head. "Are you well? You retired early last night."

A lump rose in my throat. I fought back tears and swallowed. "Yes. I simply needed to be alone."

Snaps and pops from the fire filled the silence. As if dealing with the implications of Cornelius's and my shared moment wasn't enough,

I also had to face the consequences of my broken engagement to Baze. No doubt Mother knew everything. As Cornelius had said, news traveled swiftly in London. Surely it took but the blink of an eye for it to travel next door.

I watched the fire shine off her green eyes and highlight her soft wrinkles. Shame clamped tight in my chest. I sniffled and bowed my head. "I'm sorry I let you down."

Mother frowned. "Whatever are you talking about?"

"My engagement." I tried to draw a deep breath, but my lungs ached in protest. "I've managed to bring two families down in one foolish move. We'll be ruined, and it's all my fault."

"Oh, no, my love." She leaned over the armrest, took my chin in her fingers, and turned my face toward her. "It is I who let you down. I should have known what was happening. I should have protected you." Tears sparkled in her eyes. "You did nothing wrong, not against the Fords or our family. You said no to oppression and won. And for that, I am so very proud of you."

Heavy emotion rose from my stomach and poured out in a sob. Mother stood, pulled me to my feet, and wrapped me in her embrace. The book tumbled to the floor. Weeping, I buried my face against her shoulder. The scratchy lace of her gown irritated my cheek, but I only pressed harder.

Mother held me, stroking my hair, until my cries diminished. Then she pushed me back, brushed the fringe from my forehead, and smiled. "Walk with me, dearest."

As we strolled arm in arm, past the sergeant and down the hall, remorse crept back to the forefront. I clung tighter to her and spoke, voice rasping. "How will I get through this?"

"The same way you got through your father's passing last year. The same way you get through everything." She released a heavy exhale and caressed my forearm. "By taking it day by day and walking with the Lord—and allowing Him to carry you when you cannot walk another step."

Images of Cornelius flooded back. I lowered my gaze to the floor. "He'll have to carry me for quite some time."

Mother kissed my temple. "Then it's a good thing He is always with you."

Tension melted from my muscles as peace filled the hollow cavity in my heart.

Mother stopped us near the foyer and faced me. "I'm hosting Mrs. Ford this evening for dinner. Considering the circumstances, I assume you wouldn't find much joy in entertaining her with me." She rubbed my arm. "Which is why I've arranged for you to spend the evening with your dearest friend Emily. Samuel is waiting to take you."

My hand flew to my mouth. "Samuel?"

With a smile, Mother touched my shoulders and turned me toward the door.

Standing tall and confident, albeit pale, Samuel grinned widely at his post. A gasp trapped a squeal in my throat. In two bounds, I cleared the distance between us and embraced him.

He laughed. "It is wonderful to see you, Miss Adelynn. I apologize for my absence."

I kissed his soft, weathered cheek and pulled back. "Don't apologize. I'm so thankful you're well. I've been worried."

"And I have worried for your safety." His milky blue eyes held concern. "Please tell me you have pursued more modest endeavors of late." ·

Rather than answer, I smiled and hugged him again. When we parted, he raised a critical eyebrow but didn't pry. He straightened and tipped his head. "Where to, Miss Adelynn?"

Bennett answered the door and beckoned me in with a free hand, attempting to fasten his waistcoat buttons. Dressed in casual trousers and an off-white shirt, sans a formal jacket, he looked indistinguishable from the common man on the street. Two policemen loitered near the kitchen entrance.

I looked Bennett up and down. "Going somewhere?"

"Official business tonight." He gestured to the officers. "Meet Constable Cunningham." The stout, bald man tipped his head. "And you already know Sergeant Andrews." The other, a young, handsome man, gave a small wave.

I nodded to the men, then frowned. "Two?"

"I'm not leaving anything to chance."

The concern in his eyes told me everything. I scanned the room. "Where is Emily?"

"She's resting for a bit. She's been having some pain."

My stomach lurched. "Is it serious?"

"It's been happening on and off for a few weeks now. The doctor says it's normal as she nears the end of her pregnancy." Finishing the buttons, he tugged down the hem, smoothed out stray wrinkles, and flashed a lopsided grin. "How do I look?"

"Dashing." I smiled.

He paused and studied me. "Is something wrong?"

"Wrong? No." I forced the smile to remain.

He snapped his fingers at the officers. "Lads, give us the room, please." When they'd gone, he crossed his arms and stepped closer. "You may think Baze is the only person who knows you inside and out, but let's not forget I gallivanted right along with the two of you in all of your shenanigans." He raised his eyebrows. "What's on your mind?"

Blast it all, Bennett. The last thing I wanted to do was explain what happened, but he'd always lent an attentive ear when I needed it. Besides, he was already my partner in crime. What was one more secret?

I folded my arms to my chest. "I assume you heard about our argument, mine and Baze's?"

"Indeed." He flattened his lips. "How are you handling it?"

Every emotion from that day poured out as I explained my confrontation with Mr. Ford and Baze's revelation. Then I told Bennett of my escape to the theater, of talking to Finn, and the police's interruption. Somehow, I managed to keep my composure as I explained the part where I noticed the envelope and recognized the handwriting—then was cornered by Cornelius and how I had responded.

I expected a reprimand, a harsh tone, but Bennett's expression grew solemn. "There are dark forces at work here, and it appears they know exactly how to prey upon your weaknesses." He tipped my nose with a knuckle. "We must pray, Adelynn, pray harder than we ever have. The darkness is only going to get stronger from here on."

The heavy sigh that left my mouth caught me off guard. Hearing him acknowledge the influence of that theater and the spiritual battle within filled me with a strange relief. The darkness was not all in my head. And Christ would protect me.

Bennett tapped a thumb to his chin. "You have not had a vision for some time now, correct?"

"Yes, and that's what worries me. I feel something more horrible is coming." My knees trembled. "I can't do this anymore." A lump swelled in my throat. "This has unlocked a side of myself I never knew existed, and it frightens me. I fear I'll lose control if I go back."

Bennett shook his head. "I wouldn't let you return even if you wanted to. We've discovered something new in the case." He paused. "According to the evidence we've gathered, we have reason to believe you are the target in some way."

Numbness crawled from my scalp to my toes. "What do you mean?"

"You've had visions of each crime. The victims are growing closer in relation to you. You've been involved in the investigation from the very beginning. I don't believe that's all coincidence."

"That's why you've posted a sergeant at my home," I said slowly.

"Yes. And Cunningham and Andrews will remain here."

Strangely, a sense of calm washed through me. After everything that had happened, it almost made sense. But what of my friends? My family? I could handle being a target, but if he harmed anyone close to me . . .

"You have to catch this man," I whispered.

Bennett rubbed my shoulders. "You've done more than was ever expected of you. Leave it to the lads and me. We'll take care of the rest. Focus instead on guarding your heart and mind."

Overwhelming relief nearly buckled my knees. "Thank you."

Groaning preceded Emily into the room. She used the back of the sofa for support, a hand cupping her stomach, before sinking onto the cushions.

Bennett hastened to her side and sat next to her. "Should I fetch the doctor?"

"No, it will pass." Shaking her head, she gave me a weary smile. "Thank you for coming, Adelynn."

I mirrored her expression. "Of course. I have missed you."

Bennett brushed Emily's curls from her face. "Are you sure you're all right, Millie?"

"Yes, love." She gave his shoulder a small nudge. "No need to worry." As she focused on the floor, her smile faded.

Bennett tapped his foot and cleared his throat, which drew her gaze to him. He tipped her chin with his finger. "I'm not leaving until you talk to me."

I considered offering encouragement—perhaps she would respond to a woman's coaxing—but thought better of it.

With a sigh, Emily grasped Bennett's hand and pulled it to her lap. "I don't want to let you down."

"Let me down?" He squeezed her hand. "What are you talking about?"

"I've been doing the best I can to be the wife you need and to stay healthy for the baby. But what if it's not enough?" She looked to the ceiling and blinked rapidly as her eyes reddened, yet a few tears escaped. "What if I fail to keep our child alive again?"

Bennett registered surprise, but pain squeezed my heart. Everything she had divulged to me was becoming too much for her as her baby neared—the periodic cramps likely a reminder of what she had suffered twice before.

With a furrowed brow, Bennett knelt on the floor and peered up at her. "Listen to me." His soothing tone held calm assurance. "Losing our children was not your fault. I have never thought that. Ever." His voice cracked. "You're not carrying this alone. I'm doing my best to be a good husband to you and father to this child. But that's all we can do before we have to let God do the rest, even though, sometimes, He says no to our prayers." He gulped in a breath. Sorrow rasped deep within his voice. "But we can't let that discourage us. No matter what happens this time, I'll be here to face it with you."

Fresh tears pooled in Emily's eyes. She drew him close and wound her arms around his neck. He wrapped her in his own embrace and buried his head against her stomach, her head atop his.

As they remained enfolded in each other's arms, I inched toward the kitchen to give them privacy. But as I reached the door, Emily cleared her throat. "You're like family, Adelynn. No need to leave."

I glanced back to see Emily straighten, her expression amused. She squeezed Bennett's shoulder and pushed him back. "I'm sorry to have kept you." She rubbed her tear-laden cheeks with her palms. "You have important work to do."

He wiped the rest of her tears with his sleeve. "This is more important."

"You're sweet." She adjusted his spectacles and then kissed his forehead. "Now go put your investigative prowess to work and bring justice to our streets."

"Yes, ma'am." He passed a gentle hand over her stomach, then leaned in to give it a kiss. "Wait for me, you hear?" he whispered. "Don't give your mother too much trouble, sweet Victoria."

Emily raised her eyebrows but didn't argue. Bennett chuckled, then stood, took her face in his hands, and kissed her. When they parted, he murmured, "I love you."

She blushed. "I love *you*."

Bennett helped Emily rise from the sofa, wound an arm around her waist, and led her over to me. She grasped my hand as Bennett looked between the two of us and shook his head. "That I could take this pain away from you both." He gave a sad smile. "When I return, we've much to discuss."

Chapter Thirty-Two

PAIN NEEDLED BEHIND BAZE'S CLOSED EYES. Shrill ringing filled his ears and heightened the sound of his own breathing. His nose and lungs prickled with the smell of sweat and acid. Shadowed shapes danced in dizzying patterns against his eyelids.

And so he hung there in the void, alone and distant from the world—and yet not so far away as to escape the tormenting words that trailed him. He could never be far enough.

"You will learn never to disappoint me again. I will see to it."

Father's words from that day years ago rang in his head. His father had uttered them as Baze lay swollen and half-conscious after his assault. How was Baze to have known Father would sink his talons deep into Baze from that moment forward? He'd played his adolescent son for his own personal gain, all to protect a meaningless name.

"Stop holding onto the hope that I'll utter a confession of unconditional love that will revive our bond as father and son. It is not who I am. And I can't change that."

His father had all but admitted that he viewed Baze as no more than a pawn. Even after his influence was stripped away, Alistair couldn't bring himself to acknowledge Baze as his son. He didn't even try. But Baze was free of him. He needn't give his father a second thought—so why was that all he could think about?

"He threatened my family."

Adelynn's confession assailed him once again—aggravating Adelynn. Would she never leave his mind? They were through. They had to be. She'd suffered in silence and didn't trust him enough to confide in him. She'd told everyone else *but* him.

"You wouldn't have listened. Your father's influence was too strong."

Poppycock. If anyone could have convinced him of anything, it would have been her.

"Baze!"

Something yanked the glass mug from his hand, dragging his mind back to the murky pub where he sat hunched at the bar. Cigarette smoke blended with the odors of vomit and stew. The walls and patrons spun.

Bennett slammed the mug on the countertop and swiveled Baze toward him on the stool. "What are you doing?" Bennett shouted over the ruckus.

"I'm having a drink." Baze waited for Bennett's form to stop spinning before reaching for the mug.

Bennett slid it out of his reach. "You've had more than a drink, mate."

With a frown, Baze swiped and managed to take back the mug and down a swig.

Bennett shook his head. "Easy. This isn't the time to go off. You're on assignment with me tonight. Remember?"

Baze wiped froth from his lip. "I'm not going back."

"Of course you are."

"What's the point?"

Bennett frowned. "Surely you're joking."

"Surely I'm not." Baze reveled in the burn of his next drink, of the lightness it brought to his mind. "People are dead, there's a killer on the loose, and I've done nothing but make a mockery of myself since the beginning. I never wanted this. You're better off without me."

"That's the real reason, now, is it?"

"It's what you want to hear."

They held eye contact for a long moment until Baze grunted and turned back to his mug. But before he could lift it to his lips, Bennett yanked it from his grip. Baze yelled in protest.

"I watched my mother drink herself into the gutter." Bennett tossed the remaining liquid onto the floor and slammed the mug on the counter. "I'm not about to let you start."

Baze shot to his feet, shoving Bennett and surrounding bodies in the process. Bennett lunged toward Baze but was halted by the barkeep shouting, "Take it outside!"

"I'll leave when I please." Baze waved a finger, but Bennett snagged his collar and hefted him toward the door. They skirted through a flurry of sweaty bodies until they emerged into the cool night air. Fog engulfed them.

Bennett shoved Baze onto the pavement. He hit with a heavy thud. The sky whirled, and the contents of his stomach sloshed, threatening to spew. Whether through sheer willpower or divine intervention, he kept it down, rolled over, and wobbled up onto his feet.

"What are you doing?" Bennett panted. "We've recently learned that Adelynn's life may be in danger and you decide to up and quit. What's wrong with you?"

"You'll do much better without me." Reflux burned in Baze's chest. He staggered a bit and tried to straighten his vision, but Bennett's form blurred. "You've seen that note left by the killer. I'm done playing his game."

"We don't have to play his game to beat him." Bennett curled his lip. "But you know that. You're just taking the coward's way out. You've learned some hard truths about your family, so you're giving up."

Baze spat on the ground. "What do you know about it?"

"What do I know about it?" Bennett seized fistfuls of Baze's shirt and jostled him. "I watched my degenerate father woo my mother time and time again, offering her a proper marriage and a life finally safe from the humiliation that he'd put her through. And each time, I watched him abandon her, and I was left behind to pick up the pieces. I know plenty of family dissention. But I didn't let it define me."

Baze's mind clouded as he tried to sort through Bennett's tale, but it only conjured rage. He thrust a fist into Bennett's gut, doubling him over. When Bennett recovered, he shoved Baze, which toppled him to the ground. Bennett lunged on top of him, held his chest down with an arm, and struck him square in the jaw. It elicited a crack, but Baze couldn't tell whether it came from his jaw or Bennett's hand.

Bennett cocked his arm back for another blow but hesitated, fist poised, as they panted and glowered at one another. Baze blinked rapidly to focus Bennett's blurred image but to no avail. Blood tasted bitter on his tongue. He couldn't draw a proper breath with Bennett compressing his chest.

Bennett relaxed his shoulders and sighed. With a shake of his head, he stood and stepped over Baze. Before he'd gone five paces, he turned back. "You have to realize that there are precious lives on the line." His voice grew heavy. "But more than that, we're battling against forces that aren't flesh and blood."

Baze's skin prickled. His mind dizzied.

"You can't compare your experience with your own father to a relationship with the Almighty. That's a miserable excuse, and it's time you stopped placing blame on others. Take responsibility. You'll need divine protection if you're to have any hope of bringing our killer to justice." Bennett grimaced and tilted his head. "Now, sober yourself up and do your job." His eyes softened. "And find Al. Ask her to marry you before anything else happens to drive you further apart. You'll never forgive yourself if you let her go."

Chapter Thirty-Three

THROUGH CLOUDS OF FLOUR AND SUGAR, I giggled at the dough stuck to Emily's curls. The baking endeavor had somehow turned into a tussle over who could splatter the most flour, yet we had still managed to get a finished product in the oven. The delectable scent of nutmeg and caramelized peaches filled the room.

"Enough!" Through heaves of laughter, Emily managed, "Praise the Lord for a pie already baking or we would have nothing to show for our efforts, no thanks to you."

"Me?" I lobbed a dash of flour at her. "If I recall, 'twas you who first smattered the ingredients all over us."

"Yes, but only after you nearly spilled the whole sack onto the floor."

I wiped tears from my eyes. My sides, ribs, and cheeks ached—but in a way that sent elation running through me. Anxiety had held my thoughts captive as of late, so the euphoria came as a welcome respite. Oh, to feel this joyous all the time would be a luxury.

Emily winced and curled forward, holding her breath with a hand on her back. I inhaled sharply and stared. When she noticed me watching, she waved a hand. "The midwife said this was normal, remember? Means this little one is getting ready to come." It took another long moment before she relaxed and straightened.

"Well, tell him or her to hold on one more night. I've no idea how to birth a baby."

Emily scoffed. "Neither do I."

I smirked and raised my eyebrows. "Have you settled on a name?"

"Take that up with Bennett." Emily rested a hand on her stomach, eyes downcast. "Speaking of Bennett, how do you feel about his revelation . . . that you may be a target?"

Hair prickled on the back of my neck. I snatched up a rag and began scrubbing the counter. "I know nothing more than what Bennett told me earlier. It's only a theory."

"But it would certainly explain your visions." She shook her head. "That sounds so curious to say."

"Indeed it does." I bit my lip.

"Are you frightened?"

My breath grew shallow. "I suppose I'm not quite sure what to feel. Enough has happened that it seems almost normal, I'm afraid to say."

Emily's smile warmed. "You're the bravest woman I've ever met."

I sobered and set down the rag. "I'm not brave."

"Rubbish."

"You heard my confession to Bennett, yes?" I hugged my arms around my torso. "When my bravery, as you call it, should have shone, I gave in to my fears and desires and acted upon them."

"I did hear that, yes." She squeezed my shoulder. "But the fact that you are standing here now admitting your error and seeking forgiveness is one of the greatest acts of courage. It is not a choice easily made."

I smiled and tilted my head back and forth. "Actually, I look to you for inspiration."

"Me?" She pointed at herself and flushed pink. "I'm only a simple housewife."

"Not simple. After all that's happened and all you've lost, you're willing to do anything for your family despite any consequences to yourself. You're there for Bennett at a moment's notice, and you have moved heaven and earth to make sure you are healthy for this child."

"Thank you," she whispered, stroking her stomach. Just then, she seized and hunched against the oven.

"Emily?" I held out my hands to support her.

"This little one is quite adamant." She let out a shaky laugh but remained tense. Her gaze darted to the wall clock, and a low groan emitted from her throat.

I frowned. "What is it?"

"That was"—she shook her head and huffed—"that was the fifth contraction in the last half hour."

I swallowed, mouth suddenly dry. "Is that significant?"

She blew out a terse breath, reclined back against the counter, and gave me a serious look. "I may be in labor."

My stomach dropped. When I finally spoke, my voice came out weak and airy. "So what are we to do?"

Gulping in a breath, she massaged the side of her stomach. "Thanks to all the reading I've done, I'm prepared with the essentials. Some women labor all day, while some labor mere hours. But we need to get the midwife here in time."

"Yes, we do. You certainly don't want *me* at the helm of this delivery." I gave a brief smile to try to chase away the concern on her face. I managed to draw a chuckle from her. "Now, let's sit you down. We'll have the officers fetch the midwife. Everything will be all right."

After switching off the oven, I wrapped an arm around Emily's waist and headed for the front sitting room, but we only shuffled a few feet before she pulled us to a halt. "We may have less time than I thought." She sighed, closed her eyes, and stood still for a long moment. "My water just broke."

Panic flared inside me, but I tamped it down. I ducked under Emily's arm and supported her weight. "Sergeant Andrews!" I shouted.

The sergeant appeared in an instant. He took in the situation and paled. "What's—"

"Baby's on its way," I said with a grunt. Emily grew heavier. My legs weakened. "Help us to the bedroom."

Brow firm and determined, Andrews jumped to action. He took Emily's free arm and draped it about his shoulders, then swept her entire form up into his arms. As he carried her into the front sitting room,

Cunningham watched with wide eyes from his post at the door.

Emily clung to Andrews, her face contorted in pain. "The spare . . . spare room's been prepared . . . for this."

Andrews obeyed and strode down the hall into the guest bedroom. Cunningham and I hurried inside after him and helped arrange the linens so that Andrews could lay her gently atop the single bed.

As we got her settled, propped against a pillow, I brushed perspiration from my forehead with a wrist and looked at each officer in turn. "I need one of you to find Bennett and one of you to fetch the midwife."

They shared a glance, and then Andrews said, "We both can't leave, Miss Spencer."

"But she needs a midwife to help with the delivery, and Bennett can't very well miss being there to welcome his child into the world. Sending one person would take too long."

Emily's moans cut through the silence.

I held out a hand. "Leave me a pistol. Baze taught me how to use it for defense."

Again, they didn't move. Emily's body stiffened, drawing a guttural groan from her lips.

"Please!" I raised my voice.

Finally, Andrews gave in, pulled out his gun, and handed it to me. The dense, heavy metal cooled my fingers. He leaned close with a pointed stare. "Anyone tries to force his way in here, blast 'im."

I nodded, throat tightening. "Thank you."

After I relayed the midwife's location, Andrews motioned to Cunningham, and then they departed.

I looked at Emily, who stared back through her unkempt golden curls. Her chest heaved, but for the time being, her muscles relaxed.

"Now what?" I whispered.

She filled her lungs and let out a deep breath. "Now we wait . . . and we pray."

A faint but commanding voice filtered through the floorboards overhead. The show had nearly concluded. My part was finished, at least for now. I had merely retired to my room to rest when I stumbled upon Inspector Bennett himself, snooping where he did not belong.

I stayed in the shadows and watched him sneak with quiet care from room to room. The other two officers searched elsewhere. That would be a costly mistake. What was the point of having backup if it wasn't there to back you up? I hoped he had kissed his wife goodbye.

Pain jabbed my chest. But why did he have to die? Why did any of them have to die?

We were fulfilling our revenge. It was all justified. That much was certain. At least, I thought it was.

Bile boiled up my throat. Thoughts jumbled—thoughts telling me it was right, no, it was wrong, I should abandon this quest, no, I should kill this Englishman now. The oxygen seemed to drain from the air.

My conscience felt split in two—one part devoid of morals, the other filled with the desire to do what was honorable. They were locked in a violent battle for dominance. Which one would win? Which one should I allow to win?

Fresh air. I needed fresh air to clear my head. I pulled back and slipped away to the staircase. With or without me, the plan would go on.

Chapter Thirty-Four

"YOU LITTLE NIPPER!" EMILY CURLED TOWARD her propped knees. Veins popped in her neck. Her brow perspired and her chemise clung to her form despite the cool breeze carrying in from the window I'd opened earlier.

I held her hand, rock-like in grip, and stroked her forearm until she fell back against the pillow. "The men should be back any time now with the midwife and Bennett."

I prayed my words were correct. *Lord, let them return quickly.* I wasn't prepared to help birth this baby. Other than what I had read in old medical journals I had snatched in secret from Father's study, I knew nothing of this process how long it was supposed to take or how it progressed. But I tried to keep the uncertainty from my face.

"I didn't expect this kind of pain." Emily sucked in quick, deep breaths. "If I would have known, I—"

"You still would have wanted a child. It's what you and Bennett have always yearned for."

Emily tilted her head back and stared at the ceiling, defeat hazing in her eyes. "I don't think I can do this without him."

"Don't think that way." I squeezed her sweaty hand in both of mine. We couldn't get this child out if she lost the will to fight for it. I lightened my voice. "Why don't you tell me the tale of when you first met Bennett. I've heard your first encounter was far too awkward for a blossoming romance."

She closed her eyes and huffed. "You've heard that story."

"Shh. I'm trying to distract you."

She half opened one eye, so I grinned weakly. She nodded and licked her lips. "Okay." A spasm seized her belly and punched air from her lungs. We waited for the contraction to calm before she began.

"When burglars raided my parents' shop, Bennett was assigned to the case. He was a rookie constable at the time." She gave a strained laugh. "He was so timid at first, not quite comfortable in his uniform. It took him a good while to approach my parents. He pretended to be interested in our wares, God bless him. Oh!" She arched forward, yelling through clenched teeth.

I waited until she relaxed before wiggling her hand. "What happened next?"

She paused to catch her breath. "He questioned my parents, but when I came out from the back room, his face went absolutely scarlet. He looked like a kid with his hand caught in a sweets jar. I've never seen someone retreat so suddenly."

"Did he come by to see you again?"

"Oh, yes. Many times. He always claimed to have lost his cufflinks and that he was in need of new ones. After we were married, I found seven pairs he'd purchased from us." She laughed and shook her head, then sobered. "He should be here."

"I know, Emily. Any minute now, he'll—"

Distant, rapid knocks rattled the front door. "Hello? Is anyone in there?" came a muffled male voice—but not Bennett's.

Emily and I locked gazes. I didn't dare move, though Emily's chest still heaved. "What do we do?" she mouthed.

I wasn't sure how to answer. I snatched up the pistol and swallowed. When Andrews left me the gun, I didn't think I'd actually have to use it. Could I even bring myself to do so? To harm another person?

The individual knocked again and jostled the doorknob. "I heard shoutin' comin' through the window. Everyone all right?" This time, heavy Irish inflections bled through.

Recognition piqued my attention. *Could it really be him?* I eased to a stand and inched out of the room, toward the front door.

"What are you doing?" Emily hissed.

"Hello?" The stranger shook the doorknob again. "Be you in trouble? I'd like to help, whatever it is."

After pausing briefly to say a quick prayer, I hiked back the hammer of the gun and flicked the lock on the door. Then I threw it open wide and aimed the gun—right at Finn's chest.

"Don't shoot!" He held up his hands and froze. "Adelynn? What are you doin' with a gun? What's goin' on?"

I lowered the weapon. Tension drained from my shoulders. Milky fog covered the street and draped over Finn's body like a cloak, dampening his coat and black curls. The streetlamps were but dim dots floating in the dark murk.

"What are you doing here?" I asked.

"I heard screamin', so I—"

"No, I mean what are you doing out here at this hour? Don't you have a show?"

"I've finished already." He searched my face. "What about the screamin', Adelynn? What's—"

As if to answer his question, Emily let out a growl, this one longer and shriller than the last.

Finn paled.

Trying to keep the concern from my tone, I said, "Baby's coming."

After a brief hesitation, Finn rolled his shoulders back. He removed his coat, loosened his bow tie, and rolled up his sleeves. "Best get to work then."

Chapter Thirty-Five

BAZE TRIED TO CONCENTRATE ON HIS steps as he stumbled toward headquarters, using passing benches for support. Hostile words circled in his mind like ravens searching for prey. The thoughts taunted him—revenge, sabotage, injustice—and threatened his sanity. He exhaled angrily. What did Bennett know anyway? He'd never known heartbreak of this kind. He'd never had a serial killer target him with personal notes. What right did he have to tell Baze how to act?

Footsteps sloshed behind Baze. His reaction time came up lacking, and the individual darted in front of him before he even had a chance to turn.

Andrews rested his hands on his knees, panting. "Ford, have you seen Bennett?"

Baze nearly scoffed but resisted. "He's out following a lead."

The officer swore under his breath.

"Can I help?"

"Well, the missus Bennett . . . her time's come."

"What time?"

Andrews's face boiled red. "Her baby. She's having her baby."

"She's wha . . ." Baze gripped a nearby streetlight pole to keep from swaying.

"I've got to hurry, sir. Cunningham went to fetch the midwife, so they—"

"Both of you left? You were assigned to protect them!" Baze turned on his heels. "I'll go to them. You find Bennett. He's likely at that Irish theater."

"You might have better luck locating him, being his partner."

"No, he doesn't want to see me. And frankly, I would rather not face him at the moment. Go to the theater. I will see to his wife."

Pushing past the incredible sense of impropriety—having a man who was neither family nor doctor in the presence of a woman in labor—I hurried into the spare room and to Emily's side, stepping around the fresh towels we'd assembled. "Finn's here. He's willing to help us until the midwife arrives."

As Finn approached, Emily rose up on an elbow, cheeks flushing. "Mr. Kelly!"

"Evenin', Mrs. Bennett." He tipped his head. "Though, if I'm to be helpin', you can call me Finn."

She eyed him. "Do you have experience with childbirth?"

"Some, I suppose. Back home, I used to help me parents with the ewes and their lambs."

I glared. "Did you just liken Emily to a ewe?"

He froze. "Obviously, I didn't mean it that way. I—"

Emily snorted a laugh and relaxed against the pillow. "He'll do."

Standing at the end of the bed near Emily's feet, I raised my eyebrows at Finn. "For decency's sake, you should remain by her head. Give her encouragement when she needs it."

He hesitated and looked to Emily. "You don't mind?"

She panted and lifted her hand, open and waiting. "I could use some strength right now."

He dragged a chair from the corner of the room next to the bed and sat, then grasped her petite hand, dwarfing it in his. "I'll lend you all the strength I can." Though white in the face, he managed a determined expression. "You're rather calm for one in your predicament."

"Oh, trust me, I'm anything but calm."

"Surely, you must—"

"Please stop talking." She arched forward and let out a moan. Sweat congealed on her brow and trickled down her neck. The blanket providing her decency grew damp with sweat and clung to her tense form.

Finn held her hand in both of his until the contraction ended. Color draining from his face, he looked to me with wide eyes. I nodded in encouragement. He cleared his throat and focused on Emily. "It'll be no time at all before you're holdin' your little man."

She blew out a breath. "What makes you say it will be a boy?"

"A gut feelin'. Me mam used to say 'twas the way a woman carried herself that gave it away. You have the poise and strength that one might find in a healthy boy." His cheeks reddened. "If you don't mind me observation."

I frowned. "But of course, a girl could be equally as strong."

"'Twould be less likely."

I lifted my chin. "If you ask me, there are some men I know who are anything but strong."

He scowled as though sensing the deeper meaning behind my words. "What more would you have me do?"

"You know exactly what you should do. But you're far too cowardly to do so." I leveled my gaze at him, studying those sad gray eyes. They seemed cloudier today, like drooping heather on a foggy moor. Turmoil raged inside of him, that much I could see, but unless he opened himself up to the truth, there was nothing to be done.

Finn seemed to conjure a rebuttal, but Emily's yell cut him off. She curled up. Every muscle in her body tightened. A pop elicited from Finn's hand. He winced but held on all the more.

I grasped Emily's ankle as a round head begin to emerge. "You're almost there." My stomach rose to my throat. "Just a little bit more."

When the next contraction overtook her, she pushed harder, and I helped coax a writhing, slimy tangle of limbs into my hands. Emily collapsed back into the pillow, chest heaving, smiling as the baby began to cry.

After we cut and tied off the cord, Finn took the baby in his arms so I could help with the afterbirth. All signs of agony evaporated from his face as he patted dry the wailing child with a towel and cleared the mucus from its nose. The fog cleared a bit from his eyes as he smiled wide. "Hello there, wee one. Welcome to the world."

I laughed and squeezed Emily's knee. "You were brilliant. Absolutely brilliant."

Finn swaddled the tiny baby and handed it to her. "You've a son."

Tears spilled down Emily's cheeks as she nuzzled her baby. His strained cries lessened with each of his mother's caresses. His little pink tongue rose in his open mouth, skin blotchy and wrinkled, eyes squeezed shut as though he wasn't quite ready to see the world.

All seemed not quite as dark, the terror that plagued London not as formidable. There was life here—so much life. And the light and happiness that it brought seemed strong enough to banish even the most powerful evil. Perhaps this was what we needed all along. Life. Light. Hope.

I looked to Finn. Did he see it too? Though his eyes shone brighter, fear still loomed behind them. What would it take to make him see and accept it?

Two quick raps sounded on the front door. Its hinges groaned, and footsteps pounded down the hall. Baze rushed into the room. White mist particles clung to his coat, dark sags rimmed his eyes, and deep lines creased his forehead. His eyes found me first.

My heart fluttered.

"I came as soon as I heard," he said, words slightly slurred. "Bennett was on assignment. Is Emily . . ." He stopped when he saw the rest of us, the squirming baby grunting in Emily's arms, the scarlet fluid staining Finn's arms and clothes. Baze lurched toward Finn, seized his collar, and yanked him to his feet. "Get out."

"Baze!" I jumped up and forced myself between them. "The midwife wasn't here. Finn gave us valuable assistance." The rancid stench of alcohol clung to Baze's breath. I crinkled my nose. "Have you been drinking?"

Baze ignored me and glared at Finn with bloodshot eyes. "You're not welcome here, not when you might have the blood of others on your hands."

"Basil!"

"It's all right, Adelynn." Finn wiped his hands on his trousers and tried to rub off the remaining blood. "I'll go."

"No. Don't." I caught his elbow as he passed.

Light engulfed the room, then darkness.

Oh, no. Lord, no, not again. Not another vision—not another death.

The world's light faded when a dark corridor overtook the landscape of my mind. A sliver of light marked a door at the end of the chamber. The dim illumination revealed upside down chairs, draped objects, rusted cages, chains—and Bennett. He stood twenty paces from me, and as he crept toward the door, I followed.

Bennett, look out, I tried to say, but like before, this mouth, this body, did not belong to me. I was just a consciousness along for this horrific ride.

I trailed Bennett out into the night air, heavy with mist and tension. We emerged into the alley next to the theater. I stopped, arms limp at my sides, and grinned. "Bit of a dreary night for a stroll, eh, Inspector?"

Bennett whirled, hand reaching for his pistol. When he saw me, he tensed. "I'm on assignment."

"An assignment on private property? I don't think so."

"You sound . . ." Bennett frowned, then realization darkened his features. "It was you."

I only smiled. My hand drifted to my waistband where I clutched the cold metal of a gun.

But Bennett, wonderful Bennett, noticed the movement and drew his pistol. "Don't move. My backup and I are supposed to rendezvous. They'll come looking if I don't show."

"Oh, this won't take long."

Bennett aimed at my chest. "Put both hands where I can see them." He eased forward, but when I chuckled, he stopped.

"Careful, Inspector. You don't know how the other men died, do you? Coerced into killin' themselves, as if by mind control. Isn't that right? You wouldn't want to risk your own life now, not with a brand-new son."

Bennett's pistol fell a little, a torrid mix of emotions wreaking havoc on his usually calm features. His eyes grew out of focus. "A son?"

When he refocused on me, an eerie peace fell over him. He chewed his lip for a bit, then looked me right in the eyes, almost as though looking through and seeing *me*.

He took a deep breath. "Adelynn, it's—"

I snatched up my gun and fired. A flash and pop shot from Bennett's own weapon. Sharp pain lit my side. All went black.

Chapter Thirty-Six

MIST COILED THROUGH THE AIR, CHOKING the brilliance of the streetlamps. Baze's legs ached as he half-jogged, half-stumbled toward the fray of spectators. Drops of sweat gathered on his brow.

Two shots. Adelynn had said there were two gunshots. Bennett had done it. He had caught the murderer.

Lights from inside the theater dyed the atmosphere a diluted red. When Baze reached the crowd, he shouldered through them. "Move. Let me pass. I order you to move." His own voice sounded foreign, distant.

Smoke from a cigar cloud burned his eyes. The stench of fresh horse excrement and polished leather tormented his nose. The sea of people seemed never-ending.

Up ahead, Richter held his arms outstretched, holding back the masses. When he saw Baze, he extended a hand. "No, Ford. You'd best not look."

Baze lunged through the people and batted down Richter's arm, but his foot caught a stranger's ankle in the process. He skidded to the ground. Skin tore on his palms and knees. Alone, out of the mob, mist suffocated him. He'd landed in a cold puddle that smelled of gunpowder and iron. The liquid gleamed crimson in the dim lamp beams.

Instinct told Baze not to raise his head, but his heart won the battle. He slowly lifted his gaze, following the sanguine river. It led him to a prone figure—still and familiar. Brown hair rustled in the breeze. Mist glistened off the spectacles.

Baze crumpled, buried his forehead against the ground, and screamed.

Hollow chills filled the mortuary. Though more than a dozen men clustered in the small, dingy room between bare tables and shelves overflowing with silver instruments of various shapes and sizes, the silent atmosphere did little to mask Hamilton's guttural grunts.

Baze watched as the doctor jotted notes, then read and reread them. From where he stood in the middle of his fellow policemen, Baze refused to look at the table around which they all gathered. It was too final. Too absolute. If he looked, it would become reality.

Heaviness weighed down his swollen eyelids. Aches flared in his chest with every breath. His lungs, his ribs, his muscles—everything hurt. Each labored breath he drew sent pangs of renewed sorrow through him.

"Well, my boys, best not to put this off." Hamilton's voice cut the air like a razor. Baze refused to make eye contact with the doctor, or his fellow officers for that matter. Instead, he watched the chain of a desk lamp drift back and forth—back and forth.

Hamilton cleared his throat and spoke again, this time softly. "I need to remove the covering now." No one responded, so he pinched the edges of the cloth and pulled it back. A chorus of murmurs swept through the officers as they shifted and fidgeted. Baze sucked in a breath and held it, new emotion rising to his eyes.

You have to look. There would be time for grief later. Right now, emotion and fear were the only things standing between Baze and that killer, that psychotic monster. Swallowing back his sorrow, Baze finally allowed himself to look.

Bennett lay flat on the table, face ashen and still as though hardened into marble. With his eyes respectfully closed, if one looked quickly enough, he seemed only asleep. The cloth rested at Bennett's slim waist, exposing his nakedness, his vulnerability. A puckered bullet wound disfigured his flat abdomen.

When his gaze crossed a fist-sized hole in Bennett's chest, Baze gasped. Its black and red walls burrowed deep into Bennett, exposing severed sinew and dark marrow.

"He was shot once," Hamilton said, pointing to the abdomen wound with forceps. "It was only one strike, but its effects were fatal. Perforated intestines and internal bleeding. He didn't stand a chance." The doctor motioned to the hole that provided a gruesome window into Bennett's chest. "Now this was made with a small but incredibly sharp instrument." Hamilton paused, low brows shadowing his eyes. "His heart was removed."

Horrified whispers filtered through the room. Baze went numb. What sort of sick monster—

"I'm afraid that isn't quite all." Hamilton held up a small piece of crinkled paper stained red. "This was left in its place, tucked within a wooden sphere similar to what we found on Sergeant Moseley. It reads, 'Dear Baze, now I hold both of your hearts. Enough stalling. You know where to find me.'"

Baze trembled under the stares of every man in the room. This was it—a brand-new game. The killer knew it. Baze knew it.

Superintendent Whelan coughed, interrupting the hanging silence. "Let's move out, lads. We've work to do to catch this blighter." As the officers shuffled out one by one, Whelan clapped Baze's shoulder. The sudden touch interrupted his thoughts and made him recoil. Whelan pressed his lips flat. "That brute will hang for this, Ford. We'll see to that."

After the officers had gone and Hamilton had moseyed out for a smoke, Baze dragged a chair next to the table where Bennett lay. He slumped into the seat, and his bones creaked in protest. A weak sigh escaped his lips as he looked at Bennett. "I'm sorry, old friend," he murmured, not that it did any good. Bennett was gone. He wasn't here to listen anymore, so what was the point in talking? But . . . Baze needed to confide in him. One more time.

"You weren't supposed to go this early. We still had much to accomplish together, you and I." Baze reached toward Bennett's relaxed hand, hesitated, and then grasped it in both of his. The cool touch chilled Baze's skin, and he willed the heat from his palms to breathe life into Bennett's stiff fingers. "I told Emily. She took it as well as you'd expect her to. Her parents are with her and the baby now." His eyes prickled, and he blinked away the sensation. "I hope you settled on a name for your son. Wouldn't be fair to Emily if you left her with the task after the ruckus you raised." He breathed a feeble laugh, which echoed through the bitter, empty space. "I'll look after him. I'll look after them both. They won't want for anything. You'd do the same for my family—for Al." He squeezed Bennett's hand. It resisted the pressure, the flesh falling further and further away from life.

"I'm sorry I wasn't there for you, that I was such a coward. I'm sorry—" Baze's voice caught. He couldn't continue. Some mate he was. Couldn't even find the strength to say a proper goodbye. He bowed his forehead against Bennett's fingers and let fiery tears drip from the end of his nose.

Floorboards creaked, and wheezy breaths signaled the doctor's return. Baze stiffened, waiting for Hamilton's exuberant voice to slice the silence. But instead, a gentle hand rested on his shoulder. Baze tensed.

"Do not be ashamed to mourn him, my boy," the doctor said softly. "This body is but an empty shell now. Bennett is finding eternal solace in the arms of the Lord Christ. He will await the rest of us until it is our time. And what a grand reunion that shall be."

Baze pressed his eyes shut, trying not to let Hamilton's words penetrate his grief, but they'd already sunk deep into his soul like a salve. Bennett's soul was safe now, no longer privy to pain or sorrow or evil. It didn't make the pain in Baze's heart any lighter, but it allowed him to, for the first moment since this horrible nightmare began, turn toward the path of healing.

Praying was usually the last thing Baze wanted to do, but thinking of Bennett rejoicing in God's presence drew Baze's thoughts heavenward, even if reluctantly. *I'll give you a chance. You'll need to move mountains to convince me, but . . . I'm listening.* His breathing slowed as he pictured Bennett, so confident in his faith, before repeating the prayer he'd heard so many times before. *Almighty God, commit his spirit into your hands. Bring agents of evil to justice and heal the pain of this dark world.*

Baze squeezed Bennett's hand one last time—reveling in the feel, the familiarity, the reassurance—and then let go.

Chapter Thirty-Seven

THE NEXT MORNING, BAZE STOMPED UP the drive to the Spencers' front door. Low, dark clouds blanketed the sky. Rain soaked Baze to his core. His body screamed for sleep, and his alcohol-induced buzz had faded into a splitting headache.

Constable Rollie answered the door, tugging at the tight collar around his neck.

Baze blew rain out of his eyes. "You called for me?"

Rollie shifted his feet. "She's not here, Ford."

"Who's not here?"

"Miss Spencer."

Baze's stomach tightened. "Have you checked her father's study?"

"Yes. Nothing." He cleared his throat. "Mrs. Spencer said she heard her come in, but we haven't been able to locate her since."

Baze fought off an overwhelming bout of fear. He couldn't let his mind go there, not yet. "Did Mrs. Spencer say anything about Adelynn's state, what she was doing when she arrived?"

"Said something about her sounding upset, crying maybe."

If that were the case, there was only one place Adelynn would go. "I'll find her. Keep watch over Mrs. Spencer."

Baze braved the rain once again and hurried along the path to the garden between their homes. Thunder seemed a mere rumble compared to the roaring in his chest. What would happen if he found her? How could he possibly comfort her when he himself felt crushed by sorrow?

The hedge came into view around the corner, as large and groomed as it had been when they were children. The tunnel entrance still gaped in the center.

What if she *wasn't* there? His mind drifted to the possibility of that madman finding her first.

No. Pushing aside his fears, he crouched into the foliage tunnel. It took but a moment to locate her. Though the hedge offered some shelter from the downpour, water dripped from her arms, crossed over bent knees. Her dress clung to her shivering form. Clumped hair fell loose around her face and quaking shoulders.

She stared at the ground, eyes red, tears spilling down her blotchy cheeks. As she met his gaze, her expression crumpled, and she broke into a heavy sob. Baze crawled to her side and surrounded her with his arms, holding her as tightly against him as he could without hindering her precious breath. She buried her face into his chest and cried, her muffled wails vibrating through him.

Be strong, Baze. She needs you now.

Echoing Hamilton's confident sentiments, Baze whispered against her hair. "We'll miss him. We'll miss him so much that it aches, but Bennett would not want us to mourn for him. He's rejoicing in heaven. Our pain hurts for now, but that will pass in time."

I wept as thunder echoed above and rain drummed the earth, but eventually, I quieted. Baze's words struck a chord deep within me. The notion of Bennett being safe in heaven breathed a touch of healing into my grief-stricken heart. But to think of him in heaven was to think of him gone from this world—forever.

I shook my head against the wet fibers of Baze's coat. "If only I could have seen it sooner. Maybe I—"

"No, Al. Don't talk like that. If it's anyone's fault, it's my own." He leaned his head against mine, and his voice cracked as he continued. "Bennett asked me to go with him on that last assignment. I'm his partner. I should have been there."

A lump caught in my throat. "He would say it's no one's fault, none but the one who did the deed."

"That he would."

I pulled back and looked into his eyes. "Please don't do anything foolish. Don't . . . don't go after this man." I swallowed a new sob. "I don't want to lose you too."

He hesitated. "I have to stop him, Al."

Hot tears tracked down my cheeks, and he used a knuckle to brush them away. Closing my eyes, I imagined him setting out to confront the killer and never returning. The thought sent a pang through my heart. So much between us needed to be resolved. So much needed to be said.

I opened my eyes and traced his features with a fingertip—eyebrows, cheeks, and the uneven bone in his nose. Then I placed a hand on the side of his face, his jaw rough in my smooth palm.

"I love you, Baze." I sucked in a quivering breath. "I have always loved you. I need you to know that in case . . . in case you don't—"

"Shh." He pressed a gentle thumb to my lips before cradling my cheek, warming my numb skin. "I love you too, Al."

My chin trembled as new tears sprang to my eyes. I slid my hand around the back of his neck, then drew him toward me. He resisted but a moment before surrendering and capturing my mouth in a tender kiss.

Raindrops and salty tears warmed between our lips, but it was the sweet, slightly smoky taste of him that I reveled in. I dragged my hand down his muscled chest and took a secure fistful of his shirt. He tilted my head with a firm hand, loosening my jaw so that our lips melded further and he could explore deeper. Fire ignited in me—a desire for him, his entire being.

I began trembling—whether from the chill or elation, I couldn't tell—and when he pulled back, I realized my teeth were chattering.

"Are you all right?" he whispered, brushing aside my hair and tucking it behind an ear. His eyes, soft and rich as cocoa, held me rapt. "You'll catch your death out here."

I shook my head, urging my body to lie still, but it rebelled. "Don't s-stop."

Baze studied my face, his gaze lingering on my lips, before he pulled me tight against him. "I'll take you inside." After pressing a kiss to my forehead, he scooped me into his arms and ducked out of the hedge.

I clung to him as he made for the house, tucking my face into the crook of his neck, wishing that this moment would never end.

On our way to my chambers, Baze ordered a maid to draw a warm bath and fetch fresh garments. His muscles flexed as he gripped me tighter to his chest. Closing my eyes, I buried my face into his damp shoulder.

Soon, we entered my room. He laid me atop the bed, but as he turned to go, I grasped his hand. What if he walked out that door and never come back?

"Will you stay with me?" I asked in a mouse-quiet voice.

His gaze jumped to the washroom door and then back to me, redness creeping into his cheeks.

"After that, I mean," I added. "Will you sit with me? I don't want to be alone."

His eyes softened. "I shall wait for you in the drawing room. Take all the time you need."

And take my time I did, sinking into the steaming water until it poured over my head and covered me in a safe, quiet embrace. Despite the shrouding warmth of the liquid, a chill burrowed deep in my bones. My lungs began to ache, but I remained underwater, hoping for a reprieve from voices that bombarded me.

It's your fault.

You didn't try hard enough.

Baze will blame you.

I let out a yell in a flurry of bubbles—a mere moan as the water absorbed the sound. No, those were lies, insignificant lies. Enough outside forces had influenced my mind of late—Mr. Ford, Cornelius, the killer—and I wasn't going to listen to them any longer.

Heavenly Father, fill my heart and mind with your presence. Forgive me for my error, for submitting to my desires with Cornelius. Keep my thoughts on your light. Banish this darkness and lead us to this predator. Let us find justice. And for Baze . . . help us reconcile. Don't let the consequences of my mistakes drive him away. My lungs screamed for air. *And one more request . . . give Bennett a tight embrace for me.*

As though lifted by a firm hand, I surged upward. I broke through the surface of the water into the cool air and gasped in a deep, renewing breath.

Margaret had set out an ornate evening gown for me, but instead, I requested something softer, less formal. She returned with a dress featuring a layered dark velvet skirt, a jeweled silk bodice, and a relaxed V-shaped neckline. I wrapped a shawl about my shoulders to try to chase away the rain's chill that still gripped me.

As I entered the drawing room with footfalls softened by my thick stockings, Baze hurried to my side and escorted me to the couch. In the dim light of the oil lamp and robust fire in the hearth, I caught a glimpse of his clothing. Gone were the wet jacket and trousers, replaced by dry vestments. I recognized the shirt—it had been one of my father's—and dug my nails into my palm to keep from reaching to my throat for the necklace that wasn't there.

Baze propped up a pillow and coaxed me against it, then fetched a knitted afghan to drape across my lap. When he sat next to me, I readjusted, leaned into him, and lowered my head to his shoulder.

He relaxed into me, scooped up one of my hands in his, and massaged the palm. His strong fingers burrowed into my muscles and eased my tension. As Baze stared into the crackling hearth, questions brewed behind his eyes. "I've done a lot of thinking."

"Uh oh," I said under my breath.

The slightest smile tugged the corners of his mouth. "Bennett's been right all the while."

"Is that really so surprising?"

His smile grew a tad more, and he squeezed my fingers as though telling me to hush. "Bennett believed in earnestly pursuing the things that matter most to you, with God and with life. And I need to do the same." He glanced my way. "I've kept secrets from you, Al, but I need to trust you with everything that's on my heart."

I nodded against his shoulder, my heart racing.

"The honest truth is that I blamed you for keeping your situation hidden from me. If you'd only told me, I could have helped. Or so I thought. But my father had you cornered—had us both cornered. I was paralyzed by the control my father had over me, and I did nothing to break free of it." He sighed heavily. "My excuses can't make up for the hurt I've caused you, but I need you to understand why I acted as I did."

"Your assault?" I murmured before I could stop myself.

He stiffened.

"Percy told me. I needed to know what I was dealing with before I faced your father."

He nodded and picked at a knob in the afghan. "I've never been so terrified. I tried everything to fight back, but they . . . I thought I was going to die in that alley." He rubbed the bridge of his nose. "Father was the first person I saw when I woke. It was something in his eyes— something akin to disgust. I snapped, and from that moment, I was consumed with the desire to earn his approval, no matter what it took. Even as an adult, I guess that vow clung to me in my subconscious, but now I see the folly of my ignorance. I hurt you beyond measure. Nothing I could ever say would express how sorry I am."

Tears rushed to my eyes as his words washed over me. This was his whole heart—pure and sincere. I entwined our fingers, lifted my head, and met his gaze. "I forgive you."

He furrowed his brow. "Just like that?"

"Just like that." I smiled. But as I looked into his eyes, a knot formed deep within me. More yet remained to share, this time of my own dark secrets. I lowered my gaze. "I must ask your forgiveness as well."

His eyebrows rose. "It appears tonight is one of confessions."

"Bennett has . . ." I paused. New tears threatened to form. "*Had* that effect on people."

He swallowed, fresh memories of Bennett likely conjured by my blunder, but he squeezed my hand and nodded.

"I kissed Cornelius." Nausea twisted my stomach. "It was soon after I confronted your father—and after you walked out. I was hurt and angry, so when I encountered him, I was vulnerable."

Baze stared forward into the fire, jaw tensing, eyes hardening. "After I found you with him at the pub, I wondered . . ." He pulled his hand away from mine. "Do you love him?"

"No. No, of course not." My pulse quickened. How could I explain myself without driving Baze away? I sat up and touched his wrist. "I was drawn to him but not out of love. He was alluring, and he knew the correct words to say to inflame my desires. That's not an excuse. I chose to employ poor judgement and gave in to those desires—impure as they were. You don't know how many times I've prayed that I could be worthy of forgiveness from God . . . and from you. I'm sorry."

The fire glistened on the gathering moisture in Baze's eyes. "I hate that he seduced you. And I hate that you gave in to him." His bitter tone sent a pang through my heart, but when he spoke again, his voice softened. "Though, it appears we've both displayed poor judgment as of late." He reached for my hand, linked our fingers, and squeezed. "I'm confident that God has forgiven you, and I do as well."

A sob expanded in my chest as I pressed my forehead against Baze's shoulder. God's forgiveness had already begun to mend the guilt that had weighed down my heart, but Baze's forgiveness swept away my lingering emotions.

"I have one final item to address." Baze chewed his lip and shifted his eyes. "The last time Bennett and I met, he gave me some hard advice—advice I didn't want to hear, much less follow." He swallowed. "But he was right, as usual. And before anything else happens, I'm going to act." He leaned forward, but I gripped his hand to keep him in place. "You'll need to let me up."

"Surely you can do whatever it is you want from here?"

His eyes grew determined. "I didn't get the chance to do this properly last time, so I would like the opportunity now."

Curiosity paralyzed me long enough for him to pull away and slide to the floor beside me—on a single knee. My breath caught.

"I love you, Adelynn Spencer." He gazed at me with those affectionate russet eyes, eyes that sent my heart aflutter with each glance. "I've loved you for what seems like an eternity, and that love has only grown."

He reached into his pocket—his eyes never leaving mine—and produced a polished gold ring. A single white pearl and iridescent diamonds adorned the band.

I gasped. "Is that—"

"One of the pearls from your father's necklace. I managed to recover it that night you were attacked. Even though we'd been driven apart, I clung to the hope I hadn't lost you forever." With trembling hands, he slid it onto my finger. "Will you do me the honor of becoming my wife?"

Time stood still as I lifted my hand and studied the ring. Three diamonds—an elegant teardrop gem set between two smaller round ones—framed the luminescent pearl in a half-moon curve. The silver band swooped inward and connected where jewel met pearl. Unlike the ring purchased by Mr. Ford, this one fit perfectly and comfortably. Confidence squared my shoulders, a reassurance I hadn't felt in ages. This was my choice and mine alone. No blackmail, no manipulation—only freedom.

I cupped his jaw with a hand as my chin quivered. "Yes. Absolutely, yes."

A dazzling smile lit his features as he grasped my face and kissed me. His day-old stubble scratched my chin. The faint scent of rain, cedarwood, and citrus lingered on his skin as I breathed him in. I explored across his mouth, but he was quick to readjust and capture my wayward lips snugly under his.

I pulled back to catch my breath. Baze eased onto the edge of the couch, leaned over me, and used a knuckle to brush aside stray tears I wasn't even aware had fallen. He studied me. "You're sure about this?"

I sniffled, my vision blurring. "I've never been so sure of anything."

I barely had time to get the words out before he collected my again lips with his. Heat prickled on my cheeks, my limbs, as his kiss deepened.

When we parted, Baze nudged my nose with his and touched our foreheads together. I closed my eyes. We were betrothed—officially and honestly this time. "I love you, Basil Ford."

"I love you, Al," he whispered back.

I jolted. Darkness consumed me.

No!

I lurched from my body, forced into the persona of the psychopath that I so frequently embodied, looking through the eyes that I always peered through when someone was about to die.

Please, no more!

I stood directly outside the French doors. Raindrops dripped from my brow as I peered through the fogged window, watching our engagement like a predator in the night, resting back on my haunches ready to pounce.

Baze frowned, spoke, and touched my face, while I—the other me—lay limp in his arms.

Then, just like that, I lurched back, staring up at Baze, gasping.

He went pale. "What did you see?"

"He's here." I scrambled out from under the afghan and vaulted to my feet. Baze stood with me as I clung to his forearms. My eyes locked on the French doors where a shadowed form loomed on the other side. "He's here!"

Baze swore and pawed at his belt. He snatched up his gun and backed against me, his body a shield between me and the door.

Tense seconds passed. The figure reached forward. Scraping sounds emanated from the door handle. It rattled and shook, then released a click. The door opened.

With a reassuring hand touching my waist, Baze held the other aloft with the weapon. "Show yourself," he shouted, voice strong but quivering. "Show your face, you monster."

I held my breath as the figure opened the door a bit more and hesitated . . .

Then Finn stepped into the light.

"No." My hands flew to my mouth.

Baze's fingers dug into my waist.

Finn watched us calmly, eyes hazy and dull. The heavy rain crushed his curls and weighed down his posture. With ashen skin, he wavered on his feet. One hand clutched weakly at his left side. After studying us a bit, he said, "Why so hesitant, Inspector? Go on, then. Make your arrest." He held out upturned wrists. "Isn't that what you do to murderers?"

Chapter Thirty-Eight

SHADOWS CAST BY THE HANGING LANTERN'S single flame fluttered across the prison cell's weeping walls. Despite the arched ceiling, the tight quarters grew smaller with every passing second. Wrought-iron bars stood guard over the single opaque window. Droplets plunked into a metal basin on the wall as odors from the unwashed chamber pot and neighboring cells permeated the air.

Balancing carefully on the hammock lined with a flat mattress and moldy blanket, I kept a trembling hand clamped over my bullet wound and stared at Detective Inspector Basil Ford.

Basil stared back, muscles jerking in his jaw. Dark semicircles bordered bloodshot eyes. Sleep deprived? Ill, perhaps? No. Only haunted by his best mate's final breath and memories of his fiancée's sweet kiss.

Adelynn. *Her horror at seeing me had almost been enough to interrupt my trance, especially when her prior words came rushing back.* "You can be saved."

"You killed four men." Basil's voice shattered the light of Adelynn's memory. "Good men. Sons. Fa—" His voice rasped and caught. "Fathers."

The cell door creaked. Bumped by the constable keeping watch?

"Why?" Basil clenched a hand into a fist. "Why take the life of another?"

Why, indeed.

Haze tinged the edges of my vision. Pain slithered up from my wound to pierce my skull. I winced. Lingering threads of resistance dissolved within me, surrendering to the pull I had so long withstood.

The faint light emanating from the lantern began to glisten in Basil's eyes. Crying? So unbecoming for a detective inspector. I blinked and watched a decision cross his features.

He lunged on top of me, throwing me deep into the clutches of the hammock, jamming a hand around my throat. A stray tear leapt from his lashes onto my cheek. Then anger chased the sorrow from his features. "Nothing we do to you could ever match what you did to those innocent people," he spat. "We'll hang you for this, and I hope you feel the snap of the rope as you fall."

A twinge of fright gripped me as Basil's eyes flashed. No, wait. I didn't—

"I hope you feel every one of their lives as yours is pulled down into the deepest, darkest corner of hell."

Wait, it wasn't—

Basil brought a hard fist down on my wound. Fire ignited. I screamed.

A blur of limbs yanked Basil from my hammock, out of my cell. The door slammed. Then silence.

I lay there, numb. Veins throbbed and boiled. He was right. I had no way out. I was destined for eternal darkness. No savior could pull me back from the brink.

Chapter Thirty-Nine

THE DYING FIRE SWAYED IN THE hearth, coaxing my gaze to follow it back and forth as I curled up in Father's armchair. As the flame's edges dimmed and softened, my mind drifted to Baze. I ignored the open book in my lap and caressed my new ring, the pearl smooth and cool beneath my fingertip. I breathed in, my chest swelling with the joy of our recent betrothal—but my exhale brought with it the sting of our recent loss.

And Finn . . . oh, Finn. I'd prayed he wouldn't be the one, that he hadn't been capable of such atrocities. I'd glimpsed sincerity through his music that night at the pub, and when he'd assisted with Emily and the baby, his heart had unfurled in genuine hope. Or so I'd thought. It appeared now to have been a devious façade.

I closed my eyes and replayed the events of last night—when Baze had wrestled Finn to the ground and secured his wrists in handcuffs.

"Oh, Father God," I whispered, stroking the pearl, "what is this world coming to?"

Someone knocked on the door.

I sat up straighter. "Enter."

The butler came in and approached, carrying a silver tray. A sealed letter rested on the bright metal. He bent and offered it to me.

A letter at this hour? But it was nearly sundown. I took the envelope, expressed my gratitude, and dismissed him. When I was alone, I broke open the crude wax seal. A key tumbled out and onto the floor. I stooped to retrieve it before reading the sloppy writing.

Miss Spencer, you have the wrong man. Finn Kelly is innocent. You must go to him at once or more innocent lives will be lost. Once you have discovered the truth, gather the police and come to the Empress. I've enclosed a key. Time is of the essence. — S

I lurched to my feet. The book thumped to the floor. Finn was innocent? But on what grounds? And if he wasn't the guilty party . . . then it meant the murderer still roamed free.

Sickness roiled my stomach. Who could have sent the letter? Who was close enough to Finn to have this insight?

Siobhan?

It made sense. Assuming the murderer lurked within the walls of the Empress, she would know better than anyone. Unless she herself was the killer. Of course, all of that hinged upon the letter being authentic. Perhaps it had been penned to confuse me.

Blood pumped hot through my veins. I clutched the key in a trembling fist.

I had to find out for sure. I had to get to Finn.

When I didn't find Baze at his home, I enlisted Samuel to take me to New Scotland Yard. The red-bricked buildings loomed in the shadows of dusk, haloed by the rays of the sinking sun. Inside, I searched for Baze, but he wasn't among the few officers who labored at their desks. The clicks of a typewriter drifted out from the open door of Superintendent Whelan's office. I tiptoed over the threshold and knocked softly.

Whelan looked up from where he sat hunched over his desk, a cigarette dangling from his lips. He rested his forearms on the desk and sighed. Weariness clouded his expression. "What are you doing here, Miss Spencer?"

"I need your help," I said with a quiet, calm tone as I sank into the chair before his desk. "That man Baze arrested for those recent murders, Finn Kelly . . . he may be innocent." I squeezed a fist in my lap. "I need to speak with him."

Whelan's features remained stoic as he plunked out a few more words on the typewriter. The machine gave a hollow ding, and he reset the carriage. Then he took a long draw on his cigarette, exhaled a plume of smoke, and tamped it out in a nearby ashtray.

I crinkled my nose and resisted the urge to cough.

Leaning back, Whelan stroked his full, gray sideburns. He linked his fingers over his stout stomach. "After all this started"—his voice growled as he spoke low—"Inspector Bennett kept me privy to what you two were doing."

I widened my eyes. Chills tingled on my skin. "He told you?"

"Everything." Whelan cleared his throat. "He was a good officer. Wanted me involved in case it escalated out of his control."

Trepidation, and perhaps relief, fluttered in my chest. All this time, I hadn't been as alone as I'd thought. "So you know about my—"

"*Everything*, Miss Spencer." Whelan's eyes reflected an amused sparkle. "Can't say I understand it, but you're connected to all this somehow . . . which means I trust you." He set his mouth in a straight line. "Now what's this about our suspect?"

Tears prickled in my eyes, likely triggered by the smoke lingering in the air—and my desire to right these wrongs. I laid Siobhan's letter upon the desk. "He may be innocent. And if that's the case . . ."

Whelan's nose whistled as he breathed heavily and lifted the note. He read slowly— brow furrowed, eyes narrowed, mouth twisted. Then he heaved out of the chair with a grunt and tugged up his trousers. "We'd best get a move on."

I trailed close behind Superintendent Whelan as we shuffled through the left wing of Pentonville Prison. Dim torches lit the way. Our footsteps echoed within the bare, stone walls. Whelan checked back over his shoulder. "Stay close."

I sidestepped a stagnant puddle in the uneven floor and quickened my pace, clamping a hand over my nose. The smell curdled my stomach—human waste, rotten food, mildew. Mold grew along cracks in the walls. Rusted doors with barred windows lined each side of the corridor, housing grimy criminals who sneered and whistled as we passed.

Whelan slowed, ticked my shoulder, and pointed to the last cell on the right. "He's there."

I rushed to the barred window and rose on my tiptoes to peer inside. Candlelight illuminated a hunched figure on the ground. With arms wrapped about his torso, Finn rocked back and forth on his knees and mumbled to himself.

"Finn! It's Adelynn. Are you all right?" He didn't respond, continuing to rock. "Can you hear me?" Again, no response. I looked to Whelan. "Let me in."

He shook his head. "That's not a good idea."

"Please." I tightened my grip on the bars. "Otherwise we've come all this way for nothing."

With a sigh, he dragged out his keyring. "I'm coming in with you."

As soon as the door opened, I dashed inside, lowered to my knees in front of Finn, and grasped his shoulders. "Finn, it's me. Say something."

Slowly, Finn lifted his head. Ratted, limp curls covered his ashen face. His gaze locked on mine. Thick veins reddened the whites of his eyes. His irises, devoid of color, swam empty behind a dead fog. Salt trails paved marks down his cheeks.

All words stuck in my throat. My lips quivered, body paralyzed.

"Adelynn?" Finn's voice grated like chalk drawn crooked against a blackboard. He cringed, lashed out, and gripped my upper arms.

"Hands off." Whelan tore Finn away and shoved him to the floor.

"Stop!" I rose, stepped between them, and gave Whelan a pleading look. "Please, give us a moment."

He tensed his jaw but nodded.

Finn wavered up to his knees, a hand over his forehead. "He's in my head, Adelynn." His chest heaved. "Get him out of my head!"

I eased closer to him. "Who's in your head?"

"Please." Tears rolled down his cheeks. "I can't escape." He lowered his face into both hands and yelled through clenched teeth.

My heart raced. A strange sense of calm fell over me. I knew what he needed. It was what he'd needed all along—but what he'd resisted thus far. Would his heart finally soften toward salvation?

I gave Whelan a reassuring nod before kneeling beside Finn and taking hold of his forearms. "There is hope for you. You are not yet lost. You know what must be done."

He shook his head, voice muffled in his palms. "He . . . He wouldn't save someone like me. I'm not . . . not worthy."

"Whatever you've done that makes you believe you will be excluded from grace, it's not too much. Jesus ensured that. He died for that—for *you*."

"Adelynn—"

"Please, Finn." I struggled to maintain an even tone. "The Almighty's light is stronger than any darkness the evil one throws at us. Don't underestimate that power, and don't throw away your chance at redemption for fear of rejection. Your life is too valuable. It is worth saving."

Body shaking, Finn raised his head and looked me in the eyes. Thick tears pooled in his. Breath rasped in his chest. He had the look of a man who no longer wanted to live, and for a moment, I thought he would give up.

But then he nodded. "I want to be saved." His words trembled. "I'm done walking in darkness."

I nearly laughed out loud in joy. Instead, I kept my expression calm. Gently, I placed my hands on either side of his face and squeezed my eyes shut. *Give me the right words to say.*

"Almighty Father, I come to you in humble obedience and great need. Finn's mind has been taken captive by a great evil, but now he wants to walk in the light. His heart, body, mind, and soul are yours now. Deliver him from this darkness." A cool draft raised gooseflesh on my arms. Finn grasped my arms and whimpered. "Extend your grace. Cast out the darkness that poisons his mind. Create in him a clean heart and renew his spirit."

His voice barely audible, Finn whispered, "Please . . . save me . . ."

A burst of light illuminated the cell. Wind swirled about us in a funnel. Finn's screams faded into the roar. We clung to each other as the gusts heightened.

Then it ended. The light faded. The wind dissipated. Finn sank forward against me. I clutched his shoulders and pushed him upright, holding his head steady. Eyes shut, eyebrows drawn, Finn appeared asleep, perhaps unconscious. Had his mind been so overwhelmed that it blacked out?

Say something, I urged silently, brushing away drying tears from his cheeks. *Open your eyes. Look at me. Lord, let him live.*

Finn snapped upright, gasping in a breath. I yanked my hands back. He opened his eyes and gaped. His chest heaved.

For the first time, the haze lifted. Strength, vitality, and fervor churned in his striking eyes—eyes the color of the sea on a warm, sunny day. For so long, he'd been burdened by the influence of darkness. But now he sat before me basking in the light.

A coughing fit overtook Whelan. When he recovered, he muttered under his breath, "I think I'll, ehm, go get some air," and shuffled through the cell door.

Finn and I sat in silence, staring into each other's eyes. Had I not witnessed such a display of God's power firsthand, I might not have believed it. But living proof of it sat right before me.

New tears glistened in Finn's eyes, clean and pure. Weeping, he pulled me into a secure embrace and buried his face into my shoulder. "It's gone. The darkness is gone. Thank you. Thank you, Adelynn." He drew back, now bearing a smile so bright that his eyes lit up like firecrackers. "Thank you."

I blinked away my own tears, smiling wide. "It wasn't me who saved you."

"But you never gave up on me." He stood, took my hands, and hoisted me to my feet. "I owe you my li—" He winced and grabbed his side.

The high of the moment dimmed as I led him to the hammock and helped him sit. I placed a hand on his back. "Finn?"

Waving me off, he smiled through clear pain. Now that the haze in his eyes had dissipated, every emotion shone forth like a beacon. "It's a fresh wound, so the pain is still great." He grimaced. "I will heal."

After such an uplifting encounter, any thought of death sickened me, but this had to be dealt with. My head grew faint as I labored to form the horrible words. "Finn, did you kill Bennett?"

Chapter Forty

BAZE'S STOMACH TWISTED INTO TIGHT KNOTS as he hastened to the mortuary. He should have made Hamilton send a courier. This was too soon. Since last night, he'd been plagued by a cruel juxtaposition of memories—seeing Bennett lying on the ground in his own blood but also thinking continuously of the feel of Adelynn in his arms. The thoughts tormented him. He wanted to mourn for his lost friend, but he also wanted to marry his fiancée and move on.

Inside the mortuary, he shivered at the chilled air and approached Hamilton, who bent over a microscope.

The doctor lifted his head, his bloodshot eyes relieved. "Ah, thank you for coming, my boy."

"I haven't much time, Hamilton. What is it?" Baze bit his lip. He didn't mean to sound terse, but he hadn't the patience.

Hamilton tapped his fingertips together. "I discovered something on Bennett's remains."

Discovered something. What more could they discover? Bennett was dead. The killer was behind bars. There was nothing more to discuss. Baze folded his arms. "Explain."

"As we established with the other victims, the murderer was in the midst of some sort of countdown." Hamilton paused as though gauging Baze's reaction. "In Bennett's chest cavity, I found the number two carved into his fourth rib." Hamilton stepped closer, holding out a hand. "Now, I know what you will say, my boy, but consider this. If the pattern is to be followed, there is but one victim left."

"That doesn't matter anymore." Baze massaged his temple. "We've caught the man."

"Yes, yes, yes, but he has yet to be tried and has not mounted a confession from his own lips."

"He told me to arrest him for murder." Baze pictured Kelly's proffered wrists awaiting his cuffs. "That's confession enough."

"On the contrary, your report recorded his words as being, 'Isn't that what you do to murderers?' Hardly a concrete admission of guilt. So there is a slight chance that an accomplice, or perhaps the real killer himself, is still at large."

Baze rolled his eyes and turned away, but Hamilton grabbed his arm. "Please, do not dismiss this evidence. There is one victim left, and throughout this whole endeavor, the killer has made it his personal goal to draw you in. For his every move, he has coaxed you to play the game." The old doctor's voice grew quiet and raspy. "I believe that you are his final target."

Baze wanted to dismiss the doctor offhand, but the statement gave him pause. If the theory that each victim grew closer in relation to Adelynn proved true, then it was entirely possible he came next on the list. Or Adelynn herself. Either way, they had their man, despite the doctor's insistence.

As if sensing Baze's decision, Hamilton's grip on his arm intensified. "Please, heed my words. Whatever you do to complete this investigation, I implore you to let others take control, or your life may be forfeit."

Finn took a deep breath before answering my inquiry with a quivering voice. "That is a complicated question that has an even more complicated answer."

"Please, tell me what you know." I took one of his hands and held it tightly between mine. "You owe me that."

"I do indeed." He took another deep breath. "My given name is Finnegan O'Brien. I grew up in Liscannor, Ireland, a poor village by the sea. I was but a child when I met a young orphan boy atop the Cliffs of Moher. He was so lost and alone, but I managed to save him, and he would become my truest friend. His name was Ciaran. You know him as Cornelius Marx."

"But . . . Cornelius is English." I swallowed. "He told me he was raised here in a wealthy home."

Finn shook his head. "Cornelius is as full-blooded Irish as I."

An invisible vice constricted my lungs. Numbness expanded from my core out to my limbs. I couldn't say I was entirely shocked, but I was upset that I had been lied to so extravagantly, so much so that I believed every word. Had anything Cornelius told me been true?

Perspiration gathered on Finn's forehead as his breathing grew labored. "Everythin' you think you know about Cornelius or me is wrong. In every tale he told you, he attributed his own childhood to me, but he was the one who lived that life. His mother died in childbirth. His twin sisters perished of tuberculosis. And his father was hanged for his part in the murders at Phoenix Park, but not before instillin' in his son the creed and vengeance of the IRB. After I met Ciaran and brought him home, me folks helped curb his grief. Until they were killed by an innocent skirmish turned rogue by English soldiers lookin' to pick a fight.

"We were taken in by a local IRB nationalist. He mentored us, taught us the art of illusion and how to use sleight of hand. But he also taught us his creed, his vendetta against England. Ciaran absorbed it all, and that's when he discovered his gift—or curse. Whichever you would like to call it." Finn clamped a hand over his wound and grimaced. "He found he could make people carry out his wishes, do things against their will. He could manipulate them to think a certain way, see certain images, or even act out, with just his will and his mind."

I pressed a hand to my chest as though to prevent my heart from pounding straight out of it. "So the victims who seemed to have carried out the deed on themselves . . . he was controlling them? But how is such a thing even possible?"

"Ciaran began to heal his emotional wounds in my parents' care, but when they died, something in him changed . . . something dark." Finn's gaze grew distant. "The extent to which he can manipulate one's mind is disturbin', and I'm ashamed that I allowed myself to be caught in that trap."

I shook my head, flashes of that last horrific vision coming to the forefront of my mind. "But when Bennett . . . in my vision, Cornelius didn't manipulate him. He used a gun instead."

"Inspector Bennett was different. He was like you—a strong mind, protected by a greater power that I never understood until now." Finn sighed and looked up at the ceiling. "Ciaran didn't count on that. He wanted to gain the advantage and make Bennett bend to his will. But Bennett always had the upper hand . . . hence the gun."

I closed my eyes, squeezing them against tears as I absorbed his words. "And my visions?"

"Ciaran's doing. He was able to plant the seed that night he met you at your engagement gala. You've been peerin' through his eyes, so he could alter your visions as he pleased. Even the last time, when I interrupted your moment with the inspector, he accompanied me so that he could further sow the seed of deception." Finn enfolded my hand in his. "He's been able to nudge you here and there, but beyond that, he hasn't been able to seize full control. In fact, your defenses have grown stronger since that moment. That has only fueled his desire to conquer you. It's drivin' him mad."

When I opened my eyes, the tears came, hot and rapid. I swiped at them with my free hand. "But why me? I'd never met him before all this madness started. Why is he violating my life like this?"

Finn winced. "That I do not know."

I brimmed with such rage and incredulity that I wanted to climb to the rooftop and scream until my lungs burst. This wasn't right. None of it made sense. I had answers, and yet I had more questions than when I started. Why had Cornelius targeted me? And why had he brought harm to those for whom I cared?

"If Cornelius is the one who's been killing, then how did you get this?" I tugged out of his grip and pressed my hand carefully against his hand that clutched at his injury. Fear curled into a knot at the base of my throat. "It's the very wound inflicted by Bennett that night. He shot the man who shot him."

"Ciaran needed me to take the blame, if only for a little while. He told me it was for me own good and for the good of Ireland—and then he shot me. It would be my word against the authorities', and this injury would be the only evidence they needed." Finn trembled, sweat droplets crawling down his temples. "But rest assured. Inspector Bennett's bullet dealt the intended damage. Ciaran is weak and vulnerable."

"But why frame you? He's avoided detection on his own thus far."

"He knew Inspector Bennett's death would spur the police to heighten their investigation, and he needed time to prepare. There's still one more victim."

My mouth went dry. I swallowed, a lump scraping like sandpaper down my throat. "Do you know who it is?"

"Regrettably, I do not." He met my gaze. "But he gave me a message to deliver to you."

Filling the cell entrance with his bulbous frame and casting us in shadow, Whelan cleared his throat. "Best get a move on, Miss Spencer."

"One moment." I waved my hand at the superintendent and leaned toward Finn. "What's the message?"

"Now, Miss Spencer."

"I said one moment," I snapped over my shoulder.

Whelan held his hands up in surrender.

When I turned back, Finn leveled his gaze, mystery shrouding his eyes. "'We've come to the end, Adelynn,'" he said softly. "'You, me, your one true love. Meet Baze and me at the Empress.'" Finn grimaced, as though the words physically pained him.

I gripped his arm. "Baze is there?"

"He plans to lure Inspector Ford there and trap his mind. I imagine Ford's on his way there as we speak."

"I have to get over there." I stood and rotated, but he caught my wrist and shook his head.

"Don't go alone. Whatever you do, don't go alone. I've no idea what he has planned for you, but his mind is sick. Take as many men with you as you can." He looked behind me to Whelan, then back into my eyes. "And take your God . . . our God. The battle for your mind is only just beginnin'."

Chapter Forty-One

BAZE PULLED AWAY FROM HAMILTON AND smoothed his jacket. "I appreciate your concern, but I'm a trained officer."

The doctor knit his brow. "As was Bennett."

Baze targeted the doctor with a glare and started to rebuke him, but he was interrupted by swift, scraping footsteps and a young boy entering the room. With shifty eyes and a thin, timid body, the youngster offered Baze a brown paper package tied with twine. "Delivery for you, sir. Said it's urgent."

Baze cautiously accepted the parcel. "Who said?"

"The man what caught me on the street, sir." Eyes hungry, the child waited until Baze tipped him a sixpence, then scampered away.

Baze and Hamilton exchanged glances. One mystery after another. Would this never end?

As Baze yanked away the twine, Hamilton whispered, "Careful." The well-intended warning only made Baze tear into the package faster. When the paper fell away, it revealed a hardcover novel, *The Lost World* by A. Conan Doyle. Baze's suddenly weak fingers nearly lost hold of the book.

"What is it?" Hamilton asked, leaning in.

Rolling in his bottom lip, Baze lifted open the front cover. There it was beside the book's title, the inscription he had written to Adelynn before he had gifted the book to her. But below Baze's signature, a new black message marred the page, written in a wispy, educated hand—a handwriting he knew all too well. Baze read to himself.

Adelynn's company is quite lovely, Inspector. 'Twould be a shame not to invite you to join us. You know where we'll be. Come alone.

Fury brewed in the pit of Baze's stomach, a white-hot rage that seized his muscles and inflamed his heart. But they had caught the killer. Were they wrong—or was there more than one? Either way, a lunatic had Adelynn. God only knew the torture she was enduring in his clutches. Baze couldn't let his mind wander down the path of speculation, else he'd lose himself completely. An overwhelming bout of inadequacy marched its way up his spine. He'd failed again—failed to protect her.

"Now, my boy, you need to think about this." Hamilton held up his hands. "The man is obviously provoking you. Go back to your team—"

Baze hurled the book into the wall. Its spine snapped, and pages scattered across the floor. He extracted his pistol from his belt. Trembling fingers made checking the ammunition nearly impossible. His mind already plotted ways to enter the theater undetected, find that murderer, and put a bullet through his chest.

The doctor tried again, this time with a higher pitch. "Inspector Ford . . . Basil, please don't consider his offer. To go alone would ensure certain death."

"I have to protect her. I have to . . ." Baze's voice cracked.

"You don't even know if she is in his clutches, my boy."

"I can't take that chance." The words came out laced with more emotion than Baze had intended. He cleared his throat, but the suffocating lump returned. "I will go alone." Hamilton opened his mouth, but Baze lifted a hand to cut him off. "I will go alone, but I need you to inform the superintendent of my whereabouts. Have them storm the theater." Baze flexed and relaxed his hand, trying to stop the shaking. As long as there was a possibility that Adelynn was in danger, he would act. He glanced at the doctor and drew in a shuddering breath. "Please let me do this."

Hamilton's eyes widened. His skin paled, and he nodded. "Godspeed, my boy."

Chapter Forty-Two

RAIN DRUMMED THE UMBRELLA OVER MY head and soaked the officers' jackets as we surrounded the theater from all sides. I tugged my shawl tight around my shoulders and watched Whelan and his subordinate officers as they clustered together.

The superintendent's words rang sharp. "Taylor, Andrews, get your squads ready to start the search inside, provided Miss Spencer's key does indeed unlock the door." He motioned them to move. "Richter, take your men to the side door in case our man tries to flee. The rest of you, your post is here."

Thunder rumbled above as the overcast evening sky lit with lightning. I stepped toward the huddle, prompting the officer holding my umbrella to hurry after me.

Whelan sighed. "Miss Spencer, I said you could come along if you kept out of our way."

I pointed at the squads heading for the door. "I want to go inside with them."

"No chance. It's too dangerous." Whelan chortled and massaged his temple. "Not to mention Ford'll send the firing squad after me if I let you interfere."

"Baze would understand."

Baze most certainly would *not* understand. But this was bigger than him . . . bigger than any of us. "I've spent the last few weeks gaining the trust of these people. I know this theater better than any of you. And it seems I'm the object of Cornelius's obsession. Perhaps I could draw him out and prevent unnecessary harm." I touched his arm. "I'll be among the safety of all your men, and I will respect their authority. You need me."

Planting his hands on his hips, Whelan harrumphed. The other officers exchanged glances before looking to the superintendent. After a long pause, Whelan shook his head and aimed a finger at my nose. "You stay out of the way and do exactly as we say, ya hear?"

I nodded swiftly, stomach knotting. "Of course."

Whelan began relaying the orders to Andrews and his squad when a powerful prompting filled my chest—to lift our situation up and place it in divine hands.

I squeezed into their midst and, with a firm voice, said, "We need to pray before entering."

Whelan groaned. "We haven't the time, Miss Spencer."

"You need to make time." I held him in a pointed stare, then targeted others with the same look. "Our enemy uses techniques that are not of this world. Therefore, we need to do the same."

Several of the men shifted and scuffed their feet on the ground. The superintendent frowned but eventually nodded and gestured in acquiescence. "Be quick about it."

Aware of all their gazes upon me, I bowed my head and tried to keep my words from trembling. "Almighty Father, go with us into this place. Hold back the darkness and place a hedge of protection around the mind of every man here. Deliver evil into our hands. Amen."

Feeling invigorated, I glanced about. Some of the men stood taller, their chests fuller, but others displayed expressions of boredom or indifference. No matter. The prayer would reach them whether they wanted it or not.

"Right." Whelan clapped his hands once. "On with it."

As I followed Andrews's squad under the portico and up the steps to the front door, a sinister presence settled over me, heavy and suffocating. Whispers of surrender and hopelessness tried to sway my thoughts, but I filled my mind with prayer to stave off the shadows.

The doors swung inward, opening to a gaping black maw leading into the bowels of the foyer. Cold drafts poured out in waves as though something breathed from within.

Flicking on their electric torches, the squads stepped through. They held the door for me and then let them swing shut. The air temperature plummeted, chilling my body straight down to the bone. A few of the officers swore under their breath. The torchlight illuminated the large staircase looming before us like an impenetrable barrier. Thin clouds curled upward as the men's breathing quickened.

Andrews tipped his head at me. "Stay close to me, Miss Spencer."

I followed him without a word, praying that I'd made the right choice. I knew Cornelius's methods, his supernatural secrets, and these officers were going in blind. But hopefully our prayer had been enough to protect their minds. I was tired of merely witnessing from afar the horrors that Cornelius had committed. Now was my chance to confront him. He would not escape this night a free man.

My resolve strengthened. I walked with my chin up, close behind Andrews, who led the way. He hefted his torch and squinted into the darkness, mouth twisting in a puzzled grimace.

Andrews flashed the torch beam in my direction. "Another one of your premonitions would be handy right about now, Miss Spencer."

"I can't simply conjure them at will." I lowered my voice, shivering. "Besides, they only bring destruction."

An icy breeze swirled around our heads. Eerie silence enveloped us. Andrews swiveled his head and squinted. "Something doesn't feel—"

Every torch flickered and went out. Darkness engulfed us. Gunshots erupted.

"Get down!" Andrews wrapped an arm around my shoulders and dragged me to the ground.

I landed hard on my elbow and hip. Pain laced up my arm. Muffled shots and shouts surrounded us in chaos. I covered my head with a forearm, my cheek smashed against the cold, hard floor.

Andrews's touch left my shoulder. The men's cries and frenzied commotion threw me into a state of disorientation. Who was shooting at us? How many men had fled? Were there any casualties?

An icy hand clenched my upper arm and yanked me to my feet. I gasped in a breath just as a chemical-laden cloth clamped over my face. My throat burned. I tried to struggle, but my limbs already felt heavy— and within seconds, my mind succumbed to unconsciousness.

Chapter Forty-Three

QUIET SINGING COAXED MY MIND TO the conscious world.

"And all the harm I've ever done, alas, it was to none but me. And all I've done for want of wit, to memory now I can't recall . . ."

It was Father's song again—the one he'd sing to me before embarking for Ireland. I peered through my eyelashes and found that I lay stretched out on a single bed. The small, dark room contained a roll-top desk and a wardrobe. A lone wavering candle cast weak illumination on a shadowed figure in the middle of the room. Propping myself on my bruised elbow, I blinked and managed to focus.

Straddling a chair backward, his arms crossed over the back, Cornelius watched me with serene features. Candlelight gleamed across the whites of his eyes and deepened the icy stare, made more sinister by the raven hair twisting around his face and the somber melody trickling from his lips. Despite the warm light, his skin reflected a pale sheen.

"So fill to me the parting glass, good night and joy be to you all." He finished the lyric and flashed a crooked grin.

I held my breath and stayed still, as though prey hoping its predator wouldn't notice its presence. My thoughts were still clear at least. He had yet to penetrate that defense.

"So good of you to join me, Adelynn." His tone, now fully submerged in the accent of his homeland, dripped with condescension.

Head spinning, I sat up farther until I leaned against the headboard. The effort left me winded, and I battled the confines of my corset for a deep breath. "So, everything Finn said," I whispered, "it's all true."

Cornelius pointed to himself with an exaggerated gesture. "Pray tell, what has he been sharin' about me?"

Hearing the Irish accent pour from his lips—despite his retention of the English diction—threw fuel on my resolve. My gaze darted to the door behind him, which hung slightly ajar, then jumped back to his hostile eyes. Could I distract him enough to make a run for it?

Trying to keep my thoughts from translating to my expression, I turned toward him and draped my legs over the edge of the bed. "He said you've been manipulating us this whole time. That you lived as a poor orphan in Ireland and grew into a vengeful maniac."

Amusement colored his features. "He said that, did he?"

"Not in those words. But it wasn't hard to draw my own conclusions."

"Such a clever *cailín*." He rested his chin on his crossed arms. "Go on."

"He told me of your gift. Or rather, he called it a curse." With my peripheral vision, I tried to estimate the distance between the bed and the door—perhaps ten feet—and took note of where Cornelius had positioned himself a few paces in front of the bed, leaving the space behind him unguarded. Then I directed all my attention to him. "You can control people."

"That I can." Cornelius straightened his spine, but the movement drew a slight wince. His hand drifted to his left side.

So Finn had been right about that too— Bennett had managed to injure Cornelius.

A shadow passed over Cornelius's features. His expression grew intent as he stared. His eyes twitched. Cool air raised gooseflesh on my bare arms. Heavy pressure prodded at the barriers of my mind. My skull ached and my thoughts faded, but the defenses held.

Cornelius let out a humorless chuckle. "You astound me, Adelynn. You intrigue me." He frowned. "And yet, you aggravate me. I can control all but you."

"You couldn't control Bennett either," I snapped. "Isn't that right?"

He tapped a thumb on the back of the chair. "Yes . . . but how?"

"I think you know how."

With his gaze focused on the ground, Cornelius's expression turned thoughtful, distracted.

Now!

I surged to my feet. The room became a blur. *Ten feet to the door . . . nine . . . eight—*

The chair clattered. Cornelius barreled into me. His hands latched onto my arms and yanked me off the path to freedom and threw my back against the wall. He slammed his forearm across my collarbones. I wheezed. The force kept me pinned and trapped air in my throat.

"That was incredibly foolish." He clamped cold fingers around my jaw, his thumb biting into my cheek, and pulled my face toward his. Hot breath pounded my cheek. "You won't be tryin' that again."

Once more, darkness prodded at my mind, this time more forceful. Pain shocked my spine. I gasped and struggled beneath his hold. *Don't let him in. Protect me, Almighty Father.*

"Why won't you break?" Cornelius snarled.

I clenched my fists until my nails bit deep into my palms. "What's troubling you?" I said through my teeth. "Perhaps your power is failing."

"No," he whispered, as though to himself. "Such a thing isn't possible."

The jabbing force on my mind eased, allowing me a brief reprieve . . . and a window of opportunity. I jerked my head and caught his thumb between my teeth. I bit down—*hard*. He yelled and yanked his thumb from my mouth. While he was distracted, I threw a fist into his left side with as much strength as I could muster. The next sound out of his mouth told me I'd found purchase.

I sprinted toward the door and practically leaped the last few feet.

But just as my fingertips touched the wood, Cornelius caught me. His hands clawed for leverage. Fabric tore. Limbs flailed. His arm coiled around my waist and lifted. I thrashed, throwing him off balance. We tumbled to the floor.

In a flurry of swipes, he grasped my wrists and crisscrossed them against my chest. My back slammed against the floorboards. The force punched the air from my lungs.

Keeping my arms restrained against my chest—and thus keeping me immobilized on the floor—Cornelius used his free hand to clutch his side. He bowed his head and gasped in quick breaths. Terse moments passed before he peeled his hand away and examined the blood that had soaked through his shirt and now stained his palm. His eyes found me, rage and hate pulsing behind them.

I glared back, squirming. "Bennett gave you what you deserve."

He blinked, and then a chilling grin distorted his mouth. "Such hostility. I never thought you capable." He cocked his head. "Is there no forgiveness left for me in that bleedin' heart of yours? Or have you given it all away to Finn?"

I gulped in a sharp breath. I'd told Finn there was no wrongdoing that God's forgiveness couldn't touch. But what about in this instance? Cornelius had knowingly—willingly—taken precious human life. As I stared into this man's deranged eyes, it was clear the darkness permeated his very soul. Could such a man be redeemed? If it were up to me, I'd let him rot in a cell until death chipped away at him. But it wasn't for me to decide. God could save whomever He willed—but He was also a just God, and unrepentant wickedness would receive the punishment it deserved.

"It's no matter." Cornelius reached into his back pocket and fished out a rope about the length of his arm. "I've other plans for you." He began twisting the rope around my wrists. I resisted, but he shoved my chest, which knocked my head against the floor and stunned me enough to hold me still.

As he continued winding the rope, the sharp fibers chafed. I flashed back to when Finn had showed me the magician's tricks for escaping bindings. Could it work? I rotated my wrists and pressed out as much as I could as he looped the rope. It had already pulled tight, but perhaps I had done enough.

While he tied off the knot, a distant yell pierced the room from above.

Blood roared in my ears as the familiar tone piqued my senses.

Cornelius laughed. "Looks like your fiancé's decided to join us."

Chapter Forty-Four

WHEN BAZE ARRIVED AT THE THEATER, sopping wet from rain and sweat, he came upon Whelan and a cluster of officers. Fear deepened within him, numbing his body. Had they been tipped off about Adelynn's abduction as well?

"Superintendent!" he called as he approached.

Whelan looked up and scowled. "What are you doing here, Ford? We didn't call you."

"I got word that Adelynn had been taken." Baze entered the circle of men and tried to slow his breathing. "Is that why you're here?"

"You heard wrong." Whelan shook his head. "Miss Spencer's the one who brought us here."

So the message *had* been a ruse. Baze scanned the area, heartbeat quickening. "Where is she?"

Whelan sighed and stroked his mustache. "We sent two squads in to flush out this demented blighter." His voice grew low and gravely. "Miss Spencer went with them, but they were ambushed. They haven't yet emerged, but we can't go after 'em until we have more assistance."

Whatever relief Baze felt seconds ago transformed into new fury. They had allowed Adelynn to stride straight into danger? The overwhelming urge to break something, perhaps Whelan's arm—or face—strained his muscles. He lunged for Whelan and would have swung a fist at the man had several officers not yanked him back.

Whelan's skin turned bright red as he closed the distance between them, grabbed Baze's collar, and jarred him. "Try something like that again, Ford, and I'll suspend you faster than you can blink." He shook Baze once more. "Now get ahold of yourself. You're no good to Miss Spencer like this."

Baze pulled out of Whelan's grasp and allowed himself a quick breath to calm himself, unfazed by Whelan's threats but knowing he spoke truth about Baze's state of mind. Frenzied thoughts would only put Adelynn at more risk. He threw his arms wide. "So why are you lot just standing around? Our men and Adelynn are in danger. We have to do something."

"No," Whelan snapped. "We need to regroup and wait for more backup before going in. We have no idea what the others encountered in there. I'll not send you home, but you have to stay put and shut up. One more step out of line and you're on suspension."

The order stung, but Baze wasn't about to abandon Adelynn, even if it meant putting his job—and life—on the line.

"Sorry, sir." Baze looked the superintendent in the eyes, and Whelan's demeanor tensed as though he could read exactly what he was about to do. "But I can't comply."

"Ford, don't—"

Baze weaved through the officers and sprinted toward the door, leaving Whelan's irate shouts of protest behind.

He burst into the darkness without a second thought. The temperature plummeted. Each breath he took released a swirling puff of fog. His water-saturated clothes cooled and stiffened, injecting him with an unshakeable chill.

He ventured forward slowly, his scraping footsteps the only sound in the enormous foyer. A strange heaviness weighed down his shoulders, scrambling his thoughts. He blinked rapidly, hoping his eyes would soon adjust. His toes knocked against a small oblong object. Upon feeling around the floor with wary fingers, he discovered a torch and flicked it on.

What was Adelynn thinking coming here? For once she should have listened to his warnings. For once she should have thought of the effects that her actions had on others before rushing recklessly into danger. If only that wasn't one of the reasons he was hopelessly in love with her.

But if she'd fallen into that murderer's clutches, if he dealt her harm—or worse—there would be hell to pay. Baze would make sure of it.

As he used the dim torchlight to take in his surroundings, he came across lumpy ivory linens littering the space, as though it'd been transformed into an eerie mortuary. A pair of polished shoes protruded from under one of the linens. Baze snatched the sheet away. Andrews lay face up, skin pale, eyes closed. Prodding Andrews's neck with two fingers, Baze waited for a pulse. It was there but faint. As Baze scanned the rest of the room, scouring the space with what little light he had, he came across other bodies on the floor. A quick check confirmed that they were unconscious but alive.

Faint scuffles echoed in the empty space. Hair standing on end, Baze straightened and swept the room with the torchlight. He turned around. A shadow shifted on the edge of the torch beam.

Before he could move to investigate, a person came surging at him.

He stumbled backward and caught a heel on Andrews. The force dumped him on the floor. Lunging up, he grabbed for his pistol.

"Stop, Inspector Ford! It's Siobhan."

That Irishwoman? Baze hesitated and aimed the torchlight directly into her face, lightening her already pale skin and enhancing her piercing blue eyes. What was she doing here?

Siobhan squinted and blinked, her empty hands held aloft. "I'm here to help you."

He narrowed his eyes. "Why?"

"Because this needs to end." She gestured with a hand. "Come with me."

Baze stood, keeping her centered in the torch beam. He studied her expression—furrowed brow, tight jaw, hard eyes. He inched a hand to his holstered pistol. "Why should I trust you?"

Siobhan let her arms hang at her sides. "Cornelius is your killer."

Baze's mouth fell open. Sudden lightheadedness made him sway. Cornelius. But was she telling the truth?

"I'm tired of standin' by while terror reigns and innocent people die. Someone needs to stop him, and I can't do it alone." Sorrow washed over Siobhan's features. "And . . . he has Miss Spencer."

A terrified chill slithered up Baze's spine. He forgot to breathe for a moment.

Siobhan turned. "Please. Follow me." Footsteps light and soundless, she stole through the foyer and into the auditorium.

Baze hesitated, but the heavy presence he'd felt when he first entered the building returned, this time stronger tenfold. A slight pressure on his back nudged him forward. He resisted, only to feel it intensify.

Al is here.

The mere thought of her in the midst of this darkness made him give in to the pressure and quicken his pace. He tensed to try to stop his shivering. Above all else, he needed to get to her.

Dear God, keep her safe until I can reach her. And . . . help me succeed.

The prayer warmed Baze's core as he followed Siobhan down the aisle and climbed the stage stairs after her. The dim footlights lining the edge of the stage barely provided enough illumination to see. With the curtains drawn back, the bowels of backstage stretched deep and ominous. Near center stage, Baze noticed a square hole in the floor—the trap door was open. He let his gaze wander out into the empty audience, drowned in darkness and the unknown.

A hollow crack sounded. Siobhan grunted.

Baze turned in time to see her slump to the floor. Collin loomed above her, holding a thick iron rod aloft.

"Collin, what are you—"

The boy spun and lunged.

Baze swore and jerked backward, but Collin had already reached him. He swung the rod. Blunt force struck Baze's leg.

With a cry, he collapsed onto his side. Numbness laced over his kneecap and into his thigh. Dizziness and heat coursed through him. He ran a quivering hand down his calf until he reached something sharp and slick protruding through his pant leg—torn flesh and exposed bone.

"I'm sorry," Collin said a meek voice.

Trembling, Baze lifted his head and tried to keep his vision focused. Collin stood a few paces away, brandishing the rod. Tears streamed down his cheeks.

"Collin," Baze heaved through his teeth but couldn't continue. He tensed and bent his neck as another wave of pain shrieked up his leg and torso. He fought to keep his mind clear and his body from passing into unconsciousness. *Don't let this be my downfall. It can't be . . .*

"He's makin' me do this." Collin inched forward. With a shout, he attacked.

Baze barely managed to roll aside. The rod ricocheted off the floor where Baze's head had been and left a deep gash in the boards. "Stop this, Collin." Baze used his arms to drag himself backward. "If you stop, I promise to get you home—to your brother."

Collin let out a sob. "I c-can't . . . stop."

This time when Collin swung, Baze caught the rod and yanked. Collin lurched to the floor. Baze wrapped an arm about Collin's neck, pulled the boy faceup against his chest, and pressed his other arm to the back of his head. Collin whimpered and thrashed, fingers prying at Baze's arm. Baze gritted his teeth and tightened his hold. The boy's movements soon slowed.

When Collin went limp, Baze released him and checked the boy's pulse—weak but steady. That maneuver wouldn't keep him unconscious for long. He eased Collin onto the floor.

The leg wound pulsed. Baze's thoughts dizzied. *No. Get up. You have to get up.*

Rigid, he struggled to sit up. With a quick glance to ensure Siobhan still breathed from where she lay unconscious, he shed his coat so he could craft a crude bandage. The fabric resisted his initial tugs, but he soon tore into it and lashed a strip around his calf. He held his breath against the pain, lightheaded, but managed to finish, pulling it tighter beneath his knee to slow blood flow.

A clink and the whirring of gears shattered the silence. Dread settled like an anvil on Baze's chest. He raised his head.

The below-stage lift propelled two figures through the open chasm in the floor—Adelynn and Cornelius Marx.

When the lift settled flush with the floor, Marx forced Adelynn forward several steps, his hand wrapped around her upper arm. Pieces of her dress hung from her shoulder in tattered shreds, and her loose hair curled around her neck in unruly waves. Despite the restraints binding her wrists, she appeared unharmed.

Rage fueling each muscle, Baze shifted to all fours and reached for his gun.

Marx shook his head. "Stop where you are."

A thick, dark shroud encircled Baze's mind. His hand halted, fingertips nearly touching the gun but unable to grasp it. His breath caught. *What's happening?*

Marx grinned. "It was so good of you to come." The words oozed through his lips in a thick Irish brogue.

Baze frowned, trying to connect Marx's pale face with this new voice. An Irishman. And according to Siobhan—the murderer. All this time, the Irishman invading Adelynn's mind, the one leaving the notes, the one mutilating good men, wasn't Kelly. It was Marx.

Marx's smile grew. "Now stand up. I like to look my company in the eyes."

The dense force stabbed Baze's mind. *No!* But his body ignored the command and rose. Though the majority of his weight pressed onto his undamaged leg, his mangled leg bore just enough to exacerbate his injury. Pain bubbled up from his calf and escaped in a cry.

What's happening to me? I need to . . . need to get free. He struggled to hold on to clear thoughts as the pressure increased and his skull throbbed.

Marx eased a hand across Adelynn's shoulders and drew her close.

Baze's vision blurred as he watched her recoil. He pictured tearing that monster away from her, but his limbs remained cemented in place. *God, what do I do? Show me what to do!*

His fingers twitched.

Marx's icy eyes locked on Baze. "Your mind is mine now, good inspector."

Chapter Forty-Five

CORNELIUS'S ARM WEIGHED DOWN MY SHOULDERS, but I concentrated on Baze—his eyes bleary and face the color of ash. My gaze drifted to his right calf, wrapped in a bloodied rag. Oh, Lord, what had they done to him?

Trembling, I turned toward Cornelius. His aromatic musk—verbena and sandalwood—engulfed me, a scent that had once aroused my senses. Now it repulsed me. I squared my jaw. "You've got us where you want us, so tell me why—why me? Why do any of this?"

Cornelius's smile vanished. He lifted his arm from my shoulders and moved in front of me, still favoring his left side. He reached into his waistcoat pocket and flicked up a photograph held between two fingers.

Creases and scuffs marred the image, but I could barely make out the face of a young woman holding a newborn baby. Though she appeared much younger, I recognized the woman as my mother.

I parted my lips, prickling chills sweeping across my skin.

Cornelius stared, eyes moist but harsh. "My father didn't deserve to die for what he did in Phoenix Park. He was tryin' to protect his people. It was a just action to advance our just cause. He almost walked free, but a years-long search landed him in jail. As he sat in a prison in Dublin, I scoured the land for a way to save him. Supposedly, there were Englishmen who were on our side, who would fight for us. So I went searchin'."

His lip curled into a sneer. "Oh, I found an Englishman. But the man who I'd hoped would sympathize was the very man who caused my father's demise. He didn't merely let it happen—he ensured it would happen. So I followed him that evenin', after watchin' my father dangle from the gallows. I managed to pickpocket this photograph from him, the man I now know as Thomas Spencer."

Blood drained from my face. *Father?*

No. Cornelius was twisting the story, as he always did. Father fought to uphold peace and justice between our two countries. But to a child—how old had Cornelius been?—the only truth he knew was that his father was gone for reasons he couldn't have understood . . . and after he'd already lost the rest of his family.

Realization squeezed my chest. My next breath burned in my lungs. "You're the one responsible . . . responsible for my father's—"

Cornelius grasped my jaw tight with cold fingers. "Astute observation, sweet *cailín*. I tried to influence him, but I had to resort to hiring the IRB."

Crushing grief shook my limbs. "He was fighting for you. For your people. Had he let those men walk free for their crimes, it would have hurt the Irish cause more than help it." Large, loose tears spilled down my cheeks. "No child should ever have to go through so much loss as you did. But your father was a murderer. And mine fought for justice. He did what was right, and I guarantee you he would have done it again were he given the choice."

Cornelius blinked a few times, eyes distant, as though old memories flashed before him.

I adjusted my jaw as his fingertips bit deeper into my cheeks. Anger surged past my anguish. "You took your revenge on him. So why involve so many other innocent lives?"

He refocused on me, then shoved my head away. "Thomas Spencer took my father from me and brought sufferin' upon me and my kin. I was merely repayin' the favor to you and yours." Cornelius snapped his fingers in Baze's direction. "Inspector, why don't you be a good lad and take out that gun you've so desperately wanted to use. Careful, though. It's loaded."

Baze's hand inched down and unholstered his pistol. He closed his eyes and gritted his teeth as it rose and settled with the barrel against the underside of his jaw.

Father, release his mind! I screamed in my head. *Why are you allowing this? Free him from this influence.*

Movement flashed in my peripheral vision.

Siobhan appeared behind Cornelius, iron rod in hand. She swung at his left side. It connected with a blunt *thud*.

Cornelius screamed and went down to one knee.

Siobhan's fierce gaze locked on me. "Get out of here!"

I scrambled to the side and struggled against my bonds while Cornelius lunged for her. The ropes scraped my skin, and my wrist popped, but my earlier efforts had left just enough room to squeeze my hands out. *God bless you, Finn.* I sprinted to Baze and tugged on his gun-wielding arm, but his strength bested mine. The barrel stayed buried deep into the vulnerable flesh under his jaw.

Baze's eyes remained closed, brow drawn taut. He swayed slightly, and a small pool of blood collected around his foot. As a bead of sweat crawled down his temple, his lips moved in whispered words.

I leaned closer to hear. A prayer?

Siobhan let out a strangled yelp. I glanced back.

Cornelius had Siobhan pinned facedown on the floor with her arm held behind her back at an unnatural angle. He yanked her head back and then shoved it into the floor with a dull crack. She fell limp.

Cornelius snatched up the rod and marched to the edge of the stage. He swung at a footlight. It shattered and shot sparks out into the empty audience seats. The glowing embers caught hold in the fabric. Flames sprang to life. Pain tightened Cornelius's features as he moved to the next lamp—and then the next.

With each crash, I flinched and clung tighter to Baze.

Fire spread to the second row and traveled toward the stage. Cornelius tossed aside the rod, raked a hand through his tousled hair, and straightened his waistcoat. A bloodstain stretched across his side, his wound likely reopened further from the trauma.

Then he stalked toward us.

Spreading my arms, I planted myself between the Irishman and Baze. "Don't come any closer. You believe us to be powerless, but I think you know better."

Doubt flickered across Cornelius's face, but he recovered and said, "Baze, take care of your fiancée for me."

Baze's strong arm coiled around my neck and jerked me against him. I gasped in a breath and latched onto his wrist. His rapid heartbeats hammered against my back.

"It's time to make your final move, Baze." Cornelius's eyes darkened, and he spread his arms wide. "You get to decide the last victim. Which of us will you choose? Me, your worthy adversary. Adelynn, your sweet love. Or . . . yourself."

The crackle of flames grew louder as the fire devoured the fabric seats. Its harsh glow cast us in crimson light. Raw heat singed my skin. Smoke coiled around us, stinging my eyes and constricting my lungs.

Baze hefted the gun, suspending it near my head but with the barrel aimed at his own. His body quivered.

I readjusted my grip on Baze's wrist and squirmed. "You don't have to do what he says."

"He does, I'm afraid." Cornelius's lips spread in a malevolent grin. "I've spent many years perfectin' me gift, or curse, as you might prefer to call it. You created the perfect defense in your own head, sweet *cailín*, but you neglected your love. And as you found out, all it takes is but one slim openin' for me to take hold. Once I'm in, you've lost all chances. Goodbye. The end. Baze is mine now—forever." Cornelius dabbed at his perspiring temple with the back of his wrist. "Now, unless you want to be set aflame, I suggest you make your choice. No sense in all of us perishin'."

A moan emitted from Baze's throat as he inched the gun toward his head. I lashed out and caught his arm, but he proved too strong and managed to keep moving until the gun rested under his jaw. I pulled on his arm but couldn't make it budge.

"Please don't do this. He's wrong." Sobs built within me as his forearm compressed my throat. Pain wrapped around my neck. I gulped for air and choked out my next words. "Y-your mind . . . doesn't belong to him."

Baze's arm shuddered. His chest hardened as he held his breath. He pressed his face into my hair, and his breath warmed my ear as he whispered, "I know, Al."

I gasped in sweet air. Hope sprang to life within me.

Baze dropped his arm to my waist and thrust me behind him. He took aim—then fired.

Cornelius tried to sidestep, but the bullet tore into his shoulder. He yelled and recoiled.

No sooner had Baze aimed again than tension drained from his body. He sank to the ground in a heap, and the gun clattered from his hand.

I lunged for him but couldn't break his fall. On my knees at his side, I turned his face toward me. A thin layer of sweat coated his ashen skin.

"Run, Al." He pushed my hand away. His eyes rolled back. "I can't . . . I've lost too much . . ."

"It was a noble effort. I'll give him that." Cornelius clutched his shoulder, blood seeping between his fingers. "But it's probably best to put him out of his misery, don't you think?" He limped toward us.

"Enough!" I screamed. I vaulted to my feet and stepped over Baze. A burst of warmth shot forth from my core. "Your devastation ends here. The Lord will preserve us. With His provision, whom shall we fear? Certainly not you."

Cornelius halted and paled. "Stop this."

"You've failed. Don't you see?" I balled my fists at my sides as unconscious words poured from my lips. "We wrestle not against flesh and blood but against the rulers of the darkness of this world. Therefore, all power is given to us in heaven and on earth, the power to tread over all the power of the enemy." A benevolent force that radiated peace and courage consumed my mind. The last remnants of the shadowy weight that had plagued us for so long lifted from my shoulders. "Your power is useless."

Cornelius shuddered and teetered on his feet. Air cracked in his lungs as he wheezed.

I took a sturdy step toward him. "Turn yourself in." Though I spoke with confidence, my voice quivered. "Please. Put a stop to this."

With wary movements and dazed eyes, he closed the remaining distance between us. "Your optimism is commendable, sweet *cailín*," he whispered, "but no matter what I do now, I'll not be walkin' out of here alive."

"It doesn't have to be that way." I coughed as the smoke from the rising fire burned in my throat and thickened around us. "You can choose to surrender, to face consequences for what you've done, and turn away from this darkness."

"I'm afraid not." His voice rasped. "My soul was bought long ago. There's no life for me beyond this."

"There is always hope for those who willingly choose to walk in the light."

His mouth tipped in a tiny smile. "And if I be unwillin'?"

Stinging tears filled my eyes. "Don't." I shook my head. "Please don't."

He smoothed his thumb over my cheekbone, smearing a tear. "Save your sorrow for someone more worthy of your mercy, Adelynn. I've made me choice." His fingers drifted down my chin, then dropped and seized my throat.

A gunshot pierced my eardrums. I cried out. The force of the bullet hurled Cornelius backward, his fingernails biting my skin as his hand yanked from my neck. He managed to keep his footing, but as he clutched his chest, blood spreading across his shirt, his legs shook and crumpled. He writhed on his back—then lay still.

I spun to see Baze lying on his side, holding the pistol aloft. His eyes sought mine before he moaned and rolled onto his back. The weapon tumbled from his fingers.

I sprinted to him and fell to my knees at his side. Supporting his head, I smoothed the hair from his brow as my tears dripped onto his face. My thoughts swirled. Words formed, but I hadn't the strength to speak them.

The smoke grew thicker, the fire closer. It devoured the curtains near the balcony and moved toward the stage. Coughs consumed me. I peered through the haze at the limp figures strewn about. Siobhan still lay unconscious, but Collin had begun to stir. Then I fixed my attention on Cornelius's motionless body, his wide eyes unfocused, empty.

A distant crash sounded from outside the auditorium doors.

"You need to go." Baze cringed. "I can't . . . walk."

"No. I'll help you." I draped his arm around my neck and struggled to rise. Had we come this far only to be trapped here, destroyed by this raging fire?

Another crash sounded.

Baze tried to balance on his healthy leg, but it buckled. I sank under his weight. He removed his arm from my shoulders. "*Go*, Al." Desperation laced his voice. "Please—"

One more crash shook the walls. The doors burst open. Officers poured through.

Two men took Baze from me and carried him to safety while another swept me into his arms. I clung to him as he dodged the flames and transported me away from the fire, away from the stage—away from Cornelius.

We emerged into the calm morning air. The crisp breeze filled my lungs with new, fresh breath. The first golden notes of a sunrise sang among rolling clouds in the distance. Birdsong trilled, and the faint sounds of the city routine floated on the wind. Renewed energy coursed through me.

When I noticed two officers loading Baze into the back of an ambulance, I wriggled out of my rescuer's arms, dashed to the vehicle, and climbed in next to Baze.

The young medical officer gave me a look of surprise. "Uh, miss, you can't—"

"I'm coming with you." Emotion hitched in my voice, and I struggled to hold tears back. "You'll need to examine me for injuries as well, yes?"

"Very well." He latched the ambulance doors and set to work on Baze's wound.

I sat cross-legged and cradled Baze's head in my lap. Anxiety drained from his features as he peered up at me, his rich hazelnut eyes clear and alight. He reached up and touched my cheek. I covered his hand with my own and kissed his fingers, my tears dampening his palm.

"Praise God." He sighed and closed his eyes. "Praise God for everything."

Chapter Forty-Six

SILENCE FILLED THE ROOM WHERE I sat with Baze. Doctors, patients, and orderlies bustled outside the closed door, creating a small ruckus in the background. For the moment, our door kept the unpleasant smells of sickness and disease at bay.

Baze lay sound asleep, propped against a newly fluffed pillow, arms at his sides. Heavy bags bordered his eyes and worry lines etched his forehead. He still wandered through his unconscious thoughts thanks to the sedative.

Despite the cool air, his covers were drawn back to make room for his heavily bandaged leg. The surgery had been a success as far as I knew. The surgeon had managed to save the leg but had to wire the fractured bones together with metal and screws—a method that, while necessary, could lead to a limp or disfiguration. And we would need to watch him closely for infection in the coming days.

I stroked Baze's hand with my thumb and studied his face, going over every angle, every soft curve, every minute detail. Despite the wound, he was alive. We both were. In the moment, it had seemed we wouldn't survive, but God delivered us. Thankfulness and inadequacy overwhelmed me.

Yet, a ball of remorse twisted inside my stomach.

I hadn't heard the official report, but it wasn't likely Cornelius could have survived that kind of injury. That's what we had wanted— him gone from our lives, unable to harm anyone else. I should be elated. But despite his horrifying actions, his was another life lost. Maybe it would have been possible to save him if I had more time. Maybe he had been too far gone to be saved. I would never know.

The door creaked open. I looked up to see Siobhan leaning against the doorjamb, skin pale and face gaunt. Bandages circled her chest, and a sling cradled her arm.

"What are you doing here?" I exclaimed, standing. "You shouldn't be out of bed."

She entered slowly, the loose hospital gown swishing around her knees, and stopped at the foot of Baze's bed. "The nurse told me where you were."

"Doctors said you had a concussion. Let me take you back—"

"No. I wanted to see you both." She jutted her chin toward Baze. "How is he?"

Heaving a sigh, I sank back into my chair and returned my hand to his. "We won't really know until he can start moving around."

"And you?"

I met her eyes. We exchanged an unspoken acknowledgement, knowing exactly the kind of mending we would require—physically and mentally.

"Thank you for doing what you did," I said. "If you hadn't come, who knows what Cornelius would have—"

"Best not to let your mind go there, Miss Priss." She gnawed her delicate bottom lip and crossed to me. "I should be thankin' you. You didn't give up on us. Because of you, we're free of him." She grabbed my hand, squeezed, and let go.

When she headed for the door, I called after her, "Where will you go?"

She paused and looked back, her uninjured arm curling around her middle. "Home, I suppose. I don't have many pleasant memories of that place, but this time will be different. I'm done givin' myself over to men who would use me. Cornelius was the last. And again, I have you to thank for that." She smiled, one that lit up her features in a way I had never seen. "Take care, Miss Priss."

I made to call out again but stopped myself. What more could I say? She was at peace—another mind freed.

Muscles twitched in Baze's hand. His breathing wavered.

I gripped his hand tighter as his eyelids fluttered and he peered groggily about the room. When he focused on me, I smiled and whispered, "Good morning."

"Good morning." His weary voice grated as he spoke. "How'd I do?"

"Wonderfully. The doctor said you're incredibly resilient."

"I knew my thick skin would pay off one day."

I chuckled. "Now, if only there were something we could do about your thick skull."

He grinned, then slowly let it fade.

I sobered as well. I lifted his hand to my lips and kissed the rough skin of his palm. Tears blurred my vision. "Thank you." I hiccupped a sob. "You came for me."

Baze swiped the tears from my face with a thumb. "I will always come for you."

"But he almost . . ." I shook my head. "When he controlled you, I thought he was going to make you harm me . . . or harm yourself. I thought—"

"Shh, I wouldn't let that happen." He wrapped his hand around mine. "Surrender isn't one of my strengths, that I'll admit. I already had a rubbish earthly father, and I thought I didn't need a heavenly one mucking about with my life." The corner of his mouth tipped up. "But He kept nudging me. 'Twas about time I gave in."

A laugh emerged despite my tears. I leaned across Baze's chest and kissed him. His hand wrapped around the back of my neck, winding weak fingers in my hair. He melded his lips to mine, slow and gentle.

Our kiss cut short when he jerked back and sucked in a sharp breath. He pressed his head into the pillow and released a moan through his teeth.

I stood. "I'll get the doctor."

He caught my hand before I could go and tugged me back. "Stay. Please."

Those eyes were impossible to resist. As I returned to my seat, Whelan knocked and entered. "Apologies. I don't mean to interrupt."

Baze waved a hand and then let it fall to his side. "I appreciate your stopping by, sir."

"How are you, Ford?"

"I'll survive."

"No thanks to your bullheadedness," Whelan snapped, and Baze winced. The superintendent aimed an accusing finger. "You disobeyed my orders. You put yourself unnecessarily in danger. I won't have that in my precinct. Effective immediately, you're on suspension. You'll keep your pay, but I don't want to see your stubborn hide for a good six months." Whelan sniffed and stroked his mustache. "As it happens, that should give you time enough to recover . . . and then some."

Understanding dawned on Baze's features. He nodded. "Thank you, sir."

"I don't want to hear another word of it." Whelan cleared his throat. "Now, we've finished searching the theater premises. Most of it was damaged in the fire. We recovered Andrews's and Taylor's squads. They didn't remember anything about the skirmish, but they were otherwise unharmed."

"Thank God," Baze said through an exhale. "What about the boy? Collin?"

"He's put up at headquarters at the moment. We're trying to learn everything he knows. A little hard with the language barrier, but he's been quite cooperative. Keeps asking about you."

"Tell him I'll check in on him soon."

I laced my fingers with Baze's and swallowed. "And . . . what of Cornelius?"

"We've got him in the mortuary. Hamilton's conducting the full autopsy." Whelan reached into his coat and produced a photograph. "Told me to pass this along, actually. Said it would mean something to you." He handed it to me, then tipped his head toward Baze. "Good to see you're on your way, Ford. We look forward to your return."

"Thank you, sir." Baze's voice cracked.

After the superintendent left, I held up the photograph so Baze and I could see it. The image showed a top angle of Cornelius lying faceup on a table. A hole in his sternum indicated where the bullet had struck. But above the wound, positioned between his protruding collarbones, the number one was etched into his ashen skin.

A countdown. Baze had said it had all been a countdown. Bennett being number two in a descending count had meant there was one more victim, and at the time, I believed it would be Baze or me. But this tossed all that to the wind. If Cornelius had done that to himself, then had he been planning his death this whole time? Had his corruption been so deep that he clung to it even to the end, allowing no room for repentance?

Or . . . there was another possibility. That someone *else* had finished the countdown. The thought fired every nerve within me.

As my breathing quickened and my pulse raced cold, Baze snatched the photograph away. He crumpled it and set it on the side table. "Don't let him keep your mind captive anymore, Al." He placed a hand on my face, warming my cheek and calming my anxiety. "Cornelius is dead. It doesn't matter what he may or may not have planned. He's gone. It's over."

I opened my mouth to argue but then decided against it. Maybe I was thinking too hard on the matter. Cornelius had been unredeemable in his own eyes, a belief that had led to his somber end brought about by no other actions but his own.

Blinking away tears, I nodded. "I love you."

"I love you too." His tender gaze traced my face and settled on my mouth. His hand eased my head forward.

I leaned into him and surrendered to his kiss.

Chapter Forty-Seven

THE CHAUFFEUR PULLED THE CAR UP to the bustling docks at the Port of London and parked it alongside a stacked pile of crates. Baze tried to get the door open as he fumbled with his crutches. Before exiting the car, he looked across the seat where Collin sat, taking in the atmosphere with wide eyes. Baze nudged his arm. "Are you ready?"

Collin grimaced. "What are we doin' here?"

"You'll see."

Collin nodded, hefted the pack that held his few belongings over one shoulder, and followed Baze's lead.

Dockers, passengers, businessmen, and the like poured across every inch of the docks, searching out their correct pier, hauling cargo, and bidding farewell to family members. Constant talk, sloshing water, and calling birds created a chaotic but pleasant din. The smells of fresh fish and dirty sailors returned from long voyages mixed with the exotic aromas of spices, sugar cane, and other imported goods.

Navigating through the crowd on crutches proved more difficult than Baze had anticipated. He checked back to make sure Collin followed and then continued on until he found the right dock. Workers moored a small passenger ship and set the gangplank in place. Passengers began to file off.

"I'll say this as simply as I can." Baze turned toward Collin and set down the toe of his immobile leg to provide more balance. "With everything that has happened, you've demonstrated fierce bravery and maturity. What happened last month should never happen to anyone, let alone to someone your age. But amidst it all, you proved resilient."

Collin's gaze jumped to Baze's leg and then back to his face.

Baze caught the slight wince. He placed a hand on the boy's

shoulder. "Cornelius found a way into our minds. You and I have that in common." He bent slightly to make sure Collin looked him in the eyes. "This wasn't your doing. Do you understand me? Cornelius did this to me, not you."

Collin scowled. "Then why are you sendin' me away?"

"What makes you think I'm sending you away?"

"Why else would we be here? You're goin' to put me on a ship, aren't you?"

Baze fought off a smile. "On the contrary. We're here for someone coming off of a ship." He aimed Collin toward the vessel and pointed.

Passengers continued to disembark, almost all of them lower class. Then a young man with a curly mop of red hair appeared at the top of the gangplank and made his way down.

Collin's breath caught. "Liam . . ." His arms fell limp at his sides, pack slouching to the ground. "You found him. But . . . how?"

"I'm a detective inspector. It's what I do." Baze winked. "Turns out he's been looking for you all across Ireland. It was only a matter of—"

Collin threw his arms around Baze's waist, sobbing into his shoulder.

Baze fought to stay upright on the crutches but maintained his balance. He put an arm around the boy. "You deserve a good life. Now go home to Ireland, and start living it."

Collin pulled back and brushed a wrist over his eyes. Once composed, he said, "Thank you, Mr. Ford."

Baze ruffled the boy's hair and gestured to the ship. "Go on, then."

Collin raced across the dock. The moment his brother saw him, he dropped his sack and bolted down the gangplank. They met halfway and collided in a rough embrace. Liam held his brother in a vise grip and scanned the area. When he noticed Baze, he gave him a single nod.

Baze nodded back. Then the brothers pulled away from one another and started in on a rousing conversation as though they had never been apart.

Chapter Forty-Eight

I COCKED MY HEAD AND SQUINTED at my reflection in the full-length mirror while Emily worked to pin up the last-minute alterations of my wedding dress.

Ivory satin made my skin look sun-kissed in comparison. Long gloves covered my arms three-quarters of the way. The bodice, beaded with pearls and tiny white gems, angled down along my torso and disappeared behind a small sash at my waist. Lace adorned the bodice and encompassed my shoulders and neckline where a string of pearls perched. A silk train lined in lace cascaded in layers from where it attached at my waist. It almost looked complete, save for the missing veil and hair in disarray.

"Are we finished?" I fidgeted from side to side.

"One moment. Be patient," Emily mumbled, holding pins between her lips.

"I haven't heard a sound from the boys lately. Perhaps I should check on them."

"Hold on."

I managed to stand still for a few more agonizing seconds until she nodded her approval. I hefted the skirt, stole out the bedroom door, and headed to the nearby sitting room down the hall. Holding my breath, I peered around the corner.

Settled in the overstuffed armchair, Baze reclined and held Emily's son, little Basil Allan, in the crook of his elbow. Both lay still, eyes closed, jaws slack. I stifled a giggle and rolled my eyes.

When I returned to Emily, she raised her eyebrows in question. "How do our troublemakers fare?"

"Asleep. Both of them," I said.

"As usual."

"Now, can I take this dress off yet?"

She laughed. "Very well. Turn around."

While she worked to unbutton the back, we fell silent. I caught a glimpse of her mourning dress in the mirror, the black fabric a stark contrast to my ivory gown. It had been only six months since we buried Bennett and said our final goodbyes. It had been a pleasant, sunny day, though a heaviness weighed down all who gathered at the cemetery. The police attended in their formal attire. They awarded Bennett full honors and promoted him to chief inspector. Emily had been stoic, grasping her baby to her bosom as she watched the casket bearing her husband lower into the dark grave.

And now she was here, one of her first times entertaining company since that day, helping me prepare for the moment when I would take my own husband. It felt almost cruel. What right did I have to get married after my close friend had suffered such an extreme loss?

"Please don't pity me," she said softly. We made eye contact in the mirror. "And don't feel guilty."

I almost denied her insinuation, but I let my shoulders droop. "How can I get married so soon after everything that's happened?"

"You're living life." Emily paused to squeeze my shoulder. "In fact, seeing you move forward gives me hope that life can continue after this. After Bennett . . . well, after I said goodbye, I didn't think there was anything left for me in this world." Her cheeks flushed as tears filled her eyes. "But you and Baze, and my sweet Basil Allan . . . you give me the courage I need to keep waking up every morning. So please, look forward to your wedding and don't stop yourself from feeling all the joy that comes with it."

I drew in a shaky breath and swiped tears from my cheeks.

Baze's gentle whispers drifted in from the hallway. "You're already growing so strong, Basil. You've three names to grow into, you know. Your father was a cheeky scoundrel, giving you my name, but you're stuck with it. It's not so bad. And Allan—that was in honor of my nickname for Adelynn when we were children, you know. I was trying to cover up how I felt about her, but those women will best you in the end. Consider this your first warning." There came a pause. "But your father's name is the most important. Make sure to honor him with your life. It won't be an easy legacy to live up to, but don't you worry. Your mum, Adelynn, and I will be here to help you."

Emily and I locked eyes. She smiled. "He's going to be a good father."

My heart fluttered. "He will indeed."

Infant whimpers filled the silence. "Let's remain calm. You were doing well a moment ago." The whimpers transformed into a wail, followed by Baze's pinched cry. "Emily!"

We burst into laughter. I rolled my eyes. "He could do with some practice."

"Oh, I'm sure he'll get plenty in due time." She poked my side and headed for the door. "Basil Allan needs his lunch. I'll return in a moment to help you the rest of the way out of your dress."

After she'd gone, I turned toward the mirror and looked at my reflection. It didn't quite feel real, my standing here in this moment in a wedding gown. Baze had been quieter since that day he shot Cornelius. I couldn't tell if he yet harbored guilt, relief, anger—all of those.

To make matters worse, his father had managed to escape a jail sentence and promptly came after me to follow through with his threats. Thankfully, now that he knew his father's tricks and motivation, Baze had stepped in as my protector. But as a result, Mr. Ford had cut him off and all but cast him out of the family.

If only Baze would open up to me again, like he used to. We were about to get married. We should be able to tell one another anything. Maybe he wouldn't be himself until his leg healed. Maybe he would never be himself.

A soft knock shattered my musings. "Al?" The handle turned, and the door edged open. In a panic, I lunged and threw myself against it, stopping it halfway.

Baze chuckled from the other side. "You won't let me in?"

"Of course not!" I pressed my shoulder hard against the door, but it stayed put. "I'm still in my wedding gown. You can't see me like this yet. Not until the ceremony."

The door creaked and pushed against me. Baze managed to slide a foot through the gap. "Says who?"

"Says tradition."

"Forget tradition."

An abrupt shove gave him just enough room to squeeze through the door. I whirled but was immediately caught up by him, arms wrapped around my waist and torso, lips molding to mine. We shared this passion for a brief whirlwind until he stepped back and held me at arm's length, leaving my heart pounding and cheeks blazing. His eyes tracked a slow trail up the length of my body. When he reached my face, he met my gaze and smiled a smile that sent a warm tingle to the farthest reaches of my body and soul.

He gave a low whistle. "You're absolutely stunning, Mrs. Ford."

I smirked. "We're not married quite yet."

"Oh, you're all but mine already." He wound an arm around me again, stepped close, and angled his body into mine.

Then he jolted. A cry escaped his lips as his right leg crumpled. Entangled in one another's arms, we both collapsed. I landed hard atop him. Air punched from our lungs. He moaned as I pushed off of him.

"Are you all right?" I said in a rush. "Your leg—"

"I'm fine." He averted his eyes.

"I-It hasn't been that long," I stammered in an attempt to ease the tension I felt building in him. "It may need more time before it—"

"Stop." He gripped my shoulders to push me back as he sat up. Then he massaged his calf muscle. The metal holding the fractured bone together had corroded in the early weeks of healing. Emergency surgery had come too late, leaving the leg deformed and Baze with a limp.

He grimaced. "At least give me the common courtesy of not treating me like an ignorant schoolboy. I'm crippled, Al. Let me make peace with that."

I swallowed. There it was again, Baze's bitter persona that had emerged in the months after the theater incident. He'd come a long way in terms of accepting what had happened, but every time I watched him use his new cane, another anxious knot wound its way into my body. He was clearly trying to move on, so why couldn't I? Perhaps if I let him fully accept this outcome, then I would have to accept my own. Cold sweats while I slept. Waking nightmares that swooped in without notice. Emblazoned memories of that man's touch, his cruelty.

"We all came away with scars," I whispered. "I'm doing the best I can. But it's difficult when—" A lump in my throat cut off my words. I looked at him through blurry eyes and shrugged slowly.

Strain melted from his expression. He wrapped a gentle hand around the base of my head, burrowing fingers in my hair and caressing my jaw with his thumb. "We have yet to say our official vows, but let me make a vow to you now. We went through hell and back, and it left us wounded in more ways than one. But even though I am not whole, I will be by your side in every strength and in every weakness. I will lend you support when your mind brings you down."

His words calmed my distress. I slid a hand over his wrist. "And I will lend you my strength when your body can't hold you up."

A dazzling smile lit his features. I couldn't help but grin as well. Anticipation and excitement bubbled up from within, replacing the fears that had held me captive moments ago. I pictured the tender moment when we would finally exchange marriage vows, when I would take him as my husband and give myself to him in return—wholly and completely.

My cheeks warmed. I dropped my gaze and focused on my wrinkled skirt trapped beneath his legs. I gave it a tug. "Well, this gown is utterly ruined, and I have you to thank for that."

Baze laughed. "It was worth it."

Chapter Forty-Nine

London, 1914

BRILLIANT SUNBEAMS PAINED FINN'S EYES AS he stepped through the exit of Pentonville Prison and into the street. Blinking against the light, he waited until his eyes adjusted and the busy London afternoon scene faded into view. Emotion stifled his breath, constricting his gut. It had barely been a year since he'd seen direct sunlight, but it felt like an eternity.

Praise the Lord that the prospect of forgetting his actions, much less forgiving them, didn't seem so unreachable, not since he was saved in the heart of that jail cell. Dearest Adelynn. Had it not been for her faithfulness, he'd have given up and wasted away. She and Baze had served as witnesses in his trial, and by some miracle, he was set free.

Finn rubbed his smooth jaw and joined the flow of the crowd. Only yesterday, he would have stood out as a vagabond, but he'd been allowed a shower, a shave, and a haircut. Baze had even left new clothes and personal items for his use. The stiff trousers and waistcoat were more constricting than Finn was used to after the tattered jail garb, but the close-fitting jacket allowed comfort and dignity he hadn't felt in months. Finally, he felt like a man again.

Finn took his time strolling along the streets, enjoying the feel of sunlight on his pale skin, until he came to the pub they'd designated as their rendezvous. Inside, despite it being midday, the pub was nearly half full, mostly of older gentlemen. Finn selected a table for three near the bar and ordered a Guinness while he waited. Then he set to watching the people.

Most spoke in hushed tones in civil conversation, not yet to the point of a drunken buzz. Finn found it odd. These were normal folks carrying on with their normal lives, the events of the past already forgotten. Had they cared even as it was happening?

Cool air briefly brightened the stuffy room. Finn looked up to see Baze and Adelynn coming through the door. He beckoned them over. They walked arm in arm, a look of peace and contentment on their faces.

Adelynn looked as radiant as Finn remembered, possibly even more so. Her elegant green dress lengthened her form and increased her poise. Rosiness colored her freckled cheeks and lit up her sky-blue eyes. She saw him and brightened. She left Baze's side, hurried toward Finn, and went right in for an embrace. "It is so good to see you," she said in a rush against his ear.

"And you." Finn released her and greeted Baze with a handshake. "Thank you for comin'."

As they sat, Baze hung his cane on the table and reached into his coat pocket. He produced a thick envelope and slid it before Finn. "Your ticket is there, as well as funds enough to get you on your feet. I also included Emily's address."

Finn's heart galloped. He had requested it, yes, but the thought of seeing her again struck fear to his very core. "Thank you." He stashed the envelope in a pocket. "I can't tell you how much I appreciate your help, not just now, but over this past year. Your visits kept me sane."

"What will you do when you return?" Adelynn asked.

"Perhaps go home . . . to Liscannor. I haven't seen its harbors since I was a boy. Then find some honest work, modest work. I've no desire to stand out." The couple nodded as Finn downed part of his Guinness, letting its effects ease his muscles and warm his belly. "I shouldn't tarry long, but I wanted the chance to say a proper goodbye . . . and to mount an apology."

"Apology for what?" Adelynn blurted. "You didn't do anything wrong. None of it was your doing. We know that."

"Al." Baze touched her arm. She closed her mouth but screwed her face up in a scowl.

Finn fought back a smile. There was never a moment when she didn't amuse him. But he had unfinished business to resolve. "You know and understand my situation, so I am beginnin' with you before I confront my real test. Because of my actions—or rather, my inaction— you were pulled into a fight that never should have been yours. You were hurt in more ways than one, and I had a hand in it all. I've been readin' the Scriptures and am startin' to understand more about grace and forgiveness. So . . . I'm hopin', I'm askin', for your forgiveness."

"You have it," Adelynn said without hesitation.

Baze nodded. "You've had our forgiveness since the beginning."

"But it does a man good to hear it said aloud." Finn downed the rest of his drink and waited for it to settle. The alcohol soothed him, but he felt a deeper relief far inside where the liquor could never penetrate. His soul was finally starting to mend. "It's been a pleasure, Adelynn, Baze. I've never known two finer people. I wish you all the blessin's in the world."

No sense in drawing it out. Finn slid from the chair, gave them each a nod, and headed toward the door.

He'd only gotten halfway when Adelynn shouted, "Wait." She ran to his side, lifted to her tiptoes, and brushed a warm kiss to his cheek. "If you are ever back in London, please come see us. You have to promise."

Finn winked. "Anythin' for you."

She grinned and let him go. His stomach dropped as he left her behind, but he had to move forward. There was nothing left for him now. Once he completed his final tasks, he could be on his way. Baze and Adelynn would simply fade into a memory.

Outside, Finn hailed a cab and directed it to the address provided in the envelope. The closer they got, the quicker his heart beat until he was standing on the front step and his heart threatened to thump right through his ribs. Before he could stop himself, he rapped twice on the door with a knuckle—and instantly regretted it. She wouldn't want to see him, let alone listen to what he had to say. He was foolish to think this was a good idea. It would bring him peace of mind, but what would it bring to her?

Finn turned away, but as he started forward, the door creaked, and a soft voice floated out. "Finn?"

Gulping in a weak breath, he spun. Emily peered out from the cracked door, then opened it wide. Untidy strands of golden hair curled around her flushed face—a pretty elfin face that had captivated Finn since the first moment he saw it. She wore an apron over her mourning dress, but it had failed to prevent several flour spatters on the black fabric.

Finn took a step toward her, then froze. Words clogged in his throat. Everything he had planned to say rushed out of his mind. All he could see when he looked at her was the eager face of her late husband. Then the reality of what had happened to him rose to the surface.

Emily adjusted her stance so that she leaned to one side, gripping the doorknob until her knuckles turned white. But she didn't speak, only waited.

Somehow, Finn found the nerve to open his mouth. Whatever came out, he prayed it would get his message across.

"Emily, I . . . I'm after havin' been released from prison, and I needed to see you. I helped deliver your child, so I thought . . ." He winced. Not a great start. "I mean that to say, I didn't know your husband, but he was an incredible man." Better. "He wasn't afraid to put himself in harm's way for the sake of others. But it shouldn't have happened. He should have been there for his child, not me."

Emily stared with an unchanging expression. His pulse pumped faster, and instinct told him to turn tail and flee, but he had gone too far to give up now, no matter the outcome.

"I knew what Cornelius was plannin' the whole time and I did nothin'." Emotion cracked in his voice. "My inaction got your husband killed. Cornelius isn't here, so I will shoulder the blame. I know I have no right to ask you, or even speak to you, for that matter. But I will forever regret this moment if I don't." He paused to collect himself. "Adelynn showed me the power of a new life in Christ. It absolved me of my guilt, but it can't reverse the consequences of what I did. That's why I need to ask your forgiveness. I need to know if it's even possible. If not today, maybe someday you'll find it in your heart to forgive me."

Finn studied her stoic features, trying to gauge her reaction. She chewed her bottom lip and stared back at him. Silence stretched between them. His dry tongue thickened in his mouth. Eventually, he let his shoulders droop. So she chose not to. Should he have expected any differently?

Right as Finn turned, her lyrical voice called out, "Wait."

He looked back. She stutter-stepped through the door, then ran to him and threw her arms around his neck. Bewilderment paralyzed him for a moment. Finally, he gathered his bearings and wrapped her petite form gingerly in his arms as though she might break. Her body fit snugly against his. She whispered, "I forgive you." A sob caught in her throat. "Bennett would have too."

A deep sigh escaped Finn's lungs, followed by cleansing tears. He embraced her tighter and lowered his forehead against her shoulder. Sobs shook him. A new feeling—a potent blend of joy, relief, and happiness—filled him from the inside out. He didn't know how much he had longed to receive her forgiveness until he heard her speak the words aloud. For almost a year, he'd brooded over his guilt—obsessed, really. Now he could let it go. It seemed odd, that such intense heartache could be lifted with some courage and a simple request.

Emily leaned back, but her hands lingered on his shoulders. Her cheeks glistened with tears. "You're leaving, aren't you?"

Finn loosened his hold on her, a lump crawling into his throat. "I'm goin' home."

She looked away, biting her lip, then returned her deep blue gaze to his. "Write to me. I want to know you've arrived safely."

His chest swelled. "I would be delighted to."

A soft infant whimper carried through the open door from within. Emily leaned back, and Finn reluctantly allowed her to step out of his arms. She tilted her head toward the door. "I need to see to him."

"I understand. It's time I'm on me way, so it is." He reached into his sleeve and plucked out a single flower with bright red petals, then offered it to her. "Be well, Emily."

She grasped the flower in her delicate fingers and whisked away a new tear. "Godspeed, Finn."

Leaving Emily was hard, harder even than Finn's decision to leave Ireland. Perhaps he'd see her again someday. After all, he never thought he'd return home again in his lifetime—yet here he was.

After a quick stop at a stonemason to pick up a commission, Finn hauled his new pack over his shoulder and set out toward one of the London cemeteries. It didn't matter which. Any would suffice.

Warm light washed over the city in pinks, reds, and oranges as the sun made its descent. The farther he walked, the quicker his pace. One task left and then he could go home. He was eager to be done, yet this didn't deserve to be rushed.

Headstones and monuments of all sizes and shapes—crosses, angels, slabs, and mausoleums—came into view through a dense gathering of trees. Blooming cherry blossoms punctuated the cemetery with bright pink petals. Solemn and silent, head bowed in respect, Finn padded through the grassy rows, some overgrown by ferny foliage and ivy. People of all walks of life, of all ages, of all morals, were buried here. Death held no prejudice.

Beneath a nearby cherry blossom tree, Finn squatted, set the pack on the ground, and pulled out its contents—a plain concrete slab no longer than his forearm. Like he had asked, the stonemason had etched a simple inscription:

Ciaran O'Connor
1880–1913

Finn took out a dull knife and ripped into the first layer of grass.

Soon, he had dug out an indent roughly the size of the slab. The fit was snug, but once in place, it looked as though it had been there all this time. After brushing aside some stray blades of grass, he rocked and fell to his backside, resting his arms on propped knees. He stared at the inscription, reading the name over and over and over again. He expected tears to come, but his eyes were dry, likely as weary of this ordeal as he.

"You could have been a great man, Ciaran." Finn leaned his head forward and rested it on his thumbs. "Sometimes I wish I hadn't pulled you from the side of that cliff. After all you've done, all those people you killed . . ." A lump formed in his throat. He lifted his head and focused on the name again. "I do be regrettin' not savin' your soul. My own took some convincin' before I could be saved, but I'm sorry my salvation came too late to make a difference in your life. Adelynn tried. You made your choice."

Finn scratched his nose and turned his head away to scan the angled yet proud monuments of those interred on the grounds. "I'm sorry, Ciaran." Now the tears came, loose and easy, like they had been waiting there all this time. "I'm sorry I couldn't save you. You are a soul lost, and that I will forever mourn, my friend." He rolled up onto his knees and brushed a palm over the cool concrete, tracing the sharp inscription with a fingertip.

Music from long ago came rushing back, when times were merry and carefree, when Finn had been surrounded by love, family, and goodwill. What had simply been an end to a cheery time with friends now settled like a weight in his heart.

Half-singing, half-whispering, he began, "Of all the comrades that e'er I had, they're sorry for my goin' away, and all the sweethearts that e'er I had, they'd wish me one more day to stay. But since it fell into my lot, that I should rise and you should not, I'll gently rise and softly call, 'Good night and joy be to you all.'"

Gathering his pack, Finn rose slowly with pops in his knees and a stretch in his spine. The scent of fresh flowers and a far-off bakery blew by on a gentle breeze. Waning sunlight sparkled through the shifting trees. He took one last look at the crude memorial and gave it a nod. "Good night, Ciaran."

Then he started walking and didn't look back, beckoned by the call of a distant green country and the promise of a new beginning.

Acknowledgments

Writing a novel doesn't just happen on a whim. Of all the things that make up the journey—perseverance, grammar know-how, and many late evenings editing away—one of the most important is having people around you to give you motivation and support. It's impossible to list everyone who has touched my life or this project through the years, but I appreciate all of you!

First, to my family, you've always supported my dream to be an author. Even though my answer to your questions of "Did you finish your book yet?" was almost always "Not yet, but I'm *so* close," you didn't stop asking. You urged me to keep going, to continue doing what I love, and I'm so thankful for you.

Miralee Ferrell and everyone at Mountain Brook Ink, thank you for hosting the Fire Award competition and for choosing to take a chance on a first-timer like me. You have given me so much encouragement and grace and helped affirm that I'm on the right path.

Alyssa Roat, my lovely editor, it's clear from your comments and suggestions that you understand me and you understand this book. You edited with great discernment, kindness, and humor. Thanks for helping me make this story the best it can be!

Bryan Davis, the Teen Track course you taught at the Florida Christian Writers Conference—when you critiqued my first chapter to shreds (it deserved it)—gave me the inspiration and the tools I needed to develop as a writer. You've allowed me to stay in touch over the years, responding to my emails with attentiveness and generosity, and I appreciate all of the knowledge you've been willing to share.

Shirley Helberg, you were the very first to comb through my first draft with a red pen and critical eye (bless you, because that first draft was *rough*). The funny thing is, the novel that's in our hands now barely resembles the draft that you helped to shape, but it's thanks to you that the story has blossomed into its final, polished form.

Tara Bitzan, Jamie Kakach, and Amy Chaffins, my dear friends, I'm thankful that you were willing to read my novel and give me feedback early on in the process, and you've always been there to give me a boost of encouragement when I needed it.

To my high school English teachers, you gave me the foundation I needed to build my writing career. Mr. Hartung, even though your rousing stories about cats definitely stood out, you helped me discover the love of writing and that I wanted to be a writer when I grew up. Mr. Fiskum, you helped me expand that dream and really stretch those writing muscles. You never complained when I hung around after class or bothered you during your lunch hour to ask rapid-fire questions about all things grammar related. And Mr. Hinkle, you allowed me to explore the more creative, fun side of writing and provided the encouragement I needed to keep going.

Judy Hougen and Amy Munson, my English professors at the University of Northwestern – St. Paul, your instruction and guidance added humbleness and expertise to my writerly traits. Learning how to critique and be critiqued was invaluable to this whole experience.

To all my fellow writers in the ACFW Scribes critique group, you provided thoughtful feedback, positive reinforcement, and tough love when I needed it. Thank you especially to those who stuck with me over the long haul and got to critique most, if not all, of my novel: Deena Adams, Ashley Rescot, Sherry Shindelar, Natalie Arauco, Amre Cortadino, Andra Loy, Heidi Meissel, and Gwen Gage.

And finally, to my Lord and Savior, I attribute all of this—my aspirations, my talents, and my journey. He has been faithful, and I will continue to write for the glory of His kingdom.

Made in the USA
Middletown, DE
20 March 2022